KURINJI FLOWERS

CLARE FLYNN

This is a work of fiction

Cover design JD Smith Designs

In memory of Annette Gampel, née Warburton, 1954 – 2012.

CHAPTER 1

THE BEGINNING OF JULY, and the sky was the colour of a dirty pigeon. 1936 had been a terrible year; dull, grey days, abnormally cool and unremittingly miserable. At least, that's how I remember it. I was due to be presented at Court in a couple of weeks and, for some reason, the new king had decided the presentations would be made in daytime in the palace gardens. Choosing to break with tradition and forego the solemn dignity of evening Courts in the staterooms was perverse anyway, but doing so in that dreary summer seemed like sheer bloody-mindedness. I was sure I'd have to endure the whole tedious process in the pouring rain. As it happened, it did rain: a torrential downpour. King Edward was safely sheltered under a canopy while the debutantes paraded in front of him, their coiffures flattened or frizzed and their dripping party frocks clinging to their calves like seaweed. But I was not among them. By then, I was in disgrace and exiled from London.

I hated the endless round of joyless parties, introductions to people I immediately forgot, making conversation with people with whom I had nothing in common, not to mention watching one's posture and deportment and those ghastly curtseying and dancing lessons with Madame Vacani. All under the critical eye of my mother, for whom I always fell short of expectations.

The rows between us had got worse and more frequent. I failed to share her enthusiasm for fashion and, while I loved beautiful clothes, I stopped short of spending every waking hour poring over the pages of *Vogue* or shut away in a salon getting primped and coiffed when I could be in the garden with a good book. Her hair was as shiny and glossy in its long, sleek bob as it had been when she was a debutante herself; her eyebrows formed perfect arcs; her lipstick never smudged or stuck to her teeth as mine sometimes did; and her skin was unlined, even though she was well past fifty. We were just different. My father had been the glue that bound us. Now he was gone, she could rail against me when she chose, which was rather too often in my opinion. The more she fussed and criticised, the more I tried to pull against her, to assert myself, to pit my will against hers. Me marrying well was her mission in life. Just surviving my first London season was mine.

So that dreary July afternoon, I paused in applying my lipstick and listened for the sound of her high heels clattering on the stone floor of the hall and the thump of the front door as it closed behind her. I was free for a few hours while she was at her bridge game. Free to dash over to Chelsea and spend some time with Rupert Milligan. I touched the skin on the end of my nose. I was about to get a spot. I cursed, but then realised it could be the means of my escape from tomorrow's engagements—my mother hated me to be seen in public with even the smallest blemish.

I'd met Rupert for the first time at my father's funeral. I was overwhelmed by Daddy's sudden death and, uncomfortable among the throng of mourners that came back to our house in Leighton Square, I slipped away to take refuge in the study. Curled up in the big leather armchair, the cat on my lap, I wanted to be alone with my thoughts. I didn't hear him enter the room until he was right behind my chair and reached a hand over my shoulder to cup my chin, tilting my head back towards him.

'Not quite as beautiful as your mother. But pretty enough. Her cheekbones are better, but you have a fine nose and chin. I shall paint you.'

He moved in front of my chair and stood between the fireplace and me, leaning back against the marble, with one arm draped indolently along the mantelpiece and a cigarette dangling from his lips as he looked me up and down. If I'm honest, I was a bit scared. He was tall and loose- limbed, with an effortless elegance, like a panther. His hair was greying at the temples and his face had deep wrinkles like a rhinoceros. There was nothing about him that fitted my mental picture of an artist. He was certainly not the type who went out and about in paint-smeared overalls and starved in a garret. Every inch of Rupert Milligan, from his cavalry twills to his silk cravat, spoke privilege and entitlement.

'Yes, I'll paint you and it'll be our secret. We won't tell Felicity.'

I stared at him, unable to speak or swallow, the words trapped in my throat. I wasn't used to grownups talking to me on equal terms.

He looked amused. 'Do you know who I am?'

'You're Daddy's friend, Mr Milligan...but I don't want to be painted.'

'Why not?'

'I don't know. I just don't.'

I avoided his eyes.

'Well, if you don't know, you've no reason to object. And I'd like to do it.'

3

In a sudden movement, he took hold of my chin again and twisted my head to one side to view me in profile.

I jerked away from him. 'Don't.'

He gave a slight shrug of his left shoulder and resumed his position against the fireplace. 'Richard talked about you all the time. He was very proud of you. I know he'd have liked us to meet.'

I didn't know what to say. He made me feel frightened and important at the same time. Confused.

'He said you always had your head in a book. But you didn't like school. He felt bad about that. Argued endlessly with Felicity about you being sent away. She said it would do you good, but he missed you terribly.'

He'd got my attention. I sat up straight and the cat jumped off my lap and bolted out of the room. I nodded, eager for Mr Milligan to go on.

'Have you ever tried to paint, Ginny?'

'A little. At school.'

'Are you any good?'

'Well, I like it but, in my school report, the art teacher said that I am "Only fair".'

'Only fair? Fair enough.' He drew on his cigarette. 'Ignore everything they teach you. I'll show you how to paint as a painter. How to see things, not slavishly follow rules.'

'I thought you wanted to paint me, not teach me?'

'We'll see. If you show promise, we can do both.'

'How did you know Daddy?'

'We were at Oxford together. Rowed in the same boat. At least we did until I got sent down.'

'Sent down? What did you do?'

'Made love to the master's daughter.'

I could feel the blood rushing to my face and wished I hadn't asked.

'I was on the rebound and nursing a broken heart.

Shouldn't have dallied with her—not my type at all but she was rather sweet—until she ran to her papa and spilled the beans. That was the end of a classical education for me.'

'What did you do?'

'Went to the Slade for a bit. Then I found I could make a living anyway from painting portraits, so I dropped out. Having the right connections is just as important as having talent, Ginny. Maybe more so.'

He moved across to a side table and picked up a framed photograph of my mother and studied it carefully. 'Felicity is a beautiful woman, but I think perhaps you'll turn out to be more so. Given a little time. How old are you?'

'Fourteen. It was my birthday last week; the day after Daddy died.'

He replaced the picture, glanced at his watch, then crouched in front of me, studying me in silence for a moment or two as though weighing me up, then ran a finger slowly down my cheek and tapped the end of my nose.

'Come to my studio tomorrow, Ginny. Felicity plays bridge on Thursdays so she won't know. Holbein Mews in Chelsea; the one with the green door. Three o'clock.'

Then he was gone. I could feel the cold touch of his finger on my skin long after he'd left the room.

That first afternoon when I turned up at his draughty studio, he plied me with ginger beer and chocolate biscuits and let me watch as he painted. I happily agreed to return the following week. This time he served me tea and little cakes and sandwiches he had delivered from a patisserie on Sloane Street. He talked about my father and their days at Oxford, and how they'd joined up together in the Great War, and how he served at the front in Belgium and later in Palestine, while Daddy spent the duration behind a desk in the Ministry of War.

He went out of his way to make me feel at ease and

purported to be interested in the trivial details of my life. After the holidays, when I went back to boarding school, we began writing to each other; on my part, long, over-detailed exposés of my teenage preoccupations—the plots of the books I was reading, the tedium of my lessons, the transgressions of my classmates and the unreasonable behaviour of my teachers; on his part, brief, jokey one-liners penned in black ink in his sweeping, italic handwriting, accompanying little gifts. Nothing costly: just trinkets, carefully chosen books, a set of pastels, a box of handmade chocolates, a sable paintbrush. He cemented himself into my life like lichen growing on a stone wall.

When I came home for the Christmas holidays, I couldn't wait to see him. I thought of him as a kind uncle—and my only friend. At school, I got on well enough with the other girls, but didn't really have any close friends and, at home, I always felt as though I were a paler presence orbiting the bright planet that was my mother. I took him a couple of cigars I'd found in a wooden box in Daddy's study. As I handed over the gift, I reached up on tiptoes and gave him a kiss on the cheek. He looked surprised, but also a bit pleased. That afternoon it started: first just touching my hair, then the smooth, hairless, little-girl skin of my arms and my knees above my white cotton socks. I wasn't used to touching; Mummy didn't really go in for it. But I liked what Rupert did. I stretched out on his battered sofa and let him stroke me like a well-loved pet.

Then, after I'd been home about a week, he pulled me onto his lap and I felt scared for the first time. I looked over his shoulder, examining the cobweb that was woven across the skylight, telling myself nothing was wrong. Something hard was pushing against my leg through the heavy tweed of his trousers. I didn't know what it was, but I knew it wasn't right. He held my head between his big artist's hands and brought his mouth down to mine, brushing my lips with his; then, without warning, he rammed his tongue inside. Tobacco, foul and bitter, filled my mouth; his tongue too big, making me gag. Horrid. It wasn't right, wasn't normal.

I tried to pull away from him, wanting to be sick. He stopped at once, moving his hands to my shoulders and drawing back to look at me. His face was sad, as though I'd let him down, disappointed him, come up short.

He said, 'Funny thing, inhibition, but I'm sure you'll grow out of it, Ginny.'

And so it began. He took me to the National Gallery and the Tate and gave me a potted course in art history. He talked about the human body and how essential it was for an artist to draw and paint his subjects naked, to understand the muscle groups and the way the weight of the body is distributed in different poses. Naturally, after that, it was a small step to convince me that, in order to paint me properly with my clothes on, he needed to make some preparatory sketches with them off. I was self-conscious, but he was a persuasive man and convinced me to accept what he was doing out of respect for art and his pursuit of his craft.

It was uncomfortable, standing there unclothed, as his eyes darted back and forth between the sketchpad and me as he worked. I was ashamed, conscious of my nakedness and knowing that, despite his words, it wasn't usual for a girl of my age to pose in the nude for a man. I knew Mummy would be horrified and, in my heart of hearts, I knew Daddy would have been angry too.

'Look, Mr Milligan, I don't want to do this anymore. I don't think Mummy would like it.'

His eyes showed his disappointment, as though I'd let him down. 'Of course, she wouldn't. She doesn't understand art. That's why she must never know.'

He shook his head, then turned away from me and began

cleaning his brushes. The smell of turpentine ripped at the back of my throat.

'I thought you were different, Ginny. I thought you were a free spirit. Not shallow and bound by convention. But it appears I was wrong. You're not brave enough to follow in the footsteps of the great artists' muses. I wanted you to be my Camille, my Victorine. But you're just a spoilt, unimaginative schoolgirl. Don't bother to come again. I'm not wasting time on you.'

I thought about a life without our afternoons together and couldn't bear it. 'I'm sorry. It's just...' I couldn't hold back the tears.

He moved over and put a shawl around my shoulders, then wiped my eyes with the edge.

'It's all right, Ginny. I know. It feels strange. But every artist needs a muse; a special woman that they immortalise in their work. You are mine. You inspire me to greatness.'

He eased me towards him and held my head against his chest. The buttons of the baggy white shirt he always wore when painting dug into my cheek. I breathed in the sandalwood scent of his shaving balm. I liked the idea of being an inspiration. Being a muse. Of being described as a woman. And he was the kindest person in my life; the person who cared most about me, who paid me the most attention.

He pulled back, slapped me lightly on the bottom and told me to get dressed. Then he said the words that clinched it for me.

'It's time you started calling me Rupert. After all, we're special friends now.'

The following week when he painted me, it was different. He worked rapidly, saying nothing, just looking between the easel and me as he worked the paint on the canvas. He was playing some kind of jazz music on the gramophone. I'd never heard anything like it before. I was transported by the music, losing track of time and awareness of my surround-ings, so when I felt the flat of his palm on the skin of my lower back as he adjusted my position slightly, I took a sudden intake of breath and he needed no more encourage-ment. He let his hand move on down over the gooseflesh of my buttocks, tracing their shape, and then slowly letting his fingers draw a path across my stomach. My breath quickened and my hips jerked forward involuntarily, and he stopped and stepped away from me, frowning, and told me that was enough for the day, leaving me confused, rejected and feeling dirty.

A week later, he was ready with fresh cream cakes and champagne. He pulled up a wooden chair and swung it to face away from me and sat with his chest and arms resting on the back, watching me bite into the hard shell of the meringues to the soft chewy insides, then taking my first ever taste of champagne. I winced at the astringent taste of the bubbly as it cut through the cloying sweetness of the confectioned whorls of sugar. That first taste of alcohol made me dizzy and he moved to sit beside me and kissed me again. At first, it was nice. Light little kisses that danced on my lips. Then before I knew what had hit me, he unbuttoned his flies and pulled my head into his lap. I had never seen a penis before. It was worse than his tongue in my mouth. Horrible. Dirty. Dizzy from champagne. Room spinning, his hands pinioning my head in position. The taste and smell of him drowned out the sweetness of the meringues and wine. He began making noises. A kind of low moaning. What was happening? Was he ill? Why was he doing this horrible thing to me? Just as the bile rose in my throat and I thought I'd be sick, he made another terrible groaning noise and my mouth was full of sticky, salty slime. He released his hold and sank back into the cushions and, as I spat it all out, I threw up the champagne and meringues over the studio floor. He watched me as I knelt on the floor, trying to mop up the mess with a towel, while fighting back my tears. I'd so wanted to show him I was grownup and not at all inhibited. But I'd never expected this. He reached out a hand and placed it on my head.

'Good girl, Ginny. You did very well. You've made me very happy. I love you very much.'

I wanted to kill him. I wanted to pick up his palette knife and ram it through his heart. But then he moved onto his knees beside me and wrapped his arms around me.

'Don't cry, little bird. Don't cry. It's always hard the first time. But you did so well. I'm very proud of you. That's my girl. My angel.'

It went on. Week after week and month after month. He, in turn, removed his clothes and expected me to sketch him naked. At first, this was more embarrassing for me than being naked myself but, after a while, I began to see his body as just a combination of light and shade, to be captured in sweeping pencil lines, cross-hatching and the smudging of a stick of charcoal. Rupert always critiqued my work afterwards, which gave what we were doing a kind of legitimacy. I still loathed what he did to me and made me do to him after we finished our artwork, but I did exactly as I was told. Eventually I found a way to cope; I left my body and floated above it, looking down from the ceiling as the artist's muse did whatever he told her to do. Sometimes he showed me pornography. The images wouldn't leave me, playing in my head when I closed my eyes at night and returning to haunt my dreams. I'd lie awake, knowing what we were doing was wrong and feeling afraid and ashamed. But I went along with his wishes and believed his lies.

Eventually I stopped thinking about right or wrong and let it become part of my life. Something to cope with, like being at boarding school or going to the dentist. And being without him was unthinkable. He was the only grownup who didn't talk down to me, who listened attentively to the minutiae of my day, laughing at my feeble attempts at jokes. And I glowed when he told me stories of his childhood in Suffolk, of the time he and my father jumped naked off Magdalene Bridge for a bet, of the nights they stayed out late and had to climb over the college walls and of their favourite tutor who was always drunk by lunchtime and slept all afternoon. So I unwittingly became his child mistress, while believing one day I'd become his wife. I had no thought of how the relationship was inappropriate. The age gap didn't deter me, nor did my knowledge that somewhere in the background was a wife and a clutch of children, some of them older than me. I didn't think about these things, as I was completely under his spell: bewitched, besotted and beguiled. But what of my mother, you ask? How did I keep it from her? I suppose she was preoccupied with other things; she was always distant and unapproachable. Maybe, in some strange way, I also wanted to protect her—or at least protect the idea she had of me.

That rainy July afternoon when I left the house, with a heavily powdered nose to conceal my emerging spot, I had no idea my mother was following me. Rupert and I weren't actually doing anything when she turned up, thank goodness. I think I would have spontaneously combusted had she walked in on us in the act. It was bad enough, anyway. Artie Shaw was playing on the gramophone and we were together on the chaise longue, I was in my underwear, sipping champagne and he was lying across me, his head in my lap as I stroked his hair. The studio door opened and there she was. She slumped against the doorjamb to steady herself. Artie Shaw reached the end of the disk and the needle hissed. No one lifted it off.

Rupert spoke first. 'It's customary to knock, Felicity. But always a pleasure to see you.'

I scrambled to my feet and reached for my dressing gown. Before I'd got the belt tied, she'd flung a pottery jug at him, narrowly missing and hitting the wall behind us. A piece ricocheted into my left eyebrow and drew blood. Neither of them noticed.

'Steady on. That was a gift from Celia. I'm rather fond of it. It was Moorcroft,' he said.

Her face was ugly with rage. She swept the tubes of oil paint off his worktable onto the floor, where she stamped on them, anger making her oblivious to the impact on her calf-skin Anello & Davide shoes.

'Calm down, old girl. Some of those oils are damned expensive. Do you have any idea how much ultramarine costs?'

'She's only eighteen. You've ruined her. You filthy, lecherous bastard.'

'Come on, Felicity. She's a woman with a mind of her own.'

His calm tone served to rile her further. A piece of hardboard, which he used as a supplementary palette, shot through the air and hit him in the stomach. He bent double, but was back upright before she had a chance to find another weapon. They faced each other down, like a couple of rutting stags.

'If you come anywhere near my daughter again, I'll cut your balls off and post them to Celia. Get dressed, Virginia.' Then she screamed at me like a banshee, 'Put your damn clothes on.'

I gathered up my scattered clothing. Rupert sat down, legs akimbo, one hand on his thigh and the other nursing a glass of champagne, as though he were a guest at a cocktail party. It was too much for Mummy. She lunged at him and slapped him across the face so hard that his cheek turned the colour of the Alizarin Crimson now splattered all over the studio floor. He gave a sharp cry, then retreated before she could inflict more damage heading downstairs to the safety of the bathroom he shared with the occupant of the ground floor studio.

As the door slammed behind him, she looked around and saw a stack of canvasses leaning against the wall in a corner of the room. The first one was a recent nude study of me. She looked at it for a moment, then flipped through the rest of the stack, letting each canvass fall to the floor as she jerked the next one forward. They charted my body's development from the first time he had painted me, fresh-faced, with only the faintest trace of pubic hair and still undeveloped breasts, through the following months and years. A visual catalogue of my defilement.

'The bastard. The filthy bastard.'

I'd never heard her utter even the mildest form of profanity before that day. I'd never seen her so angry. Then I realised she was crying. I'd never seen her cry before. Not even when Daddy died. She collapsed onto her knees and let out a guttural sound like a wounded animal.

What had I done?

CHAPTER 2

THE SHORT TRIP back to Leighton Square seemed to take forever. The silence was punctuated by muffled sobbing from my mother. I was dry-eyed. I was surprised she was taking it this way. I'd expected anger, recriminations, threatened sanctions. She was behaving as though she were the guilty party and that made me feel worse; the petulant defiance that usually characterised my response to her criticism gave way to shame and embarrassment.

I wasn't sure how I felt about what had happened. I still believed I was in love with Rupert, but knowing this was the end of our affair brought a sense of relief, a lifting of a burden I hadn't realised I was carrying, until now I felt its absence. I'd lived for our afternoons together; for his stories, for his views on politics, religion, art and literature, and the worsening situation in Germany and for the little nuggets of gossip about his society clients. The young men I met at social functions were pale and shallow in comparison. But the entry of my mother into our secret world had cast it in a different light.

She told me to wait in the study and went upstairs. When

she returned, her customary poise restored, along with her makeup, I expected to be read the Riot Act, but she sat down beside me on the chesterfield and reached for my hand.

'How long, Virginia?' Her voice was gentle, soft almost. Not her usual brisk, barking tone.

'I don't know...'

'Tell me. When did it start? When did you meet him?'

My voice was a whisper, 'Five years ago. At Daddy's funeral.'

Her nails dug into the skin of my hand. I expected her to yell at me, hit me even, but her eyes swam with tears. 'And you've had intimate relations with him?'

I nodded.

'When did it start?'

I looked at the closed door and wished I could run through it, out of the house and a million miles away.

'Ginny, I need to know. When did he start doing things to you?'

I forced the words out, 'A few weeks later. When I came home from school for the Christmas holidays.'

She gave a little gasp, and then her arms were around me and she pulled me into her chest and kissed the top of my head. 'Dear God, you were just a child. I'm so sorry, my darling. I've let you down. I wasn't paying attention. I should have known. I'll never forgive myself. Did he hurt you?'

I pulled away in surprise. 'It wasn't like that. Rupert loves me. He's loved me for a long time. And I love him, too. He's going to marry me.'

This time it was she who pulled away, recoiling from me and pushing herself into the corner of the sofa. 'Don't be ridiculous.' Her words were spat out. 'He has no intention of marrying you. Not that it would happen while I've breath left in my body. Don't you get it? He's exploited you, abused you.

You were a child. You're still practically a child. He should go to prison. And we must get you to a doctor.'

'No.' I clutched at her arm. 'Please, no, I love him. It's not his fault.'

'Don't be ridiculous. You didn't even know what you wanted. You'd just lost your father. You were young and vulnerable, and he took advantage of you. The stinking, rotten beast.'

'Don't. It wasn't like that. He's kind. He cares for me.'

She twisted the rope of pearls that hung around her neck, gathering them into her hand and squeezing them, as though trying to force out the sand and water that had formed them.

'The only thing Rupert Milligan cares about is himself. I hate to do this to you, Ginny, but you need to know. He's a philanderer with a string of mistresses and numerous, discarded, past conquests. If they stood in line, they'd stretch the length of the Mall.'

'That's not true.'

She laughed drily. 'I'm afraid it is, darling. That's one of the reasons why I didn't marry him.'

I felt like I'd been hit in the stomach.

She said, 'We went out together for more than a year while he was up at Oxford. And then I found out he'd been seeing other women all along. He's a persuasive liar and plied me with plausible explanations until he'd convinced me it was all a series of misunderstandings. We got engaged to be married.'

I was about to interrupt, when she said, 'Yes, darling, he's a convincing liar, but I broke off the relationship as soon as he introduced me to your father because I knew at once I was with the wrong man.'

'Why didn't you tell me this before?'

'Why on earth would I? It wasn't important. It was ancient history. If it had been up to me, your father would have had nothing more to do with him but, for some reason, he insisted on keeping up the friendship. Maybe he felt guilty? Rupert was the one who usually succeeded with women, and he was in shock when your father swept me off my feet.'

I tasted bile and prayed for her to stop talking, but she carried on, oblivious to my distress.

'As soon as he found out I was leaving him for Hugh, he began an affair with the daughter of one of the college staff— the dean or the master, I think. A schoolgirl, barely sixteen. When he ditched her after a few weeks, she told her parents and there was a terrific scandal and he was sent down.'

I tried to look away, but she grasped my hand and jerked me towards her.

'He met Celia soon after at the Slade. He got her pregnant and tried to pretend the child wasn't his, but her father wouldn't let him get away with it. Not that Rupert took too much persuading once he found out she came with a trust fund. See what kind of a man he is?'

Before I could reply, her hand shot to her mouth. 'My God. You're not pregnant, are you?'

'Of course not.'

'I suppose he made sure of that, didn't he? Once bitten. The little shit.'

Then she insisted I tell her everything. How, as soon as I looked mature enough, he'd given me a cheap wedding band and sent me off to the Marie Stopes clinic to be fitted with a contraceptive device. How we met when I was supposed to be shopping or meeting school friends.

WHEN I'D FINISHED, she put her head in her hands. 'I've let you down, Ginny. I should have been more careful. You're so naïve, so trusting, so...gullible.'

I started to protest, but my words sounded hollow, even to me. 'He's going to leave Celia. He loves me. You're wrong. You don't know him like I do.'

'What he did to you has nothing to do with love, and everything to do with jealousy of your father and hatred of me. That and his own sick mind and inability to keep his trousers buttoned.'

She saw the disbelief on my face and gave a sigh. 'His speciality is married women. He taps them for money. And he's not very choosy. Everyone knows he's been having a liaison with Lady Beresford for the past ten years, while carrying on with her stepdaughter for the past three or four. And then there are the artist models, who are happy to serve double duty. The day of your father's funeral he asked me to have dinner with him. I told him that he wasn't welcome in this house, and Hugh's death made no difference to how I felt about him. It seems he went straight off and started to work on you. I was too wrapped up in my own grief to realise he'd try that. Well, that, and the fact you were a child. I didn't think even a rat like him would be capable of that.'

Her voice broke again.

I sat beside her trying not to believe what she was saying, but knowing it was the truth. I wanted to cry, but the tears wouldn't come. I felt nothing. A cold, empty hollow where I'd thought my heart was meant to be. She looked at me sadly. I wanted her to reach out and hug me again, to make it all right, but she didn't and couldn't, so I just stared at my shoes and wished it were a dream and I'd wake up to find the world as it used to be.

On an impulse, I asked, 'Why did Daddy avoid going to the Front in the war?'

'What are you talking about?'

'He had a desk job, rather than fighting.'

'Who told you that?'

I looked away. She grabbed my hand.

'Good God. That's the giddy limit. Your father never spoke of the war because it was too harrowing. He won a medal for gallantry. He was terribly, terribly brave. That useless, dilettante Milligan was the one behind the desk. Pulled strings at the War Office. Now do you see what kind of man he is? A filthy coward and a liar, not fit to clean your father's boots. It was the damn war that killed Hugh. His heart was weakened. He lived on his nerves. He was never the same afterwards.'

And then a hideous thought struck me. 'You and Rupert? Did you?'

The force of her words made me shrink away from her. 'Are you asking if I had a physical relationship with Rupert Milligan? What do you take me for? A cheap trollop?'

My cheeks burned at her words. A cheap trollop. That's what she thought of me. She touched my hand.

'I walked down the aisle a virgin, and I'd thought you would, too.'

The bell rang for dinner, but I couldn't face eating and escaped to the sanctuary of my bedroom. Looking out onto the bleak, rain-drenched garden, I started to feel angry. Angry with myself for letting this happen. Angry with Rupert for all the lies he'd told me. For the way he'd made me think of my father as lacking courage. And angry with my mother for keeping so much from me, for being so removed. Rupert had never given me the slightest indication he had once cared for her—that he'd actually asked her to marry him. If she were to be believed, he'd toyed with me, but had really wanted her.

From my window seat, I saw the dark, grey sky was broken up by a few lighter patches, as though someone had spilt some bleach over it. Everything was monochrome; the colour in the flowers appeared to have leached away. Rainwater pooled on the garden table and dripped onto the stone flags below. The rain had battered the lavender plants into bent submission and soggy rose petals were scattered on the ground. This time, last year, I'd sat out there, day after day, bathed in the scent of lavender and roses, painting and reading in the shade of the fig tree. Now, my life was ruined.

The next morning, hunger forced me to venture downstairs. I went down early, hoping to be out of the dining room before my mother put in an appearance, but there she was already, behind *The Illustrated London News*, pretending to read a feature about duck-billed platypuses. I knew it was an act, as she never read magazines unless there was an article about someone she knew; she just looked at the pictures and criticised people's dress sense.

Keeping the magazine in front of her, she spoke, her voice business-like, leaving no doubt that the moments of tenderness of the previous day were not to be repeated, 'We can't undo what's done, but from now on I'm not letting you out of my sight. I don't blame you. He is entirely culpable. But you've been deceitful, Virginia, seeing him in secret and lying to me. We brought you up to know better than to consort with a married man. I've told Proud he's not to be given entry here, nor are you to accept any telephone calls from him.'

I'd have swum the Thames from here to Oxford rather than see Rupert Milligan again, but I resented her talking to me as though I were a ten-year-old, so I sat mute and sullen, making a tower from sugar cubes, as I knew it would annoy her.

She sighed, then smiled, her lips making the shape, but her eyes telling a different story. 'Righto. Onward and upward. Dinner at the Pagets' tonight and I have a hair appointment at half-three. Frederick can fit you in, too, I'm sure.'

'I don't want to go to the Pagets'.'

'Very well. Just this once. I'll make our excuses, but you can come with me to Frederick's. I don't want you alone in the house today. Not good for you to mope. Is that a spot on your nose?'

I scowled at my porridge, but was relieved that, at least, I had a reprieve from the evening engagement.

'I hate it.'

'Hate what?'

'Coming out. The season. The parties. The whole debutante thing. Can't we just stop? I'm sick of getting dressed up night after night and being on show all the time. It's horrid. It makes me feel like a piece of meat in a butcher's window. People sizing me up.'

She peered at me over her reading glasses. 'Don't be petulant. It's a rite of passage. You have to do it. How else will you get married? There are thousands of girls who'd give anything to be in your shoes; to be presented to the king; to meet so many interesting people; to spend time partying and dancing till dawn. Really, Ginny, you're impossible sometimes. I absolutely adored my first season. I can remember how excited I was as though it were yesterday.'

'But that's just it. I'm not *you*! I'm *me*, and I'm telling you I don't find it exciting at all. It's an ordeal. As soon as I cross the threshold, I long for it to be time to go home.'

'I've worked really hard to make your coming-out a success. And it's only a couple of weeks until you're to be presented.'

She narrowed her eyes like an owl's, and said, 'I'll tell the Pagets you have a bad headache. But it's business as usual from tomorrow, Virginia. The season's nearly over. Henley next week, then we're on the home straight to Court. Do buck up. It's not a lot to ask. And sit up straight, you're slouching again. Shoulders back.'

WE WERE INVITED to an exhibition in a gallery in Cork Street. It was likely to be crowded and full of the usual bevy of braying boys, simpering girls and lots of Mummy's friends, but I was looking forward to it. My mother had no interest in art, so I'd have some uninterrupted time to enjoy the work while she gossiped with her chums.

The show was a collection of landscape paintings by contemporary artists, known collectively as the Blackmore Group. Philip Osborne, the gallery owner, was an acquaintance of my father's, and a couple of works from the gallery hung on the walls of Leighton House.

The place was packed; the popping of champagne corks, chinking of glasses and drone of conversation had reached that horrible background buzz where it's impossible to hear anyone unless they yell in one's ear. Everyone who was anyone was there. My mother swept inside, fox fur tails trailing, with me, as usual, a couple of steps behind. She was soon gathered up by a group of women, and I was free to inspect the art.

The Blackmore Group appeared to make up in popularity what they lacked in talent. Their work was dull; mainly traditional vistas of the Suffolk coast and countryside, but most of the pictures were already badged with a little red sale dot. When I'd had my fill of cloudscapes and seascapes, I drifted to the back of the gallery and stepped into another room on a lower level. This wasn't part of the main exhibition, but there were about twenty people crushed into the narrow space.

Then I saw Rupert; he had his back to me and was in conversation with Philip Osborne. The crowd parted, and I found myself moving towards a pair of oil paintings on the back wall as the assembled throng closed in behind me like the incoming sea.

I raised my eyes to look at the pictures. Instead of the landscapes that adorned the rest of the gallery walls, I saw my own image. I was smiling, my hands folded in my lap, my teeth matching the pearls around my neck and my pink lips matching my cashmere twinset—a classic *Country Life* cover pose. Why was it there in a landscape show, particularly when Rupert had no connection to the Blackmore group?

And, then, I saw it. What everyone else was looking at. A second portrait, identical to the first but, this time, minus the twinset—in fact, minus everything except the pearls. I'd never seen the painting before. My face was turned to look downward so the features were masked by a cascade of hair, but the skin tone, the way the light fell and the blue upholstered chair left one in no doubt that it was the same woman in the same place. The same pearl necklace circled my throat but, this time, my arms were behind my lowered head, elbows bent above naked breasts and every detail perfect, right down to the little brown mole beside my navel and the colour of my pubic hair.

I tasted bile in my throat. People were staring at me. Nudging each other. Whispering. Pointing. My face burned. *God help me. But I don't even believe in God. The room spinning. Let me die. Let me out of here.*

As if Mummy had an in-built antenna, she appeared at my side and reached for my elbow. Without a word, she led me back through the gallery. We passed through the crowd, faces blurred, voices a low thrumming accompaniment. I looked over my shoulder. Rupert was watching, champagne flute in his hand as we moved towards the door.

I was as exposed and naked as the painting. Unpeeled. Bare. Skin flayed. Utterly humiliated. Not that I cared for anyone in that room; I had no real friends among them, but

Rupert's betrayal was so absolute it was like a knife in the stomach.

I heard a woman speak in a stage whisper, 'Of course, it's her. She's not fit to be presented to the king.'

'Isn't she Felicity Dunbar's daughter?' said another voice.

And then we were through the door and into the street, where I gulped in great breaths of smoggy air and fought back my tears.

When we were inside a cab, she spoke first, 'To do that to you... to punish you like that, just to hurt and humiliate me. He's never forgiven me. How could he stoop so low? And as for Philip Osborne...he'll have known it will ruin your reputation, the gossip it'll cause, that people will think you posed willingly for it like a cheap tart. He's just chasing after free publicity for his little, tin-pot gallery. And your father spent a fortune in that place over the years. Gutless cowards—both of them.'

Yet again, I realised it wasn't about me. My mother had made it clear it was all about her. She had her legs crossed and was twirling her raised foot round and round, first clockwise, then anticlockwise. She did this a lot. I'd always assumed it was her way of showing off her pins, but, right now, there was no one to see except me.

'Right, Ginny, chin up. There's no question of your being presented anymore. We can't stay in town. Everyone will be talking. We'll lie low until the fuss has died down. Of course, he didn't show the paintings of you as a child. He's not that stupid. He'll have destroyed the evidence. He needs to be punished, but what can we do?'

'I just want to forget about it. I don't want anyone else to know what happened.'

'Of course. Your reputation is at stake. No one must know.' She frowned. 'But I wish Hugh were alive. He'd have given Milligan a good pasting. Thrashed him. But, then, if he'd been alive, it would never have happened anyway.'

We drove in silence for a few minutes. The windows of the cab were all steamed up, but I feigned an interest in the streets as we drove along, even though I could see nothing. All I could think was that I hated Mummy as much as I hated Rupert.

After a while, she put her gloved hand on my knee and gave it a squeeze.

'I know what we'll do. We'll go and stay with Pud for a while. Get out of London until the fuss has died down.'

Pud was her younger sister, who'd made what was— according to Mummy—an injudicious marriage to a farmer and had been living in the Yorkshire Dales ever since. By rights, she should have been the black sheep of the family— former debutantes weren't supposed to marry hill farmers, especially ones who spoke with a regional dialect. But, while my mother couldn't stand her brother-in-law, she adored her only sister. I'd spent many happy holidays up there when I was a child. Mummy only ever stayed there on sufferance, preferring to get Pud down to London to stay with us without her husband, Roger, who, of course, needed to tend to his flock. Over the past few years, my desire to see Rupert had caused me to fabricate reasons to stay in London rather than visit Pud.

'But you hate it up there.'

'I know. All those smelly sheep, muddy fields and Roger skulking around. But I know you love seeing Pud and she's not been in town in ages,' she said.

A wave of relief washed over me at the prospect of liberation from the rest of the London season and from Rupert Milligan. 'I could go on my own. You don't have to come.'

'Out of the question. My eye's on you until there's a ring on your finger.' She looked thoughtful. 'I won't have your prospects ruined because of him.' She paused a moment, then added, 'But we're going to have to set our sights a bit lower. It might have to be a foreigner? Perhaps an American?' She spoke the words through clenched teeth, her nose wrinkling as though there were a bad smell under it. 'Or someone in the colonial service? Someone who won't know what's happened. But we'll leave it a while, shall we? A bit of country air, then maybe the south of France? What do you think?'

I knew she wasn't really interested in my opinion, so I wound down the window and stared at the soot-encrusted buildings.

'Mummy?'

She looked at me absently.

'Why did you follow me to the studio? What made you suspicious?'

'People were starting to talk. You were seen arm in arm with him leaving the British Museum.'

I cursed my own stupidity and Rupert's reckless disregard for my reputation.

'I didn't want to confront you about it until I was sure,' she said. 'It seemed preposterous, completely unlikely. I didn't even know you'd met the man. I thought it was a case of mistaken identity, or that you'd asked him to paint your portrait as a surprise for me. I waited outside for half an hour, praying it wouldn't be anything sordid. In the end, it started to pour down and I'd forgotten my umbrella. And I had to find out.'

She looked away and fiddled with the clasp of her hand-bag. I got the sense that the subject was closed.

I seethed with resentment at her. Looking back now, I understand that she was only trying to do her best; trying to get by without my father, doing what she thought was the right thing. She'd shielded me from the worst of the realities she faced. Daddy had left her with little money. He'd been an academic and came from old money, which means 'not-very-much-left-of-it-money', and being blessed with a big brain, had dedicated himself to the study of subatomic particles on a meagre research scientist's stipend. He blew most of the family money on an over-optimistic investment in a cousin's business venture, so Mummy was left with the house in Leighton Square and a widow's pension of subatomic proportions. She couldn't help it that motherhood didn't come naturally to her. Her own mother had been a tight-lipped matriarch, who'd shown neither her nor Pud any sign of affection.

The morning after the gallery debacle, resenting my mother's clampdown on my movements and desperate to reassert my independence, I slipped out of the house while she was on the telephone. The sun had come out and, although it was weak and watery, the world looked better. I headed on foot for Regent Street to nip into Dickens and Jones for a couple of pairs of stockings. I enjoyed walking through the streets of London, a habit I'd shared with my father—one my mother thought unfathomable.

As I ambled along, humming a dance tune in my head, I told myself everything was going to be fine. I'd got what I wanted: a reprieve from my season. Yorkshire would be a blessed relief.

I had to jump out of the way to avoid being knocked over by a deliveryman with a handcart at Piccadilly Circus, so I almost missed spotting my friend Rita Carruthers emerging through the doors of Swan and Edgar. I called out to her, eager for a chat, maybe over coffee and cakes at the Café Royal, but she swept straight past me. She must have seen me; she couldn't possibly not. Blind and deaf to me, she signalled a passing taxicab. I hurried after her, thinking the sound of the traffic had drowned me out, but she jumped into the cab, slamming the door behind her, and the taxi pulled away from the kerb. I'd been snubbed. There was no doubt at all. Rita had been at school with me and was one of perhaps three or four fellow debutantes whom I classed as friends. Not anymore.

My sin was getting found out. I was sure I wasn't the only debutante who'd lost her virginity. I suspected Rita was afraid my disgrace might be contagious—and my stripping to pose for an artist was the kind of thing shop girls and waitresses did for a bit of extra cash; the stuff of dirty, seaside postcards. Not something girls like us did.

I returned home to Leighton Square, all fight gone and ready to submit to Mummy's will.

CHAPTER 3

THE FIRST COUPLE of months in Yorkshire were grim. The weather was foul from the moment we got there; a dragging on of that wet and miserable summer into autumn.

We were a quiet household. Pud was cheerful, but occupied with the daily routine of a farmer's wife. Mummy was subdued and Pud's husband, Roger, rarely opened his mouth, except to put food in it. He was a bit scary, with a constant frown etched on his well-weathered face, like a gargoyle. Not for the first time, I wondered why my aunt had married him. She had a sunny disposition, and it was inexplicable to me that she could be happy with a man who looked as though he'd start a brawl at a moment's notice and without provocation. Not that there was any actual evidence of him being the trouble-making type; he spent most of his time in the fields or shut up in one of his outbuildings doing something to his tractor. He was gone long before I was up, taking a packed lunch Pud prepared for him each morning. It was only during the evening meal that he shared a table with us, and then he let the three of us talk amongst ourselves, while he chewed silently and stared into the middle distance. He and

Pud had no children and it was hard to fathom what could have brought them together.

Occasionally I'd see Pud walking out through the fields to bring Roger some food and, once, I came upon the pair of them sitting together on a stone wall. They had their backs to me and were out of sight until I crested the hill behind them. I didn't intend to creep up on them. She was leaning into his body, her head resting on his shoulder and he had his arm about her waist. They were laughing and looked completely comfortable together as if their bodies had melded into a single entity. I suppose I'd always taken it for granted that Pud thought the same about Roger as I did: that he was a dull, grumpy man. I'd imagined she'd only married him out of some kind of desperation. But this little vignette shone a different light onto their marriage and I realised that it was not what it seemed. I felt a little guilty, knowing I had witnessed what they supposed to be a private moment. Before they could spot me, I hurried back the way I'd come.

From then on, I watched Roger more closely and several times caught him as he looked at Pud, his face transformed by a tender expression so different from his usual frowning disgruntlement. I wanted to ask her about how they'd met, but it felt too intrusive. I suppose I could have asked my mother, but I knew she wouldn't welcome the question. Besides, she made it apparent on a daily basis that Roger was unworthy of attention; she treated him like a family retainer rather than a brother-in-law—someone whose rightful place was below stairs, safely out of sight. Pud, if she was aware of this, chose to ignore it.

I spent dry days sketching and watercolour painting, and wet ones reading or battling through the wind and rain across the hills seeking occasional refuge and a half of best bitter in the various local pubs scattered around the country-side. I never mentioned that to my mother. She wouldn't have approved of me entering a public house, let alone drinking beer. The first time was nearly the last, as I wandered unthinking into the public bar and was met with hostile looks and mumbled disapproval from the assembled men, until the barmaid nodded her head at the door to the saloon and suggested I'd be more comfortable in there on my own in front of the fire.

In the course of these lonely hill walks, with only the grouse and sheep for company, I had plenty of time to reflect on what had happened. I knew I'd been used by Milligan, then thrown away like a well-chewed rag doll that a dog gets bored with. Eventually, I walked so much and thought so much that I couldn't bear to think about him anymore. One morning, as I sat on a rocky outcrop munching an apple, watching the sun force its way through the clouds, I decided it was time to stop moping. I was free of London and the treadmill of the season. The time had come to think about what I wanted for my future, instead of dwelling on my past.

Our time in Yorkshire must have been a torment to my mother. Since my father died, she'd kept herself busy with a relentless schedule: bridge games, hair appointments, concerts, tea parties, dinners, visits to the opera and lengthy telephone calls with her friends to conduct post-mortems on the previous nights' events to dissect the credentials, looks and pedigree of the young men whom she presumed to be in need of me as a wife. It honestly never occurred to me that all this was to help her forget the loss of my father and to help set me on a path to a secure future. I just assumed she did it to make my life as beastly as possible. Here, in Yorkshire with no one around her but me and Pud, she must have been at a loss for what to do. I did suggest she join me on my rambles over the hills, but she gave me a horrified look and claimed she had no suitable footwear. Pud had the good judgment to arrange for her to participate in a bridge party to give her something to do.

When she'd gone, I curled up in front of the range in the big, but cosy, kitchen, contentedly reading a book, while Pud was baking scones. I was glad to be free from Mummy's restless pacing and frequent sighing. Roger, who usually went to the village pub in the evenings, probably to avoid the remote risk of being drawn into conversation with Mummy, was fast asleep in his chair, his elderly dog spread out at his feet. I'd never heard the dog's name and thought it possible she'd never been given one. The sweet smell of the scones filled the kitchen, the clock ticked loudly, and I looked at Pud as she wiped her floury hands on her apron and readied another batch of scones for the oven. For a moment I contemplated telling her everything. I knew Mummy had spun her a yarn about me finding the season a strain on nerves still fragile after losing my father four years earlier. I doubted that Pud believed her but, if I told my aunt what had actually happened, she'd feel sorry for me. I didn't want to be seen as a victim. I hated the way my mother had described Rupert as a predator, as much as I hated what she'd told me about his infidelities. So I kept my confidences and, instead of opening up to Pud, I buried my nose in my book until my mother returned from bridge in a state of high excitement.

'Ginny, I met someone interesting this evening.'

She turned to her sister and gave her a quick hug.

'Thank you so much, Pud, for suggesting Mrs Butterford's bridge party. You're such a clever girl.'

Pud wiped a floury hand across her brow.

'What happened, Fliss? I thought one game of bridge was much like another. And there you were, moaning this morning that the people there were likely to be—what did you say?—"*rather common*", wasn't it?' She winked at me.

'Nonsense, Pud. You make me sound like a snob.' She pulled her hat off and slung it carelessly onto the sideboard.

'I have such good news, Ginny.' The pitch of her voice could break glass and gloomy Roger awoke from his snooze. Doubtless sensing this was something he'd rather not hear, he got up from the chair, clicked his tongue to summon the old sheepdog and went out the back door, the dog's paws padding softly over the stone flags behind him.

Mummy lowered herself into Roger's empty chair, flapping at it first with her gloves, in case the dog-with-no-name had deposited any stray hairs there. 'Please put your book down, Ginny. This is important.'

I complied with a sigh and looked at her with as eager an expression as my limited dramatic talent permitted.

She carried on, her head swivelling to address Pud and me in turn, 'I met a woman this evening who has recently returned from India.'

'Mrs Tilman? I didn't know she was a bridge player,' said Pud.

'A rather indifferent one. But what's so exciting, is she has an unmarried son of just about the right age—I'd say seven or eight years older than you, Ginny. He's here on leave from India and he's staying with his mother. I only met him briefly when he came in the motorcar to collect her and was kind enough to give me a ride home so Mrs Butterford wouldn't have to come out.'

'Really. You can't possibly think...'

'Think? I don't waste time thinking, Ginny—I *act*! I've already set the wheels in motion, darling. I've asked them both to join us tomorrow for tea in Harrogate. It wasn't appropriate to invite them here.' She looked around the room, then flashed a smile at her sister. 'I couldn't impose on you, Pud, in that way, not with you so busy and this place being so...remote. I think you're going to like him, Ginny. I know how frightfully fussy you are, but I've a jolly good feeling about this one.'

'I'd hoped we'd got over all that. I've told you I don't want to be married—I'm actually thinking of going to university.' I wasn't. I was actually thinking of going to art school but knew I'd have to find a better moment to break that piece of news to her—I'd do it by degrees.

'Don't be ridiculous, darling. Everyone wants to be married. No one wants to know a girl who's too clever and bookish.' She rushed on, overcome with excitement, 'Now there's only one tiny snag. But, actually, I don't even think it's so much a drawback as a blessing in disguise.' She hesitated. 'The young man will be going back to India fairly soon. He owns a tea plantation.'

She paused a moment as Pud took the first batch of scones into the scullery, then continued, *sotto voce*, 'I realise it's not what your father and I had in mind for you, but we can't be too choosy now. Of course, as they've both been in India and don't mix in the same circles as us, they won't know anything about *"you know what"*. He intends to spend his entire leave here in Yorkshire. He has business to do in Leeds and wants to spend as much time as possible with his mother. Isn't it marvellous, darling?' She clasped her hands together and looked at me nervously. She was bouncing her crossed ankle up and down.

I tried to be annoyed with her, yet I wasn't. I'd burnt my boats in London, but I didn't want to give up on the art school idea. The best course was to play along with her until this chap disappeared back to India. Then I'd drip feed the idea—perhaps with Pud's help.

'What's his name?'

She beamed at me and glanced at Pud, conspiratorially. 'Anthony. He told me he likes to be called Tony, which I think sounds rather common, so you can stick to Anthony. He'll get used to it. And he went to a fairly good school. Wilder-brooks, down in Dorset. Not quite Eton or Harrow, but not too bad.'

'Steady on, Mummy. I haven't met him yet.'

'No, but I've such a good feeling about him. When I met Mrs Tilman, I sensed at once we were going to get along. Her eyes lit up as soon I told her about you. She confided she's hoping Anthony will find a nice girl to settle down with. The poor woman's been keeping house for him, but she wanted to come home to England. That's why he has such a long leave. I think finding a suitable girl is quite a challenge in India.'

I wanted to suggest he think about advertising for a housekeeper but, as Mummy was in such a good mood, it was better to keep it that way.

She went on, 'Did I say he's a tea planter? I did? That's jolly good news too, as apparently they only grow tea high up in the hills, so it won't be too hot for you.'

Pud spoke at last, 'Don't you think you're getting a bit carried away, Felicity? They haven't even clapped eyes on each other and you've already married them off. Ginny may hate him on sight. She's still young after all.'

'Don't be tiresome, Pud. I'm sure Ginny will give Anthony a fair chance.' She turned to me again. 'Won't you, darling?...Did I tell you he's frightfully good looking? Tall... thick, blonde hair... blue eyes. Perfect manners.'

I shaped my mouth into a rictus smile and picked up my book. 'Right-o. I'll keep an open mind and look forward to meeting him tomorrow. But I can't promise...'

'An open mind is a good start. Now off you go and get your beauty sleep, darling.' She took the book from my hands.

That night I couldn't sleep for what felt like hours. When I did drift off, I slept heavily and dreamed I was walking down the aisle to be married. As I reached the altar, the bridegroom turned away and I looked down to see my bridal gown was missing. I was standing in front of a packed church, stark naked apart from the bridal veil and a string of pearls around my neck. I watched the congregation file out of the church in silence, leaving me there alone at the altar rails, covering my nakedness with my hands as Rupert Milligan's laughter rang in my ears.

MY MOTHER HADN'T EXAGGERATED about Tony. He was probably the best-looking man I'd ever seen. He struck me as an outdoorsy type, with a tall, muscular build, blonde hair, tanned skin and the bluest of eyes. He had lots of finely drawn, white lines where he must have habitually screwed his eyes up against the sun. When he sat down beside me, I felt very small. He was unlike the pallid young men I was used to, with their drawling, bored voices, their brilliantined hair and their pre-planned conversational gambits. He was also a world apart from the arrogant sophistication of Rupert Milligan; I soon found out Tony Tilman had no pretensions. If he had something to say he said it. If he didn't, he kept quiet and listened to what others said and, if no one spoke, he made no attempt to fill the silence.

His manners were impeccable, practically falling over himself trying to pull a chair out for my mother and directing a charm offensive in her direction. He took little notice of me at first, shaking my hand, and then turning to speak with her. I felt a tug of jealousy as she flirted with him. I'd never come near to her skills in that area, feeling gawky and ill at ease when expected to play the game, so I turned my attention to his mother.

Marjorie Tilman was a large lady with a huge bosom like a shelf and poor dress sense. Under her tweed suit, a floral-

print, satin blouse strained under the force of her embon-
point, so that gaps were visible between the buttons,
allowing glimpses of the flesh pink of her girdle. There was a
cloying scent of gardenia about her; talcum powder rather
than perfume, I suspected. Her hair was in an old-fashioned,
crimped style that I guessed she hadn't altered in years. She
was the kind of woman my mother wouldn't normally have
given the time of day, but I decided I liked her. She was reassuringly ordinary.

'Virginia, how lovely to meet you.' She grasped my hands.
Hers were pale and her tiny delicate fingers were out of
proportion to the rest of her. 'Felicity told me so much about
you. Tony and I have been so looking forward to this afternoon. I hope you find Yorkshire agreeable?'

'Most definitely. I've always loved it up here. The
scenery's so wild and the air's so fresh. Such a change from
smoky, old London.'

'I missed the West Riding frightfully when I was in India.
Not that India lacks its own charms,' she added quickly. She
placed a hand lightly on my arm, as though to reassure me.
'Travancore is beautiful. The mountains are stunning. Clean
and cool. Not like the coast, which can be hot and stuffy. The
area where we live is not unlike Yorkshire. But milder in
winter, of course.'

She looked at her son for reinforcement or reassurance,
but my mother interjected, 'Yes, do tell Ginny all about India.
She's always wanted to travel there.'

This was news to me, but my corroboration was
evidently deemed unnecessary, as she ploughed on without
it, 'Ginny's grandfather, my late husband's father, was
stationed in Madras for several years. He was a Major
General in the British Army in India.'

'How awfully interesting.' Mrs Tilman's expression didn't
match her words. Ignoring Mummy's comment, she went on,

'My late husband and I met in 1906 when my own dear father was in the Indian Civil Service and Walter, Anthony's father, was a tea planter. You must have heard of Tilman's Teas? Until he went to school over here, Tony grew up in India, didn't you, darling?' She flashed him a look of undisguised adoration. Perhaps Tony was as embarrassed by his mother as I was by mine, as he only grunted in response.

There was a hiatus in our conversation, punctuated by the serving of tea and cakes. I looked around the room at the vast, glass ceiling and rows of plaster Grecian columns. The place was filled with the rumbling of conversation and the clatter of teacups. I felt shy in the presence of the blonde Nordic giant, but couldn't help stealing the occasional glance up at him as I chatted to his mother and he listened to mine. He was so like my mental image of a Viking warrior that I was already starting to imagine him in a horned helmet, tossing me over his shoulder and carrying me off to his longboat. The prospect was both scary and exciting.

He interrupted my reveries, prompted no doubt by a sly kick under the table from his mother. 'Isn't it a bit dull up here after London, Miss Dunbar?'

'Not at all. I don't think I'm really cut out for the London season—it's a bit overwhelming and I'm not keen on all those dinner parties. And the dancing. I'm afraid I have two left feet. And endlessly practising to curtsey ready for Court made me feel a bit like a performing dog.'

As the words rushed out, I wanted to take them back. I was terrified he'd ask me about being presented; obliging me to confess I'd missed my Court. Mummy had heard and the alarm showed in her eyes. But Tony Tilman just looked at me with a blank expression, so I pressed on, trying to dig myself out of the hole. 'I mean you see the same people all the time and everyone's jockeying for position and trying to get noticed. It's all talk about who was at so and so's the previous night and who will be going to such and such? All frightfully tedious. I much prefer it up here. Open space and quiet. I suppose that means I must be more *Country Life* than *Tatler*.'

He looked puzzled, frowned, then lifted his eyes up to mine and smiled, and it transformed his features. His face went all crinkly round the edges of his eyes where the white lines disappeared and my tummy did a little belly flop.

'Would you like to take a walk around the garden, Miss Dunbar? I'm sure our mothers are keen to dissect last night's game of bridge.'

I jumped to my feet. 'I'd love to.'

Gosh, it was a strain at first. Small talk clearly wasn't his thing. I think he told me that this was the place where Agatha Christie had been tracked down when she went missing a few years back. I probably prattled on about the weather and plays I'd seen in London and that sort of trivia, then tried to find out whether we had any chums in common. We hadn't.

Round and round the gardens we went, he with his hands in the pockets of his overcoat and his eyes fixed straight ahead, me skipping along beside him, trying to keep up.

'Tell me about India,' I said.

I'd hoped asking him about something so familiar would bring him out of himself, but he had little to say. It was as though his own familiarity with the place were universal. I had to drag the information from him with a series of what he probably thought were stupid questions. Verbal description was clearly not his forte. I'd be better off reading books, looking at paintings or watching newsreels. His India was confined to a few meteorological statistics, population numbers and the acreage of his tea plantations.

I struggled on, plugging the gaps in the conversation, terrified he might bring up the London season and my missed Court. I'd have had to dream up an excuse as to why I'd not been presented—but the gods were smiling on me, as he didn't ask. Perhaps he was as little interested in, or impressed by, the London season as I was. After all, he'd spent most of his life in India, so probably wouldn't be aware of what the whole silly business involved. I began to relax.

Then he came to the point. He stopped walking and, still looking straight in front of him, said, 'Look, Miss Dunbar...'

'Do call me Ginny.'

'Look, Ginny, I'm not going to beat about the bush. I'm not much good at this kind of thing. And not a lot of time left before I sail. Sorry, it's dashed awkward...'

'It's quite all right. Go on.' I tried to look encouraging and flashed him a smile.

'I wanted to say, would you mind? I'm starved of company here, stuck in that house, just the mater and me. Would you be game for going to the pictures with me this evening? There's a musical on at the new Odeon with Bing Crosby and Ethel Merman—sounds good fun. If we go to the early show, then we could have a spot of dinner together afterwards. I could pick you up in the motor and run you home later. Maybe you'd like to get out of the house too? But if you're busy this evening...perhaps another time?'

He looked mortified and my heart went out to him. I wanted to give him a hug and tell him it was all right and I felt just the same way.

'Yes. I'd love to. Tonight is perfect.' I wasn't sure about the choice of film, but the prospect of sitting in a darkened theatre beside Tony Tilman was not without appeal.

'Only you seem awfully nice and I'm—'

I interrupted him, 'It's all right. I do understand. Please don't apologise.'

For a moment I was terrified he was going to propose to me on the spot. I knew then with absolute certainty he was going to propose eventually—but I didn't want the embarrassment of it being before we'd even started courting. I didn't even flatter myself it was a case of love at first sight on his part. He was a man in a hurry. I could almost touch the desperation in him.

His face was unable to mask his relief. He was nervous. I wondered if he was as much under the maternal yoke as I was.

He said, 'Thank you. I'm not used to this courting caper. In India, there's just the other planters' wives and a few ladies at the club and absolutely no one as pretty as you.'

Under his shock of blonde hair, his face was reddening through his tan and he looked away, as if fearful he might have overstepped the mark.

I felt a wave of affection for him. He was so gauche and vulnerable. The contrast between his diffident manner and his physical presence was marked.

'Now you're embarrassing me, Tony. Come on, let's go and tell the old girls the good news.' And I took his arm and let him lead me back into the hotel.

SITTING in the cinema in the dark beside Tony Tilman I wondered what it would be like to be kissed by him, to have those big muscular arms around me. I'd only ever kissed one man, unless you count Roddy MacBride when we were eight and playing sardines at the Hendersons'. I was curious how it would feel with someone else, someone so different from Rupert.

About twenty minutes into the film, he reached for my hand and held it until the end. His skin was warm and his hands were large and I liked it. I felt safe with him. Strange to feel safe, you may say, but that's how it was. Perhaps I was still unsettled by the recent events and there, in the dark cinema with Bing and Ethel warbling away on the screen, I felt looked after, cared for, secure.

Tony was a model of gentlemanly conduct. Apart from the covert handholding—which ceased as soon as the house lights came up, he didn't lay a finger on me. He was so far from my first impression of him as a marauding Viking that I was beginning to think he didn't find me attractive. All I got at the end of that evening, and the one that followed, was a quick peck on the cheek. I might have been his elderly aunt. Over our late supper he said little, leaving me to keep up a virtual monologue. He listened intently, but asked few questions and offered little information about himself. Every girl enjoys an appreciative audience, but I did wish he gave more back.

I was right about the proposal though. The third time we went out together he drove back to Pud's and, after turning into the yard in front of the farmhouse, he switched the engine off, leaned across and kissed me on the mouth. He barely brushed my lips, so that the kiss was over almost as soon as it began, leaving me unsure whether to be relieved or disappointed. And then he popped the question. Even though I'd expected it—and my mother had assured me it would only be a matter of time—I wasn't prepared when it happened like that. There was something curiously impersonal about the whole thing. It was the only long leave he'd had in the past four years, so I suppose he wanted to make the best of it.

I spoke, suddenly nervous, my voice echoing in the darkness of the parked car, 'Crumbs, it's a bit unexpected. I don't know what to say.'

'Just say yes.' He took my hand and squeezed it. 'Please.'

'But we barely know know each other.'

'We know a jolly sight more about each other than the average Indian does when he marries. Lucky if he's seen a photograph before he lifts his bride's veil on the wedding day. Not that I'm suggesting we follow Indian customs.

Certainly not. Damned uncivilised. But when there's so little time, one has to grab hold of what chances arise. I'll be back in Travancore in less than two months.'

'Golly…'

'I know it seems fast. But you'll love Mudoorayam. I know you will. And you're such a game girl, Ginny, you'll fit right in. You're frightfully good at the old chitter-chatter, so you'll get along famously with everybody at the Club—all the gang there is very welcoming. And you've no idea what a difference it will make to me having you there. It's pretty grim for a chap on his own.'

I waited, hoping for a declaration of love, for him to give me some sign of feeling or affection. I'd hoped to be swept off my feet, the way it happened at the pictures, and I felt a bit let down. His proposal was all about how marrying me would make his life easier. Maybe that makes me sound ungrateful, bearing in mind my situation, but I still hoped I might be able to grab a bit of happiness, even if it didn't come wrapped up in a title as Mummy would have liked. Handsome as Tony was, I couldn't imagine seeing him over the toast and marmalade every morning.

Eventually I spoke, 'Tony, thank you. I'm honoured and flattered but I can't accept. I'm sorry. I know you'll make someone a wonderful husband, but I can't marry you. I want to study art. I'm not ready to be married. I'm not sure I'm even going to marry at all. Ever.'

Before he could reply, the car door was wrenched open on my side and there was my mother, a fox cape draped around her shoulders, stamping her feet on the frosty ground and pushing her head into the car to talk across me to Tony.

'You need a nice warming scotch, Anthony. That'll set you up for the drive home. Come on, you two. Inside. Far too cold to be sitting out here. My sister is keen to meet you, Anthony. Come on, hurry up, it's freezing.'

She dug me in the ribs, so I got out and Tony had no choice but to follow. Pud was waiting for us in the hallway and, after making the introductions, Mummy left Tony with her and hustled me into the kitchen.

She shut the door behind us and leaning against it, asked, 'Well? We were trying to see what was happening out of the dining room window. I saw him kiss you. Did he propose? You looked as though you were talking seriously.'

'Yes, he did ask me to marry him, and I've said no.'

I hadn't expected her to be ecstatic to hear this, but she gave a little cry that was strangled in her throat before it was fully born. She stepped towards me and clutched my arm. Her eyes were brimming and her fingernails dug into me.

'You have to marry him, Ginny. For heaven's sake. You like him, don't you? You said you did. You've been out with him three times now.'

'Three times. Listen to you, Mummy. Three times is nothing. I don't know him. How can I possibly marry him? I like him, but I don't know him enough to commit the rest of my life to him. You must see that? Besides, we have nothing in common. And I told you. I want to go to university.'

She looked stricken. 'I only want your happiness, darling, but I know you better than you know yourself. You're a clever girl, but you're certainly not the academic type. I wasn't married to your father for nearly twenty years without knowing what that entails, and it's definitely not you. I'd hoped you'd meet someone suitable during the season. I've worked tirelessly to make that happen, and I know that's no longer possible and I don't want to go into all that horrid past history, but you must see this is your best chance. Anthony Tilman is polite, handsome; he comes from a decent family, he has good prospects and he'll provide for you. I hate the thought of you going to India and not being near to you, but I can't be selfish and this is a new beginning for you. You must see that, darling.'

Her words flowed on like a river in flood and I could hear the near panic in her voice. 'It's so hard for me without your father. I do my best. God only knows I do. And it's what he would have wanted. He would want to know you were settled.'

'No.'

'What do you mean, no?'

'I mean I'm not marrying Tony Tilman. And I know Daddy wouldn't push me into doing something I don't want to do.'

She snarled in exasperation and started to answer, but then Pud's head came round the door.

She spoke quietly, so our guest wouldn't hear, 'Mr Tilman's about to go.'

Mummy narrowed her eyes at me, then followed Pud out of the kitchen. I trailed behind her to join the awkward farewells in the hall. I almost relented when I saw Tony's face. His expression reminded me of a statue of the martyred St Sebastian gazing in supplication to heaven. As soon as the front door closed behind him, I slipped upstairs.

Unable to sleep, I heard voices on the landing and padded barefoot across the bedroom to eavesdrop. They were at the far end of the long landing, outside my mother's bedroom door.

'Are you sure about this, Fliss? It's terribly quick. Surely Ginny should get to know the chap a little better first? She's so young. Why not go with her to India to see what the life's like? Find out what she'd be letting herself in for? Give them a chance to get to know each other? You have rather flung them together. I know you want her settled, but isn't it more important she's happy?'

'I know what I'm doing.'

'But is he right for her? He seems awfully quiet.'

'She likes him, Pud. Really she does. She's just a bit mixed up.'

'But does she love him?'

'If not yet, she will do. Just a matter of time. She's been through a lot lately, and I don't want to go into all the details, but believe me she'll be a lot better off out of London and settled in India. Trust me.' Then, with more certainty, as though trying on the idea for size, 'Yes, I'm sure it's the right thing.'

A few seconds of silence followed and I was about to creep back into bed, when I realised they were still there, their voices lower.

'What's really going on, Fliss?'

'What do you mean?'

'You haven't told me why you missed Ginny's Court. And don't tell me it's because she wasn't enjoying coming out— you wouldn't have let that stop you.'

'What are you implying, Pud? That I was forcing my daughter to go through something she didn't want to do?'

'Of course not. But it was very sudden. You can't blame me for thinking there must be more to it. Come on, tell me. You know how I care about Ginny.'

There was a brief silence then my mother said, 'I didn't want to tell you this and I don't want Ginny to know I've told you, but she was in a liaison with someone unsuitable.'

'Good grief. Who?'

'It doesn't matter. They were indiscreet and her reputation is ruined. An older man.'

'Who was it? Tell me, Fliss. For goodness sake. I'm Ginny's godmother.'

There was a long pause, then my mother spoke his name.

Pud gasped. 'That's dreadful... but to get her away from Milligan, you'd be prepared to let her marry *anyone*?'

'Of course not.'

'And it's not just because it was Rupert? Are you sure of that?'

I could hear the sting as my mother slapped her sister's face. 'How dare you? Are you implying I still have feelings for that man?'

'You were engaged to him.'

'How could you? And how dare you presume to tell me how to manage my own daughter. You've no children of your own, so you're not remotely qualified to lecture me about mine.'

A door slammed shut, then I heard my aunt's footsteps as she made her way to her room.

Next morning I went into the dining room for breakfast, to a silence intensified by the loud ticking of the longcase clock and the occasional dull thump of the tail of the dog-with-no-name on the wooden floor. There was no sign of Roger. Pud and my mother were sitting at opposite ends of the table, Pud reading the newspaper and my mother giving her full, undivided attention to an inspection of the back of her own hands. When I announced I was returning to London and I intended to apply for a place at art school for the following year, Pud slipped out of the room, leaving me to face Mummy alone. It was not as I expected. Instead of objecting, she listened in silence, shook her head, then told me with a tone of resignation that she wanted only the best for me.

CHAPTER 4

I̲t̲ ̲w̲a̲s̲ strange being back in London without a mantelpiece groaning with invitations. My mother didn't complain about being forced to keep a low profile but, after all those weeks in Yorkshire, she was anxious to renew her acquaintance with her hairdresser and her dressmaker. I threw myself into organising my portfolio of artwork. What surprised me most was the way Mummy took on the task of helping me find a place at art school as her next project.

'If that's what you want, Ginny. If you're really sure, I won't stand in your way. I just want you to be happy. But I hope this is not down to that man's influence on you and you wanting to be like him?'

I assured her that was the last thing I wanted and I showed her the few paintings I'd done while we were in Yorkshire.

'I know nothing of art, Ginny, but these do seem awfully good. I'll have a word with Viscount Hambledon and see if he has any suggestions. According to Patricia, he's been chairing some committee to review the future of art education. If anyone knows, it will be him.'

She left me going through my artwork, desperately trying to pull together those that I thought might impress a prospective admissions panel. Rupert Milligan's coaching had mainly consisted of him telling me when things were not good enough and encouraging me to throw them away and start again. I looked at the meagre stack of work that was left and told myself it was about quality not quantity—and I was proud of what I'd done.

And so it was, that less than a week after returning to London, I found myself heading to Campden Hill for an interview with F. Ernest Jackson, the Principal of the Byam Shaw School of Art. To my surprise, Mr Jackson was a Yorkshireman, from Huddersfield. He had made a reputation for himself designing posters for the London Underground, as well as propaganda posters during the War.

He examined my scant portfolio in silence, then leaned back in his chair and polished his spectacles. 'Miss Dunbar, your work shows some promise, but you need to apply yourself more assiduously to your craft before being considered for serious study of art. These are daubs. Sometimes happy accidents. Like this.' He pointed the stem of his pipe at a watercolour of the Yorkshire Dales. 'These little touches of colour redeem what would otherwise be an insipid piece, but there's no attention to detail. No considered design. No craft. Until you have developed your powers of observation and concentration, you will never make a painter. Only when you have seen what is there, can you decide what to put in and what to leave out. Look more. Draw more. How many hours a day do you devote to your art?'

I didn't know what to say. Had he asked hours a week, I'd have still had to exaggerate. Averaged across the year, it was probably a few hours a month. I looked down and said nothing.

'I thought as much. You're a dabbler, my dear. A hobbyist.

You need to practise your art every day. It's not about trying to be perfect. It's about trying to improve.'

He picked up a charcoal study—one of the few Rupert Milligan had praised. It was a drawing of one of his arms. I was proud of it and waited for Mr Jackson's endorsement. Instead, he glanced at it and put it down again.

'Be yourself, Miss Dunbar. I sense you're trying to emulate someone else. You will only make an artist if you stop trying to be someone you're not. My advice to you is to go away and do nothing but draw. And every day. Leave your paints aside and concentrate on your draughtsmanship. Come and see me again in a year and I'll give your work another look. But, if you carry on like this,' he slammed the portfolio shut and pushed it back across the desk to me, 'we will be wasting each other's time. You'd be better off getting married and concentrating on bringing up a family. The world of art is not the most welcoming to women and I will only accept those I consider to be exceptionally gifted, as they will be taking a place that would otherwise be afforded to a man, for whom art will be life and livelihood.'

I was crushed by Mr Jackson's words, although I knew them to be true. I had nursed the foolish hope that he would applaud my creativity, strew metaphorical flowers at my feet and open wide the doors of the Byam Shaw to me. I wandered around Kensington Gardens feeling humiliated. I suspected my mother had set me up for a fall, and I was irritated with myself for my naiveté and my hubris. I saw myself as Mr Jackson must have seen me: a spoilt girl with an over-inflated idea of her own talent. As the fog thickened and the afternoon turned to dusk, I sloped back to Leighton Square.

I was barely inside and starting to take off my coat when the doorbell rang. Proud, our elderly retainer, was enjoying a rare afternoon off and, when I opened the door, there was

Rupert Milligan, grinning at me, a beribboned cake box in one hand and a bottle of champagne in the other.

'I've brought meringues. Your favourites.' He stepped past me into the house and put the box on the hallstand. 'I've just run into Valerie Davenport and she told me she saw Felicity at the hairdresser's this afternoon. She reckoned she's good for a couple more hours, so I thought I'd scoot around here and cheer up my favourite girl.'

'Get out.'

He gave me his lazy patrician smile, a man used to getting his own way. 'Come on, Gin. There's no need to be mad at me still. It was just a bit of a prank. Old Phil Osborne and I got wellied one night and I showed him the paintings, and he bet me ten pounds I wouldn't let him put them in the exhibition. You know what it's like, Gin. A man has to live. And you couldn't even see your face in the nude one. And they were both bloody good. In fact, Phil sold the nude for forty guineas so I've bought you a little gift.' He reached in his pocket and pulled out a little box, then moved towards me, his arms stretched out as though about to draw me into a kiss. I jumped away, pressing my back against the wall, trying to get as far as possible from him.

'Aren't you remotely sorry for what you did?' I said. 'For wrecking my reputation? For all the promises you made about marrying me?'

'Come on, Gin, they weren't real promises. You know I'd never leave Celia. There's the children to think about. Not to mention my main source of income.'

'You disgust me. You're a creep. A bully. A…pervert.'

'Come on. You wanted it as much as I did.' He put his hand out to touch my hair.

'I was fourteen,' I screamed at him. 'I was a child. You stole my childhood. You poisoned it. You've ruined my life.'

I was tempted to strike him in the face with my handbag, but all I really wanted was to be rid of him, so I opened the front door and stepped outside, slamming it behind me and quickly locked the mortise. I ran down the street through the heavy smog, caring not whether he'd be able to find a spare key and effect his escape or be trapped in the hallway until either Proud or my mother returned and released him. I was oblivious to the biting cold of the afternoon, tears of rage running down my face. I gulped the air as I ran, not caring where I was going. And I couldn't see anyway; the thick fog blotted out the shapes of the familiar buildings and muddied the effect of the street lamps.

I didn't get far. At the corner of Leighton Square, I crashed into someone coming round the corner and, after he caught my fall, I realised it was Tony Tilman. Before I knew what I was doing, I was clinging to his lapels and sobbing into the rough tweed of his overcoat as I felt his arms encircle me and hold me tightly against his bulk. The same sensation I had in the cinema swept through me. I felt safe, cared for, anchored. He started to turn me back towards the house, but I pulled away.

'I don't want to go home yet.'

We were close to a pub so he shepherded me inside the deserted lounge bar and ordered us both large brandies, then watched in silence as I drank mine down in little burning gulps.

'What on earth's wrong, Ginny? What's upset you? Gosh, I hope it's not seeing me again?'

I looked up at him though my tear-filled eyes. 'I'm actually jolly pleased to see you. I didn't expect to meet you again, but I'm glad I have.'

His face reddened and he looked down, suddenly shy. 'What's the matter?' he asked.

I hesitated for a moment before telling a half-truth, 'I had a big row with Mummy. She's not terribly keen on the idea of me going to art school.'

'I see.'

And then, before I knew it, I was telling him about Mr Jackson and his verdict on my work. He nodded his head solemnly and patted my arm to convey sympathy, but must have found it difficult to understand and empathise with my experience.

We fell into silence, until I asked, 'What are you doing in London? And here in Leighton Square?'

'Came to see you.'

'Me? Why?'

If he found me rude, he was too polite to acknowledge it. 'You left without saying goodbye.'

'Sorry. That was bad-mannered of me.'

'I did spring my proposal on you. Didn't give you much of a chance to get used to the idea or to get to know me. In such a darned hurry, I took it for granted you'd understand. I'm not so good at the old courting. Haven't had much experience. The mater gave me a bit of a ticking off, actually, for botching it.'

He picked up his leather gloves and slapped them absently against the edge of the table. 'To be perfectly honest, I've been walking around the bally square in the fog for an hour or so, trying to pluck up the courage to knock on your door. Almost did a runner back to King's Cross, but didn't dare face the mater without at least having had a go.' He had a sheepish expression.

I wondered if he'd witnessed Rupert's arrival, but if he had, he made no mention of it. Thank heavens for the fog.

'A go? At what?'

He looked away, his voice quiet, 'Wanted to see if I could persuade you to give me another chance. Maybe take it a bit slower this time? If you don't want to think about it, I'll buzz off and leave you in peace but, if you're willing to give me a go, you could come out to India and visit and, if you like it, we could get engaged over there and think about getting married here next year. The mater would come along, Mrs Dunbar, too, if she'd like, so all above board. Or you could stay at the Club? Then, if you don't like India or me, you can come back to England and we'll forget all about it. I won't hold you to anything. I know it's a jolly big step. Only, Ginny, I really hope you'll give me a chance as you're the most smashing girl and I don't like the thought of you being snapped up by some other chap. What do you say?'

He looked into my eyes and, this time, his expression was so sincere and so eager and anxious. I didn't even mind that he still hadn't told me he loved me. He was probably like Mummy; taught to button up the emotions and keep them safely under control. It didn't mean he didn't feel anything.

Seeing Rupert Milligan had made me realise there was no way I could go back to living in London. I would never be free of him. And, even if I worked single-mindedly on my drawing and persuaded Mr Jackson to think again about admitting me to the Byam Shaw, I would be even closer to Milligan's milieu. And, so, I decided, then and there. I downed the last drop of brandy and laid my hand over Tony's and said, 'I'd like to marry you, Tony. And right away. Before you go back. Just as you first suggested. I don't need to think about it anymore.'

I was rewarded with a smile that lit up the dingy pub. 'Really? You don't want to see what it's like out there first? Sure it's not all a bit rushed for you?'

'I'm sure. I just needed a couple of days for it to sink in. I've never really liked London and India will be an adventure. I'm looking forward to it.'

'And art school?'

I hesitated for a moment, then said, 'Mr Jackson's probably right. I'm not good enough to be a professional artist. I can carry on painting as a hobby. I'm sure there will be heaps of interesting subjects for me in India.'

He leaned forward and planted a kiss on my forehead, then took my hands in his. 'You won't regret it, Ginny. I promise you. I'll take care of you. I'll do all I can to make you happy. Can't wait to tell the mater.'

'Mummy will be happy too. She thinks a lot of you.'

We sat on in the pub making plans for the wedding. Tony had business to do in Leeds and I was only too happy to return with him to Yorkshire to avoid any possibility of seeing Milligan again. I wasn't sure how my mother would react to going back, since she'd left on bad terms with Pud, but it turned out she was so overjoyed I'd changed my mind about marrying Tony that the relief came off her in waves. She even flung her arms around him in an uncharacteristic display of affection.

I never got to find out who let Rupert Milligan out of the house. Proud was too discreet to mention such a thing, and my mother was so overwhelmed with the news of my coming nuptials that, had she known, she wouldn't have mentioned it anyway. And, possibly, Milligan, being the slippery creature he was, found a way out himself through a window or via the servants' quarters.

Tony and I went twice a week to the pictures in Harrogate and I dined with him and Marjorie once a week. During the day, he was busy with tea-related business in Leeds and both our mothers were busy with planning the wedding. I found it hard to enthuse about the size and shape of table centres and decided it was politic to leave them alone to the inevitable wrangling over the seating plan.

I wanted a modest, quiet ceremony and knew that what had happened in London would constrain my mother's worst excesses and limit her options on the guest list. Tony invited a couple of dozen school friends, as well as a few distant relatives. I prayed none of them would be aware of my recent role as artistic model.

I'd expected our new status as a soon-to-be-married couple would lead to Tony taking a few more liberties with me, but he was a model of gentlemanly behaviour; a stark contrast to my former lover. If I had a fleeting doubt about his lack of passion, I pushed it aside and presumed things would be different once we were married. And, to be honest, he hadn't really inspired any feelings of passion in me; just a sense of calm and order, as though at last I'd passed through a stormy sea and was safely back in harbour.

Tony was to sail ahead to India a few days after the wedding to arrange for his house there to be fixed up for me, and Mummy insisted I needed time to acquire a wardrobe appropriate to life in the colonies. I was to join her at Leighton Square after the honeymoon so we could do my shopping together in town. Evidently, she believed the presence of a diamond ring and a gold band would wipe out all traces of my sullied reputation should we run into any of her friends. Looking back now and seeing her in a kinder light than I did then, I believe she wanted to hang onto me for a bit longer but, at the time, I was annoyed at what I thought was a pointless delay. I was becoming excited about the prospect of a new life in India, not knowing what to expect but sure that it had to be better than the London season, and I longed for the safe margin of a three-week voyage and over five thousand miles to separate me from Rupert Milligan.

The wedding was to take place in the Berkshire village where my mother had been born and married. As it was November, I tried to rule out the horrors of a white bridal gown; a source of great anxiety after my recurrent nightmare of my wedding dress dematerialising on the steps of the altar. Mummy was horrified when I suggested a tailored suit. 'I don't want to hear that idea again. It would be advertising to the world and the Tilmans that you're not..., you know.'

In the end, we settled on the ivory silk gown that had been made for my cancelled Court debut.

There was only time for a three day honeymoon before Tony's return to India. I was hoping for Paris, but he vetoed the idea.

'No time. No sooner there and we'd have to turn round and come back to be in time for my ship.' So it was Eastbourne.

CHAPTER 5

ON THE MORNING of my wedding day, I sat in the hotel drawing room flipping nervously through *The Times*, waiting for the bridal car. Without my father to give me away, Pud had offered up Roger to do the honours. Mummy wasn't too thrilled, but there was no suitable alternative. I'm sure old Roger wasn't very happy either, but then he was never very happy anyway.

Reading the paper was preferable to sitting, unoccupied, listening to the ticking of the clock and the spitting of burning logs in the fireplace while Roger paced up and down the room in silence, sucking on his pipe. At least Mummy wasn't around to fret about the newsprint getting on my hands or my gown. *The Times* that morning was full of the story of the burning down of the Crystal Palace. There were photographs of the flames consuming the enormous glass building. It seemed portentous; this imperial landmark crushed and destroyed just as I was embarking on my own exploration of the far flung corners of what was beginning to be clear was a dying empire. The words of Mr Churchill said it all for me: *"The end of an age".* It felt like the end of one for me, too—but the start of a new, better one, I hoped.

In the car, Roger cleared his throat, looked embarrassed, then said to me in his thick Yorkshire accent, 'Raight, I orpe tha'll be as appeh in 't marriage as our lass and I ave bin in ours.'

I muttered my thanks and tried not to look surprised. I couldn't imagine Roger and Pud happy with each other. In fact, I couldn't imagine Roger being happy at all. Then I remembered that day I'd caught sight of them together on the dry stone wall. I suddenly felt lonely and in need of my father. I leaned over and took Roger's hand. He didn't react; just carried on staring out of the window, but he didn't pull away and, as we took up our positions in the church porch, he gave me a little nod of encouragement and what was the shadow of a smile.

Moving slowly up the aisle to the sound of the thundering organ, I kept my eyes fixed on Tony as he waited at the altar rails, his eyes shining. He was so handsome, so tall, so reassuringly solid, like a big sturdy tree; but, as I spoke the vows, I shivered and wondered whether I was doing the right thing. It had all happened so fast. Pud was right—I was young and inexperienced in life. But I also knew I'd been damaged, and Tony was offering me a new beginning.

A voice cried out inside me as I stood there beside him. *You've not told him the truth. He'll find out and he won't want you anymore.* Then the organ roared into life again and, the next thing I knew, he was leading me back down the aisle past the ranks of smiling faces. Mrs Tony Tilman.

I barely saw Tony at the reception. Once the food and formalities were concluded, he got steadily squiffed with his friends. They sang old school songs with increasing raucousness and diminishing tunefulness, while I sat with our mothers and a few of his friends' wives and girlfriends.

He'd always been so polite, so correct and dignified, but here he was, transformed into a brainless, braying idiot. I wondered if he was looking for Dutch courage before our wedding night, or just grateful to have a chance to carouse with the boys after several weeks stuck in Yorkshire with Marjorie.

My mother-in-law had arranged for a driver to take us to Eastbourne. As soon as we got into the motorcar, Tony fell asleep and slept all the way there, snoring loudly, his head lolling uncomfortably on my shoulder. When we reached The Grand Hotel in the early hours of the morning, the driver and hall porter half-dragged and half-carried him inside and held him upright in the lift that took us up to our suite, where he immediately passed out, fully clothed, on top of the bed. I took off his shoes and pulled the counterpane over him, then put on the satin and lace nightdress Pud had given me as a wedding gift. I studied my reflection in the looking glass and ran my hands over the soft fabric, tracing the contours of my body. Then, determined not to cry, I climbed into the other side of the bed and fell asleep straight away.

The next morning, when I emerged from the bathroom, Tony was still comatose. His Hollywood-handsome face was covered with a dusting of stubble, but he looked as peaceful as a sleeping baby and I decided not to wake him. I went for a walk along the seafront past the newly built domed bandstand, with its lines of empty deck chairs, as the winter sea crashed loudly against the shingle of the beach. The sky was heavy and an icy wind blew in off the Channel over the regimented beds of the Carpet Gardens.

What on earth was I doing here? I barely knew the man I'd left sleeping in the Grand Hotel. Here I was in a place I didn't really want to be, with a virtual stranger, whom I was about to follow to the other side of the world, to live in a place of which I knew even less. But what was the alternative? Stuck in Leighton Square with nothing to do, shunned by society and fearful of running into Rupert Milligan? With Mummy increasingly anxious about my future and I increasingly consumed with regret about my past?

I pulled my fur coat around me, a present from my mother to mark my eighteenth birthday; the biting cold made the prospect of India appealing. What had I got to lose? Apart from the silver fox coat—I wouldn't need that in India. But I was annoyed with Tony for getting drunk, and I was nervous about this stranger who was so different from the quiet, respectful chap I had known in Harrogate, so I lingered as long as possible on my walk, trudging the length of the pier, stopping to watch the men fishing off the end.

When I walked up to the entrance of the big, white hotel, Tony was hovering in the lobby. 'Thank God, Ginny. I was jolly worried. Thought you were angry and gone back to London.'

He led me into the dining room where they were still serving luncheon to the last few stragglers.

'When did you rise from the dead?' I asked.

'Won't happen again, old girl. I promise. Not a good start I know. Hadn't seen the chaps for ages and afraid I let rip. Wanted to let the old hair down a bit. Sorry. Overdid it, didn't I?' He ran a hand through his shock of blonde hair and his face had the expression of a little boy caught trying to smoke his father's cigar.

He carried on, 'What have you been up to, darling? Out there all on your own?' He nodded towards the picture windows overlooking the sea.

'It's Eastbourne, not darkest Africa. No wild animals or scary natives. I've been walking along the seafront, dodging the bath chairs.'

He gave me a blank look, as though I were speaking to him in Swahili.

He tried again. 'We can go out and have a bit of a mosey around after lunch. If you're game, that is.'

'I think I've already exhausted the pleasures of the promenade.' I was deliberately being beastly.

'I'm sure there's plenty more to do and see. How about Beachy Head? White cliffs and lighthouse and all that...or maybe you're tired after all that walking and you'd like to lie down for a while?'

I thought of the satin nightdress and said, 'I'm not tired at all. I'd love to go to Beachy Head.'

We passed the short drive up to the cliff top mostly in silence. His fingers brushed against mine, but I pretended not to notice and, before he could take hold of my hand, I shoved it into my coat pocket and turned to stare out of the window of the taxi as we drove up above the town and over the rolling downlands, empty but for the drifts of grazing sheep.

Side-by-side, on the cliff top in a howling wind, we looked down at the black and white striped lighthouse, which rose out of the grey-green, chalky sea. I felt melancholy and a bit dizzy and instinctively reached for his hand. I was thinking about my father again and how everything had been horrid since he died. Tony squeezed my hand, but kept silent, for which I was grateful. We tramped about on the downs for a while, getting colder and colder, until I spotted the Beachy Head Hotel and steered us in the direction of a warming Whisky Mac.

We got back to the Grand with a couple of hours to spare before dinner. I didn't know what to expect but, as he helped me out of my coat and leaned in to kiss me, my mother's words rang in my ears. *'Whatever you do, don't let him find out you're not a virgin. He's a decent man and doesn't deserve to be hurt.'*

I'd tried to argue with her, troubled by what I knew was deceit. 'As he's a good man, then surely it's wrong to lie to him?'

'Don't be a little fool, Ginny. Do you want to wreck your marriage before it's started? If Tony wants an annulment, where will you be then? Darling, trust me, I know I'm right about this.'

I was nervous, despite the fact Rupert Milligan had done his level best to give me a comprehensive education in the arts of the bedroom—or maybe it was because of that. I went into the bathroom and got out of my clothes and into the satin night-gown. When I stood in front of Tony, I was trembling and it was all too easy to give him the impression it was my first time. But, in the final analysis, I don't think he'd have noticed if Mata Hara had been in bed with him, as it was over almost as soon as it began. Afterwards, he was apologetic and solicitous of me. I was relieved we'd got it over with, but a bit deflated, like opening a birthday gift and finding it was just a box of handkerchiefs.

When I emerged from the dressing room of our suite, ready for dinner, he grinned at me—I suppose in apprecia-tion. I was wearing an evening gown in midnight blue, closely fitted, with an asymmetric neckline, a cinched waist with the bias cut skirt gathered slightly on my left hip. He jumped up from where he was sitting on the edge of the bed and held out a velvet box. Inside was a pearl and diamond filigree necklace. It was delicate and rather beautiful. He put it around my neck and then, as though embarrassed, muttered that we would be late for dinner.

The strains of the chamber orchestra rose to meet us from the lounge hall as we went down the stairs. The sweet-ness of the strings was complimented by the lush sound of the Mustel organ. They were playing *Limelight*, and the violin soared above the rich double bass before the other instruments swept in to join them. I felt a sudden release of tension and slipped my hand into his. I decided I was going to miss him when he left me in a couple of days. I felt warm inside and happy for the first time I could remember.

He was quiet during the meal. His conversation rarely strayed from cricket, rugby, the weather, and the clues from that morning's *Daily Telegraph* crossword. As usual, I had to take the lead. Not that it was particularly hard. I had, after all, spent the London season trying to do the same with a long procession of supposedly eligible men and chatted away to him happily.

I asked him again about India, 'Do you love it, Tony?'

'Suppose so. Never really thought about it. Grew up there and was miserable when I was sent back here to boarding school. Couldn't wait to get back.'

'What did you miss about it?'

He shrugged. 'It's just what I was used to. Home. Suppose I felt much freer there.'

I nodded in encouragement, waiting for him to elaborate, but he lapsed into silence again.

We danced a couple of stiff waltzes. Fred Astaire wouldn't need to watch his back but, then to be fair, neither would Ginger Rogers. My debutante dancing lessons at the Vacanis' dance school in Piccadilly had done little to address my poor coordination. I'd managed to master the royal curtsey—a skill that would be of no help to me now. But I was feeling so happy, I determined not to let anything spoil my mood. We moved into the bar for a nightcap and, sitting there beside him in the mahogany room with the lights from the chandelier lighting up the rows of crystal glasses, I reflected that what had started as a bloody awful day had turned out rather well.

When we got back to our suite, I took off the necklace and slipped it back into its velvet box. 'Thanks again for my beautiful necklace, it's absolutely perfect. I love it, you clever thing.'

'Good show.' Then matter-of-factly, he added, 'Actually the mater picked it out. I don't have much of a clue about these things. Glad the old girl picked a winner.' Then he climbed into bed beside me, flicked off the light, said goodnight and dropped off to sleep straight away.

This wasn't what was meant to happen on a honeymoon. I assumed it must be my fault; that I was undesirable, unpleasing. My sense of self-worth had been calibrated by Milligan's voiced appreciation for what we did together. He had heaped praise upon me—I realise now, to encourage me to go further with him each time. Tony, in contrast, was silent. I interpreted this silence as disappointment in me. The romance of the orchestra had kindled a sense of romance in me, but had failed to move my husband.

Worried I had disappointed, on our next and final night in Eastbourne, I took it upon myself to try to remedy matters, drawing upon what I had learned in Holbein Mews. Tony was lying on his back and I pulled back the bedcovers and moved headfirst down the bed, undid the cord of his striped cotton pyjamas and took his limp penis into my mouth. He hardened immediately, but jumped up as though electrocuted and pushed my head away.

'Good God! What the hell do you think you're doing? Where on earth did you pick up that trick?'

I was stung, retreating back up the bed and sitting up against the pillows with my legs drawn up in front of me. Despite his evident disgust at what I'd tried to do, he was aroused. He grabbed me and flung me down on the bed and took me quickly, coming almost at once with a great cry I feared the guests in the adjoining rooms would hear. Afterwards, I curled myself into a ball, cheeks burning with shame and humiliation. I thought he had gone off to sleep but, then, his voice cut through the darkness.

'I don't know what made you think that was a good idea. It's not something a decent woman does to her husband.' My heart hammered inside my ribcage when he added, 'Look, I hope this doesn't mean you've been with a man before?'

The lies flowed. It was a case of self-preservation. I was terrified that what my mother had said would come true, and the disgrace I thought I'd avoided would drag me back down and ruin my life.

'I'm sorry. I'd no idea. One of my married girlfriends told me it's what men like. I thought you weren't happy with me. That you didn't want me. I thought maybe if I tried that...'

'She can't be a nice girl. Maybe some men do like that sort of thing, but it's not something a woman should do to her husband. For heaven's sake, Ginny, that was the giddy limit.'

I started to sob. I so didn't want to, but I couldn't help it. All I'd wanted was to please him, and here I was sabotaging my marriage before the honeymoon was over. Tony turned over in the bed and put his arms around me.

'Don't cry, darling. It's not your fault. I expect your so-called friend was having a joke at your expense. Let's just forget all about it. I'd never expect you to do something degrading like that for me. I have far too much respect for you. Now go to sleep. We'll forget all about it.'

He kissed me lightly on the top of my head and turned on his side and was asleep in moments. I lay there in the darkness, silently cursing Rupert Milligan and my own still childish ignorance. I looked at the dark bulk of Tony's body next to me, willing him to wake up, turn over and take me in his arms again. But he slept on, oblivious. When the scream of seagulls signalled the imminent dawn, I grabbed my dressing gown and went out onto the stone balcony to watch the light come up over the wintry sea. I leaned on the balustrade, shivering as the outline of bare pine trees, twisted and bent by years of wind, emerged from the darkness. It was hard to imagine the sun ever shining down on the tennis courts, denuded of their nets for the winter. It all looked so bleak.

Three days later, I waited on the quayside at Tilbury as Tony's ship moved away from the dock. Looking up at his diminishing figure against the railings, waving to me, I willed myself to miss him but was unsure I would. Our honeymoon had not proved to be the breathless romance I had hoped for. Tony was down to earth, considerate and utterly reliable; qualities I valued as they translated into safety and stability. His rectitude was the polar opposite to the turpitude of Rupert Milligan. But I yearned for that mythical desire, joy and rushing blood I witnessed when I went to the pictures— longing, passion, love. Not sex, as that was never on the screen in those days, and sex was something I associated with shame, furtiveness and deceit; something that had got me into big trouble, first with my seducer, and now with my husband. No, sex was definitely to be avoided where possible —but a little romance? Who wouldn't long for some of that?

As my mother ushered me away from the dockside into a waiting cab, I wished I'd argued the case more strongly for going with Tony. She could have had some dresses made and shipped out after me, and I could have roughed it a bit while the work on our home in India was going on. She seemed to sense my mood and immediately went into military mode to head off any possibility of me wanting a bit of maternal comfort.

'Righto, I've made a list. Marjorie Tilman says this Muddy-what's-it place isn't exactly Park Lane and the social life centres on what they call the club. Sounds absolutely frightful. Like the Pony Club. I know what those colonial types are like. They just sit around all day, bossing the natives about and getting pissed. No need to spend a fortune with Norman Hartnell. I know you're lucky to have Anthony in the circumstances, but you're going to have to watch your spending, Virginia. He's not exactly made of money. In fact, had I realised...never mind.'

After delving around in the depths of her handbag for her compact, she began to powder her nose. 'We'll have one or two signature pieces made for day wear and evening, and then bulk out the rest of your wardrobe with off-the-peg. No one there will be any the wiser. Shall we start off at Marshall & Snelgrove?'

Day followed identical day of her barking orders at the various poor women fitting me and making alterations. Then, just a week after Tony left, the king abdicated. I didn't feel sorry for the poor man; if my debutante days had taught me anything, it was that being on show all the time is no cause for pleasure. He was probably well out of it and lucky to be free to spend his life with the woman he loved. After all, he wasn't going to need to watch his spending as Mummy had so bluntly put it. And he could choose his place of exile. I, on the other hand, had no say in mine.

I found it easier to say goodbye to my mother than to Pud, who had come down to London to see me off. Mummy was determined to show no emotion at the prospect of separation from her only child, possibly for years. Pud, on the other hand, was teary eyed and wouldn't let go of my hand.

The day started out as a classic London pea-souper, with smog shrouding the buildings when we drove through the City and out to the docks. As the fog lifted, I looked through the window at the smoke-blackened offices and warehouses crowding claustrophobically around us and was glad to be going. I felt a frisson of excitement at the adventure ahead of me.

We found a porter to carry the impressive collection of trunks and bags my mother had insisted were essential to my survival, then she and Pud came on board to inspect my cabin —first class and for me only—and declared it passed muster.

Pud slipped a copy of *Wuthering Heights* into my hand, and said, 'Something for you to escape to if India gets too hot and you're missing the Yorkshire weather.'

Mummy, unsentimental, breezed through it all. 'Now, don't forget, darling, you must introduce yourself to the Finchingtons.'

When I didn't respond, she carried on irritably, 'For heaven's sake darling, you never listen to a word I say. Bunty Finchington came out the same year as me. We were great chums. She was a maid of honour at my wedding. It's such a shame we didn't get a chance to see them in London. They came down from Scotland yesterday. Their daughter has just produced their first grandchild. They're based in Delhi. Bunty's husband, Ian, is something terribly important in the colonial service.'

She narrowed her eyes at me. I felt like a butterfly pinned in a display case. 'They're bound to be seated at the captain's table, so make sure you're included in their party. I've written to Bunty that you're on board; so let's go and call in on her now so I can do the introductions. The purser will show us their cabin.'

'No. Please. I'm a bit tired. I want to lie down for a while. I promise I'll meet your friends, but in my own time. Why don't you both head off now—I hate goodbyes.'

She looked at me with an expression I took to be disapproval, wrapped up in poorly disguised gratitude, and, after proffering a heavily powdered cheek, gave me a quick hug and hurried out of the cabin without a backward glance. According to Pud, she cried in the car all the way back to

Leighton Square. Pud told me this years later, after Mummy was dead. Had I known at the time, I would not have believed it.

Shortly after they'd left, there was a knock at my cabin door. Fearing it was Bunty Finchington, I threw on my dressing gown so I could pretend to be about to take a bath. But it was Marjorie Tilman.

'May I come in, Virginia?' There was a coolness in her voice.

I stepped aside to let her in. 'How kind of you to come and see me off. It's a shame you've just missed Mummy. The ship's leaving in less than an hour.'

'This won't take long.' Her voice was curt and she didn't return my smile. 'May I sit down?' She unpinned and removed her hat and settled herself into a chair. I remained standing, leaning against a side table.

'This is not an easy thing to say, but say it I must. My son believes he's made a good choice in you as a wife and I have no wish to disabuse him. For one thing, it's too late, and, for another, it would break his heart. His happiness is paramount to me.'

I knew what was coming.

'But make no mistake about it, Virginia, I am marking your card. I have already spoken to your mother about the things I've heard about you and your involvement with a married man. Felicity tried to pass it off as malicious gossip and, then, as misguided youthful spirits on your part and the lack of the steadying influence of a father, but I'm not so easily fobbed off. I want you to know if you do anything to hurt my son, you'll have me to answer to—and I can be a formidable enemy.'

Until now, I'd witnessed nothing but sweetness and smiles from Marjorie Tilman and here she was now like a snarling she-wolf protecting her only cub.

My voice was a stutter. 'I...it...I didn't...does Tony?'

'He has no idea. And I mean to keep it that way. I mistakenly believed you to be the innocent creature you appear. Not some trollop who takes her clothes off for married men. I don't want to hear a whisper about anything else of this nature. Is that clear? I am presuming, based on your mother's assurances, you have had no further contact with this man?'

'No. Nothing,' I was whispering, but inside, my heart was hammering and I was angry. Angry at the way she'd ambushed me. Angry at the way she'd humiliated me, and angry that my mother-in-law now had a hold over me that I knew she would not hesitate to exploit.

CHAPTER 6

THE VOYAGE TOOK JUST under three weeks. We stopped at places with names familiar from the school geography lessons I had paid so little heed to: Gibraltar, Algiers, Marseilles, Malta, Port Said, the Suez Canal and Aden. I drank in the sights, drunk on the colour and novelty after dreary, grey London and wished for someone to share it with me. I tried to imagine Tony beside me, but I was still haunted by Eastbourne. I imagined him pacing up and down the decks, bored by the confinement and without the distraction of the *Daily Telegraph* crossword and sports reports. Had I made a mistake marrying him? What lay ahead of me at the end of my journey?

But the longer I was at sea and the nearer we got to India, the more I romanticised my new husband, transforming him into an intrepid adventurer, like the flimsy nonsense of the Hollywood movies I loved. Without reality to confound my dreams, I pictured him as a doughty Errol Flynn, a man whose good looks were matched by a swashbuckling, self-confident charm. In India, he would be in his natural element. I began to approach our future with renewed optimism.

The ship, *The Viceroy of India*, was only eight years old and was plush, modern and comfortable. For the first few days at sea, my sleep was interrupted by the sound of weeping coming through the thin cabin wall. I was next door to a woman returning to join her husband in India after depositing their two young children at their British boarding schools for the first time. She was one of many such women on board, devastated at being parted from their brood. I wondered if Marjorie had cried like that when she left Tony at school for the first time. Somehow I doubted it.

Once we reached the southern Mediterranean, I would sit in a deckchair for hours, shaded by an umbrella, reading novels and swimming in the salt-water pool. Although a little lonely, I was relieved not to have my mother breathing down my neck, telling me to stop slouching, chivvying me to go to the hairdresser or hurrying me off to my next engagement. I worked with pencil and sketchbook, drawing quick little studies of my fellow passengers, careful to avoid detection. The days passed happily, but the evenings were a bit of a trial. Dining on board was terribly formal and every bit as bad as the dinners I'd endured during my brief London season.

As my mother had preordained, Bunty Finchington took me under her wing. Everywhere I went on the *Viceroy of India*, there was Bunty with her husband, Ian, a few steps behind. I became adept at giving them the slip, apart from at dinner when it was out of the question.

I wanted to lie low in case anyone on board knew my story. Sometimes London feels like a village. But no one knew, or if they did, my proximity to Bunty provided a protective shield. Ian Finchington rarely spoke. He carried a lot of clout in government circles and must have been the kind of man who works miracles behind the scenes, but he was hard to engage in conversation and I inwardly groaned when I was seated next to him at dinner. He treated me like an inconsequential girl, unworthy of his time. Bunty made up for him. A leading light among the diplomatic wives, she was one of those women born to colonial life and had an endless capacity to engage anyone in conversation.

There was an unspoken hierarchy on board, which dictated where everyone sat at dinner. My acquaintance with the Finchingtons meant I joined the senior civil servants, sundry diplomats, peers and dignitaries; otherwise, I would probably have been seated with the melancholy mothers. The army officers sat together, as did the planters, who turned out to be a hard-drinking, rowdy crew. Had Tony's behaviour on our wedding day been more typical of him than he'd let on? Last of all in the hierarchy—the British equivalent of the Untouchables—were the *box wallahs*; a motley crew of commercial travellers, traders and businessmen who, whilst looked down on by everyone else, had the most money and the best-tailored clothes.

Bunty was quick to set me straight about what to expect in India.

'The whole place is a nightmare, my dear. Filthy-dirty and awfully inefficient. Don't expect anything to work. It will drive you completely round the bend. But, I promise, before long you won't want to leave.' She had a laugh like a tinkling bell, belying her ample frame and booming voice.

'You'll be homesick, I promise. Begging your husband to let you come home.' She laughed again and nudged her husband in the ribs. 'Won't she, Ian? Remember what I was like? Bawled my head off every night for months, didn't I?'

He merely nodded and stroked his luxuriant moustache absently.

She went on, undeterred by his reticence, 'Fear not,

Virginia, India will get you in the end. Always does. Once it's got you, it'll never let you go.'

'I'm looking forward to it.'

'Good show. Some advice—don't let the *dhobi wallah* near your best clothes.'

'The what?'

'The chaps who do the washing. All your beautiful gowns will be in shreds if you let them near them. Get your house-keeper to wash your fine silks for you. Only give the linens and household stuff to the *dhobi*. They create havoc with buttons. Smash them to smithereens. Beat the clothes with stones. Terribly primitive. That's India for you. But they do a grand job with the linens.'

'Thank you. I'll remember that.'

She laid a hand on my arm for emphasis. 'Then food. Milk and water *must* be boiled. You can't be too careful, Virginia. Indian personal hygiene leaves a lot to be desired—the cows aren't clean, nor are the hands that milk them. We don't want you getting dysentery or cholera. Make sure you go into the kitchen every day and check the servants are washing the cooking pots properly. If they know you're keeping an eye on them, they'll stay on their toes. I always do an inspection straight after breakfast. I turn the pans upside down and make sure they're clean outside and in.'

She wagged her finger at me as though I were a tweeny maid and she was the head housekeeper. 'And the other thing you should know, my dear, not that it will apply to you of course, but you should be aware...'—she lowered her voice —'there's an awful lot of hanky-panky that goes on.' She dropped her voice to a conspiratorial whisper, 'When the heat gets unbearable, the wives head for the hills. The husbands stay down on the plains and get up to no good with the native women. Lots of the wives are at it, too—many military regiments are stationed in the hills. Shocking.' She lifted her eyebrows semi-comically. 'So many marriages end up on the rocks. But, of course, you're going to be in a hill station anyway and your husband will be there with you all year. Not that I'm for a moment suggesting...but don't be surprised if you find out there's a lot of it going on anyway, especially at the club. People get over-familiar, and there's a lot of drinking and loose behaviour and late night parties. When I was in Simla, there were affairs going on right, left and centre. Wasn't that so, Ian? Scandalous. It would never happen in England. People seem to drop their morals in India. Must be the heat.'

I looked across at the table of planters who were happily making inroads into the ship's whisky supply and it was all too easy to picture my husband among them.

WHEN WE REACHED PORT SAID, before passing through the Suez Canal, it felt that we were really in the Orient—although, almost everywhere we sailed by had the British flag flying. It was hot and sunny and little bum-boats crowded around the ship. They were packed with dark-skinned Arabs, clamouring to sell their wares: cheap trinkets, leather goods, pottery, prayer mats and carved animals. Camel trains moved along the banks as we made our stately progress through the canal. In the Arabian Sea, I leaned over the ship's rails and watched the flying fish leap out of the water, the sunlight turning their scales into precious jewels. Most men on board now wore solar topis, the old India hands referring to them as Bombay bowlers. Whilst there was no doubting the protection they offered from the fierce heat, I couldn't help thinking the men looked absurd; the caricature British gentleman abroad.

On the final leg from Aden to Bombay, there was a fancy dress ball. My attempts to absent myself from the festivities were in vain. Bunty wouldn't entertain my excuses. Once the party began, I started to enjoy myself, helped no doubt by the free flowing champagne and the high spirits of all the passengers now we were near our destination.

My costume was a lacklustre attempt at Maid Marian. A man dressed as a Mexican, complete with sombrero and a stick-on Zapata moustache that fell off halfway through the evening, asked me to dance. An old buffer had just tried to put his hand on my knee under the table, so I was grateful to be rescued. I intended to have just one dance and then slip away to my cabin for an early night.

My dance partner had one of those bland, forgettable faces. I do remember he had light brown hair, as it didn't match the black, false moustache. He was a good dancer though; much better than Tony. When our waltz ended, he didn't relinquish his hold and we kept on dancing. My feeble footwork was disguised as he guided me around the floor so expertly that I began to feel quite graceful. I happily let him monopolise me. After several more dances, all the swirling around was making me feel tipsy so I excused myself and went on deck for some air. I decided to go up to the boat deck, where it would be quiet, then head back down to my cabin.

I got to the top of the companionway and sensed him behind me and, before I could turn around, he shoved me up against one of the lifeboats.

I didn't try to push him away or call out. I just leaned back against the side of the boat and let him kiss me. Perhaps I was hypnotised by the balmy Arabian night under the twinkling stars and the distant soft strains of the ship's orchestra. Maybe it was because I was drunk and didn't know what I was doing, but I don't think that was true. It wasn't anything I can explain in a rational way. It was as though a little voice inside my head was saying, *"You're bad, Ginny, and this man knows it.*" Of course, he couldn't possibly have known about my reputation. We didn't mix in any of the same circles. In our brief conversation while dancing, he'd said he was a musician from Birmingham, now playing the saxophone in one of the ship's bands as he wanted to see the world and the money was better than playing in nightclubs at home.

The kisses became more urgent—then he grabbed my breast, pushed his leg between mine and his tongue into my mouth, his body pressing me against the lifeboat. His tongue darted about inside my mouth like a reptile's, small and hard, while he squeezed my nipple as though tightening a screw. Sour taste of tobacco. Rough stubble. Cheap aftershave. A wave of nausea hit me and I pushed him, catching him off guard.

He looked surprised for a moment, and then grinned. 'Come on, love, don't play hard to get. You know you want it. You've been leading me on all evening.' And he put his hand on my bottom and jerked me back towards him. That stale tobacco smell again, an unhappy pairing with the cloying cologne. I swung my arm out and caught him a blow across his face, my diamond engagement ring drawing blood from the corner of his lower lip.

'Take your hands off me. I'm a married woman.'

He put his hand up to his face, felt the blood, and then his lip curled into a snarl. 'Why don't you act like one then? Prick teaser.'

He threw me a look of utter contempt, and then bounded off down the companionway and back into the ballroom.

He'd treated me like a tart in a back alley. I was ashamed. Had I given off a signal I was prepared to have sex with a stranger? I'd been cast in the role of slut by Marjorie, by Milligan, by my own mother and by all the people who'd paraded past my portrait in Osborne's; they all saw me as a floozy, a tramp, a woman of easy virtue. When the man from

Birmingham danced with me that must have been what he saw, too. My self-respect was so low and my spirits so battered, that I took that as the truth and sought no other. The fact he was a chancer, taking advantage of my inebriation, didn't cross my mind.

Back in my cabin, I saw there was a gash in the skirt of my organza gown where it must have caught on a nail. I hung it on the outside of the wardrobe door as a silent reminder of my stupidity. The night before we were due to reach Bombay, I slipped the frock over the side of the boat and watched it float away in our wake, like Ophelia.

When we were docking in Bombay, I saw the man again. He was leaning on a railing talking to a girl who was a singer with one of the on-board bands. I don't think he even recognised me.

CHAPTER 7

I SAW India long before we arrived. The dark bulk of the Western Ghats rose out of the ocean like an emerging whale and appeared on the horizon long before the city of Bombay was visible. The decks were crowded with passengers, relieved or, no doubt, in some cases anxious, that the voyage was coming to an end. As we sailed into port past the yellow basalt triumphal arch of the Gateway of India, I imagined my father saying, '*You've gone and done it now, Ginny. No going back, my girl. Go for it.*'

It didn't take long to spot Tony. He was a full head taller than anyone else on the quayside. And, yes, he, too, was wearing an awful Bombay bowler. I realised I was nervous about seeing him again after so long. My new beginning. My second chance.

Before I could make my way down to meet him, Bunty Finchington thrust a proprietary arm through mine and marched me down the gangplank, with Ian following behind like her devoted page. I was irritated. I'd harboured visions of running into Tony's arms and being swept off my feet, but the presence of the Finchingtons would put paid to that. I longed to be wrapped up in a big bear hug so I'd forget my encounter with the Birmingham bandsman. But, when Tony materialised in front of us, romantic thoughts faded when I realised I'd been building a picture of him with little resemblance to reality. He leaned towards me and gave me an awkward peck on the cheek, a brief squeeze of the shoulders, a sheepish grin and a muttered, 'Darling', before turning his attention to my travelling companions and, once they took their leave, to the supervision of my luggage and its deployment among several Indians he'd recruited for the purpose. He looked slightly ridiculous in khaki shorts, solar topi and long socks. The blonde Nordic warrior had transformed into a younger version of Lord Baden-Powell. As I was thinking this treacherous thought, a large drop of sweat ran down my neck and set a course between my shoulder blades to join the growing line of moisture around the gathered waist of my cotton frock. My hairline was damp, and I felt the tickle of a fly as it landed on my collarbone. The heat was bestial and the humidity unlike anything I'd known before. A physical assault.

I sat on top of my trunk and fanned my face with my hat. All around was chaos: brown-skinned people in a state of minimal dress, their skinny frames hefting heavy luggage as though it was as light as a couple of cushions. And a cacophony of sound: celebratory blasts from the Viceroy of India, greeted by answering horns from vehicles on the quayside and tugs in the harbour, bicycle bells, cowbells, the roar of traffic, the scream of seabirds circling above and diving for scraps of food carelessly thrown onto the water. And the colours: the brilliance of the women's *saris* enriched by the harsh glare of the afternoon sun—blinding whites, vivid reds, purples and oranges and vibrant yellows as eye-piercingly bright as rapeseed fields. I looked down my pale blue, poplin dress and the spreading patches of dampness that darkened it. Drab and out of place against the carnival of colour around me.

Then there were the smells: rotting fish, rotting meat, decaying garbage, sewage, cow dung, cloyingly sweet burning incense, hot pavement, cooking food, the scent of flowers, the heady aroma of spices and the acrid smoke from impromptu cooking fires. I was a bit nauseous but, at the same time, excited. The fog and cold of the London winter might have been on another planet.

We were to travel south by train before heading by car into the hills to Tony's home—I couldn't yet persuade myself to think of it as mine—in the town of Mudoorayam, a journey of more than two days from Bombay.

Despite the deafening noise, the profusion of people, the strange smells and the oppressive heat, I took to Bombay and was disappointed not to have a chance to linger longer, but Tony could spare no more time away from the plantation. I looked out of the taxi window as we passed a cricket maidan, where a sizable crowd was watching what looked like an impromptu game. Such a scene felt out of place on a pitch encircled with palm trees in the heart of the bustling city, instead of on an English village green or behind the walls of Lord's.

The short journey took us through streets filled with people, pushcarts, rickshaws, bicycles, stray dogs, parading cows and skinny horses; a teeming mass of humanity and untamed nature. It overwhelmed and excited me. Whenever the cab stopped in the traffic, a crowd of beggars surrounded us, hands outstretched, many of them huge-eyed, malnour-ished children. I was fascinated and horrified to see women cooking food in the street, washing their naked children at the kerbside, while men slept on the pavement in the shade. And the beggars—crawling on legless trunks, lepers with missing noses, twisted figures limping along with all manner of deformities. My cosy, privileged upbringing had not prepared me for this—I'd never seen anything like it, and it shocked me to the core. Tony, oblivious, just stared ahead and consulted his wristwatch every few moments, as though he expected time to move at a faster than normal pace.

We were driven up to the front of Victoria Station, which was about a million times more impressive than its namesake in London. An enormous pile of honey-coloured stone, with domes and spires and gargoyles; it was more like a palace or a university than something as prosaic as a railway station. It was crowded inside. There were beggars lying down out of the harsh sunlight, seeking peace in the oblivion of welcome sleep. Vendors of sweets and cigarettes worked their way up and down the platforms, and men pushed carts carrying segregated drinking water, yelling *"Hindi pani"* for the Hindus and *"Mussulman pani"* for the Muslims. And everywhere were legions of travellers, sitting patiently on the ground beside their baggage.

When our train came, the waiting crowd greeted it with a roar as it came to a halt, belching smoke, soot and steam. Bearers bustled around us loading my copious quantity of luggage into the baggage car and installing big blocks of ice under our seats to cool the air in the carriage. When the train pulled out of the station, beggar children still clung to the windows and people clambered up over the carriages to ride on the roof.

In contrast, our own carriage was a tranquil haven, well-appointed, with pull-down sleeping bunks and a tiny, self-contained toilet with washing facilities. The windows had gauze as well as Venetian blinds to shut out the world—and the blinding sunlight. Tony sat down opposite me. Now that, at last, we were alone, I thought he would show me a sign of affection, but he wiped his brow with a handkerchief and said, 'Good Lord, Ginny. You have an awful lot of kit.'

'Sorry. Blame Mummy. Anyone would have thought she was outfitting half a dozen people. Have they managed to stow it all away?'

He wiped his brow. 'Of course. But we won't get it all in the motor at the other end. I'll have to send the driver back later to pick up what we can't squeeze in.'

He looked irritated. Our reunion had not got off on the best footing. I looked at him sitting there, his handsome face flushed with the heat and his legs below the khaki shorts, browned by the sun and dusted by a fine covering of gingery blonde hairs. I felt a rush of affection for him but, before I could say anything, he got up and moved to the carriage door, saying gruffly, 'I'm going to have a smoke. I'll leave you for a while to settle in and get changed.'

WE REACHED ERNAKULAM JUNCTION, the station for Cochin, at the ungodly hour of four-thirty in the morning, yet the place was jammed with people meeting relatives. It was a carnival atmosphere. I was exhausted from the train journey and overwhelmed by the heat. I'd hoped sea breezes in Cochin would mitigate the suffocating temperature, but there didn't seem to be any wind at all. The air was heavy and humid. My dress was soaked across my back and under my arms, and my hair was plastered to my head as soon as we stepped away from the fan-cooled train with its blocks of ice into the chaos of the station. Tony played his imperialist hand strongly I thought, barging through the crowd, barking displeasure at any unfortunates in the way. We were greeted by our Indian driver with a tray of cool drinks and little sweet cakes. Then, after he and Tony had sorted out arrangements for the temporary storage of my excess luggage, he drove us out of the city.

The dawn broke as we began the climb into the Western

Ghats. The air was fresher, cooler and clearer than in the lowlands. We strained our way up a winding road, frequently potholed and with steep banks of lush vegetation on either side. The journey was punctuated by warning blasts from the motor's horn whenever people were walking in the road; more, I felt, because our driver liked the sound of the claxon than for any regard to the safety of the pedestrians.

The dark rocks rising above the roadside were dissected in places by fast flowing streams and waterfalls; a tropical paradise with the early morning sunlight dappling through the trees and lighting up the vivid-blue morning glory flowers that were draped over the undergrowth like floral bedspreads. The birdsong provided a tuneful accompaniment; strange, whooping sounds and little, coloratura arpeggios, unfamiliar to my English ear. The scent of cardamom filled the air as we drove past spice plantations. The blue-grey peaks of the distant hills pierced the mist, like desert islands in a pale sea. It was a kind of wonderland and I found it utterly beautiful. Despite the draw of the scenery, the motion of the car eventually lulled me to sleep, my head resting on Tony's shoulder until he gave me a gentle prod in the ribs.

'Nearly there, darling. Mustn't miss the first sight of Mudoorayam.'

I looked through the open window. The vegetation on either side of the road had changed markedly. We had entered tea country. The slopes were now vivid green, regularly ribbed with darker parallel lines—pathways between the tea bushes. It was like a huge carpet of green corduroy velvet or the ripples on a wet sandy beach when the tide's gone out. Protruding from the strips of green was the occasional big, grey boulder and areas where red soil was exposed, like bunkers on a golf course.

'Grandpapa planted the tea estate in the 1880s, when he

was a young man. A great man, a true pioneer. Worshipped him when I was a boy. This was all forest. Quite an undertaking.'

'He cleared and planted this all by himself?'

As always, he took me seriously. 'Course not, darling; hundreds of Tamil workers did the clearing and planting. He supervised them and managed the whole process. We used to own all this land—20,000 acres of tea.'

'You don't own it all now?' This was a surprise.

He shook his head. 'None of it. Grandpapa died when I was 15 and Father passed away the year after. The mater thought I was too young to take it on. She was cut up about Father dying so suddenly and wanted to go back to England, so she sold up in a hurry for a price much less than it was worth. Afraid of the responsibility I suppose, as I was still at school. Part of the deal was that I'd eventually get to work on the place as manager. Can't blame the old girl really, but she'd have been better off hiring a manager till I finished school and keeping the plantation in the family. Bit short-sighted. Unfortunately, she took some bad advice and invested the proceeds in stocks and shares just as the Depression hit, and the rest is history.'

I wondered if my mother had found this out. It would account for her tart reference to Tony's lack of means.

'Did she lose everything?'

He shrugged. 'Still has the place in Harrogate and a few houses she lets in London. Not a lot of rent. Not exactly in the poorhouse, but we were a damn sight better off before.'

'Who owns all this land now?'

'Bell's Holdings. Own half the tea in Travancore. Not to mention thousands of square miles in Ceylon. They kept the Tilman brand name. Nice for me, of course.'

'What a pity. Don't you resent having to work for them?'

He gave me a puzzled look. 'Course not. Why the devil

should I? Not their fault the mater didn't have a clue about money. I'm happy to be working in the tea business - even if it's not *my* business anymore. They pay me a decent whack. Absolutely nothing to complain about.' His tone had become sharp and he looked affronted.

I put my hand on his arm. 'I'm sorry. I didn't mean to imply you were complaining. It's just...'

'Look, I'm darned lucky. Could be out of work. Thousands of men are.'

'But it must be hard knowing all this could have been yours?'

'Not at all. Tilman name is still over the factory gate and stamped on the tea chests. Bell's treat me well. Confident they always will. Good British company. Long heritage. Right values. Trust them completely. They won't sell me down the river.'

I turned to look back at the green hillside and saw it was peppered with people, scattered along the pathways between the green velvet of the tea plants. Keen to change the subject, I asked, 'Are they picking the tea? How come the leaves are still green—don't they have to wait till they've turned brown?'

He looked at me with a fond expression, his momentary irritation forgotten. 'Silly girl. Tea only turns brown when it dries out once it's been picked, withered, rolled and cooked. A fermentation process. The pickers pluck only the top shoots, called flushes. Bushes have to be kept at the right height so they can reach the flushes—or they'd grow into enormously tall trees. The women do the picking, and the men do the pruning. That's why they're all flat-topped.'

I knew he was about to give me a dissertation on the finer points of tea growing and harvesting. He hadn't been so animated since I'd met him. Tea was clearly his passion. I had a feeling it wasn't going to be mine. Not that I don't enjoy a nice cup of Earl Grey, but understanding the secrets of its cultivation has never been a pre-requisite to my enjoyment. It was enough for me to appreciate the landscape.

He went on about tea varieties and the historical development of tea in India, while I tried to look interested. Then, we rounded a corner, and below us Mudoorayam was spread out at the confluence of a couple of rivers. As we went down into the valley in which it was nestled, it struck me that this was *it*. Until now it was a journey, but now I'd arrived and I didn't much like what I was seeing. I felt nostalgic for grimy, old London. The town looked undersized and scruffy, the outskirts covered with ugly shacks and food stalls. I couldn't imagine living here. The prospect of being stuck here for the rest of my life made me even glummer. Tony was too busy pointing out landmarks and attractions to notice my dismay: the temple, the mosque, the churches, the Valley Ridge Hotel, the market, the tennis club and the cricket maiden.

How had I ended up here? As if in response, I looked up to see heavy black clouds moving across the sun, darkening the sky. The resultant gloom made the place look even worse: dirty, shabby, inconsequential. Although I was dog-tired and desperate for a cup of tea, I was glad when he told me our house was a few miles outside town in a valley in the middle of the tea gardens.

Ahead of us the hills rose, blanketed by the ubiquitous green corduroy velvet rows of tea bushes. Just as I thought we'd never get to the end of this journey, we pulled through a stone-pillared gateway and, there it was. Home. A long, brick-built bungalow, surrounded by lawns and flowerbeds, with a green-painted tin roof, edged like a paper doily with white wooden coving. A veranda ran around three sides, one of which was glassed-in like a conservatory. The place was more like a sports pavilion or a scout hut than a home. Trying not to let the disappointment show in my face, I tried to picture myself on the veranda with its covering of sinuous flowering vines, sipping ice-cold lemonade in the cool of the evening. The garden was full of mature trees of more varieties than I could count or recognise, a broad, well-groomed lawn, rose beds and a mass of colourful flowers growing in the red soil. But, the house itself, was small. Smaller than I was used to anyway. I felt a twinge of homesickness for Leighton Square, with its sweeping marble staircase, polished parquet floors, tall windows and spacious, well-appointed accommodation.

'Here we are, old girl. Home, sweet home.'

Four native men and a woman were lined up to greet us as we got out of the car.

Tony led me towards them by the hand. 'This is my bearer, Thankappan, and his wife, Nirmala, who was my *ayah*. She took care of me till I went to boarding school. They've been in the family since before I was born and do a splendid job of managing things and looking after me here. And they're looking forward to looking after you, too.'

He turned to face the couple, beaming and gesturing towards me.

'Meet the new *Memsahib*.'

Introductions followed to the cook and the *mala*, who looked after the gardens, and to a young man named Venu, who was the *chokra* or houseboy responsible for carrying food in from the cookhouse and generally assisting Thankappan.

They all stopped short of my hesitantly outstretched hand and, instead clasped their hands in front as if in prayer and bowed slightly, then took to enthusiastically shaking their heads from side to side, while grinning at me and flashing incredibly white teeth. I let my hand drop and looked at Tony, who nodded reassuringly, and, when I turned back to face them, they grinned and made their funny sideways nods again.

Thankappan and Nirmala looked elderly, but were only in their fifties. Both had very dark skin. Nirmala was stout, with thick, black, oily hair, dry-cracked feet and a roll of fat visible between her *sari* and her silk *choli*. Her husband was about six inches shorter, a wisp of a man, with legs like sticks under a pair of long khaki shorts. They reminded me of lean Jack Sprat and his fat wife. I was about to head inside the house, when Tony took me by surprise and grabbed me in his arms, swinging me off my feet and carrying me over the threshold, to the accompaniment of laughter and handclapping from the assembled servants.

'Have to do things properly, darling. Welcome home.' I buried my head in his neck, relieved the distant manner he had shown since I'd arrived in India had disappeared.

Inside was dark and a bit gloomy; the windows all shuttered, needlessly I thought, given the disappearance of the sun. But it was bigger than it looked from outside.

He put me down inside the red, clay-tiled hallway and turned to Nirmala. 'Get the cook to see the *Memsahib* has some tea and something to eat, and then she'll want a bath and a rest.'

Then, to me, 'Righty-ho. Off now, Ginny. Time and tide and all that. Relax and explore the house. See you tonight.'

After a cursory peck on the cheek and ignoring my protests, he was through the door and heading back down the driveway to the motorcar and its waiting driver.

Nirmala led me into a dark, formal dining room, with heavy chandeliers suspended over a big mahogany table. When I'd drunk some tea and half-heartedly picked at the unappetising attempt at a sandwich, I had a bit of a prowl around. Each aspect of the house looked out onto a different part of the tea gardens. Miraculously, the sun reappeared and the clouds raced out of sight over the tops of the mountains, lifting my spirits as they departed. There was one enormous mountain, a gigantic outcrop of bare rock, and other lesser ones covered with grasslands or forest. Spread out below were tea gardens up and down the slopes of the valley.

The house, all on one level, was in a V-shape, with two long corridors running away from the central entrance and with the dining room at the apex. There was a spacious drawing room looking onto the rose garden at the front and leading into the covered veranda that ran round the side and the back of the drawing room, with windows facing the mountains.

The bathroom was in an annexe, tacked onto the main house in a kind of lean-to. There was no proper plumbing; the lavatory, universally referred to in India as the "thunderbox", was just a wooden seat with a metal bucket underneath. A poor, low-caste chap, an untouchable, known as the "sweeper", had to empty the bucket into a cesspit concealed somewhere in a thicket of trees at the outer limits of the property. Taking a bath entailed the servants boiling water and filling the big zinc bathtub that sat in the centre of the clay-tiled floor. Afterwards, when one pulled the plug, the dirty water ran out of the hole and across the floor into an open drain. Thankappan politely warned me that this water egress was also an occasional ingress for uninvited snakes and to check before venturing inside the room. He showed me a hand bell to summon assistance, but as I soon discovered, he always checked the lie of the land before either Tony or I ventured across the threshold, and I suspect he may have stood guard outside the exit pipe to clobber any would-be serpentine party crashers. I couldn't imagine what my mother would say when she came out to visit us. It was hard to imagine her dignity surviving a close encounter with a thunderbox or a poisonous snake.

The bungalow had been built about ten to fifteen years earlier, but the furniture consisted of heavy Victorian sideboards, old-fashioned high-backed chairs and velvet upholstery, all in sombre colours. While the bedroom and the drawing and dining rooms had been freshly painted in readiness for my arrival, the rest of the house didn't appear to have been touched: all bottle-green paint and brown anaglypta. Tony's home improvement efforts, during the past five weeks, had stopped short of a full overhaul. One thing was certain; the place would look a lot better with a coat of white paint. Maybe I had a project to keep me occupied? The velvet-covered furniture would have to go, too. I'd arrange to have some new stuff shipped out from Heal's.

When Venu carried my luggage into the master bedroom, I was taken aback for a moment by the twin beds. My parents had shared a bed for their entire married life and, while I knew many couples slept separately, it had always struck me as slightly odd. Tony had made a special effort here as the room was freshly papered and the smell of wallpaper paste still lingered. I wasn't sure which bothered me most—the separate beds or the bilious blue roses. Then I told myself separate beds would be a boon in hot weather.

Tired from the long train and road journey, I collapsed gratefully on top of one of the beds and slept soundly until woken by the sound of Tony banging the front door.

He came into the room with his tie off and his shirt half undone and looked surprised to see me there. 'Sorry, darling. Didn't realise you were lying down. Did I wake you up?'

'You did actually.' I pulled myself up. 'But I'm happy to be awakened. What time is it?'

'Half-six. Need to get a move on and get changed and up to the club for drinks before dinner.'

I reached up and pulled him down onto the narrow bed beside me. 'I think that can wait a bit, can't it? Don't you want to welcome me to India properly?' I opened the remaining buttons on his shirt and slipped my hands up his ribcage and eased his arms out of the sleeves.

'Yes. Rather. But it's hardly the right time.' He coughed nervously.

I slid across the bed and reached for my dressing gown. After what had happened in Eastbourne, I wasn't about to give him any more cause for doubt about my level of sexual experience, but I felt hurt, rejected. He must have sensed this, as he moved behind me and wrapped his arms around me and reached down to untie the gown.

What followed was, if I'm honest, as awkward and unsatisfactory as our honeymoon efforts. It wasn't for lack of enthusiasm on the part of either of us. It was just that we didn't seem to be attuned to each other. I supposed most married couples require time to get to know each other. I'm not laying the blame at Tony's door. Our timing was out, as though we were dancing to different tunes, and there was an awkwardness about the whole thing that resulted in us constantly apologising to each other, like novice tennis players when they serve the ball into the net. Maybe it would get better with time and practice.

WE SET off to the club, heading into the town and then branching off on a road that wound its leisurely way beside a river. The town looked lively after dark, with crowds of Indians buying fruit and vegetables at the corrugated iron stalls that ran round the periphery of the busy market hall, bathed in the warm light of dangling electric bulbs and hurricane oil lamps. The distinctive smell of the place wafted through the open car window and I remembered how, when visiting Paris as a child, the first thing I noticed was the way it smelled: an indefinably different smell to that of the streets of London so it was impossible not to know we were abroad. Mudoorayam's smell was even more foreign. I tried to distinguish the different aromas, but they were all unfamiliar. The smell of India.

The club, or *The Planters' Club*, to give it its full title, was in a secluded area by a reed-filled river, just outside the town. It was away from the hurly-burly of the town, accessed by a narrow concrete bridge and hidden from the road by willow trees and dense vegetation. A wide veranda surrounded the two-storey building with a scalloped and pillared wooden canopy that reminded me of the stations on the Metropolitan District Railway Line. Several bungalows were ranged around the vast lawn that spread out behind the main building. The club also boasted a nine-hole golf course, tennis courts and a cricket maidan. We could have been in deepest, darkest, Surrey. The grounds were enclosed by white railings and the building was bathed in bougainvillea. The low rumble of voices and the strains of a familiar dance tune met us on the crisp evening air and mingled with the sound of crickets. I was nervous. As we went through the heavy wooden door, my stomach lurched and I gripped Tony's hand.

I was introduced to a lot of people, whose names I instantly forgot. I felt a belated admiration for Bunty Finchington's facility for instant recall of the names of every person on the *Viceroy of India,* and wished she were around to cover for me now and that I'd asked her to share with me how she did it. Tony knew everyone. It was just like our wedding all over again—he, transformed into an overgrown, public schoolboy surrounded by a bunch of braying chums, and, I, the awkward outsider at the party. They were all old India hands and inspected me with unashamed curiosity. I was clearly this week's hot news—which said a lot for what little happened in this out-of-the-way town. One of the women, tall, regal and with a face resembling a shrew, marched up to me and grabbed my hand in a vice-like grip.

'Lilian Bulstrode-Hemmings.' She pumped my hand. 'And you're Tony's new wife? Practically a child bride.' She seemed to find this hilarious. 'Delighted to meet you, my dear. Old Bunty Bullfinch telegraphed to ask me to look out for you. Marvellous girl, Bunty.' Then, slightly conspiratorially, she added, 'Can't imagine what she ever saw in that old duffer she married; although they do seem to be devoted to each other. No accounting for taste, eh Virginia? Mind if I call you Ginny? I know Tony does, and we don't stand on ceremony here at the club.'

I tried to get a word in, but she steamed ahead without drawing breath, 'We were all so pleased when we heard Tony had got married. You've got a good man there. There were broken hearts all over Travancore when the news got out. He's such a popular fellow. And so good looking.' She nudged me in the ribs. 'Well done, you.'

I wondered if she would be equally effusive to Tony about what a terrific girl he'd managed to snag—but I doubted it. I decided Lilian was one of those women who believe men to be a superior race and we should be grateful for any crumbs they might scatter in our direction. This snap judgement was one of many I was forced to reconsider when I got to know her better.

'Come along then, Ginny.' She affected an American accent, 'Stick with me, kid, and I'll make sure you meet all the right folks.' She gave me a knowing look. 'And I'll tip you the wink on whom to give a wide berth.' The woman certainly fond of her clichés.

I looked around for Tony, but he was deep in conversation with Lilian's husband, Theo. She steered me past them, her hand gripping my elbow, ensuring there was no escape. She led me along corridors lined with sporting trophies and

95

wooden honour boards that listed past club secretaries in gold lettering. She pointed out the card room, the reading room, the skittle alley, then let me peek through the glass panel in the door to the gentlemen's bar; a hallowed "Men Only" sanctum we were not permitted to penetrate, and which was evidently a mausoleum for murdered wildlife, judging by the trophies on the dark, wood-panelled walls. She showed me the ladies' bar—tiny, the billiard rooms— two, both huge, until, eventually, we entered a book-lined room with a roaring fire and only one occupant ensconced in a wing chair. As soon as she saw him, Lilian tried to propel me back towards the door. Too late. He lowered his newspaper and his commanding voice stopped her in her tracks. It was deep and resonant like a double bass, and very plummy.

'Put her down, Lilian, and let me have a proper look at her.'

With a sigh, she said, 'I was hoping we might postpone the moment when the dear girl has to meet you, Hector.' She rolled her eyes at me. 'Mrs Tilman, meet Hector Channing, the Planters' Club resident cynic and thoroughly disreputable old gossip.'

'And I love you too, Lilian.' He rose slowly to his feet from the depths of the chair and stretched a languid hand to me. 'I'm delighted to meet you, Mrs Tilman. What a pretty little thing you are, too. Now, don't listen to anything this wicked witch tells you. She loves to be the centre of attention here at the club, and she has no doubt realised her star is now in the descendent with your arrival. Isn't that so, Lilian, darling?'

'If you've quite finished, Hector? I need to get Mrs Tilman back to her husband. Dinner is about to be served.'

I smiled at Hector, and he narrowed his eyes and took a step back. 'I have a funny feeling we're going to be friends, Mrs T.'

'Please call me Ginny, Mr Channing.'

'Oh, no. I much prefer Mrs T. But do please call me Hector. Now, when are we going to get our friendship properly off the ground? I'll have to show you the sights of this one elephant town, and I need to know everything about you; all your guilty little secrets—how a lovely little thing like you has come to be exiled to a place like this. You must have some interesting stories.' He dipped his head slightly to one side, and I instantly knew he already knew all about me. I could feel the blood rising up my neck.

'Look, Lilian, I do believe she's blushing,' he said.

Lilian sighed again and ushered me from the room, calling back over her shoulder, 'You're incorrigible, Hector. Leave the poor girl alone.' As we walked back to the dining room, she patted me on the arm. 'Take no notice of him. He's harmless really, but he has an odd personality. A conversation with him is like going for a swim in a vat of sulphuric acid. One always feels one comes off the worse for it.' Then, lowering her voice to a whisper, she leaned towards me, 'I think he bats for the other side.'

CHAPTER 8

THE NEXT MORNING, over breakfast, I suggested Tony give me a tour of the tea gardens and the factory. He looked startled.

'Why on earth would you want to do that, darling? Bit of a rum idea, don't you think? Can't imagine what you'd find interesting at the factory. Loads of noisy machines. Not your thing at all.'

I felt a bit squashed. My face must have shown my disappointment as he immediately relented.

'I'll send the car back later and Savanaram can drive you through the tea gardens. Not a lot to see, mind. Few dozen women plucking on the top division, and half a dozen men driving the bullock carts between the weighing points and the factory.' I smiled. Tony boiled everything down to production processes and was blind to the landscape all around us.

'I meant I'd like to go on foot and see how the ladies do the picking.'

One eyebrow rose. 'Wouldn't you rather have the driver

98

take you down to the club? Not the done thing for white women to walk around the estate. Need to watch the sun or you'll end up looking like a coolie. Not good at all.' He laughed, then said, 'Club then?'

'I can't think of anything worse.' The words were out before I could stop them.

His expression was if I'd insulted him personally. I tried to recover. 'I mean I'm still tired from all the travelling, and making conversation with people I barely know is a bit daunting, but a walk in the sunshine would do me good. I can go to the club another day. And I really don't need to be driven around.'

There was a look of incomprehension on my husband's face, so I plunged on, 'I thought I'd take a sketchbook and do a bit of drawing—the ladies picking the tea leaves, the patterns the rows of tea bushes make, all those beautiful tall trees, the mountains. It's all so terribly beautiful. I think I'll be able to paint here forever without running out of inspiration.'

He frowned. 'If you think so, darling. Sorry can't spare the time to show you around. Sure you really want to? Frightfully hot today.'

'I'll take a sunshade and find a tree to sit under while I draw.'

'Very well, but Venu will go with you. Just in case.'

'I won't get lost. I won't go far. Promise. I don't want one of the poor servants having to tag along.'

'Out of the question. Can't have you wandering around unaccompanied. Unlikely to meet an elephant in the daytime, but don't want you stepping on a snake or getting lost. Hillside's jolly steep. If you happened to fall, it could be a dashed long time before someone found you. Not a good show at all. Besides, you'll need Venu to carry your water bottles and something for you to sit on. Going to have to sort you out a horse. Although, I still think you'll find everything you want up at the club, without gallivanting round the estate.'

'I'm not awfully keen on riding, Tony.'

'Won't get far here without a horse.'

'I suppose so. But...'

'I'll sort it out later in the week. You drive?'

I shook my head.

'Righto. We'll sort that, too. Teach you myself.'

'That would be wonderful. If you have time.'

He grinned at me. 'I'll make sure I have time.' He came round the table and dropped a kiss on my head. 'But, today, if you're dead set on going out on foot, then Venu goes with you.'

The tea gardens began at the boundary of the bungalow's carefully cultivated garden. Venu led me onto a broad dirt track from the gateway, past hedgerows peppered with *lantana*—pink and yellow flowers that looked nothing special from a distance but, close up, were stunning—perfectly formed rosettes, pink clustered around yellow. We were accompanied by jays hopping from bush to bush. All manner of butterflies danced around us. The air was fresh—it had rained overnight, and the light intensified the emerald mosaic of tea plantings. The track led past a section where about a dozen women were plucking the flushes. They wore brightly coloured *saris* and dropped the leaves into sacks on their backs. Backbreaking work. But they seemed happy, chattering away and calling out to each other as they worked. Some waved at me shyly so I returned the compliment. I wished I could understand what they were talking about—complaining about the boss, perhaps, or hatching marriage plots between their unmarried sons and daughters?

The rest of the morning passed rapidly as I sketched and

painted. Then I wandered back along the track, following the women, who were now carrying their full sacks of leaves on their heads to the weighing point, where three or four men loaded them onto the scales and then onto bullock carts. The carts, known as *bundies*, were just wooden platforms suspended over a pair of wheels with a protective canopy of bamboo matting. As soon as each cart was full, its chanting driver drove it down the hill to the factory. I sat watching, mesmerised by the swaying motion of the cart and the dull echo of the oxen's bells as they made their descent. Venu carried my bags and flapped along in his chappals, with his skinny legs like ebony-coloured chicken drumsticks.

Tony was already at the dining table when I walked in. He looked pointedly at his watch.

'Frightfully sorry. I didn't realise the time,' I said.

'Luncheon needs to be prompt. I've work to do, decisions to make. The boy had instructions to get you home on time. I'll reprimand him.'

'Please don't blame poor Venu. I kept spotting interesting things on the way back and asking him questions, and then I stopped to draw a quick study of a flower I've never seen before as I want to look it up in the Flora of India book I saw in the drawing room.'

He sighed. 'Don't make a habit of it, darling. Like to set an example to the workforce by keeping strict hours. News would be all over Muddy if the boss was late back after luncheon. I have responsibilities. Can't expect you to know that, but hope you'll try and understand it, Ginny, eh?'

Feeling like a naughty schoolgirl, I nodded and got on with trying to eat the meal. Already, on my first day, I was coming up short in Tony's idea of the plantation manager's wife. I mentally wrote my hundred lines—*Must try harder*.

I WAS in the garden reading when Hector Channing materialised, casting a shadow across the pages of my book. I'd found the perfect spot—a wooden bench that circled a huge tree I later discovered was a fully-grown tea plant. The circumference of the trunk must have been about twenty feet and some of its branches rose upwards, perpendicular to the main boughs like gravity-defying aerial roots. It was covered in lichens and parasitical plants and it was a favourite haunt of the local birdlife, so I was able to read not only sheltered from the sun, but with full orchestral accompaniment, albeit at the risk of an occasional unwelcome splash from an incontinent songster.

'I've come to rescue you before you succumb to terminal boredom, Mrs T.'

He took the book from my hands and looked at the spine, then tossed it onto the bench beside me.

'Georgette Heyer? On first impressions, I'd not have expected you to be a reader of romantic tosh. I'm going to have to educate you, my dear. I shall draw you up a reading list. We can't have you sitting here all day pining for a Regency buck. Tony will never live up to it.'

I had to shade my eyes from the brightness of the sun. Squinting at him like that put me at a disadvantage. 'I really don't need you to tell me what I can and cannot read thank you, Mr Channing. Nor do I require rescuing. What can I do for you? I suppose I shall have to offer you some tea.' I instinctively wanted to be rude to him, as if he expected it of me.

'Can't stand the stuff. The only "T" I like is the one with a "G" in front of it. We can get a few of them later on at the club. Now get a move on. I'm going to show you around town. And call me Hector, for heaven's sake.'

His tone brooked no challenge, so I offered none. He stretched out a hand and yanked me out of my chair.

At the end of the driveway, there was a waiting *tonga*. The driver tapped the horse with his whip and the decrepit-looking nag shuffled forward. It looked frail; skin stretched across bones, but was soon trotting along happily enough. I looked sideways at Hector, his long legs encased in linen trousers and his jacket crease-free; a feat I have never managed to replicate where linen is concerned.

The *syce* dropped us in a crowded street full of stalls and kiosks at the centre of town. People were sitting on stools, getting their hair cut in the open air. The road was jammed with *tongas*, wandering goats and the odd untethered cow, mingling with motorcars, motorcycles and a couple of buses packed to the gunnels with humanity. All the vehicles were honking horns at the pedestrians, creating a discordant symphony.

Hector said, 'Let's start off at the markets. They're bazaars really. The centre of the universe for the locals, but a no-go area for most Europeans—they prefer to congregate at the Mudoorayam Supply Association and the Post Office. The MSA has stuff shipped in from Bombay and Calcutta and you can order by catalogue for delivery there, although your servants will buy all the general provisions here and in the vegetable market next door. Come on, it's fun.'

The first section of the market consisted of a warren of narrow alleyways of open-fronted wooden shacks housing mostly tailors and garment sellers. Men and a few women were working, each in a tiny cubbyhole stall, fronting the alleyway, marking out suiting with tailor's chalk, cutting out pieces on the tiny counter tops or sewing on their treadle machines.

Hector stopped at one of the stalls and spoke to the man behind the counter, collecting a bag from him.

'Marvellous chap, Faisal. Does all my tailoring and

repairs. Can run me up a suit in twenty-four hours. And, as for his invisible mending...'

The place was a hive of industry and, everywhere we walked, smiling faces and nodding heads greeted us. The second part of the market was a wide, concrete, central street with a tin roof over it, and open-fronted shops on either side, each raised on a concrete platform slightly above street level. Men in *lunghis* perched on top of full grain sacks and whizzed the beads of their abacuses backwards and forwards in a frenzy of calculation; shops were crammed with colourful bolts of fabric, plain and patterned, silks for *saris* and heavier woollen suiting; and there were stalls with huge metal dishes, laden with spices—cardamom, turmeric, cumin and many others Hector couldn't identify, as well as heaps of lentils and trays piled high with dried beans and pulses. Flower sellers wove heavily scented garlands for people to wear around their necks en route to the temple. As we passed one of the flower stalls, its owner jumped up and placed a garland around my neck, waving Hector away when he tried to pay for it. Kiosks sold a rainbow of sweets and sweetmeats, others had shelves stacked high with little pots and potions, remedies for every imaginable ailment, baskets and buckets and bowls. The kiosks were brimming with merchandise, every square inch covered with goods and— when the walls and surfaces were full—the shopkeepers hung merchandise from the ceiling on strings. It was an explosion of colour and noise. Everywhere was the buzz of commerce, as men bartered and haggled over the prices.

The crowds and the strange mixture of smells over-whelmed me; a combination of sweat, spices, sawdust and flowers, and I shrank back when anyone came close. Hector realised this and placed a hand on my arm in reassurance.

'You're quite safe, they don't bite. These are the kindest and warmest people. Just relax.'

Several of the stall holders knew Hector and made that funny little head movement I had seen from Nirmala and Thankappan. He swapped greetings with them in what he told me was Tamil.

'A little bit of local language goes a long way. Try and pick up a few words. They'll love you forever if you do. Most of the British couldn't give a damn. They behave as though they're still in the home counties and the Indians are invisible.'

I crossed over to one of the stores selling fabric. On the cardboard core of the bolts of cotton were the words "Made in Manchester."

Hector pulled a face. 'I know. It's a disgrace. The raw cotton is grown and picked here, then sent to England to be made into cloth and shipped back here again, where most people can't afford to buy it.' He pointed to a stack of rough white cloth. 'This is all most Indians can afford—although the little man with the spectacles wants them to make their own instead of buying it. It's known as *khadi*. That's a good word for you to learn.'

'Mr Gandhi?'

'He's been trying for years to get his countrymen to boycott British imports and spin their own cotton. And he has a point. The people grow and sell their cotton for a few *rupees*, then we send it away for our higher paid workers and expensive factory machinery to process, and send the finished cloth back on British-owned and run ships to sell back to them at inflated prices—fine if you're a *maharajah* or a doctor or their like, but the average Indian can't possibly afford it.'

'That's not fair.'

'It's not, Mrs T, it's not.'

'So why do we do it?'

'Because we can. It's called running the empire. We've

been getting away with it for centuries. But our days are numbered. It's only a matter of time before we have to throw the towel in and give them what they want—what is, after all, their right. Then, they'll probably kick the lot of us out. They'll be glad to see the back of us.'

'Are you a communist, Hector?'

He roared with laughter. 'Of course, I'm not. Far too fond of my creature comforts. But I do support Indian home rule. And when they send us packing, it's no more than we deserve after two centuries plundering their riches.'

I must have looked alarmed, as he carried on, 'Don't worry. It won't be for a while yet. Years probably. But it will happen. It's inevitable. And it means you'll get a reprieve on your sentence at some point. I bet you've been worrying you'll be stuck here for life?'

'How did you guess?'

'You're an intelligent young woman, Mrs T, even if not well informed in current affairs. Someone with too much spark to want to be in an Indian backwater for the rest of her days.'

'You're wrong,' I lied. 'London's become a bit of a bore.'

He jerked his head back dismissively. 'Don't try to pull the *khadi* over my eyes. You're like me. An exile. I know you were a bad girl, darling, but your secret's safe with Uncle Hector.'

'I don't know what you're talking about.' I shivered in the warmth of the afternoon.

'Come now, don't be coy. I know all about your idea of an adventure and, until now, it's involved stripping your clothes off for disreputable artists, rather than hanging around hill stations.'

I slapped him across the face, to the amusement of the Indians around us, who all stopped what they were doing and stared at us, trying to stifle their laughter, and eager for the next instalment.

'I suppose I did ask for that, didn't I?' He placed his palm over his now livid cheek. 'But if we're going to be friends, we need to be honest with each other.'

'I never asked to be friends with you. I may be young, but I'm not stupid, and I can't bear being patronised, especially by older men who think they can push me around.'

'I'm sorry. I overstepped the mark.' He tilted his head and looked at me with a woebegone expression. 'Forgiveness, please? The G&Ts are on me this afternoon. And I'll lend you a couple of good books to read.'

'I'm perfectly happy with Georgette Heyer, thank you very much. I happen to think she writes rather well actually.'

'Come off it.' I could tell he was as relieved as I was to get off the topic.

'She's funny. I've laughed out loud a few times. How many books make you do that? And if I want to lose myself in a world of Regency bucks, then I will. Who the hell do you think you are? You barely know me. You've got a diabolical cheek, Hector Channing.'

'I know I have. Thanks to the blow you landed on it. It's burning like hell.' He frowned and pouted like a little boy, and I couldn't help smiling.

'Don't make fun of me.' I tried to sound cross, but I wasn't anymore.

'I wouldn't dream of it. You're far too formidable to trifle with. I may even give Miss Heyer a go. Anyone who can make one laugh out loud has to be worth a glance. There's little enough to laugh about these days. Let's head off for that gin and tonic, and you can tell me all about what you got up to with your society artist, darling. And, then, it will be our little secret. My lips will be sealed forever.'

I don't know why I liked Hector, but I did. There was a vein of cruelty in his humour, but underneath it I detected a vulnerability. He had managed to create an intimacy between us, despite so brief an acquaintance. And he was a grownup, about twenty years older than me and, yet again, the little girl in me was flattered by the adult attention.

We settled into rattan chairs in the sunny garden at the club. It was quiet—a bridge afternoon, so the memsahibs, who would normally be cluttering up the lawn, were inside around their green baize tables. Mummy would have been in heaven.

Wanting to steer our conversation away from my indiscretions, I decided to get him to do the talking.

'What are you running away from then to end up in an Indian backwater, as you put it?'

'Touché, Madame. Shall we just say that, like you, I was guilty of an indiscretion and leave it at that?'

'You'll have to do better than that. Nothing less than full disclosure.'

He sighed and looked up at the sky. 'You're a bit of a minx aren't you, Mrs T? I can see I'm going to get very little past you. Very well then... But you'd better not breathe a word of this and, if you do, I will deny it and exact a fearful revenge. I was caught *in flagrante* with a cabinet minister.'

I'd just taken a slug of gin and went into a coughing fit. Hector handed me a linen napkin.

'Have I actually managed to shock you? Surely not?'

'I wasn't expecting that. It was a bit of a surprise.'

'That I'm a queer, darling?'

'No, I did suspect that might be the case.'

'There was I thinking I was being all strong and manly. I obviously can't fool a woman of the world like you.' He raised his glass to clink it against mine, 'Cin-cin, darling.'

'Was there a scandal?'

'Fortunately, not. But it was a mess. His wife of thirty years caught us. She was meant to be in Cheltenham. Got suspicious and came back early. Obviously, she didn't want anyone else to find out her husband had a predilection for young men. I think she hoped—in vain, of course—that he'd make it to PM one day, and the voters wouldn't be too thrilled about a pederast running the country, so she gave me a thousand pounds and said if I didn't clear off she'd tell my family. As that would have put the kibosh on the old trust fund, I decided to do as she asked. I scarpered off to France at first, then back to India in '29 when the markets crashed. The trust fund took a hell of a battering, and the little that's left goes further out here. And I must confess that singsong Indian accent has positively aphrodisiacal qualities.' He finished his drink and raised his arm to signal to a waiter to bring replenishments.

'There you have it, Mrs T. My sordid, sorry story. I hope I haven't scandalised you?'

I shook my head. 'I find your honesty refreshing.'

'Good. Then you're ready to reciprocate?'

I shook my head. 'Not until we've finished with you. You said you came *back* to India. You'd been here before then?'

'After Cambridge, I joined the Indian Civil Service and spent three years in Rawalpindi as a district officer.'

'What did that involve?'

'Wielding an immense amount of power over an extraordinary number of people at the tender age of twenty-three. I collected their taxes, meted out justice, listened to their complaints and refereed their fights and petty squabbles.'

'Golly! Did you like it?'

'Strangely enough, I did. I liked it a lot. Even though I often questioned the fact that an English greenhorn like me was able to come out here and lord it over so many people in their own land. I only went into the service because a chap from the ICS came along to Trinity and told us all we'd have a lark and get a decent pension at the end. Their entrance exams were reputed to be the toughest. And I do like a challenge. But it didn't seem fair that I should have a God-given right to rule over so many people without their consent.'

'Is that why you left?'

'You have an annoying habit of asking difficult questions. No. I wish I could say that my conscience got the better of me, but I was thrown out.'

'Not because you...?'

'Yes, you've guessed. Only, that time, it was impossible to cover up. I was caught in bed with my bearer. So, not only had I committed the unforgivable sin, I'd done it with a native. One is not supposed to sodomise one's servants. "Not very British." So, that was that. I was sent home on the next boat. A Cambridge chum fixed me up with a job as a Parliamentary aide and you know the rest. That's me. Hector Channing—the man who made the mistake of mixing his career up with his personal life. Not anymore. Much easier not to have a career at all. Now it's your turn to spill the beans.'

I looked into my glass, watching the tiny bubbles bursting, then spoke in a rush, keen to get it over with, 'There's not a lot to tell. An artist painted me naked. It's infra dig for a debutante to be an artist's model, so there was a lot of talk. I had to withdraw from my Court presentation. My mother was not amused.'

He studied me intently, then said, 'You're holding out on me, Mrs T. Debutantes don't usually take their clothes off for artists like that. Someone must have convinced you to do it.'

I blushed, swallowed, and then decided to get it over with. 'He was a family friend. And I don't see what's wrong with it. The galleries are full of old masters with naked bodies all over the place. I'm not ashamed.'

'A family friend? While I might have been convinced you'd perform such a generous act for a great artist, I can't see you doing it for a family friend. Far too embarrassing.'

I looked away.

'You were having a thing with him, weren't you? Fair's fair. I told you everything and you need to do the same. It will go no further.' He swept a finger over his mouth. 'My lips are zipped.'

He had an instinct for truffling out information.

'Yes, I had an affair with him. Like you, I was found out. By my mother. She was absolutely furious.'

Hector raised an eyebrow and motioned me to go on.

'He was a friend of my late father's. It would have been the end of it, only he exhibited a compromising painting of me, alongside a formal portrait. My mother was desperate to marry me off to a duke or something. That idea went right out the window.'

'And did you want to?'

'Want to what?'

'Marry a duke or something?'

'I don't think I really knew what I wanted. I'm not even sure I do now.'

He gave me an arch look. 'Really? Marry in haste, repent at leisure?'

'Gosh, no. I didn't mean that at all. It's just that everything's happened so quickly. If you'd asked me six months ago, I'd never have dreamt I'd be living in the middle of India.'

'It's hardly the middle. Clearly you were reading Georgette Heyer under the desk when you should have been paying attention in geography.'

I pulled a face, but he carried on, 'Were you in love with this artist?'

I hesitated. 'No.'

'You don't sound very sure.'

I took a deep breath. 'He bowled me over. He was interesting. I was easily influenced, and he was exciting. Maybe it was the subterfuge...'

Hector raised an eyebrow.

'Well, perhaps not just the subterfuge.'

'Go on.'

'Look. I was naive. Lonely, too.'

'"*Loneliness is the first thing which God's eye named, not good.*"'

'Excuse me?'

'Milton, Mrs T. Clearly you weren't paying attention in English either.'

'Are you always such an intellectual snob?'

'I fear so, my dear. I'm a product of the English public school system with a sponge-like capacity to absorb stuff. Sadly, I also have a sponge-like capacity to sponge. At least, that's what my father always said. But I've never managed to find an occupation that offers an opportunity to show off all my useless knowledge.'

'You could have been a teacher.'

'Good God, woman. What a hideous thought.'

I laughed at the evident distress this idea caused him.

'Why was someone as beautiful and intelligent as you lonely?' he said.

'How can anyone really know *why* they're lonely?—just that they *are.* I didn't have a lot of friends at school. I wasn't *un*popular, just not very close to anyone. I was a bit shy. Daddy dying left a big gap in my life, and I don't think I ever really got over it. Rupert's connection to my father drew me to him. He talked about him all the time. About stuff they did when they were young. At Oxford. I think he missed Daddy, too. We had that in common. And he taught me to paint.'

'Rupert?' He looked thoughtful, and I inwardly cursed at my carelessness. 'It doesn't sound terribly romantic. A lovely little thing like you ought to be swept off her feet by an eligible man, not seduced by an ageing Lothario. I don't think Miss Heyer would approve.'

Perhaps recognising my discomfort, he changed the subject. 'Tell me about your parents.'

'Daddy died the day before my fourteenth birthday. It's ruined birthdays for me ever since. I don't get on with my mother very well. Since his death, it's been awfully strained between us. I suppose she was keen to see me settled down. I don't know why, but I always have the feeling she blames me for him dying.'

'Why on earth would she do that? How did he die?'

'He had a heart attack.'

'Why do you think she blames you?'

'Maybe blame is the wrong word. But I feel she's always resented me. She and Daddy were awfully close, and so were he and I, and I can't help thinking she felt I'd stolen some of his affection from her.'

I'd expected him to disagree or try to reassure me but, he just listened, then asked, 'What was he like?'

I thought for a moment. 'He had a serious face that softened when he smiled. He was a good listener, thoughtful, with a great sense of fun. No matter how busy he was, he always had time for me. Clever—a research scientist. What else? Loyal to his friends. Loved art and opera and walking— which is something Mummy didn't like at all. He and I did that together. He lost both his brothers in the War, one at the Front and the other to pneumonia and, then, both parents to influenza—so Mummy and I were all he had.'

'Were he and your mother happy?'

'Yes. Even when I was a child, I could tell they adored each other.'

As I said the words, I felt overwhelmingly sad and far

from home. I looked at my watch. 'I'm long overdue to get back. How do I call a *tonga* to take me home?'

'They wait at the gates, but I'll escort you, Madame.

As he helped me slip my cardigan on, ready for the ride home, he said, 'You haven't told me how you and Tony met.'

'If he hadn't come along, I'd still be stuck on a moor in the middle of Yorkshire with my mother nagging me about my bad posture and making me feel as though I'd ruined both our lives. I'll always be grateful to him for saving me from that.'

'Good old Tony, riding in on his white charger to rescue the damsel in distress and carry her off. Must say I'd never have thought he had the gumption to play the hero.'

'It wasn't like that at all.'

'What was it like then?'

'Our mothers sort of flung us together. I think Mummy was pretty desperate that, after the nude portrait business, she'd never get me off her hands. And his mother was just as keen that he find a wife.' I paused, then added, 'But I liked him at once.'

'Really?' he raised an eyebrow. 'Reassuring that at least you liked him. So it was, as Miss Heyer might say, "*un mariage de convenance*"—I didn't think it was his devastating wit and charm that swept you off your feet.'

'Must you always be a complete, unmitigated, rotter?'

'Sorry. I've overstepped the mark again, haven't I? But you are a little prickly where Tony's concerned.'

'Maybe it's because he's my husband and I love him.'

'Maybe. But, somehow, I doubt that.'

'You're impossible.' I reached for my handbag and accidentally knocked my empty glass off the table. Feeling slightly drunk, I strode away from him across the lawn. My attempt at a dignified exit was short-lived, when I tripped over my loose shoelace and landed on my knees. He helped me to my feet.

'Come on, let's get you home, Mrs T. And we'll call a truce. I can't let you ride round Muddy alone in a *tonga*, half-sloshed. What on earth would Tony say?'

CHAPTER 9

As the weeks passed, I came to understand why the expatriates loved the countryside around Mudoorayam. It wasn't so much for its own unique charms, as for its surprising resemblance to what they'd left behind at home. The rolling hills and verdant valleys could be mistaken for parts of the English countryside or the Scottish Highlands, and the British had done their level best to reinforce that impression by the building of neat bungalows and the creation of carefully curated gardens.

The climate was often close to that we had left behind in Great Britain, a mild and gentle contrast to the scorching heat of the plains and the sweaty, hothouse atmosphere of the coastal cities. Up here, the winter days were mild, the nights cold but never freezing, and the summer months were warm and sunny. The benevolent climate and the nostalgic scenery had led to the town becoming a popular escape for many of the British civil servants and government officials posted at lower altitudes. But, when it rained, Mudoorayam lived up to the name the expats affectionately used—"Muddy".

Used to rising at a fashionably late hour in London, I had to get used to a rude awakening here. Every morning at around five-thirty, a chap known as the head conductor sounded a big brass gong to wake up the tea workers. It echoed across the valley, and was repeated an hour later to muster the gangs for the day. It was worse than the military: a trumpet, sounding reveille, would have been more tuneful.

Tony found a horse for me, a little bay mare. I wanted her to have an Indian name, to his bemusement, and christened her "Naṭana", which Hector told me was the Tamil word for "dancer". I took advantage of the dawn wakeup call and often rode out on Naṭana before breakfast. The tea gardens were their most beautiful in the early morning, shrouded in mists with low clouds over the mountains and a wonderful limpid light that made them seem almost mystical. My solitary rides introduced me to another side of India, away from the bustle of the Muddy market or the narrow snobbery of the British club. When I rode into villages, children—usually with an entourage of scabby dogs, would run out and follow me, reaching their little hands to stroke my horse. I always carried a bag with boiled sweets to give them, and their happy smiles and giggles as they ran alongside lifted my spirits.

While I grew fond of the countryside and the bustling Indian market, the rest of Muddy was slightly quaint and too English. It didn't feel as though I'd travelled halfway round the world. But, then, I'd spot an exotic bird in the club garden, hear the trumpeting of a distant wild elephant in the night or disturb a flock of peacocks on top of a row of tea bushes. Seeing the flash of their cobalt-blue plumage and spectacular tails showed I was, indeed, a long way from Leighton Square.

One Sunday evening, Tony and I were on our way home from the club later than usual. Everyone had gathered in the lounge for a rant about the independence movement. The evening had started off well enough. We'd arrived to be greeted by the sound of Hector accompanying himself on the piano as he sang Noel Coward songs. But, after dinner, the conversation degenerated as the post-prandial *chota pegs* were consumed. I hated it when they talked politics at the club. Not because I wasn't interested—although granted, until coming to India, I had not shown the slightest concern —but because it brought out the pettiness in so many of the British, including to my disappointment, Tony. I sat in the corner of the club lounge, in a bit of a sulk, too cowardly to launch a riposte, but annoyed by the bigotry on show. Mr Gandhi was their target. One of the men, Roger Throckley, a spice plantation owner with a red nose and an enormous belly, was being particularly obnoxious.

'The man needs a damned good hiding. Give him the birch till his skinny legs snap off. That would stop all this nonsense.'

Tony responded, 'He's cracked up to be a holy man, praying and meditating all the time, but if you ask me he's a damned pervert. Sleeps with his niece apparently. Dirty old man.'

'But Mr Gandhi's celibate,' I said.

Throckley started laughing. 'Don't tell me your little lady's a fan of the man? Need to set her straight Tilman, old boy.'

'Why anyone would want to follow a man who runs around wearing what looks like a baby's nappy I can't imagine,' said a woman I took to be Throckley's wife.

'To think he was called to the bar. Education wasted on him, bloody fool.' And so it went on.

I looked over at Hector but, instead of challenging them, he rolled his eyes, picked up his book and headed for the quiet of the library. I wanted to join him, but I knew it would annoy Tony.

Avoiding Tony's annoyance was becoming a priority for me lately. He'd started making cutting comments or frowning and sighing whenever I mentioned Hector. I sensed it was down to discomfort with Hector's sexual orientation—something he barely tried to conceal. To me, it didn't matter in the slightest—my parents had had one or two friends of ambiguous inclinations and never gave it a moment's thought. Most of the people at the club acted as though he were part of the gang, but I sensed they talked about him behind his back, and one or two of the men, Tony included, appeared to see him as an affront to their own masculinity. Hector's sympathy with the aims of Indian nationalism was another black mark against him.

We left the club in a crowd of people, and snaked our way in a convoy of motorcars towards the town. Tony's face was set in concentration and I could tell he was getting ready to say something. Eventually, he spoke, 'You were awfully quiet tonight. What's wrong?'

'Nothing.'

'Come on, old thing, Spill the beans. You're miffed about something.'

'I just hate it when everyone piles in with the insults about Gandhi.'

He laughed. 'Is that all? Why should you care about that old fool?'

'I think he's a wise man. And I think it's pathetic that they're all afraid of a man whose only weapon is prayer and passive resistance.'

'For God's sake, Ginny. Play the game. You've been spending too much time with that Channing fellow. Filling your head with nonsense. Don't like it at all. Can't you make a bit of an effort to get along with the people who count here?'

'The people who count? Who might they be?'

'You know as well as I do, darling. People like the Blakes and the Carvers and the Worthingtons. Jock Bentley, old Throckley and the Hendersons. Practically everyone in the club apart from that nancy boy.' He laid a hand on my knee, but I brushed it off.

'Don't call him that. I don't want to get along with people who are narrow-minded and petty. I was brought up to show more respect. Mr Gandhi is an educated man and a man of God, even if it doesn't happen to be your God.'

As soon as the words were out, I regretted them. It would only make matters worse between us. Whether I approved of his views or not, he was my husband and I had to get along with him. Direct confrontation was hardly the way to marital harmony.

Before he could respond, the cars in front of us screeched to a halt and we had to do the same. We sat for a moment in silence.

'Probably an animal in the road. A cow or maybe an elephant.' He reached past me into the glove compartment and took out a small cloth bag. 'Stay here. Don't move.'

He got out of the car and was swallowed up by the darkness. After several minutes, a bulky shape moved across the road in front of the cars ahead of us and up a bank on the other side. I heard branches snapping. The night was pitch black with barely any moon, and the shape was swallowed up in the greater darkness of the trees and undergrowth.

Tony leaned into the car through my wound-down window. 'Sit tight. It's an elephant. Off the road now, but it could come back.'

He pointed to a spot where the forest bulged out in a kind of promontory above us, forcing the road into a sharp bend. I squinted into the blackness; in the middle of the forested bank was the unmistakeable outline of an elephant in profile, standing stock-still.

I felt a rush of excitement. I'd heard the distant trumpeting of elephants and seen them hauling timber, but I'd not yet seen one out in the wild. 'Can we go and have a closer look?'

'Don't be daft. Can flatten a car in a moment. Imagine what it could do to you.' As he spoke, the elephant's trumpeting broke the silent night. The sense of loneliness, fear and loss in its call was palpable.

'What are we going to do?' I whispered.

'Sit still and keep quiet.' He walked away and I lost sight of him in the inky blackness. Then it dawned on me that the bag from the glove compartment contained a gun, and he was planning to kill the creature. I tensed and shut my eyes, waiting for the sound of a shot.

A truck drew up and a group of Indian men jumped out. I could hear Tony speaking to them, his words having an immediate effect on the men. They moved as a group onto the bank on the other side of the road. One moment the elephant was there, and the next it was gone, crashing through undergrowth carving its own path into the forest.

Tony tapped the roof of each of the cars ahead of us, and one by one, they released their brakes and began to roll silently down the hill. When the queue had cleared, he got back in, returned the cloth bag to the glove drawer, eased the handbrake off and we began to slide after them silently down the hill. Only when we had reached the bottom and out of earshot of the elephant did he fire up the engine

'They won't kill it, will they?' I asked.

'Not allowed. Elephants are protected. They'll lead it back to its herd. They know the hills and the wildlife better than you know the back of your hand.'

'Who are they?'

'Tribal people—Muduvans—guides and hunters. Keep themselves to themselves, but they got me out of many a scrape when I was a boy. They're called the "back people."'

'Why?'

He shrugged. 'Haven't a clue.'

His lack of curiosity was alien to me. I wanted to know everything—things it never occurred to him to wonder about. He took so much for granted.

Eventually, he spoke again, 'Not much more than a calf. Must have got separated from its mother.'

'If it was only a calf, surely it wouldn't have done us any harm?'

He laughed. 'Weighed about three tons. You wouldn't want it to sit on you. Last year, a young rogue male threw a bloke off his bicycle. Picked him up in his trunk and smashed him back down on the road. Every bone in his body broken.'

'Goodness! Did he die?'

He nodded.

'How frightful. I've always thought of elephants as being sweet and friendly—like Babar.'

'Females are docile enough when they're domesticated. Adult males are a different matter. This one was a youngster. Probably cut off from the herd. Maybe injured. Everything can be the enemy then. The Muduvan will help him find his herd. They can smell elephants.'

'Smell them?'

'Not just elephants. They can identify different animals from the smell of their dung.'

I wrinkled my nose. 'What language were you speaking to them?'

'Tamil.'

'How did you learn it?'

'Spoken it since I was a child. Muduvan have their own

language, but it comes from Tamil and they understand the gist of it, so we get by. Most of my workers are Tamils. '

I twisted in my seat to look back at the seemingly impenetrable, dark forest behind us and wondered if the elephant would find his mother. I hoped if he did, she'd be pleased to see him again.

'Tony, was that a gun?'

'What?'

'The thing in the bag from the glove compartment.'

I moved to open it, and he snapped at me, 'Leave it alone.'

'It was a gun. Were you going to shoot the elephant?'

'Don't be daft. Wouldn't shoot an elephant with a small pistol like that. Well, only as a last resort.'

'Have you hunted elephants?'

'Not here in Travancore. Not allowed.'

'Why would anyone want to kill an elephant?'

'For sport. For the tusks. For the fun of tracking them. For the shooting.'

'Hunting them seems so cruel and pointless. They're beautiful. They look so wise. I sometimes think men just do it to look brave. Heroic even. But it isn't brave at all. Not when you have the guns and they have nothing.'

I saw he was frowning, his jaw set firmly. We drove the rest of the way in silence. I'd seen another side of my husband tonight. At first, I'd liked the way he'd naturally taken charge of the situation—the scoutmaster had turned back into Errol Flynn. But I wasn't happy that, given the right circumstances, he could probably shoot an elephant in the blink of an eye. I hated the tired cliché of the British colonials, eager to shoot game just to plaster the trophies over the walls of their homes and their clubs. But, as we pulled into the driveway, I realised I'd put my foot in it again. *Just button it, Ginny. Think before opening your mouth. You have to adapt to his world. It's your world now.*

TONY WORKED long hours at the plantation and the tea factory, then usually went straight to the club in the evening to meet me in time for dinner or drinks. He went down to Cochin for the fortnightly tea auctions and travelled inland to Coimbatore and, occasionally, to Bombay. He would be away for days at a time on these trips and never offered to take me along.

'It's business. Can't be worrying about entertaining you, Ginny.'

'But you wouldn't need to. I can look after myself. I just want to have a look around and see what those places are like.'

He stared at me over the top of the Times of India. His mouth was open and, not for the first time, it struck me he looked slightly stupid.

'It's India, darling, not Eastbourne. Have you any idea how hot it is in Cochin at the moment? You can't just wander around. You're a white woman, a *memsahib*. Not done to wander around these places alone, and I can't spare the time to ferry you about.'

Then, seeing my crestfallen face, he softened his tone and put a hand on my arm and gave it a little squeeze.

'Is it awfully dull for you here, darling? Maybe if you made a bit of an effort to get involved with the other women at the club, you'd find there's a jolly lot going on. Plenty to do. Tennis, bridge, croquet, amateur dramatics. Take your pick. I've got work to do and can't spend time keeping you amused, much as I'd love to do that, old girl.'

He gave me his crinkly-eyed smile and I felt ashamed and smiled back. But I knew I wasn't going to follow his advice; I had little or nothing in common with the *pukka memsahibs* from the club. Getting dressed up in costume and joining the amateur Thespians with their booming, stilted delivery and exaggerated gestures was about as enticing a prospect as being burnt at the stake.

Whenever Tony was around, he was affectionate, in his stiff-mannered way. He brought me little gifts back from his trips: a jasper bracelet, a pair of star sapphire earrings, and countless trinkets and ornaments. To be honest, they were rarely to my taste, and I understood why he'd co-opted Marjorie to choose my wedding gift, but I feigned delight, and loved seeing how making me happy made him happy.

He kept his promise to teach me to drive and showed infinite patience with my incompetence at hill starts—essential for driving in the Western Ghats—as well as my pathological tendency to stall the engine whenever my foot touched the clutch. When, in mounting frustration, I revealed a capacity for a well-chosen expletive worthy of a barrack room—learned from a classmate in the Lower Fourth when I was thirteen and didn't know what the words meant—he just shook his head and asked me to try again. At the end of each lesson, he got me to slide across, and he took over the controls and drove us to the club for a well-earned gin and tonic.

But, despite his kindness, I was living with a stranger. Perhaps I was too young to be married. I'd experienced little enough of life and seen little of the world, going straight from boarding school to my short-lived debutante career. I shudder at the callow girl I was then. I think now some of my chippiness and often jaundiced view of the world was a protective mantle from what I feared the world might throw at me. And, after what Rupert Milligan had done, I found it difficult to trust anyone, even my husband.

I was lonely. Lilian Bulstode-Hemmings was kind but she was often away, travelling with Theo. I asked her how she'd got him to bring her along when Tony refused to take me on business trips.

'Theo needs me as there's a lot of glad-handing to be done. Part of the role of the D.O.'s wife. Very different from Tony's job, of course. He couldn't have you there when he's conducting business. And he's quite right, Virginia, it's not done to wander around unaccompanied. To be frank, I can't imagine why you'd want to go to Cochin. It's so much nicer up here where one can breathe.'

The club wives, like me, had followed their husbands to India and, while many of them may also have been bored and lonely, all excelled at putting on a brave face. With no talent for tennis nor interest in card games, it wasn't easy for me to build rapport. And I couldn't help but be repelled by their blinkered views on the importance of empire and the unassailable hegemony of the British.

That left Hector Channing.

He turned up at the bungalow regularly and we'd sit in the garden talking. One afternoon, he took me to visit the Hindu temple. Hector was the only British person I knew who showed any interest in the way of life of the indigenous population. Knowledgeable about the town and its people, he didn't give off that air of superiority and condescension that the other expatriates did.

I jumped at the chance to go with him. I wasn't keen to get to know any individual Indians, but I was interested to find out more about their customs and culture. I didn't want to admit it, but I was slightly afraid of the local people. Not that they would do me harm—despite the constant rumblings among people at the club about the independence movement—all I ever saw were smiling, happy faces. No. I was afraid of their difference from me. The dark brown of their skins, their glossy, raven hair, the little wooden hovels they lived in that were pitch dark inside, and their strange alien smell: slightly sweet, pungent and spicy with a base note of sweat. It was fear of the unknown. Fear at an atavistic level. I hesitate to say this now but, despite my protestations against the bigotry of the rest of the British, I think then I also felt superior to the Indians, viewing them, as many of my countrymen did, as people of lower intelligence. People to feel sorry for. I had absolutely no basis for this judgment as I rarely spoke to any of them, apart from Thankappan and Nirmala and I knew nothing of their lives. It was blind prejudice and ignorance. My admiration for Gandhi was theoretical—based on his moral certainty and strength of purpose—and the fact he had yet again been slung into prison; it had not been put to the test by a close encounter with a real Indian. I felt vaguely uncomfortable with myself about this, and stopped short of actually giving it serious thought and would never have mentioned it to Hector.

As we drove up the hill to the temple, Hector turned to me. 'Imagine, if it hadn't been for The Cork Street Scandal, you'd be cavorting and flirting your way around London with the fast set, instead of swanning around here with an old queer finding out how the other half live.'

'The Cork Street Scandal? Is that what people are calling it? Gosh, I'd hoped it would be long forgotten.'

'You are so deliciously egotistical, darling. I can assure you the exploits of one, now long departed, insignificant, little debutante made scarcely a ripple on the great lake of London life.'

'Well, please don't call it that, Hector. It makes it sound like the Cato Street Conspiracy.'

'I'm impressed, Mrs T. You stayed awake in at least one history lesson, then. So what shall we call it?'

'Let's not call it anything. I'd prefer we didn't refer to it at all. And I didn't exactly cavort around London, I certainly wasn't in the fast set and I've always been absolutely hopeless at flirting.'

'Really?' he raised an eyebrow. 'I've heard you were said to be the belle of the ball.'

'I can't think where you got that from.'

'Rumour has it most of the chaps were queuing up to get down on their knees to you, until you managed to get bowled out for a duck.'

'I think to say they were queuing up is a bit of an exaggeration. There certainly wasn't anyone in particular.'

'My spies back in Blighty tell me you were on course to break a lot of hearts. But not popular with the other girls. Not surprising, really.'

'It's hard to make friends. I don't know why.'

'I'm beginning to think that, underneath that cool and superior exterior, you're actually shy.'

I looked away.

'I think there's a little girl inside who's overwhelmed by it all. Maybe your confident exterior is a flimsy cover for someone who's been forced to grow up too quickly.'

'And I suppose your name's Dr Freud?'

'I'm no psychiatrist, darling, but I think I can recognise a kindred spirit.'

The *tonga* pulled up at the bottom of a long flight of white steps. We jumped down and Hector took my hand and led me up them. When we reached the top, slightly breathless, he untied his shoelaces and removed his shoes.

'Indians are barefoot when they go into a temple or mosque. Most of the British refuse to do it, so I'll understand if you have scruples. But I happen to believe they are as entitled to our respect as we are to theirs. In fact, more so. It's their country after all.'

I slipped off my sandals. The concrete felt slippery under my feet from an earlier rain shower. I tried to ignore the slightly greasy feeling and tried not to think about all the naked Indian feet that had trodden there before me. I followed him into the white-painted building, past the big, gaudy, plaster goddess who stood guard at the top of the steps like a figurehead on a schooner. She had jet-black, wavy hair, swooping black eyebrows and a tight *chola* stretched over ample bosoms. She didn't look holy enough to be at the entrance to a temple. I'd expected someone more modestly dressed. The temple was cool and shaded inside, and I saw a monk sitting on the floor in the corner banging a muffled gong. I stood on the threshold, breathing in the heavy scent of incense inside the building.

Hector showed me around the building as though it was his personal fiefdom, telling me the names of the various gods and what they symbolised. I told him I wanted to do some sketching. Painting always helped me feel calm, centred, peaceful and replaced my loneliness. When I drew or painted, I focused on the task and my head was blissfully free of thoughts. Hector approached the chubby monk, had a few words, then nodded to me.

I made a quick study of one of the painted deities: a turbaned and garlanded male with two sets of arms, standing on a cobra. Then, I sat beside Hector on the steps outside, our backs to the temple entrance, looking out over the valley, with Mudoorayam sprawled below us in the sunshine, an untidy tangle of buildings inside a big green bowl. The white-painted Catholic Church with its spire, the tallest building, faced down the stone-built Church of England structure, where most of the British went every Sunday, and the Muslim mosque on the opposite side of the river. The river itself wound its slow and indolent way through the town, its banks strewn with discarded rubbish between reeds and willow trees. I made a few quick sketches of the statues around us and the town below us.

Drawing forces me to look beyond the first superficial impression and really see a place for what it is. The way light and shadow falls, the pattern of colours, the interplay of shapes. Even the most mundane things present themselves with a special beauty when you really look at them. As I drew, I found a kind of charm in the scruffy, little town that had tried to squeeze itself tightly into the space between the rivers, but had been forced to overflow in a haphazard sprawl. Everywhere on the riverbanks and the roadsides were long, white, trumpet-shaped flowers, hanging in clusters, the whiteness of the flowers brilliant against the green foliage.

I burrowed in the depths of my bag for my little tin paint palette and began to paint the muddy river and its banks festooned with litter and flowers. Hector had fallen asleep in the sunshine, his panama hat over his face. He was one of the few white men I knew in India who refused to wear a solar topi. He woke and looked over my shoulder at my work.

'Mmm—you're actually not that bad at it.'

'You don't have to sound so surprised.'

'I'm not surprised, Mrs T. And I did say you're not bad. Which is not quite the same as saying you're good.'

I jabbed the paintbrush in his arm.

'Why are you always attacking me, woman? Slapping my face and stabbing me with sharp instruments. You're dangerous company.'

'Well, stop giving me cause, you beast. Tell me what those white flowers are, Mr Know-It-All.'

'*Datura*. Or angel's trumpets to badly educated philistines like you. They grow everywhere around here. Don't try to eat them, darling. They're highly poisonous.'

'I'll bear that in mind.' I put a dab of paint on the tip of his nose.

He shook his head and wiped the paint off without

complaint. 'What will you do with all this then?' he asked, gesturing at my sketch book.

'I'll probably use the pencil sketches as studies for larger paintings. There's a little bedroom at home I'm using as a studio. It gives me something to do and helps pass the time.'

'Well, well, Mrs T, do I detect a note of dissatisfaction with your lot?'

'Of course not.' I hated the fact he was always able to read me. 'I'm not dissatisfied at all.'

'Save the indignation, darling. I know you don't mean it.'

I paused for a moment, then decided to open up. 'It's just I sometimes feel a bit useless.'

'Useless?'

'Tony has his work. He's always busy. All I do is loll around reading or painting all day.'

'And what's wrong with that? You can't expect me to sympathise with your underemployment. I haven't done a day's work in years. Look at me—retired since I turned 30. And painting strikes me as a rewarding and fulfilling occupation.'

'It's only a hobby. Like reading. I'd really like to do something useful.'

Hector leaned back against the balustrade and roared with laughter. 'Good God. Next thing you're going to offer to visit the widows and orphans. I'm sure if you have a word with the lovely Lilian, she'll add you to her roster of volunteers for good works.'

'Gosh, I don't mean that. I'd be absolutely frightful at that sort of thing. But I feel I'm lacking in purpose. And I suppose a bit guilty. I did want to go to art school, but my mother was dead against it. Her only measure of one's value is based on whom one marries. And as it happens my work wasn't considered good enough. All I've done with my life is learn a load of things that are absolutely pointless now. Like how to curtsey to royalty and how to organise a seating plan without offending people. And Tony's away so often.'

'Neglecting you, is he?'

'I didn't say that. He works hard, and he's obviously awfully good at his job and terribly passionate about tea. But I'd like to feel I had something I could be equally passionate about.'

'Well, shouldn't you be passionate about him?'

I looked at him to see if he was taunting me again, but he actually looked sincere.

'I am, of course. He's my husband.'

'Doesn't necessarily follow.'

'Well, I can assure you, Hector, I care for him very much.'

'Well then, I imagine your problem will be solved before too much longer.'

'What do you mean?'

'It can't be too long before you find another use for that little bedroom.'

I was puzzled for a moment.

'Come on, girl. You know that's what's expected of you. Preservation of the Tilman line. A tiny Tony or a Junior Ginny.'

I sighed and looked out at the hills and, without my intending to tell him, the words followed; I found it impossible to keep things from Hector. 'Nothing seems to be happening on that front.'

'Really?' The arched eyebrow. 'You do surprise me. I'd have thought you'd be at it like a couple of rabbits.'

I slapped his arm playfully. 'For heaven's sake, Hector, have you no shame?'

I wasn't about to discuss my married life with him—that was a step too far, and Tony and I weren't exactly going at it like a couple of rabbits, as he so charmingly put it. During the later years of my time with Rupert, I used to look at him when he was painting me, seeing how he was totally absorbed in his art and knowing in a short time his brushes would be put aside and we would be having sex. The anticipation was always more thrilling to me than the act itself, which I endured rather than enjoyed. I suppose it was the knowledge that I could make a man like him desire me. But, with Tony, it was never like that. When I looked at him, I saw a sensible, solid man, handsome but lacking any sense of the erotic and very little of the romantic. In my head, sex was associated with clandestine meetings and fear of discovery. I hated the intimacy of it; the smells and secretions and the way it was all so awkward and undignified. My first experiences were under duress, when I was too immature to understand fully what we were doing and why. I suppose I had been hoping marriage would have changed all that; that Tony would make me desire him, so I could wipe out the memories of Milligan and be healed and restored. But, then, I had no understanding that physical attraction has more to do with what is inside a man's head than the features that adorn it. I couldn't deny Tony was caring and considerate of me. He may have had little to say, but he was a generous listener and I had no reason to doubt he cared for me, even though the word "love" had still not passed his lips. To be fair, I had not said it either.

I sometimes asked myself what was wrong with me. I admired Tony in some ways. He was good at his job, popular, a reliable husband and, as far as I knew, a faithful one. Why could I not settle for my lot? Why did I want more? And why should I have more? After all, I was damaged goods and ought to be grateful for my second chance. But the difference between us became more apparent as time went on. The difference was exemplified in the way we saw the world. I loved to paint the brightly coloured laundry hanging on washing lines throughout the town and its surrounds. I was building up quite a collection of laundry paintings. Wherever there was a dwelling, the women found a space to sling up a line, or laid out their laundry on top of bushes or on the grass. I loved the patterns the colours made against the dark green of the trees or reflected in the dull brown of the river or were illuminated by the brightness of the afternoon sun. When children came across me painting, they shyly peered over my shoulders at the subject, realised what it was, and then giggled and ran to tell their mothers, amazed anyone would think painting washing worthy of the time and effort.

Tony wandered into my studio one evening while I was working. He glanced at the half-finished painting and said, 'Bit primitive isn't it, Ginny? Like a child would paint.'

I tried not to feel wounded by his words; by the way he threw his comments out so lightly, as if painting was such a pointless pursuit that nothing he said could cause offence.

'Why all these washing lines? What's wrong with a nice picture of some flowers or a portrait? Painting people's washing seems like a damn waste of paint.'

He laughed and flipped through my sketch book, stopping at a drawing of the market square in the town.

'No, no, you've got it wrong. You've missed out the building next to the market hall. The big, ugly, concrete one. You've made it look as though the market stretches further than it really does. And where's the clock tower?'

'It's not a technical drawing, Tony. Or a photograph. It's called artistic licence. I chose not to put every detail in.'

He frowned, grunted, and said, 'It's almost seven. Get your skates on, old girl or we won't have time for a drink at the club before dinner.'

This way of seeing things reflected our characters and view of the world; his literal approach, all attention to detail, and my preference for paring things down to their essentials, to simple shapes, colours and the impact of light and shade.

One morning, he was still at the breakfast table when I walked in. This was unusual; he was an early riser and was mostly long gone by the time I surfaced. He looked at me over the top of the newspaper, his face creased with worry.

'Japs have invaded Shanghai. Bloody awful business. One of the chaps I was at school with works for an oil firm there. Hope he got out before it happened. It's going to be a god awful mess.'

It all seemed too far away for me to be really interested, so I nodded and reached for the toast rack.

He went on, 'There'll be trouble in Europe, too, before long. That horrible little Kraut throwing his weight around. There's a piece here about the rate Germany is rearming. Sounds like he's thrown the entire nation into making munitions. Doesn't look good. Another war coming. And those dashed stupid, goose-stepping soldiers, parading everywhere and threatening to take over the Sudetenland.'

'Thank goodness we're out of it all over here. And I'm sure it won't come to anything serious. Hitler's just trying it on. It's all just posturing. There can't be another war in Europe, surely? Not after the last one. That was the whole point, wasn't it?'

'Don't bank on it, old thing. As for being out of it here— we're actually stuck in the middle with the Japs on one side and the Germans on the other. And that bloody Gandhi fellow and his gang are making things worse by getting in the way and banging on all the time about independence.'

'It is their country, after all. Hector reckons if the various factions had got together, instead of always falling out with each other, they'd have had home rule long ago.'

He looked at me for a moment as if I was stupid and then shook his head. 'I've told you before, don't listen to the tripe Hector Channing spouts. He's a failure. Thrown out of the Civil service. Man knows nothing. Far too chummy with the natives. He'll be running round in a loin cloth before long.'

I knew I was on dangerous territory, but I pressed on regardless, 'Hector's been in India a long time. Maybe not as long as you, but he does understand what's going on.'

Tony folded the newspaper and put it down. 'He knows nothing of the Indian mind. These oriental fellows can be dashed cunning. Same throughout the empire. We old hands know exactly how to handle them. My family has been here for generations. Johnny-come-lately types like Channing just don't get the picture.'

He got up, came round the table and dropped a light kiss on the top of my head, then went off to work. I buttered a piece of toast and reached for the marmalade, jar. As I was about to dip the spoon inside, I saw the blobs of butter smearing the pellucid orange surface. I'd lost count of the number of times I'd asked him not to dip a buttery knife into the jar. I dropped the toast back on the plate, appetite gone.

CHAPTER 10

'HAVE you ever been in love, Hector?'

'The eternal question, Mrs T.'

'Well, have you?'

'Yes.'

'With your cabinet minister?'

He roared laughing. 'Good God, no. I never really cared for him. It was just the thrill of transgression. Although, I did enjoy our hotel room assignations and the odd occasion after hours in his office in Whitehall.'

'In his office?'

'Yes. With the red ministerial box on the table and the portraits of past ministers on the walls. I can't tell you how thrilling it was with the risk of getting caught and imagining all those serious meetings taking place around the big mahogany table where we...'

'All right, Hector. Please spare me the gory details. So, who was he?'

'You know me better than that, my dear. I'm never going to tell you his name. He's famous enough that even an igno-rant, under-educated debutante will have heard of him. Even one who prefers Georgette Heyer to reading *The Times*. And, besides, his wife swore me to secrecy. I'd be thrown in the Tower.'

'I didn't mean the cabinet minister, silly. I meant who were you in love with? Was it your bearer?'

'Certainly not. Fond of him as I was, the dear boy.'

'Was it a long time ago?'

He hesitated a moment. 'Not so long ago.'

'How did you know you were in love?'

'I suspect, my dear Mrs T, this conversation is less about your curiosity over my emotional history and more about your own?'

'No. I'm interested in hearing about you. Human nature fascinates me.'

He snorted in derision. 'Now why do I struggle to believe that one?'

'I can't imagine. It always interests me what people see in each other. I've often wondered about my aunt. She's married to a lugubrious Yorkshireman. I've never understood what she sees in him. I can only imagine he must have been different once.'

'*Le coeur a ses raisons que la raison ne connait point.* But I expect you weren't paying attention in French lessons either, were you, darling?'

'I know what it means. I speak French well, actually. Just not who said it. The heart has its reasons which reason knows nothing of.'

'*Parfaite*. It was Pascal.'

'Not very helpful advice.'

'But very true. I'm sure your aunt's husband, who is in fact correctly referred to as *your uncle*, is seen in a different light by your aunt. He may have talents and depths, which you will never know of.'

'I find that hard to believe. We must have exchanged

about five words in the whole time I've been alive. Although, he was sweet in the car on the way to my wedding. He gave me away. Pud seems happy enough, so there's got to be something keeping them together.'

'Pud? Well, if she's anything like her name, maybe he was the only man prepared to take her on.'

'Don't be mean. She's thin as a rake and rather beautiful. She acquired the name as a child and it stuck, long after anyone could remember why she had it in the first place. Roger doesn't call her that though. Just Mummy and me.'

'What does he call her?'

'Goodness. I've no idea. Maybe her real name, which is Margaret. But I can't actually remember him calling her anything.' I rolled my eyes. 'Maybe he has a pet name for her that he only uses when they're alone. That would be romantic, wouldn't it?'

Hector shrugged. 'Speaking of hidden attractions, you've never explained what you saw in the handsome Mr Tilman? Apart from the fact that he rescued you from your bossy mother. Somehow, I wouldn't have put you down as someone who'd just fall for a pretty face?'

'He's a good man.'

'Do me a favour, darling.'

'Well, he is. He's kind and generous and caring to me. Decent. Reliable. Solid. Safe.'

Hector yawned theatrically. 'You could have bought a dog for that.' Then he realised I was not enjoying the banter. 'You're not in love with him though.'

I didn't like the way the conversation was heading. 'What makes you say that? I don't know whether I am or not.'

'Then you've answered my question. If you were, you'd know.'

'Do you really think so? I'm not even sure I know what love is. That's why I asked you if you'd been in love.'

'There's a difference between loving someone and being in love.'

'Well, that's obvious. I loved my father and I love Pud and I suppose, even my mother, in a way. And Tony. But I'm not sure if that's the same as me being in love with him, because it doesn't seem that different from what I feel for my family...just a bit weaker...more diluted. That sounds awful, doesn't it? But he makes me feel cared for. That's important to me. You know, since my father died. And I suppose he saved me.'

'Cut it out, Ginny. You didn't need saving. You don't need to be so melodramatic. And I don't like to hear you sounding self-pitying.'

I tried to be flippant. 'You haven't met my mother, or you wouldn't say that.'

'Come on, the old girl can't be any worse than mine was. When I was fifteen, she suspected I was a queer and threatened to tell my father, who would have written me out of my trust fund. She agreed to keep it from him on condition I went to see her friend, a Jesuit priest, for spiritual guidance and correction.'

'And did you?'

'Of course, I did. I went to confession. I read all the books he gave me about avoiding temptation, wore out the rosary beads with countless Hail Marys and acts of contrition, and then declared I was cured.'

'Did they believe you?'

'People will believe anything if they want to. My mother was a staunch Catholic and was convinced I'd be destined to burn in hell if I didn't reform. So, when I told her I had, she was delighted. You have to understand Catholics believe what I do is a sin and a choice. They don't understand it's who I am. Much easier to let her be deluded. Then we're all happy.'

'Can't be much fun though, living a lie?'

I thought I detected a flicker of sadness in his eyes, but he breezed on, 'What makes your mama such a battle axe?'

'She's not actually a battle axe. She just has impossible expectations for me. And for her, being married is like religion. She'd have sooner slit her own throat than risk having the humiliation of an unmarried daughter. I don't suppose she's even now recovered from her disappointment at me only marrying Tony, rather than a member of the aristocracy. Especially once she realised he didn't actually own Tilman's Tea anymore. She's a terrific snob. But then, she does seem to like him. I mean as a human being. Probably because he made such a fuss over her, and did the nearest thing he does to flirting, with her.'

'She sounds a formidable woman. I have a mental picture of her as a merry widow, surrounded by admirers and disliked by every woman within a mile.'

'How on earth have you got that impression? Men adore her, yes. And she is very beautiful. Even though she's positively ancient now—nearly fifty. She may be popular with men, but she prefers the company of women. She has tons of friends. And she's never seriously looked at any other man than Daddy. I don't think she'll ever marry again.'

'You're actually jealous of her, aren't you Mrs T?'

I spun round and stared at him. 'What on earth makes you say that?'

'Just a sense I get.'

'Well it's a wrong sense. Why on earth would I be jealous of my own mother?'

'Well, you tell me, darling. How about the fact she was happily married to your father? That she's wildly popular and has lots of friends? Or possibly even that Tony, dear boy, seems to have been charmed by her, too? And maybe it's something I detect in your tone of voice when you talk about her.'

'How dare you.' I took a slug of my drink, then slammed the glass down on the table. 'You have a bloody cheek.'

'Don't shoot the messenger.' He counted the points out on his fingers. 'You told me she adored your father and he, her. Whatever else you say about your devotion to him, you clearly don't have that kind of relationship with Tony. And, yet, the cold fish that is Mr Tony Tilman was inspired to behave flirtatiously with your mother. More than it seems he has ever done to you.'

I felt the tears rising but was determined not to give him the satisfaction. 'That's ridiculous. All of it.'

He looked at me and looked away again immediately. 'I'm sorry. My mistake. I haven't met the woman, so who am I to speculate?'

'Exactly. You haven't, so you shouldn't.'

'Will I get to have that pleasure?'

'I don't know. I'm not sure she's too thrilled about the idea of coming to India. Not really her cup of tea.'

I realised the ice was chinking in an empty glass and reached across for the gin bottle. 'Time for a top up.'

'Don't you think you should go a bit easy?'

'What are you saying?'

He looked at me unsmiling, and then slid his hand across his own glass as I moved the bottle towards it.

'Don't be a bore, Hector. Since when have you said no to another tipple?'

'Since now. I fear I've been leading you astray, Ginny. I'm not risking Tony punching me on the nose for turning his wife into a dipsomaniac.'

'Don't you dare call me a dipsomaniac.' I smacked him in the chest.

'You can't even pronounce it, darling. Anyway, it's time I

was going. A parcel of books arrived from London today and I can't wait to get my nose into them. See you at the club tonight? And mind you don't have too many more of those in the meantime.' He tapped the side of my glass.

I was annoyed with Hector, but I knew he was speaking the truth. I was hitting the bottle with too much zeal. I just hadn't realised it was noticeable. I was trying to take my mind off the fact I felt so lonely and miserable and my fears about not yet expecting a baby. I was starting to wonder whether I might have a fertility problem. I wouldn't be the first woman to have sought consolation in a bottle of gin, especially here in the far reaches of the empire.

IT RAINED COPIOUSLY IN MUDOORAYAM. We had two big doses every year as we were on the receiving end of both the south-west and the retreating north-east monsoons. In England, I'd had an image in my head of a sunny Indian subcontinent with a brief annual burst of refreshing monsoon rains. But it rained as much as it was reputed to do in Manchester. I hated the way it turned the roads to mud, filled the sky with threatening black clouds and hammered a loud percussion on the tin roof of the bungalow.

I was spending a lot of time in my "studio", which I tried to make as attractive as possible, buying colourful rugs in the market and draping bright coloured *sari* silk over one wall. My plan had been to fill the other walls with my work, but there wasn't a lot of that being produced these days. Most of the time, I curled up in an armchair, sometimes reading, but more often just staring out of the window at the interminable rain dripping through the tall teak trees in the garden.

Our first wedding anniversary was looming, and I wanted to surprise Tony by organising something special to celebrate. The thought of marking the occasion at the club was not an appealing one. My dilemma was whether to plan something and risk that Tony might have already arranged something. In the end, I decided to trust in him. I bought him a pair of gold cufflinks, but doubted whether he would ever wear them. He lived in khaki most of the time.

On the day, unusually, I awakened before he did and slipped out of my bed and moved across the gap to his. I leaned down to kiss him.

He took hold of my shoulders and eased me away from him.

'Sorry old thing, have to get a move on. Big backlog of orders to clear because of the machinery breakdown in the factory last week.'

I groaned. 'Can't someone else deal with it? It's our wedding anniversary. Didn't you remember?'

'Of course, I did. And sorry. That's what being the boss means. Needs must, Ginny. Needs must. Make it up to you later.'

He grabbed his dressing gown and headed down the corridor to the bathroom, his leather slippers slapping his progress on the clay-tiled floor.

I suppose I shouldn't have been surprised. He hadn't managed to stay awake for our wedding night, so why would he behave differently on our anniversary?

The romantic dinner *a deux* I'd hoped for turned out to be a big bash at the club. He'd told all and sundry it was our anniversary, and I had to face drinks and dinner followed by a mass sing-song around the piano in the lounge, with Theo bashing the ivories and Lilian leading the community singing. If someone had told me I'd be celebrating my first year of marriage by singing *The Lambeth Walk,* I'd have told them they were crazy. I looked over at Tony. His face was flushed from a few too many whiskies, and he was grinning from ear to ear. It was clearly his idea of the perfect way to spend one's wedding anniversary. There was only one way to get through the evening, and that was by slugging back the scotch, too. I suppose I'd been foolishly optimistic to think he might have planned something special. Maybe all those years stuck away at boarding school had given him a fondness for institutional life. I'd expected married life to be more about us, and less about mixing and mingling with the entire community.

It was two in the morning when we staggered out and into the car. Both half-cut. I studied his face as he drove, then reached out and ran my fingers through his hair and he didn't pull away. He didn't say anything, so I began to imagine him saying things Tony would never say. The last *chota peg* had gone to my head. There, in the dark capsule of the car, I wanted him with a hot, dirty, desire. So what if I was playing a part? It was working for me. I thought about what we would do when we got home. We wouldn't speak. He'd take me in his arms and carry me to his bed, hot with desire for me, and we would make love as never before. Tonight would be the start of something different. A new phase in our marriage.

In the bathroom, my reflection in the looking glass was a bit blurry-eyed. Not the glamorous seductress I was intending to be for him. I pushed my hair back from my face and applied some more lipstick. *You'll do, Ginny. You'll do.* I slipped my finger between my legs and felt the wetness and thought of my husband waiting in the bedroom for me. I gave a little gasp of pleasure.

But he was already asleep. Snoring, mouth open, shirt undone, tie trailing onto the floor, but the rest of his clothes still on. Damn him.

I lay awake, nauseous, regretting the whisky and wondering if things would always be like this and, if so, would I come to accept it? Why were we always on a different page? As the first light broke through the edges of the shutters, I drifted into a restless sleep.

HECTOR and I were in my garden. I was finishing off the last touches to a painting, and he was slouched in a deck chair watching me work.

'Has he managed to put a bun in the oven yet?'

'Don't be coarse, Hector. Sometimes you're the giddy limit.'

'Just anxious for you. I know you're keen to put one of those empty bedrooms to good use.'

'No, if you must know, I'm not expecting a baby.'

'Not trying hard enough? Tony failing in his husbandly duties?'

'Hector, please. You're embarrassing me.'

'I very much doubt that, Ginny. A worldly wise woman like you?'

'Shut up. It's not a joking matter.'

He looked suitably contrite, so I carried on, 'I meant that despite...all that...I can't seem to conceive.'

I couldn't imagine saying this kind of thing to my mother, and certainly not to Tony. Then I felt guilty at betraying what I knew Tony would consider our private business. But I couldn't stop now, and I'd been going mad with worry. I trusted Hector not to discuss this with anyone else.

'We never talk about it, but I'm sure he's as aware of it as I am. He's really keen to have children. We're both only children and, he told me when we first got married, that he'd love to have a big family. He's not said anything about me not expecting yet, but I can tell it's bothering him. The other day at breakfast, I said I had something to tell him and his eyes lit up, and he was positively crushed when I said I was planning to get my mother to send me some more art materials and did he want anything sent out from London at the same time.'

'Why can't you talk to him about it?'

'I'm a bit afraid to, I suppose. I keep hoping it will be all right soon, and if I raise it with him and he isn't actually worrying about it, it will make him start to worry. And I might be making a mountain out of a molehill.'

'I'm sure you are, my dear. All I can offer in the line of consolation is that my sister was married for six years before producing her first brat and then went on to drop four more of them, including a set of twins.'

'Golly. I don't think I'd want that. Too much of a good thing.'

'Well, stop worrying and, instead of feeling guilty about your painting, try getting really good at it and leave nature to take its course.'

I didn't take Hector's advice—well, not about stopping worrying—but I was doing a lot of painting again. After all, there was little else to occupy me and I felt less guilty about slapping the paint about than I did about sitting around reading. I'd not really heeded his other advice—to ease back on the drinking. Instead, to avoid him commenting, I was starting to do it in secret. I kept a little flask of gin in my handbag and slipped a slug into tonic water, while pretending to be abstemious. I don't know why I imagined it would fool him.

My reticence about raising the baby question with Tony was due less to a desire to save him worrying and more to a fear I would be opening a wound that might not heal. I was afraid I wasn't making him happy. It didn't even occur to me he wasn't making me happy, either. I felt it was all my fault. And drinking more than I should was my temporary escape from guilt.

Then, to my surprise, Tony raised the unspoken question one morning at breakfast. He'd been short tempered with Nirmala when she brought him his tea and had been making disgruntled noises from behind his newspaper. It was beginning to get on my nerves, so I spoke up, 'You're awfully cross this morning, darling. What's the matter?'

He folded the newspaper and placed it neatly on the table, then folded his napkin and laid that across his plate. He cleared his throat, then looked down and brushed a few crumbs from the tablecloth into his hand and added them to the plate. Finally, he raised his eyes to me.

'Tricky to talk about, darling.' He coughed again. 'Might be a good idea for you to see Doctor Banerji.'

I paused with my piece of toast mid-air, then dropped it back onto my plate. 'I'm not ill. Why do I need to see a doctor?' I could tell my voice sounded shrill.

He was about to respond, when Nirmala stuck her head around the door to ask if we'd like a fresh pot of tea and more toast. Tony bawled at her as though he'd caught her stealing the silver.

When she'd scurried away, he began again, 'Beginning to wonder if something's wrong. The mater bangs on about babies in every letter, and I'm getting sick of giving her the bad news.'

I might have guessed Marjorie would be behind this. My reply was sharper than I intended.

'Your mother should jolly well mind her own business.'

'No need for that, darling.'

Tears of anger started to prick at my eyes, but I fought them back. 'I'm not going to be prodded about and have intimate things done to me by a strange doctor. I won't. I just won't.'

'Look, old thing, I know it can't be nice for you. I do

understand. If you're bothered about seeing Banerji, we'll go to Cochin and you can see an English doctor there.'

I hissed back at him, 'I've told you I'm not ill. I don't need to see any doctor. How do you know I even want to have a baby? You haven't even asked me. Maybe I don't want one at all.'

'Don't be silly, darling, of course you do. You're upset. Sorry, I handled it badly. Look, maybe you should have a chat with Lilian. She's a sensible woman. Has children of her own and bound to know all about these things. Could be quite simple. Matter of us doing it at the right times. Sorry, this is a bit embarrassing. The mater says...'

'I'm married to you, not to your mother, and I don't want her knowing intimate details about our personal life.'

'Calm down and don't be silly, old thing. I haven't discussed any intimate details. It's just that she thinks by now we should be seeing some results.'

'That's ridiculous. She only had one child herself. As did my mother. My parents were married quite a long time before I came along. Why the hurry? I'm not even twenty-one. There's plenty of time. Surely?'

My voice trailed away, and I realised I was sounding positively whiny.

He reached a hand across the table and laid it over mine. 'It's just...you know how it is, me being her only son. Desperately wants to be a grandmother. Understandable, Ginny. She's not getting any younger. Surely you can see that?'

'So this is all for Marjorie? What about me? Don't I have a point of view? Next thing you're going to tell me is you only married me because the mater told you to.'

As I said the words, I realised they were possibly true. I began to cry. I hadn't wanted to do that as I was afraid he'd rush round to comfort me, and then I'd feel constrained to give in and agree to see Dr Banerji. But his face was expressionless as he rose from the table and moved to the doorway.

'Dry your eyes and buck up. Need to be sensible about this. I want you to see a doctor. Your choice which one. Need to get it sorted out and that's an end to it. Don't let the side down.'

And then he was gone, leaving me to sob quietly at the table until, fearing the return of Nirmala, I fled to my room.

I SAW DR BANERJI. I didn't want to, but nor did I want Tony to think my reluctance was based on the fact the local doctor was an Indian although, if I were honest, it was. The thought of being poked around by a native horrified me, and made me think of all those cold afternoons in Holborn Mews when Milligan touched me and made me feel dirty.

It wasn't as bad as I feared. Banerji had a nurse in the room with him all the time and she was a white woman— well—a pale-skinned Anglo-Indian lady. He asked me about the regularity of my monthly cycle, gave me a mercifully brief examination, pronounced that everything appeared to be in working order, and advised me to keep on trying.

'It's not automatic, Mrs Tilman. Some ladies fall in the family way the first time they have marital relations. Others take a long time. The best thing is not to worry about it. It will happen in the end, I'm sure. You're young and healthy. You and Mr Tilman need to be patient. There's plenty of time. Please remember to have sexual congress around the midpoint of your monthly cycle. That is the most fertile time.'

He pulled a calendar from under the piles of paper on his cluttered desk, and drew lines and circles on it to explain the way my fertility varied across the month.

'If you have any more questions, please don't hesitate to

ask.' He extended his hand to me to draw the consultation to a close. He smiled with what I took to be a mixture of kindness and pity, and held open the door as the nurse ushered me out of the surgery.

Tony was less than thrilled when I gave him the glad tidings.

'Is that all? We need a second opinion. You can come with me to Cochin and see another doctor there. Banerji's a good chap, trained in England, but he's a GP. We'll get a specialist to look at you.'

'Please, Tony. Stop making a fuss. It's making it worse. The doctor said worrying makes having a baby harder. We need to forget about it and let nature take its course.'

'All right, but I still want you to see a specialist.'

I felt hounded. I dreaded our love-making. It was an ordeal: anxiety on my part and a grim determination on his. It was as though he was trying to get a difficult job done— and one in which I was always letting him down. I just lay there, praying for it to be over.

His solicitude began to grate on me and, when I saw that look in his eyes around the due date each month, I wanted to shout at him, *"No I'm not pregnant yet. I'm sorry. I'm trying my best."* But I said nothing and felt increasingly helpless against the intractability of nature.

I thought of writing to ask my mother's advice, but feared it would not be forthcoming. We'd never talked about such things—at least not until that afternoon at Holbein Mews—and I didn't want to rub salt in what I suspected had long been a personal wound for her in her own inability to produce more children after me. Maybe infertility ran in our family? Pud had not had any children, either.

I thought about talking to Lilian Bulstrode-Hemmings, but I was intimidated by her. She was much older than me and I sensed she disapproved of me, so I wasn't confident enough to test her as a confidante.

My visit to the specialist confirmed what Dr Banerji had already said. His advice was to be patient and have lots of sex.

Tony, disappointed not to have an instant solution wafted under his nose, barely spoke to me during the four hour drive home. I stared out of the car window without taking anything in.

Despite the doctors' advice, we were having sex less than before and the requirement to focus on the calendar made it like a military manoeuvre. On the prescribed nights, Tony would return from the bathroom, hang his dressing gown on the back of the door, then pad across the floor in his striped cotton pyjamas and leather slippers, taking care to line his slippers up under the bed, before slipping into my bed. He would usually mutter something along the lines of 'You all right?', kiss me perfunctorily and then climb on top, his penis poking through the flap of his pyjamas like a railway signal. I lay underneath him, watching the ceiling fan slowly circling, as he pushed himself in and out of me with his eyes closed. When he was finished, he would roll off, kiss my forehead, ask me again if I was all right, then slip out of my bed and into his and go straight to sleep. Job done. I would lie there wide awake, wondering why this was happening to me. There seemed to be little pleasure in the act for him, and there was none at all for me. Occasionally I'd close my eyes and pretend he was a movie star from *Picture Post*. It never worked, and then I was angry with myself, as well as with him.

While I realise now that Rupert Milligan had abused me, at the time I had felt there was a connection. With Tony, sex was just fumbling about in the dark. It negated me. It made me feel as though I wasn't myself. I know I'm making it sound really horrible. To be truthful, the sex itself wasn't always that bad. Mostly it was hurried, over soon, to my relief. The more fundamental issue and the probable underlying cause for our difficulties was that Tony and I made no connection. We had little or nothing in common. He should have married a nice, jolly, practical girl; a younger version of Lilian or Bunty, capable of organising his life for him and being eternally cheerful.

I AVOIDED THE CLUB, often pleading tiredness or a lack of appetite and taking advantage of Tony's frequent absences to stay at home in the evening. The hard-core members assembled there and drank heavily from sundown until about 8 or 9 o'clock, when they staggered home for dinner or went to one of the frequent parties. The conversation was always the same. The women talked about their children and the shortcomings of their servants, the men talked of sports and game-hunting, and all of them reminisced about people and events I knew nothing of. It was a close-knit world and I didn't belong in it.

Stung by his criticism of my drinking, I also avoided Hector. But it didn't last long; he was not a man to be shunned and came looking for me. And, after a few minutes banter, I forgave him. No point in alienating my only friend in Muddy. And he never mentioned the drinking again.

The thing most on my mind through these lonely times was having a child.

Why was I so desperate for one? It wasn't a case of wanting to make Tony happy. Not anymore. I liked the idea of having someone to care for. Someone to love, and who would love me back. Someone who wouldn't be finding fault all the time. Someone who'd just accept me for who I am. And, most of all, I hoped having a baby would somehow validate me as a wife and a grownup, capable of getting something right, instead of always mucking things up and disappointing everybody.

But, then, everything changed. It was the middle of the morning and I was sitting on the veranda trying to read, when the post boy cycled up the drive. He jumped off, slung his bicycle on the gravel and ran towards me shouting,

'Telegram, *Memsahib*. Telegram from London. I wait for answer?'

I took the brown envelope from him and read the message FELICITY IN HOSPITAL UNCONSCIOUS - STOP - COME HOME - STOP - PUD

I'd always thought Mummy was indestructible. Her being in hospital was more than my impoverished imagination could conjure. And unconscious? My brain scrambled. I stared at the flimsy piece of paper and didn't know what to say.

The post boy coughed and hopped about from one leg to another, so I said, 'Yes, let me write a reply.'

I grabbed the proffered pencil and scribbled *"On my way love Ginny."* with a shaking hand on the form he handed me.

I telephoned Tony at the factory, and he dropped everything and drove home. He was an absolute brick and went into general manager mode to organise everything, making phone calls and sending telegrams. He got Theo Bulstrode-Hemmings to pull some strings to get me on a Tata mail flight from Bombay to Karachi, where I could pick up the Imperial Airways flight to London.

I'd never been in an aeroplane before and, although terrified at the prospect, it was the fastest way to get to London. As it was, the journey took almost a week. The flight from Karachi stopped numerous times for refuelling, loading and unloading cargo and passengers.

I couldn't take seriously the fact my mother was lying

unconscious in a hospital bed, and couldn't help but be excited that, at last, I was going home and I was actually going up in an aeroplane. Theo had found out through the Foreign and Colonial Office that Mummy had had a fall, but was in a stable condition, so I wasn't particularly concerned. I pictured her sitting up in a glamorous bed jacket, complaining about the colour of the bedspreads, bossing the nurses about and demanding to be released immediately so she could get her hair done.

Despite costing a king's ransom—I overheard Theo telling Tony the Imperial flight alone was over 170 pounds—the aeroplane was hardly the height of comfort, especially the first leg from Karachi, which was in a land plane furnished only with wooden benches. The engines and propellers were deafening, so I had a headache most of the way. Things improved once I got on the Imperial flight and I ticked off the places as we landed and took off again, impatient to be home: Bahrain in Arabia, Basra and Baghdad, Lydda in Palestine and then, at last, to Alexandria, where we switched to a more comfortable flying-boat. After a brief stop in Athens, we spent the night in a hotel in Brindisi, where I was kept awake by Italian sailors in the street outside, before we took off at dawn for Rome and got to Southampton in the late afternoon. I took the boat train into London, where I fell into a cab and went straight to the hospital.

The green, ceramic-tiled corridors smelled of Jeyes Fluid, and the realisation struck me that I'd just flown halfway across the planet because my mother was ill. I felt a mixture of exhaustion and dread. When I got to her ward, a belligerent-looking staff nurse crossed her arms over her ample chest, and said, 'Visiting hours ended half an hour ago. Come back tomorrow.'

Irritated by her smug smile, I barked back at her, 'I've just spent the last seven days travelling day and night from southern India, so you can jolly well bend the rules and let me in.'

Without bothering to reply, she turned away and picked up a pile of manila folders and carried them into an adjacent room. I was saved by the arrival of a more accommodating ward sister who asked me to follow her.

'Mrs Dunbar is very poorly. She's unconscious. I can't let you stay long. If you come in tomorrow morning, the doctor will explain everything.'

'How long has she been unconscious? When will she wake up?'

'You need to speak to the doctor.'

She opened the door to my mother's room, and I caught my breath. Mummy lay there pale as an alabaster statue. There was a mask over her face attached to an oxygen cylinder, but I could tell from the faint rasps not a lot of oxygen was getting through. I took her hand. It felt strange to be doing that. She would hate it if she were awake. She'd thought it vulgar and common to show one's affection in public.

I sat beside the bed, stroking her hand. It felt very thin and very cold. I began to talk to her, realising as I did that she was going to die. It was as if she was tethered to life by just a gossamer thread. I could feel her slipping away from me.

'Mummy, it's Ginny. I got here as fast as I could. Please wake up.'

There was no reaction, so I carried on stroking her hand, fighting back my tears.

'I know I've been a big disappointment to you, Mummy. Please get well. I've got so much to tell you. Please, please, wake up. I need you.'

Then I could help it no longer, and I began to cry; big tears rolled down my face and ran into my mouth where I felt their salty tang. I fumbled in my handbag for a handker-chief and wiped them away. Then, I took her hand in mine, and thought for a moment there was a slight pressure back from her, the faintest sense she was trying to squeeze my hand.

'Mummy? Can you hear me?' But the sensation passed, and there was nothing more, so I must have imagined it.

The belligerent staff nurse appeared in the doorway. 'You'll have to go now. The night sister will be doing her rounds shortly, and you don't want to get me into trouble. Visiting is at nine-thirty tomorrow morning.'

Actually, I didn't give a damn if I got her into trouble, but I was too tired and weak to argue.

CHAPTER 11

Pud opened the door at Leighton Square herself. She'd been watching out for me from the drawing room window. She gathered me into her arms and hugged me tightly, then pulled back.

'My God, Ginny. You're wasting away. You're a bag of bones. And you must be exhausted? And starving? How was the journey? You're later than I thought. Were you delayed?'

'I've been to the hospital.'

'I didn't want you to do that on your own. I told you to come straight here. Did they let you in?'

'Eventually.'

'So you've seen how poorly she is? I'm so sorry, darling. I couldn't tell you all that in a telegram.'

'She's dying, isn't she?'

She put her hands on my shoulders, and nodded. 'Yes. I'm afraid she is.'

'I knew as soon as I saw her. Oh, Pud.'

She slipped an arm around my waist and led me to a chair.

'What happened? They said she had a fall?'

'She was getting ready to host a bridge game, and realised she hadn't laid out enough pencils, and the silly girl ran upstairs herself to fetch them. What the hell are servants for?' Pud's voice was unsteady. 'Coming back downstairs, she caught her heel on a stair-rod, tripped and fell. One of the pencils punctured her lung.'

I covered my mouth in horror.

'She hit her head on the newel post and fractured her skull. The doctors said right away she had little chance of recovery. Each day, she's been weaker and her breathing is barely there anymore. Fluid on the lungs and internal bleeding.'

'Dear God. I knew it was bad when I saw her. She's so frail, so fragile and weak. But they told me she was stable when I left India.'

'We didn't want you to be in a panic all the way here, as you couldn't have got here any faster. Do you know, Ginny, if we could foresee how we'd end up, we wouldn't have the strength to live our lives. It's so sad. She was always so alive and so strong. So grounded. I can't reconcile that with the person lying helpless in that bed.'

Her voice was choked. 'I think she's been hanging on till you could get here.'

'Do you think so?' I couldn't hide the need in my voice. 'I thought for a moment she tried to squeeze my hand, but I must have imagined it.'

'I don't think you imagined it. She was so proud of you, Ginny. You were so precious to her. Her only child. So wanted.'

I looked at her in amazement. 'Come off it, Pud. I know she's dying, but you don't have to lie about her.'

'I'm not lying, Ginny. She loved you very much. She just found it hard to show it. She and Hugh were overjoyed when you were born after they'd waited so long. She'd given up hope of having a baby. Fliss has never been demonstrative, and then with Hugh dying...she wanted the best for you, but your going to India sapped her spirit. She believed was the best thing for you, but she was lost without you. You gave her purpose.'

I took a slug of the large whisky my aunt handed me and kicked off my shoes, curling my feet up under me in an armchair in front of the fire. And then I began to cry.

WHEN WE ARRIVED on the hospital ward the next morning, the nurses' station was unattended, so Pud and I walked arm in arm along the corridor to Mummy's room. The door was open, but the bed was empty and stripped bare. A nurse appeared.

'You're Mrs Dunbar's relatives?'

We nodded.

'I'm sorry, but she passed away during the night.'

WE BURIED her with my father in Brompton Cemetery, after a well-attended funeral service. She had been well-liked: all those bridge pals, fellow debutantes and school friends. The church was packed. I felt as though I'd been hollowed out. My relationship with her seemed a lost opportunity. Another person I'd disappointed and let down. My own mother.

After the service, the interment was to be witnessed by just Pud and me. As the coffin was lowered into the ground, I sensed a slight movement behind the trees. I looked up, momentarily distracted from the awful finality of throwing my clod of earth into the hole. There was no one there. I hung onto Pud's arm and I asked myself if I'd ever really known my mother?

We walked away from the graveside and were at the gate

when I took one last look back. There was a figure by the grave, head bowed, dropping roses one by one into the hole. Rupert Milligan. Pud must have seen my face, as the next moment she grabbed both my arms and pinned them to my sides.

'Let it go, Ginny. Leave him. He can't do any harm.'

I tried to twist free of her. I wanted to scream at the top of my voice. I wanted to rain curses on him. I wanted to run across the graveyard and hammer him with my bare fists.

'How dare he come here? It's his fault she's dead. If it weren't for him, I'd never have gone to India and I'd have been here to fetch her bloody pencils for her.'

My voice was distorted and I couldn't see through my tears. I don't know how she did it, but Pud got me out of the graveyard, onto Brompton Road, and into the waiting funeral limousine.

'Ginny, you can't stop him wanting to grieve for her, and he has a right to pay his respects.'

'No, he hasn't. He has no right at all.'

'He was engaged to her once. He loved her. Believe me, I know. It doesn't excuse him in any way. It doesn't alter the fact he's an unprincipled, corrupt, snake, and I'd like to kill him myself. But he can do her no harm now, and there's no point giving him the satisfaction of making a scene. It's not worth it. And he can't hurt you any more, either. Forget him.'

She put an arm around me, and I sobbed into the sleeve of her coat on the way back to Leighton House.

Pud was a rock. She stayed in London until it was time for me to sail back to Bombay. As there was no hurry this time, I plumped for the stately comfort of the Peninsular and Orient, rather than the stop-start noisy progress of the aeroplane. And, perhaps, I was trying to delay my eventual return to life in Muddy with Tony.

On our last evening together, Pud and I shared a whisky

at the fireside. It had become our little ritual. Roger had attended the funeral, but had left again on the next train. Livestock can't be neglected for long. I was relieved to have the opportunity for more precious time with my aunt.

'Can I ask you something, Pud? Something personal?'

She looked up at me. 'Fire away.'

'Are you and Roger in love?'

She tilted her head slightly. 'What makes you ask all of a sudden?'

'I've often wondered. He's so different from you. You're so kind and friendly and loveable and cheerful and he's so...'

'Grumpy?'

I blushed. 'Well...he's not the most talkative of people.'

'That's true enough but, yes, we do love each other.'

'How did you meet? I always meant to ask Mummy about it, but I didn't dare.'

'Your mother was never keen on Roger. She made it clear she disapproved of us getting together.'

'How did you get together? You and Mummy were both debutantes, and I can't imagine you meeting Roger during the London season.'

She laughed again. 'Good Lord, no. I finished my season engaged to be married to someone else. Someone different.'

'I didn't know.'

'His name was Monty Goring. Or to give him his full title, The Honourable Montague Goring-Ferguson. Son and heir of Lord Sunderland. My first love.'

My mouth was gaping like a goldfish's.

She looked serious, and her eyes took on a faraway look as she stared into the glowing fire.

'Monty was killed in the war. Silly boy was far too brave. He was leading a party of men to reconnoitre an area near the enemy lines. They were ambushed and two of the group were shot. He went back for them, dragged the first chap off a barbed wire fence and carried him across a ploughed field to safety. Then, instead of getting the hell out of it himself, he went back to get the other fellow and the Germans ploughed him into the field in a hail of bullets. He got the VC for it, posthumously. Much good it did him.'

'How terribly sad. And Roger?'

'He came to visit me after the war. He was the corporal Monty pulled off the wire.'

'My goodness.'

'He hero-worshipped Monty. At first, I was angry when he turned up and didn't want to see him. But he kept coming back. He just wanted to talk about Monty and, eventually, I realised so did I. That's how it started. We comforted each other and shared memories and stories. Roger was his batman. They'd served together since the beginning and Monty died just three weeks before it ended. He shouldn't even have been in the reconnaissance party. Batmen were supposed to be behind the lines, polishing shoes and brass buttons and running errands. But that day they'd taken a lot of casualties, so Roger offered to go out with them. He blamed himself for Monty's death. Thought it was his inexperience that led to him getting shot. And he was full of guilt that Monty sacrificed himself to save him.'

'What about the other fellow?'

'Already dead, I think. Or if he wasn't, he was by the time the Germans finished blasting at him and Monty.'

'Golly, Pud. I had no idea. How sad. How truly awful for you.'

'Not really. I've been happy with Roger. And I think I've made him happy, too. At least, as much as he'll let himself be. Terrible thing, guilt.'

We lapsed into silence for a moment.

Then, hesitantly, I asked, 'Did you ever want children, Pud?'

'Not really. Neither of us particularly wanted them. We didn't *not* want them, either. I mean, if they'd come along we'd have been pleased I suppose, but it never happened. I think we were actually relieved in a way, as it doesn't seem right somehow, to bring a child into a world like this one. Right now, especially as it looks like we might have yet another war. What kind of future will there be for us all? Besides, Roger and I have always been enough for each other.'

I must have looked surprised as she carried on.

'We didn't have that head turning, butterflies in the tummy, joyful, kind of love I had with Monty, but now I know we have something much better, something more durable. We really, really, care for each other. It's as though we can read each other's thoughts. We don't need to speak. And he's the only man I've ever made love with. Monty and I never did, of course, as we weren't yet married. And I'm glad about that now. I couldn't have hoped for a better husband than Roger. He's the love of my life. And I never would have met him if Monty hadn't saved him and sacrificed himself. Roger and I were meant to be together.'

She laughed again. 'Of course, my parents had a fit. And your mother was absolutely horrified. She wouldn't speak to me for weeks. Then she and your grandmother tried to convince me I was marrying beneath me. A common soldier. A corporal. A batman, for heaven's sake. My father threatened to have him flogged.'

She laughed again at the memory. 'And then your lovely father stepped in. Hugh didn't join the argument—he simply befriended Roger. Took him under his wing, and by his actions got the message across that Roger was a "good chap". Mama and Papa couldn't really ignore that. After all, your father was far better connected. Our side of the family made their money through industry, whereas your father came from old money. So, if Roger was good enough for Hugh, he must be good enough for them. Fliss was in awe of Hugh and worshipped him, so she dropped her hostility to Roger. She never fully accepted him, but at least she stopped hurling verbal hand grenades at him.'

'I'd no idea about any of this. Was he already a farmer?'

'His family scraped a living from a smallholding. His elder brother died early in the War. When we married, we moved up there and Roger took over from his father and began to build the farm up, gradually buying more land. It had been neglected by the old man. He never really got over Roger's brother dying.'

'It must have been strange for you, Pud. Going to live on a hill farm in Yorkshire. Not exactly what you were used to.'

'A blessed release. Unlike your mother, I hated the whole London society thing. The only thing that made being presented at Court bearable was meeting Monty. After he was gone and I married Roger, I was glad to get away. Not that married life was easy—at least, not at first. I can't tell you how many times I walked to the end of the farm track and stood waiting for the omnibus into town. Every time I wanted to run away, Roger came looking for me and brought me home.'

'You and he argued then?'

'Never. I told you—we loved each other. No, it was his mother. She was a devil who dedicated her declining years to making my life a misery. She thought I wasn't good enough for her only surviving son. I suppose I was pretty useless at first. I took a long time getting used to the isolation of that place. I'd always had servants to do everything for me. It was a rude awakening. We had to pump all our water from a well, and I had to learn to cook and clean. But each time, when I stood by that dry-stone wall in the wind and rain, as soon as I saw Roger coming down the lane for me, it all felt different.'

The room was starting to feel chilly, so I put some more logs on the fire. Taking that as a signal I wanted to keep talking, Pud poured us each another whisky. So much for my recent attempts at sobriety—and, yet, I felt clear-headed.

She chinked glasses with me, then curled up in the armchair again, her stockinged feet tucked underneath her. 'How about you, Ginny? How is married life?'

I sighed, and shook my head.

Pud put down her glass.

'It takes a while to get to know someone. You were married so fast. You barely knew each other. Give it time.'

'It started out quite well, but it's getting worse, Pud. He was awfully kind and considerate when we first married. He had me on a pedestal and, now, I've well and truly fallen off.'

She took a sip of her scotch. 'What do you mean?'

'He wants me to be the perfect wife and I haven't a clue how. I find it hard to like the people he likes. To fit in. We've absolutely nothing in common. He wants us to have a child, and I can't manage that either. I've seen two doctors and they both told me to be patient, but, meanwhile, I know he blames me.'

'And what about you? What do you want?'

'Well, a baby, of course. I want that, too. At least, I think I do. And I suppose I want to be a good wife. I'd like to get something right in my life. I keep on messing things up and letting people down.'

'You're too hard on yourself. You didn't let your mother down. Yes, she was upset about what happened, but she was angry with that toad Milligan, not with you. And if she blamed anyone else, it was herself. She talked about you all the time. She lived for your letters.'

'Did she really?'

'Of course. I know she could be an irritating woman at times. She was my sister, so I had a lifetime of her. She may have been an unmitigated snob, but she did really care about you. She struggled to show her emotions. Always did. She didn't exactly have a good example in her own mother. All we ever got from her was criticism—and on high days and holidays, a proffered cheek. We certainly weren't showered with love and affection.'

I stared into the glowing fire.

Pud said, 'And why are you assuming the failure to conceive is your fault? It could just as easily be down to Tony. Have you considered that? Maybe he should see a doctor himself? It does take two to make a baby. It's not entirely your responsibility. Not that fault or responsibility enters into it anyway. You can't control your own fertility.'

'I suppose so,' I said doubtfully.

'Do you love him?'

I stared into the flames of the fire.

'I don't know. At first I was sure I didn't, then I thought I did. Now, I don't know at all. I want him to care for me, but I can't make him do it. Sometimes, I think he despises me. And then, I think sometimes I feel that about him.'

'Can you talk to him?'

'No. That's the biggest problem. It's as if we speak different languages. Sometimes I say something, and he looks at me as though I'm talking double-Dutch. The only time he gets excited about anything is when he talks about growing tea or games and sports. We're completely different.'

'And in bed? Do you have anything in common there?'

I blushed to my roots. I wasn't used to having such an intimate conversation with anyone—let alone my aunt.

'Well...it's never been very...and, since all the trying for a baby became such a big thing, it's... well, it's been really awful. When we do, it's as if he's only doing it because he has to—he marks the dates when I'm most fertile on a calendar. Otherwise, I don't think he'd want to do it at all.

And I find it so horrible, so mechanical, marking dates off a chart.'

Pud frowned, then swung her legs out from under her.

'Come on, Ginny. Don't let it get you down. Things will get better I'm sure. It can take ages to conceive. If you really want it, the gods conspire against it. Give it time. Now, come with me. There's something I want to give you.'

She took me into what had been my parents' bedroom and opened a jewellery box and took out a gold locket. Inside was a lock of blonde hair. She put the locket in my hand.

'That's your hair from the first time it was cut when you were a baby. She wore it all the time until they took it off her at the hospital before her operation. She would have wanted you to have it.'

She fastened the locket around my neck and then leaned forward and kissed me on the brow, and I flung my arms around her and hugged her tightly.

I couldn't sleep that night. Maybe it was the whisky? I kept thinking about Pud and Roger and then about Tony and myself. I couldn't imagine Tony and I reading each other's thoughts, let alone my ever having the look in my eyes Pud had when she talked about Roger. And, in between it all, I thought about Mummy and how wrong I'd been about her. I knew now she'd loved me, but she'd never understood me and that, combined with the undertow of jealousy between us, had proved to be a corrosive combination.

I DIDN'T KNOW it at the time but, as my ship sailed out of Tilbury Docks, Neville Chamberlain was climbing the steps to the aeroplane that would bring him back from his historic Munich meeting with Hitler. Not that it would have meant much to me anyway. Most of the time, I thought politics was for other people. I associated it with complicated debates about borders and thought it bore little relation to my own life and experience. I knew nothing of the Sudetenland or whether it should be annexed by Germany. I don't imagine I was alone in this, particularly among the Muddy expatriates. Europe and its affairs were a long way away. Little did I know then that, once war broke out, it would affect even those of us tucked away on the slopes of the Western Ghats.

Tony met me from the train at Cochin. I thought of that first time, when he'd travelled all the way to Bombay and been waiting at the dockside for me. I'd still had the cards in my hands then. He still held me in regard. Now the cards were all in his hands.

He looked pleased to see me. I wondered if, like me, he'd come to the conclusion the end of our enforced separation was a good opportunity to start a fresh chapter in our marriage. That was how I was going to play it, anyway. He clasped me briefly when I got down from the train carriage and looked sincere when he told me how sorry he was about Mummy dying. But, then, he had been fond of her.

I told him a little about how it was, seeing her in the hospital, but it was as though now she was dead and he'd expressed his condolences, he wanted to forget all about it. I think he found my dwelling on whether or not she'd been aware of my presence, either unnecessarily sentimental or, possibly, a little macabre.

I had little to report to him about his own mother. To my relief, I'd seen Marjorie only briefly. She came to the funeral, proffered a heavily powdered cheek for me to kiss, glanced at my still flat stomach with ill-concealed disappointment, spoke a few words of condolence and then retreated. Pressing business, no doubt bridge-related, had necessitated her return to Harrogate straight after the funeral.

As usual with Tony, I had to initiate most of the conversation and it didn't take long for him to update me on all that had happened in Muddy since my departure. After a brief account of club trivia, he lapsed into silence. I decided I'd have to make a superhuman effort to win my husband back.

'How are things at the factory?'

He stared at the road ahead. 'Same as ever.'

'What does that mean?'

He sighed. 'Darling, you're not interested in that kind of thing.'

'But I am. I want to know more about what you do.'

'It's dull. No need to know about all that.'

I pressed on valiantly for a few minutes, but he was obdurate.

'For God's sake, Ginny. What's got into you? We both know the business is of no interest to you, and nor should it be.'

'I want to understand more what your work is about. I want to take an interest.' I hesitated for a moment, then placed my hand on his shirtsleeve. 'I think I've been a bit too wrapped up in myself.'

He sighed and raised his arm to brush away a fly that had landed on his forehead, thus giving me a brush off too.

'What's brought all this on?'

'I've had a lot of time to think. Mummy dying and everything. The only family I have in the world now is you and Pud. Things between us haven't been too good lately, so I'm going to turn over a new leaf. I'm going to try to be a better wife.'

He exhaled slowly and turned the corners of his mouth upwards into what he evidently hoped would pass for a smile. He took a hand off the wheel and placed it on my knee. He didn't say any more but, apart from changing gears, he left his hand there for the rest of the journey home.

A FEW MONTHS after my return to India, I realised I'd missed my monthly period twice. I told Tony and he was overjoyed. That evening he came home laden with flowers. He lingered over breakfast the next morning, and was still sitting there when I came down for mine. Not that I ate breakfast really. I just sipped the squeezed juice of an orange and a cup of weak tea. He leaned forward, elbows on the table, eyes shining.

'Doctor Banerji will see you this afternoon. Want him to keep an eye on you.'

'He'll be able work out the date we'll have the baby. They have charts for that sort of thing, don't they?'

He nodded and carried on, 'Thankappan is getting some chaps in to paint the nursery. Nirmala will take care of the baby when it comes—just as she did for me. We'll take on someone else to help with the housekeeping. And I've wired the mater to come out. She'll be company for you. Haven't told her the good news yet. A baby on the way will be a wonderful surprise for her when she gets here. Want to get her out here before more trouble breaks out in Europe. Looking bad. Better to get her here sooner than later. If a war starts, it could last months. Travelling could be tricky.'

My heart sank at the prospect of Marjorie descending on us, but I couldn't complain about Tony's enthusiasm for the baby coming. And I supposed Marjorie would be mollified by the prospect of a grandchild. And I'd got the old caring and affectionate Tony back again. The doctors and Pud had been right. All it took was a little time. I didn't like the sound of Nirmala taking charge of the baby. I wanted to do as much as possible myself for my baby.

Later that day in Dr Banerji's waiting room, I sat opposite the portrait of George VI which was hung incongruously beside a lurid painting of a Hindu god. The deity had the usual extra helping of arms and was carrying what looked like a bunch of grass or herbs, a conch shell, a golden container and a bundle of papers. There was something vaguely repellent to me in these gaudy-coloured, many-limbed creatures but, at the same time, their sheer flamboyance fascinated me. Looking back now at the Ginny I was then, I am ashamed at my sense of racial superiority. The reluctant debutante was now an even more reluctant *memsahib*, in a country I hadn't made any effort to understand. I picked up a copy of *The Lady's Companion* and flicked through the pages without taking in what was printed there.

The doctor asked me about my monthly cycle, then examined my breasts with cold, freshly washed hands and asked me to get on the scales. After registering my weight, he frowned and signalled me to sit down on the other side of his disorderly, paper-strewn desk. 'Mrs Tilman, I am sorry, but it does not seem you are having a baby.' His words didn't sink in for a moment. 'You are severely underweight, and I believe this is what has caused the interruption in your monthly cycle. Can you think of any reason why you've lost so much weight since the last time I saw you?'

I stared at him, mute. I didn't know what to say. I didn't know what to feel. I didn't feel anything. Just empty. Disbelieving.

'Are you eating enough?'

My voice was barely a whisper, 'I don't have much appetite.'

'Anything to cause you stress or anxiety?'

'Trying to have a baby is difficult in itself.'

He looked at me, and I realised he thought I was referring to sex.

I blushed and hurried on, 'I mean, I worry a lot about whether it will ever happen. If I'm even capable of having a child? If there's something wrong with me? Now I'm sure there must be.'

'I've told you, Mrs Tilman, you are perfectly healthy. There is absolutely nothing to worry about.'

'That's easier said than done.' I wanted to add—*What the hell do you know about how I feel?*—but thought better of it.

'And I understand you have been bereaved?'

'Yes, my mother.'

'Please accept my sincere condolences. And your father, how is he?'

'He died some years ago.'

'I see. Losing a parent, especially your remaining one, can have an effect on your health and wellbeing and, most particularly, on your appetite. I'm going to prescribe you some iron tablets, and I want you to make sure you eat three full meals every day. Please avoid alcohol as well. We need to build up your strength and, when you are menstruating again, I see no reason why you can't have a healthy baby. I would like you to write down what you eat every day, and come and see me again in one month. I am sure we will have you right as rain before long, but you must eat a healthy diet and get plenty of rest. It will not happen otherwise.'

I sat there mute. Paralysed. I couldn't speak. I couldn't move.

'Do you understand what I have said, Mrs Tilman?'

I nodded.

'Do you think there might be a reason for your lack of appetite?'

I shook my head. 'I don't know.'

He took off his glasses and polished them carefully. I realised he was a younger man than I'd thought. His eyes were dark and rather soulful.

'Are you happy here in India, Mrs Tilman?'

I hesitated. 'I'm getting used to it.'

'A serious lack of appetite can be due to feelings of unhappiness.'

'But I'm not unhappy.' I shook my head, a feeling of panic rising.

'You don't like the food? Is it your cook? Maybe you need to find another?'

'I don't know. I don't really feel comfortable eating.' I hesitated.

'I see. And what causes this discomfort?'

I thought back to the voyage on the *Viceroy of India,* and the words of Bunty Finchington with all her admonishments about what to eat and what to avoid, and how the servants were unclean and I suppose, somehow, subconsciously I was afraid. Afraid of India, or more importantly, of Indian people, of my own servants, even of Dr Banerji.

'I'm not used to spicy food.'

He looked at me gravely. 'Mrs Tilman, it takes a little time for the delicate European stomach to adjust to our cuisine. But, once you do, you'll find traditional English food a touch bland and will want to spice up your meat and two vegetables as you call it.'

I knew my aversion was less to the spices than to the hands that prepared them—about the only meal I ate readily was breakfast, as the toast popped straight out of the toaster that sat on the sideboard and the marmalade was Keiller's from Dundee, spooned out myself from the jar. I didn't like the idea Bunty Finchington might be right about Indians not washing properly, and I was scared of dying of cholera or some other hideous tropical disease.

Dr Banerji spoke again, 'We eat spicy food for a good reason—it is actually good for the constitution. I studied to be a doctor at the best medical school here in India, and then spent three years at your Saint Bartholomew's Hospital in London. I like to think I know the best of Western medical science and, yet, I also believe our more ancient traditions still carry much wisdom and veracity. One should take the best of east and west.'

'The best of east and west,' I echoed him

'Very good, very good. Now here's your prescription. One tablet three times a day with meals. I'll prepare some dietary suggestions for you to pass to your cook. Do please give the curries a chance and, with time, you will grow to love them. Avoid alcohol. Once you have gained a little weight, I am sure you will soon be gifted with a child.'

And, with that, he rose from behind his desk, put on his spectacles again and ushered me towards the door.

How was I going to tell Tony? When I broke the news, over dinner that night, he looked at me with a blank expression, as though he hadn't heard what I said. I repeated the doctor's diagnosis.

He pushed his chair back and spoke slowly, 'You're telling me you're not expecting a baby at all, and you can't even expect to conceive until you gain some weight?'

I nodded and looked down, finding the weave of my linen skirt a source of sudden fascination.

'So you've been starving yourself half to death? Who the bloody hell do you think you are? Mahatma Gandhi?'

He didn't wait for an answer, but left the room, banging the door behind him. I picked up my fork and made myself swallow a piece of roast chicken, despite the gagging feeling in my throat.

CHAPTER 12

IT WAS TOO late to stop Marjorie coming, but I was grateful Tony hadn't told her I was pregnant. When she arrived in Muddy—Tony went all the way to Bombay to meet her ship— she fussed over us both and behaved as though our conversation on the *RMS Viceroy of India* had never happened. Tony and I put on a united front—the picture of the happy couple— as if we both sensed things would be better for us if Marjorie thought everything in our garden was rosy. She swept into the house as though she owned it—and I suppose she once did. She was enveloped in her habitual gardenia talcum smell, which now mingled with a sour undercurrent of sweat.

'I've brought you a present, Virginia. A little gift, but a special one. An heirloom, in fact. My mother-in-law gave it to me when I married and I intended to give it to you as a wedding present—but better late than never.'

She handed me a neatly wrapped, heavy parcel. Inside was a copy of *The Complete Indian Housekeeper and Cook*, a hefty Victorian tome that looked as enticing as the complete works of Euclid in ancient Greek. I flipped it open and read on the title page, in her old-fashioned copperplate *"To Virginia - to help you become a pukka memsahib"*. I wanted to fling it at her, but instead I plastered on a cheery smile and thanked her as graciously as I could, while Tony grinned approval and poured the drinks.

I contrived not to be alone with her. She adored the club and spent as much time there as possible. Having spent years in Mudoorayam, many of her friends from those days still lived in town and were anxious to see her.

If I sound less than charitable about my mother-in-law, it's because that's exactly how I felt. By now, I'd reached the conclusion her behaviour towards me in the cabin of *The Viceroy* was more indicative of her personality than the sugary sweetness she coated me with whenever Tony was in earshot, and which so smacked of insincerity now. When we were alone, she seized every opportunity to make a catty comment, to point out my many shortcomings as the wife of the plantation general manager. I couldn't help thinking Tony must have been itemising these failings in his letters, as she was familiar with the whole catalogue.

'I'm not convinced you're in control of the domestic situation, Virginia. Nirmala needs a firm hand and much more guidance. All servants try it on if you're not careful. You must stay on top of things.'

She commented on the clothes I wore and how I did my hair. 'Those shoes aren't at all practical—the grass is wet today. Run and change them, dear.' Or ' You need to talk to the *ghai wallah*—I'm convinced he's watering the milk. These natives will always take advantage of a slackly run household.'

Her words were usually accompanied by a facial expression that was a cross between frowning and disappointment. When Tony was around, she was all charm and reasonableness, so when I tried to tell him privately she was being impossible, he wouldn't believe me.

'Don't be silly, darling, the mater adores you.'

One afternoon, when I believed her to be at the club playing bridge, she caught me having a little weep on the veranda. I'd been thinking about my mother, and how I wished I'd understood her better and had the time to make up for letting her down.

'What on earth are you crying for, Virginia? What's happened?'

'I'm just a bit blue today. Thinking about my mother. I'll be all right now.'

I blew my nose and was about to go back indoors, but she stayed my arm and indicated I should sit down again.

'I want you to buck up, Virginia. No point in tears. Can't abide blubbing. It's not the done thing at all. In fact, I've come to the conclusion that's the problem. You need to develop more backbone. It's what's expected. You're emotionally overwrought. You live on your nerves. Tony needs a rock as a wife, not a cry-baby. He has more than enough to worry about without worrying about you too. Your role is to ease his burden, not add to it.'

'What are you saying? What burden?'

'The burden of responsibility. He's the head of the house, the boss of the plantation and the factory. He has hundreds of coolies to deal with and dozens of managers and clerks. And with the possibility of a war coming and all this independence nonsense, he has to keep a closer eye than ever on his workforce. He has to worry about crop yields and tea prices, pests and diseases and all manner of things that are too complicated for you to understand. You, on the other hand, need to concentrate on *your* job, which is to be a good wife to him. Making sure he has nothing to worry about when he crosses the threshold. Being supportive and dedicating yourself to his comfort. Your domain is the home, and you should be spending most of your time in it or pursuing suitable activities at the club.'

She paused for a moment, then smoothing her skirt down over her plump thighs, she carried on, 'I keep hearing about you gadding about all over Muddy—sitting on steps and walls and painting pictures of the natives in full public view. More than one little bird has told me that you've been seen in all kinds of unsuitable places in the company of that dreadful Channing man. For heaven's sake, Virginia, have you no shame? The man's a homosexual.' She mouthed rather than spoke the last word. 'It won't do at all. Think of Tony's reputation. That is paramount. Do you want to make him a laughing stock at the club? Seriously, Virginia, I despair. A girl of your education and good breeding should know better.'

My jaw was somewhere around my collar bone and I was lost for the words to respond, but I didn't get a chance anyway as she was still in full flow.

'I always dedicated every waking moment to the happiness of my husband and the wellbeing of my son. Obviously, you've lost your mother, so I'm going to put your behaviour down to that and make some allowances, but I want you to see this as a clarion call. I hope I won't have to raise these matters with you again? Understood?'

She leaned forward and patted me on the knee.

I wanted to yell in her smug, jowly, face but, of course, I didn't. I just nodded dumbly. I was actually afraid of her. Intimidated. I knew I could never be the kind of wife she was talking about. I wouldn't even want to be. But if I couldn't be that person, I should never have agreed to marry Tony. Everything was such a mess.

I knew it was only a matter of time before the baby question came up. Marjorie waited until the penultimate day of her stay with us and asked me to join her in the drawing room. Picking up the teapot she asked,

'Shall I be mother?' A moment's pause, then, 'After all, that's not a role you're qualified to perform, is it Virginia.'

She handed me a cup, and I put it down at once, fearing I might be tempted to fling its contents in her direction.

'That was cruel and unnecessary,' I said.

'Cruel? Cruel? No, the way you misled my poor son is cruel. He was absolutely devastated when he discovered he was not to be a father after all. How could you?'

'How could I?' My voice was shrill. 'How could I? How do you think *I* feel about it? And what the hell business is it of yours anyway?'

'Don't you dare use cheap language with me. Now you're showing your true colours, and it's not a pretty sight.'

'Do you have any idea? Do you know what it feels like to want to have a baby, to believe it's happening at last, only to find out it that it isn't? Do you have any bloody idea at all?'

'Stop that. I can't bear foul language. You sound like a guttersnipe.'

'I'm desperate to have a child. Every bit as much as Tony is. Probably more—as I think he just wants one to keep you off his back. My failure to conceive is a cross I carry daily. And it's unbearable to have you throwing out beastly, heartless, comments like that.'

'Sometimes one needs to be cruel to be kind. It's quite clear, Virginia, you've been irresponsible and foolish in your behaviour and have not done all you could to make having a child more likely. I speak specifically of what Tony says is your tendency to practically starve yourself and to overindulge in alcohol.'

'What?'

'I am his mother and, as such, I have every right to say these things. If you want to have my son's child, then you must start to behave more responsibly and with more dignity. Your own mother is not around to give you counsel, and I know she would be ashamed of you if she were alive to hear you now.'

I stood up. 'You've gone too far. Bringing my mother into this. I will not be at dinner or at breakfast. I will not leave my room until you are gone. You are a mean and spiteful woman. This is my home, and you're no longer welcome in it. I have nothing more to say to you.'

For a moment she struggled for words, the veins on her neck bulging, then she hissed at me, 'I should never have objected to him marrying Daphne. It was the worst mistake of my life. You may come from the top drawer and think you're better than the likes of us, but you're not a patch on that woman and you're simply not cut out for this life.'

Then she left the room, slamming the door behind her.

When Tony came home that evening, he burst into the house calling my name and I thought Marjorie had already got to him and he was taking her part.

'Terrible news.' His voice was excited, belying the words. 'We're at war.'

After all the rumours and false alarms and pointless peace agreements, it was finally happening.

'Get a move on, Ginny. Need to get to the club. I'll have to cancel the mater's trip tomorrow. Thank God, it happened before she'd left. Can you imagine if she'd already set off? Doesn't bear thinking about.'

'But she can't stay here.'

'What do you mean? Where on earth do you expect her to stay? This is her second home.'

'It could be months. Years even. Look at the last war—that was four years. She can't live with us indefinitely.'

'Why not? Plenty of room. This was her home for twenty-odd years.'

'Maybe she could stay with one of her friends.'

'Don't be daft.'

'Tony, please. We had a huge row this afternoon. She said some frightful things to me. I can't stay under the same roof as her.'

'For God's sake,' he didn't attempt to disguise his impatience, 'if you've had words, then go and apologise to her. She's not getting any younger. You have to make allowances. Probably all a misunderstanding. Storm in a teacup. Find a way to muddle along with her. I can't be worrying about this. Far more important things happening in the world than the two of you squabbling. Sort it out, Ginny. Don't ask me to take sides.'

But the implication in those words was that he already had.

So that was that. I was not to be rid of her. It was only later on I remembered I hadn't asked him who Daphne was.

CHAPTER 13

DESPITE THE FACT we were now at war, nothing much changed at first in the way of life in Mudoorayam. The Viceroy, Lord Linlithgow, managed to upset both Mr Nehru and Mr Jinnah by declaring war on behalf of India, then telling them after it was done. As far as I could gather, Gandhi, for his part, thought it would be a good idea for everyone to surrender to Hitler and Mussolini. I was beginning to have doubts about him.

The war felt distant. There were no bombs raining down on Britain in those early months, but life had changed for Pud and Roger, who had accepted a consignment of evacuees.

Meanwhile, the other war, the one between me and my mother-in-law, raged on. I behaved civilly to her in front of Tony, but avoided addressing her directly. I couldn't understand how Tony failed to notice the catty comments she made to me. Maybe he chose not to hear them—years of practice enabling him to tune her out completely. I had not mastered that skill and sat there biting my tongue when she made her digs, determined not to take the bait.

I was deflated, ground down by Tony's expectations and my failure to conceive—and probably by India, as well. It still overwhelmed me, this funny little town, tucked away among the hills in the green folds of the tea gardens. I was alien, with nothing in common with my compatriots, and wary of Indians, despite the kindness I saw in their eyes and the broad smiles that revealed shining, white teeth. The racial tensions and sporadic bouts of violence between Hindus and Muslims that filled the pages of the *Times of India* were not evident in Muddy.

I still hadn't asked Tony about Daphne. I was afraid to find out about her, afraid he too might say he regretted not marrying her. Was she a Yorkshire lass? Or worse, someone out here? I'd not met any Daphnes at the club and no one mentioned anyone with that name. I wouldn't have put it past Marjorie to invent her.

TONY WAS in Coimbatore for several days and Marjorie was at a bridge party, when Hector turned up after supper and offered to take me to a public meeting in town.

'An opportunity to advance your education, Mrs T. A chance to meet some of the locals. You're shut away in a little colonial bubble and, since Tony's not around to tell you not to, it's too good an opportunity to miss.'

'What kind of meeting?'

'It's a lecture. A chap from the Congress party drumming up local support.'

'You're right. Tony would tell me not to.'

'So?'

'I don't think I should go.'

'You've a mind of your own, Ginny.'

'I know. And my own mind thinks I shouldn't go.'

'Please come. I promise you it will be interesting.'

'I don't like politics.'

'That's just because you haven't tried to understand them. Besides, tonight's not really politics. It's about *satyagraha*.'

'Now, you've absolutely settled it. I'm not going. I'm not going to a lecture about something I can't even pronounce, let alone understand.'

'*Satyagraha* is the Sanskrit word for truth-force and is Mr Gandhi's philosophy of non-violent civil disobedience. The struggle to escape from the yoke of the mighty British Empire.'

'Sounds exactly like politics to me.'

'It's a chance to get an insight into the lives of the local people. Tony will never know. I doubt any other Brits will be there.'

'That's supposed to encourage me?'

'Yes.'

I thought for a moment. I liked the sound of non-violent civil disobedience—I might pick up some tips for dealing with Marjorie.

'Very well, then, I'll come. As long as you're sure there won't be any trouble?'

The meeting was held inside the big vegetable market in town. Men were crowded into the spaces between the empty market stalls, most of them sitting on the floor. The only white people I saw were a man I recognised as an Anglican priest and another—a teacher at one of the local schools. I didn't know either personally. Hector and I stayed at the periphery, seating ourselves on a couple of empty crates. Some of the men looked a bit hostile when we first arrived, but Hector's presence provided automatic immunity from too much scrutiny and, after a few minutes, they got used to my presence and stopped staring, focusing instead on talking to each other and then listening to the speaker.

Like most things in India, the proceedings started late.

Three women on a raised platform, the only other females present, were hard at work spinning cotton to make *khadi* cloth on star-shaped, wooden, spinning wheels. The evening began with practical demonstrations on how to construct the *charkha* on which to spin the yarn. While it was unlikely I'd ever need this skill, I found it interesting and enjoyed the frisson of excitement I got from being in that crowded hall, knowing Marjorie would violently disapprove.

After the spinning, a stout man, clothed entirely in white *khadi* cloth, addressed the crowd in Hindustani, in an aggressive tone. It was a bit of a rant. Beside him, another man translated his words into Tamil, giving Hector time to translate into English for my benefit. The gist of it was that *khadi* was not just cloth, but the living symbol of Indian history, heritage and pride, the means of empowerment of the Indian people and the way to free them from the rule of the British. He quoted Gandhi, saying, *"The wearer of khadi is like a man making use of his lungs"*. While he spoke, the women carried on spinning, oblivious to his words. I couldn't help thinking it was a bit of an over-claim that a homemade spinning wheel and a bit of rough cloth might be the means of bringing about the overthrow of the British Empire. I was even less convinced once he got onto the topics of sexual abstinence, poverty and diet. It turned out I was not the only one. When the speaker finished, a man who was hidden from me by a pillar began a slow handclap. I leaned forward to try to see him, but the pillar blocked my view. When he spoke, I assumed from his accent and his perfect English that he was British, but his words showed he was not.

'Very creditable, sir. Far be it from me to criticise Mr Gandhi, but it's will take a lot more than spinning cotton at home every day to drive the British from our country. This is just a distraction, a sideshow and a diversion from the real issues at stake. We've been dragged unconstitutionally into declaring war by our colonial masters. And all you want to talk about is spinning thread and living in an ashram.'

Several people began shouting. The man behind the pillar was unmoved and carried on, 'I'd like to know how you, Mr Mohan Gupta, think *satyagraha* will make a difference. Let's suppose all the good people here tonight go home, start spinning, start praying and stop buying British-made goods. Do you imagine the politicians in London will notice? Not even the Manchester mill owners will. We are a mere drop in their ocean. You are deluding yourself, and everyone here, if you think it will make any difference. And, what's worse, you're diverting attention from the real struggle that must take place. Nothing much has happened yet in the war against Hitler but, believe me, it will and, before long, many of us could be drafted into fighting, forced to risk our lives for a quarrel not of our making.'

The noise level erupted in the room, and it was clear the words had struck home. Mr Gupta spoke again, this time in English, 'Sir, I respect your views, but I cannot possibly condone violent struggle. That is not the way. Remember what the Mahatma said, *"I see God in every thread I draw on the spinning wheel"*. God will help us. God will support our peaceful struggle.'

'So you think it's right to stick to peaceful struggle for our own freedom, yet also right to be dragged into what is bound to be a violent struggle against Germany on behalf of the British. Where's the sense in that?'

'Are you saying we should condone fascism?' asked Mr Gupta.

His invisible interlocutor shouted back, his voice angry, 'I'm not condoning fascism. I'm saying we need to wake up and grab control of our own destiny.' He paused, then said, 'What's the point? We're all wasting our time.'

He pushed his way through the crowds and out of the

market. As he passed us, Hector took my arm and led me outside after him.

The man sat on the edge of the stone fountain in the middle of the market square and began rolling a cigarette. Hector steered me over to him.

'Ginny, let me introduce Jagadish Mistry. He's recently arrived in Mudoorayam and is Tilman Tea's new land surveyor.'

'Jag, this is Mrs Ginny Tilman. Your boss's wife.'

The man looked up and stared at me coldly, then recovering his manners, jumped to his feet and held out his hand. I hesitated a moment, then took it. It was the first time I had shaken an Indian's hand. His grip was firm and his skin was smooth.

He looked at me with a curiosity I thought was brazen. I wasn't used to Indians looking me in the eye. They were more deferential. I'm not saying they should have been. Just that's how they were. Jagadish Mistry was certainly not deferential. Not even close.

All of a sudden, I wanted to go home and wished I'd never agreed to come.

'I'm pleased to meet you, Mr Mistry. Hector, I need to get home.'

Without waiting for Hector's reply, I set off towards the end of the market square where the *tongas* were lined up waiting, leaving him to say goodbye to Mistry and hurry after me.

'I must say, Mrs T, that was rude of you. Jag's a good fellow.'

'I wasn't rude. Just tired. It was crowded in there, and I'm a bit queasy. I want to get home. And, anyway, I did meet him.'

He looked at me sideways. 'What did you think?'

'I thought it was all a bit dull, if you must know. And I

can't help but agree with your friend about it taking more than a bit of cloth to get rid of the British. Mr Gandhi is not very practical, I'm afraid. And if he waits for God to bring about change, he's going to have a very long wait.'

'Never mind that. What did you think of Mistry?'

'Why?'

He shrugged, grinned, and I groaned. 'God, Hector, please don't tell me. I don't want to know about it.'

He looked wounded. 'I can't imagine what you're getting at?'

'You're incorrigible. Far from broadening my local knowledge, this was all a pretext for you to show off your latest conquest. So how long has it been going on?'

He sighed. 'It hasn't, and I doubt it ever will. A chap can but dream.'

SINCE THE DAY war was declared, Marjorie appeared to be following the same tactics as Germany and its Phoney War, and I was left awaiting an attack that never came. This made me nervy and jumpy. I'd become so demoralised by her presence and by Tony's preoccupation with work that, despite the doctor's recommendation that I avoid alcohol, I was drinking more than ever. I was using it as crutch against my moral cowardice. I'd not made a good show of my marriage —my husband consistently took the part of his mother rather than his wife—and I failed to confront him about it. But marriage was a one-way ticket, so I'd have to make the best of things.

Most days, once Marjorie went to meet her friends, I sat in the garden on a bench at the back of the house, or in a deckchair on the lawn beside a tall *spathodea*, the African tulip tree, with its brilliant, flame-coloured flowers. These trees grew everywhere around Mudoorayam, their big orange blooms exploding like fires across the hillsides. They helped prevent the thin soil from washing away during the rains. The local people extracted the bark, leaves and flowers to treat malaria—so they called it the malaria tree. Since living here, I'd developed a passion for trees. There were so many and of such diversity of species, size, shape and colour. Some were curved like broccoli or lollypops, others tall and thin as spindles. They grew densely packed in clumps of woodland, straggled along the edges of roads and tracks, stood sentinel along the ridges at the tops of the high ranges above the tea gardens or popped up like lone guards in the middle of the neat rows of tea, providing shelter and preventing erosion. So many different shades of green; a whole palette's worth, set off by the rusty red of the soil.

I spent a lot of time reading. Hector's vast library provided me with a steady literary diet. The latest offering was Tristram Shandy. I groaned when he'd handed it to me, doubting I'd find anything of merit in a picaresque eighteenth-century novel. But I was won over by the way Tristram's life story got told, despite all the seemingly impossible barriers that prevented its telling and the way it ran off in wild tangents and digressed into fascinating side stories so you never got to the bottom of what was going on. Complicated, just like life. Yet, despite the crazy distractions of the book, the hot and sticky afternoon made it hard to concentrate.

After an hour of wool-gathering, as my father used to call it, with the book open in my lap, I called Thankappan to summon a *tonga* and set off for the Hindu temple. I knew it would be closed until later in the afternoon, so it would be quiet up there, and I'd be alone to paint undisturbed on the terrace outside.

I loved being up there with the town spread out below and the tea bush-covered hills rising above it. I watched the local people going about their business in the distance. At this time of day, most of the memsahibs would be holed up at the club playing bridge or smashing tennis balls around a court, so there was little risk of being seen in town by anyone I knew.

I filled my empty jam jar from a little tap behind the temple. I wanted to capture the lazy, dirty river with my watercolours. The river was low, awaiting the rains; its banks appeared stranded, separated from the narrow stream by a wide strip of bare soil and debris. I liked the unkempt nature of the place and the contrasts; the rectangular shapes of the wood and concrete shacks against the curve of the river, the soft green whorls of the tea gardens counterpointed by the pure white of the angels trumpets which grew profusely on the river banks. There was a narrow, wooden footbridge, congested with people going to and from the centre of the town.

I worked away, content in my solitude and heedless of the passage of time, until my concentration was broken by a voice I recognised.

'Not the most beautiful of vistas, Mrs Tilman? Why should this merit your artistic endeavours? Just a dirty river and a lot of shabby dwellings.'

The man from the *satyagraha* meeting was leaning against one of the pillars of the temple staring at me. That same arrogant expression. As if he was sizing me up.

'How long have you been there?' My tone made the words harsher than I'd intended.

He pushed himself off the wall. 'Sorry. I didn't mean to intrude.'

'You're hardly intruding. It's your temple, not mine.'

'Actually, it's not. I'm an unbeliever.'

'You're not a Hindu?'

'Well, I suppose it depends what you mean by Hindu. If

you mean am I a member of the indigenous population of the Indian subcontinent, then, yes I am. If you mean do I follow one of the many diverse religions of said subcontinent, then, no I don't.'

I decided he was a pompous ass. I picked up my pencil and carried on drawing, determined to ignore him and hoping that would make him go away. But he walked behind me and looked over my shoulder. I put my pencil down and closed the sketchbook.

'Do go on, Mrs Tilman. Don't let me stop you. I'm fascinated by the process of painting. Perhaps because I don't have a creative bone in my own body.'

'Everyone has the capacity to be creative—they just forget how to exercise it.' Now it was I who sounded pompous.

'In that case, I have total amnesia.' He laughed with a deep, sonorous, laugh. 'What are you going to paint?'

I hate people watching me paint. It's ghastly. Feels like being choked. It stops the flow. I picked up my brush, and paused, waiting for him to move away. He leaned over and examined the watercolour study, then crouched down beside me to look more closely. It made me nervous. I hoped he'd take a quick look, nod politely and leave me in peace. But he didn't. He stayed there. Close. Too close. I could hear his breathing. As he squatted there, I looked at the brown skin of his wrists where they rested lightly on his thighs. He had beautiful hands. I had a sudden compulsion to reach out and touch him. I looked away, unable to breathe myself. *Pull yourself together, Ginny.*

At last, he got up and moved away to lean over the wall and look down onto the river.

'I can see what you're doing now. It's beautiful. The way you've caught the light playing on the white flowers. The blocks of colour of the buildings against the green of the tea gardens. Not much of a view when you just look at it, but what you've done to it is so different, and yet so true to what's there. You really see, don't you?'

I looked at him in surprise.

'You have a gift, Mrs Tilman. Most people—I include myself—look at this view and just see ugliness, but you look beyond that. It's as though you see the essence of things. A dirty backwater becomes a thing of beauty—you convey so much more because you bring out the way one object relates to another. It's remarkable. I'm impressed.'

I couldn't help smiling. Then, disconcerted by his fulsome praise, I lowered my head to carry on with my work. I didn't want him to notice the effect he was having on me. He made me feel uncomfortable, vulnerable, exposed. When he looked at me, I felt as if he could really see into me; see beyond the outside and see me as I really was. It was extraordinary. He was a total stranger. And, yet, it was so.

I painted on, aware he was watching me intently. 'Shouldn't you be at work, Mr Mistry?'

He sighed. 'Yes, alas, I should. I was on my way back to the plantation office when I saw you up here and thought I'd check to make sure all was well. Not many English ladies sit alone outside a temple. But I can see you're perfectly happy here, so I must end my malingering. I hope you won't spill the beans to Tony?'

The familiar way he used Tony's Christian name made me frown momentarily.

'Well, yes, I am perfectly happy and, no, I won't tell my husband I saw you. Why on earth would I?'

He shrugged, and I realised I'd been rude and dismissive. He was about to go but, suddenly, I didn't want him too. I looked up at him, and said, 'I thought what you said the other night at the meeting was interesting. I'd been thinking exactly the same thing myself.'

He laughed. 'That we should adopt violent insurrection to

throw you and your countrymen out? That sounds like treason to me, Mrs Tilman.'

'No. I mean it seems a bit ingenuous to believe self-sufficiency and this truth-force business are enough to achieve what are pretty ambitious political aims.'

'You think our aims over-ambitious?'

'I didn't say that. Just that it will take a bit more than weaving cloth to get the British to give up what they believe is theirs.'

'And do you think it's rightfully theirs?'

'Of course not. I think it's time to let India govern itself.'

'How magnanimous of you.'

His sarcasm cut me.

I tried again. 'Sorry, this is never going to sound right. And I don't pretend to understand much about politics, but I don't believe we should still be governing India and it seems to me there's a lot of exploitation goes on. I suppose you think I sound patronising. It's probably impossible to explain myself properly, so I shouldn't even try.'

I dropped my pencil and he bent down to pick it up for me.

'I don't think you sound patronising. I was surprised to see you at the meeting and, even more so, when Channing told me you were Tony's wife.'

I should never have embarked on this line of discussion. I'd walked into a place I didn't want to be.

'I'd be awfully grateful if you wouldn't let on I was at that meeting. My husband isn't terribly keen on some of my efforts to get to know more about India.'

He looked thoughtful. 'You are an unusual woman, Mrs Tilman. So you want to know more about India? And you think independence is a worthy aim. I'm sure from what I know of Tony, he'd never approve of those views.'

'He wouldn't at all.' The words were out before I realised I was being disloyal.

Mistry said nothing for a while.

'I must heed the call of duty. One day, I will show you some more interesting scenes to paint.' He gestured towards my sketch book. 'If you can make that dirty river appear beautiful, I can't imagine what you might do with the high ranges.'

'Maybe my style is better suited to the more mundane scenes here. The trivial and the everyday. I don't think I could do justice to a broad panorama. I'd find it intimidating.'

'I very much doubt that.'

He nodded to me, then moved behind the wall of the temple and down the long flight of stone steps. I watched him descending, noticing the way he way he moved, his easy nonchalance, his comfort in inhabiting his own body. At the bottom, he climbed onto a motorcycle and pulled on a pair of goggles. Before he kick-started the ignition, he waved up at me. Then the engine roared into life and he was gone.

I picked up my paintbrush, but the inclination to paint had left me.

CHAPTER 14

TONY, Marjorie and I drove home from the club in stony silence. I tried to make conversation with Tony about the progress of the war, but he pretended not to hear and I could feel Marjorie's eyes boring into the back of my head.

I turned sideways in my seat to look at Tony as he drove. His mouth was turned down and his chin thrust forward. Definitely annoyed about something. I hated trying to talk with him with his mother breathing down my neck and listening to my every word, but the silence was worse.

'What's wrong, Tony?'

Silence.

'Please, darling, tell me what's the matter? Have I upset you in some way?'

Marjorie leaned over the back seat and put her hand on Tony's shoulder. 'If you won't tell her, then I will.'

'Keep out of this, Mater.' He swung the motorcar off the road onto a gravel patch, so the tyres screeched and I was jerked forward, banging my head on the windscreen.

'Hey! Steady on. What on earth's up?' I asked.

'Do you do it deliberately? Try to make a fool of me?' His usually quiet voice was rasping and loud.

'I don't know what you're talking about. I'm not a mind reader. For heaven's sake. Tell me what's wrong.'

'As if it isn't bad enough you running around town with that arrogant pansy, but now you're hanging around the Hindu temple.'

Mistry had told Tony after all.

Marjorie chipped in, 'And going to political meetings. Don't forget that.'

Tony swung round and yelled at his mother to shut up. I'd never witnessed him raise his voice to her like that and, by judging her cowed reaction, neither had she.

This gave me courage. 'What's wrong with going to the temple? It's interesting. I sketch there. The statues are so colourful. And the monk there is awfully nice, and he gave permission for me to paint there and doesn't mind at all, so I'm not offending anyone. I've been a few times. I'm not in anyone's way. There's usually no one around in the afternoon, anyway.'

'Don't you understand a bloody thing? It's not *done*. It's not appropriate. The Indians don't like it. You've been here long enough to know they have their places and we have ours. We respect their territory and they do ours. You wouldn't get them hanging round the club like that.'

'But they're not allowed in the club.'

'They are if invited, but do they come? When did you last see an Indian there—apart from official occasions? They don't come because they know it's ours and we like it that way. Barred from the clubs altogether in some towns. We never had to do that in Muddy because they don't take liberties. Prefer to keep things separate. That's how you need to behave, too.'

'But there was no one there to see me. Just the monk. I

only go when it's closed—never during the services. I like it up there. It's quiet. There's so much to paint. All those marvellous statues and the view over the whole town.'

'Hang your painting. There's trouble enough brewing with the natives without you stirring up more by poking your nose into their stuff. We walk a fine line here and we follow the rules. These things work because everyone knows where to draw that line. We keep off their side and they keep off ours. By hanging around their damned temples with all your painting clobber, you're giving them ammunition. For God's sake, Ginny. Show some common sense. We're at war. We need their cooperation more than ever.'

I started to feel angry. 'I didn't have my painting clobber as you call it. Just a sketch book, a pencil and a few water-colours. I didn't even take my easel. I was respectful, and I even took off my shoes.'

'You did what?' His voice rose to a screech. I'd never seen him so angry before. Apoplectic.

'But I was doing exactly what you say. Respecting their traditions. They remove their shoes before entering the temple grounds, so I did the same.'

'My God! You've no sense at all. Why don't you just put a bloody *sari* on while you're about it and splash some paint in the middle of your forehead? You stupid little fool. We're British for God's sake. Not natives. We don't run around like Gandhi in bare feet. I forbid you to go there again. And no more hanging around with that nancy boy Channing, either. And, as for political meetings, words fail me, Ginny. Grow up, for God's sake. Play the damned game.'

I was about to protest when he started the engine and swung the car back onto the road.

'I mean it. And I don't want to discuss it any more, Ginny.'

I STOOD IN THE HALL, leaning against the heavy mahogany table, dreading the thought of making the telephone call. I'd waited until Marjorie was out of the way and Nirmala and Thankappan were in their own quarters at the rear of the house eating their luncheon. I didn't like to think of the servants listening to my conversations. Nirmala was always creeping up behind me when I wasn't expecting her. I wondered whether Marjorie had asked her to spy on me, then I decided I was being ridiculous. I wasn't bothered so much about Thankappan. He was shy and respectful, always keeping his distance and avoiding eye contact. Nirmala, on the other hand, appeared to be amused by my domestic inadequacies. Her former role as Tony's *ayah* gave her added standing, and I didn't feel comfortable with her.

Taking a deep breath, I closed my eyes and picked up the receiver and asked for Hector's number. The operator connected us and he answered after the third ring.

'Hector, it's Ginny.'

'How delightful. I was just thinking about you.'

I was anxious about what I had to say so plunged right in. 'Tony's angry. Someone told him about the *satyagraha* meeting and that I've been up to the Hindu temple to paint. I think it must have been that Mistry chap. He saw me up there and must have mentioned it to Tony.'

'Why would he do that? Not like him.'

'I neither know nor care why he would do it. The net result is Tony doesn't want me to go up to the temple anymore.'

'Why not?'

'Apparently I need to respect the dividing line between the Indians and us, and not stir up trouble with the independence movement.'

Hector's laughter boomed down the wires. 'My dear Mrs T, I doubt even a woman of your own impressive talents has the capacity to incite the gentlemen of the Congress party into insurrection by sitting outside a temple painting the scenery and quietly observing a demonstration of yarn weaving.'

'He thinks it's inappropriate.'

'He's a bloody fool.'

'Don't say that. I hate you being horrid about Tony. It makes me feel disloyal.'

'All right, but I can't believe you've done me the honour of a rare telephone call just to tell me Tony's not happy with you visiting Indian holy places.'

'No. There's more.' I hesitated. 'Look, Hector, I think we need to see a bit less of each other for a while. Well, actually, not meet up together at all anymore.'

'You think? Or Tony says?'

'Don't make this harder for me.'

He waited in silence for me to carry on.

'He doesn't want me spending time with you. Not alone. Obviously, if we meet up in public at the club, that's different.'

There was a silence, then he began to laugh again. 'He's afraid I'm leading you astray, is he?'

'Yes.'

'You need to tell him he's being an idiot.'

'He's my husband. I must do as he says.'

'My arse, you must.'

'Hector! Really.'

'You're not going to listen to him, are you? Besides, he'll calm down after a few days. It will all blow over.'

'I'm trying my best to make my marriage work.'

'That doesn't mean letting him be unreasonable and petty-minded. For Pete's sake, Ginny, I thought you had gumption.'

'I'm sorry. Please try and understand how hard this is.

Marjorie makes matters worse. She's put him up to it. If I'm ever to get shot of her living here and breathing down my neck, I have to get Tony to fight in my corner instead of always taking her part. My seeing you aggravates him. I wish it wasn't like this, but I have no choice. I'm frightfully sorry. I'll miss you dreadfully. Goodbye and God bless.'

I hung up the telephone as he was repeating my name. I was a miserable traitor, unworthy of his friendship.

Soon after I cut poor Hector, I found the book. It was in the drawer of Tony's desk in the study. I was looking for a roll of sticking tape. The cover caught my eye; wrapped in brown paper—the way we'd covered our text books at school —as if someone wanted to conceal the contents. Not the kind of thing I thought Tony would bother to do. Curious, I flipped it open. It was a manual; a guide to married life. At the back were fold-out, full-colour drawings of sexual organs. I felt myself blushing and immediately jumped up and closed the door. I didn't want Marjorie wandering in and finding me looking at it. Too embarrassing for words. I was shocked Tony would have bought such a book. It seemed so unlike him. There was a complicated graph entitled "Ovarian function, Rhythmic Vital Curve and Menstruation". I sat down with the textbook in my lap, and tried to make sense of the coloured dots plotting body temperature, and charting the birth and death of an ovum. Words like "mucous membrane" and "glycogen" swam before my eyes. Horrible. No wonder he was so attentive to my dates. He was treating my impregnation like a scientific project to eradicate a fungal infection in a tea plant. But this was evidence he must be really determined to do his bit on the baby front. A sign he was committed to the marriage and to me. I found the biology repellent. Unromantic. Horrid, if I'm honest. It made me feel a bit sick to think of him reading this in secret. I flicked back through the body of the book, shocked by the detailed descriptions of all kinds of sexual positions in the chapter titled "Sexual Communion". Tony had clearly skipped those bits. I was about to put the book back in the drawer when I found a slip of paper inside the flyleaf with the words—*Hope this helps! Love Mater (Granny in waiting) x*

That night, when Tony pattered across the space between our twin beds and climbed on top of me, it was as if Marjorie was standing at the foot of the bed watching us.

TONY BROACHED the subject of our hosting a dinner party as I struggled to eat one of the cook's least appetising creations: a plate of sliced hard boiled eggs, spicy cauliflower curry and tinned pilchards—no wonder I'd been losing weight.

'I'm inviting some of the chaps from work for dinner. Can you sort something out with the servants? Nirmala knows the drill.'

I put down my knife and fork. 'A dinner party? Here? What's the occasion?' We had never done any entertaining at home before.

'Have to push the old boat out every now and then. I'm the general manager. It's expected. Want to lay on a bit of a do for Goddard's retirement. Haven't done it before now because... well, just haven't got round to it.'

'Who will you invite?'

'Usual crowd. Rogers, the company engineer, and his wife. You've met her. Valerie. Funny little woman. Short. Looks like a mouse.'

This was going to be an ordeal. 'Who else?'

'Couple of the senior planters, Goddard, of course, and Johnson. Goddard's a bachelor and you know Mrs Johnson, big woman with the high-pitched voice.' Seeing my blank expression he added, 'Come on, Ginny.'

Marjorie seized the opportunity. 'You must make more effort, Virginia, dear. As the GM's wife, you must fly the flag and get to know the troops.' She gave a laugh that was brittle and false. Surely Tony could tell it was all an act?

I ignored her and looked at Tony. He sighed. 'Then there's Bailey - he'll be on his own - and the Wilkinsons.'

At last a name I recognised. 'Yes, I know the Wilkinsons. Recently arrived. He has a big, bushy moustache and she has blonde hair and is expecting a baby.'

As soon as the words were out I wished I hadn't said them, as a frown immediately settled on his brow and Marjorie gave a theatrical cough, then excused herself from the table.

I reached for a notebook and pencil and scribbled down the names. Tony carried on eating.

'And an Indian chap, Jagadish Mistry. Good type. Recently joined.'

I prayed I wouldn't give myself away. 'An Indian?'

'Yes, an Indian. You don't have to sound so shocked.'

'I'm not shocked. It's just you don't normally...'

'I told you he's a good chap. Sound. Land surveyor. It's a work thing, Ginny. Wouldn't ask him otherwise.'

The moment for me to confess my prior acquaintance had passed. Now what was I to do if Mistry let the cat out of the bag when we were introduced? Then I remembered he'd already told Tony about our meeting at the temple and the political meeting. So why hadn't Tony called my bluff? Perhaps it was some kind of a test? If so, I'd just failed it.

'Is that it then?' I asked.

'Up to you, darling. We chaps will be talking business, so you may need some more ladies for you and the mater to chat to. You can always ask Lilian.'

I forced myself to ignore his patronising tone and the way he was lumping me with Marjorie.

'What will we give them to eat?'

'Can't I leave anything to you, Ginny? Just sort it. You've been to enough fancy dinners in your time. Should be able to come up with a menu.'

'But the cook can't cook.' I pointed at the plate in front of me, where I'd done little more than rearrange what passed for food around the china, trying to disguise the fact I'd barely touched it.

'Get him to follow a recipe.'

'He can't read.'

'Well, read one out to him.'

'He barely speaks English. I communicate with him through Nirmala.' The truth was I didn't communicate with him at all. 'And, with so many guests, I don't want it to be a disappointment. I don't want to let you down, darling.'

He got up from the table. 'For pity's sake, Ginny, can't expect me to spoon feed you. You've little enough else to think about.' He paused in the doorway. 'Don't wait for me to turn in. Pile of paperwork to catch up on.'

I hadn't a clue what to serve the guests. I'd never paid much attention to food. My mother had ruled over the domestic management of Leighton Square and never involved me. She knew I'd be as interested in that as I was in discovering the rules of bridge. Here, in India, the food our cook served up was an abomination—a kind of Indianised hybrid of English classics like the meals we'd had a school, but with an often ill-conceived Indian twist. And all with tough meat. Chewy mutton and stringy chicken. Puddings that were all variations on caramel custard. How was I to design a suitable menu for a formal dinner? Then I realised I was being pathetic. How had I arrived at this state of clueless incompetence? *Buck up, Ginny.*

I telephoned Lilian and asked her to meet me for lunch at the Club. She sounded surprised, but pleased. When we arrived, she was delighted to find shepherd's pie on the club lunch menu.

'Comfort food. Nothing like it. I'm having the tapioca pudding afterwards. Just like schooldays, but they cook it a damn sight better here.'

I was struggling to finish the generous helping. Everything, even shepherd's pie, had a vaguely curried aftertaste.

Lilian leaned across the table and patted my hand. 'How's it going? Getting used to Muddy? There are worse places to be. Theo was in Calcutta for seventeen years, and I practically expired from the beastly heat there. Used to escape to the hills for months—but not so good for married life being separated like that.'

I hoped this wasn't a prelude to a lecture on how to do my duty to king, country and husband by producing a child—or worse, a confession that Lilian had been indulging in the kind of thing Bunty Finchington told me went on when the wives took to the hills.

She carried on, blind to my concerns, 'Muddy's a marvellous place. Theo is due to retire in a year or two, and we have a house in the New Forest waiting for us. I suppose I'll adapt, but I can't imagine it.'

'How long have you been in India?'

'Most of my life. I was born here, then sent home to boarding school. I met Theo when I spent the Easter holiday with his sister in 1901. He swept me off my feet. Hard to believe it, eh?'

She laughed and tapped me on the arm. 'He was rather dashing in those days. Mind you he always will be to me.'

She was lost in thought for a moment. I envied her. It reminded me of the way Pud had talked about Roger. I couldn't imagine having that look in my eyes when I talked about Tony, but I wished I did.

'Has Theo always been in the colonial service?'

She nodded. 'We started out in Africa. Nairobi. I missed India dreadfully. My parents were living in Dacca, so Theo applied for an Indian posting and we haven't budged since—apart from the odd passage home to see his people. He misses England, and I suppose since we've lived here most of our married life, it's his turn. He's been bringing home the bacon all these years and our children and grandchildren all live over there. It will be jolly nice to spend more time with them. But enough about me, Ginny. You called me for a reason. Spill the beans.'

'Are you and Theo free a week on Wednesday to come to us for dinner. It's just some chaps from Tilman's. It'll probably be a bit of a bore, but...'

'Well, I can tell you right now, Theo can't make it. He'll be at Government House for the annual audit. But if you don't mind having this old broiler on her own, I'd be delighted.'

'Thank you, Lilian. That's such a relief.'

'You didn't need to invite me to lunch in order to invite me to dinner—must be something else?'

'It's rather embarrassing.'

'Heard it all before, my dear. Spit it out.'

'It's the menu. For the dinner. I haven't a clue. I normally leave everything to the cook, but now Marjorie's living with us...she and Tony expect me to organise it, and I've no idea where to start. I can't even give the cook a recipe book and ask him to get on with it, as he can't read. And he's an awful cook. I'm terrified it won't be up to scratch, and Marjorie will have something else to complain about.'

Lilian leaned back in her chair and roared with laughter. 'You poor little thing. I know just how you feel. I was terrified of my mother-in-law, God rest her soul. And Marjorie

Tilman puts mine in the shade. She's always been a dreadful bully. Likes to get her own way. Can't be easy having her under the same roof. Of course, I'll help you. I'll even lend you my cook.'

She reached across the table and gave my hand a squeeze. I wanted to jump up and hug her.

CHAPTER 15

THE DAY of the dinner party I was nervous, afraid of letting Tony down and fearful of the inevitable criticism from Marjorie. No matter how well it went, I knew she would find something to gripe about.

Her attitude seemed to have infected Tony. I wasn't capable of making him happy anymore. How had it come to this? Was there a specific event, a moment when he began to look at me in a different way? The man I'd met in that Harrogate hotel had been shy and diffident and eager to please. The man who'd got drunk and missed our wedding night had been apologetic and bashful. The tables were now well and truly turned. He didn't shout at me or get angry. He just absented himself, put a distance between us I was finding harder to narrow. The little gifts he had bought me on his trips away became less frequent, then stopped altogether, although the trips hadn't. Now, I was glad if I managed to get by without the creasing of his brow and the look of slightly mystified disappointment, as though he was trying to work out what exactly was going wrong. Every time I saw the disappointment in his face, it was matched by a corresponding look on Marjorie's, telegraphing *"I told you so"*. I wondered if they were both imagining how things might have been different if he'd married the mysterious Daphne.

Because he'd disapproved of Hector, I'd given up the only person in Muddy I regarded as a friend. I'd renounced my best friend. And it still wasn't enough. If only Hector could have been here tonight to give me some moral support.

The planters fell into two categories: the administrators, who got their thrills from balancing the books and titrating soil samples, and the explorer types, who got theirs from tramping through jungles and swinging their theodolites. I had no common ground with either group. Marjorie, however, was as expert as her son was in the nuances of tea production. Yet another black mark on my score sheet.

Lilian came up trumps with the menu. She not only dispatched her own cook to help out in the kitchen, she suggested the courses and helped with the seating plan. India was even more hierarchical and based on precedence than London—particularly where the Indian Civil Service was concerned.

All day I went in and out of the kitchen—a place that had hitherto been *terra incognita* to me—to check on progress. The warm smell of melting sugar, the aroma of roasting lamb —well—mutton actually—as always— and the bouquet of spices filled the air every time I entered. Venu polished the silver on the veranda, while Thankappan polished the glass-ware in the dining room. Remembering Bunty Finchington's advice, I clattered about lifting pan lids and inspecting the bottoms of the pans. Ammu, the cook, must have thought I'd lost my mind. I was probably in the way, but I was greeted with smiling and nodding every time I stood beside him or Sulu, Lilian's redoubtable cook.

I picked flowers from the garden. At least an indolent ex-debutante could manage an artful arrangement of a few blooms in a bowl. Then I fussed about the dining room, adjusting the placement of the candelabras and napkins and filling fingerbowls with lavender and lemon.

That night I put on a dress I'd never worn before. It was probably *de trop* for Muddy, but I needed some confidence. Floating cream silk chiffon, cut on the bias with scallop-shaped fringes of silk thread. When I'd been fitted for it back in London it had skimmed my hips loosely—but now I could see the curves of my body through the soft fabric. I must be gaining weight at last. Doctor Banerji would be pleased. Studying myself in the looking glass, I liked what I saw. A bit more flesh suited me. I'd always thought my breasts were a bit flat but now they looked just right. I sprayed on some Joy and went to ask Tony to fasten my necklace. I chose the little pearl and diamond one Marjorie had chosen as his wedding present and hoped that would put them both in a good mood, but he barely glanced at it, or me, as he fastened the clasp.

Everyone arrived together—no doubt after an aperitif at the club. Except for Jagadish Mistry. He stood apart from the group. I tried not to make eye contact when Tony introduced us, afraid the Indian would remind Tony we'd already met and reopen the topic of my visits to the temple. But he picked up my cue and behaved as though we were complete strangers.

Tony appeared unaware of anything out of the ordinary, and I realised it could not have been Mistry who'd betrayed me. I felt a wave of gratitude—and relief. As I accepted his handshake, I knew in pretending we'd never met before, I'd given something of myself away. He and I were now co-conspirators in a deception of my husband. I'd crossed a bridge, and I didn't know how or if I could get back. I was annoyed at my own stupidity and at Mistry for playing along with it. I turned away, leaving him standing there alone.

When Thankappan sounded the dinner gong, Goddard, a bumbling bachelor with bad breath, jumped up to escort me into the dining room and, as the guest of honour, was seated beside me, so I had to listen to his increasingly lecherous comments throughout the meal and constantly brush his hand from my knee. Lilian was on his other side and recognising my plight, strove to engage him in conversation. I was rapidly changing my point of view about her. She was turning out to be a good egg.

On my other side was Cecil Wilkinson, the scientific advisor chap. He talked to me about soil erosion and drainage schemes, and I went into a bit of a trance. At least the food was going down well with the guests. I still didn't have a lot of appetite, and picked at my roast mutton, but I was quite light-headed. I'd had a large G&T for Dutch courage before the guests arrived, followed by an even larger one when they got here, and now as Cecil rabbited on about pH values, I let him top up my glass with more wine.

Through the buzz of conversation I overheard Marjorie, Mr Mistry and Mr Rogers, the company engineer. Marjorie was clearly smarting from being seated next to the only Indian in the room.

'I hope you're not involved in all this independence nonsense, Mr Mistry?' she asked. 'I told my son the other day he must be vigilant in stamping out such talk in the company. You, as an Indian in a senior position, must help set a good example.'

Rogers coughed and interjected, 'Mrs Tilman, the viceroy has promised independence will be granted once the war is over.'

'He doesn't mean that. Once it's over, it will be back to business as usual I hope.'

She turned to Mistry. 'Educated Indians such as yourself

know which side their bread is buttered on. Isn't that so, young man?'

Mistry's face was inscrutable. 'Buttered bread has never been a staple of our diet, Mrs Tilman. But it's clear, despite the blustering rhetoric of your Mr Churchill who has always held my country in contempt, Britain can no longer hold onto India. It simply can't afford it. Once the war is over, the British government will be drowning in debt. And there's only so much they can squeeze out of a country that struggles to feed its starving populace. The cost of running India is outstripping the return. After the war, home rule will be an inevitability.'

The veins on Marjorie's neck were bulging and her face was red. I could see her forehead was glazed with perspiration. I wasn't the only person who got under her skin. I started to feel more kindly disposed to Mr Mistry.

She looked as though she was about to choke. 'Really. Anyone with half a grain of intelligence would realise Indians are simply not capable of governing themselves. They're like children.'

The whole table went silent.

Tony interjected, 'Now, mother, we agreed, no politics at the dinner table.'

Rogers tapped Mistry on the shoulder and, while I couldn't tell what he was saying, it was clearly intended to mollify him. I don't know whether it worked, but Mistry and Marjorie kept their backs turned on each other for the rest of the evening.

We finished the main course, but there was no sign of Nirmala and Thankappan to clear away the plates and bring dessert. I excused myself, and went to investigate progress in the kitchen. I felt slightly dizzy. I made it to the kitchen, banging my hip into the sideboard in the hall on the way. Damn, that would mean a whacking great bruise tomorrow.

As I entered the kitchen, Nirmala and Thankappan jumped to their feet and rushed past me to clear the table.

The dessert was on the table in the pantry: a Queen of Puddings. Sulu had done a spectacular job: towering mountain peaks of fluffy meringue, in a dish set on an enormous silver platter. I decided to carry it to the table myself: the crowning glory of a successful evening.

The dining room door was open, and I went through with the pudding as Thankappan and Nirmala made their way out. Swerving to avoid them, I caught the toe of my shoe on the rug and tripped. The Queen of Puddings left my hands and fell onto the parquet floor, and I followed after it, landing on hands and knees in a custardy mixture topped with meringue. It was slathered all over the floor in a glutinous, multi-coloured mess.

The conversation stopped, and I could feel as well as hear the shared intake of breath. A momentary lacuna: I'd fallen, like Alice in Wonderland, into a hole. Then the pain seared through me, clearing my fuzzy head. My ankle. Activity all around me. Hands lifting me, helping me to my feet. Thankappan and Nirmala scooping the remains of the Queen of Puddings from the floor.

'Oh, what rotten luck,' said someone.

'Frightful shame, Ginny.'

Mr and Mrs Johnson supported me as I hopped into the drawing room. Lilian snapped out instructions to the servants to bring coffee, chocolates, cheese and biscuits. Tony gave me a look I took to be a mixture of disappointment and disgust. I knew in that moment he didn't love me anymore. If he ever had. What surprised me more was that I cared so much. That I cared at all.

The guests clustered around me, solicitous, making light of what had happened, anxious to show it was all fine. I looked down at my beautiful, cream, bias-cut gown, now spoiled by a big, dirty stain around the knees. Ruined. I hobbled to my bedroom to change.

I was about to fling myself on the bed and weep with shame and anger, but then I thought about my father. I so rarely thought of him these days but, suddenly sober, he felt very close. I heard his voice in my head saying, *"Come on Jenny-Wren, don't give up. Keep on fighting."* And then the words of a song from a Fred Astaire film Tony and I had watched on our honeymoon in Eastbourne, something about picking yourself up and starting all over again.

I pulled open the wardrobe doors and jerked another gown off its hanger. A powdered nose and a coat of lipstick later, I was ready to face them all again. I unclipped the pearl and diamond necklace and replaced it with an emerald one Mummy had given me for my fifteenth birthday, my first grownup present from her. It was perfect against the pale, chartreuse silk of my dress. I took a deep breath and went back to rejoin the party.

The guests were downing port in the drawing room. The atmosphere was lively and voices loud, drowning the gramophone music. I looked over at Tony. He was drinking his coffee as though it were hemlock. There was no sign of Marjorie.

I sat down beside Lilian, who patted me gently on the knee. 'Marvellous party, Ginny.'

I gave her a grateful look. 'Sorry about Sulu's pudding.'

'Most of this lot are too pissed to have noticed. Now excuse me, my darling girl, but I must be away. I sleep so badly when Theo's not at home and, unless I'm in bed by midnight, I won't get off at all. I'm going to slip out quietly as I don't want to break the party up. You can say my goodbyes for me. Toodle-oo.'

And with another pat on my knee, she was gone.

Jagadish Mistry was watching me. Before I could move,

he took Lilian's place on the sofa beside me, leaning back easily into the cushions and crossing one leg over the other as though he were in his own home. I shifted my weight to widen the gap between us.

'Another beautiful gown, Mrs Tilman.'

He looked at me as if he was seeing me without the gown, and I felt the blood course up my neck into my face. I wondered what he would look like too without his elegant suit, but pushed the thought out of my head. I was ashamed. He was an Indian for heaven's sake. And I didn't like him at all. He wasn't going to get the better of me. Not tonight. Besides, Hector had designs on him. But I knew as well as Hector probably did, there was no possibility of that succeeding.

'Why don't you like me, Mrs Tilman? Have I offended you in some way?'

I spat the words out. 'Yes, you have. I don't know what gives you the right to tell tales about me to my husband.'

He was taken aback. 'I have absolutely no idea what you're talking about.'

'Of course, you do. You told my husband I was at the temple and went to that political meeting.'

He shook his head. 'I told no one we'd met there. If you recall, it was I who was worried you might tell Tony you had seen me when, by rights, I should have been working.'

I was nonplussed. 'So who? How?'

'I can't help you there, I'm afraid. It most certainly wasn't me. Besides what's wrong with your being at the temple? You weren't doing any harm.'

'Unfortunately, my husband doesn't agree. He thinks it was disrespectful and likely to offend... you people.'

'I don't see how you sitting on a step looking at that ugly view is going to offend anyone, although I'm not sure what you mean by "you people".'

'I'm sorry. I have offended you. I seem to be making a hash of things lately.'

'I've already forgotten what you said.' He flashed a smile at me and it lit up his face. 'If the temple is out of bounds, I hope you'll allow me to show you some other places to paint.'

'I'm perfectly happy painting in my garden. There's plenty to occupy me.'

He looked crushed. Ashamed of my rudeness I said, 'I understand you're a surveyor.'

'Yes. But don't let's talk about such uninteresting details, Mrs Tilman. You don't want to review my curriculum vitae.'

I looked around for a potential rescuer, but everyone was deep in conversation and the formerly attentive Goddard was snoozing in his chair. 'What would you like to talk about then?'

He shrugged. 'About you. Why you're in India. What you do all day besides paint beautiful pictures. Who you are. That kind of thing.'

I couldn't help myself. 'Don't let's talk about such uninteresting details. You don't want to review my curriculum vitae.'

He laughed and looked at me again, full in the eyes. I had to look away. The man was really annoying me. I suppose I expected him to be deferential, servile and polite, like most of the Indians I'd met. But he was bold to the point of rudeness.

He spoke again, his voice indolent, educated, 'All right. You win. I joined Tilman's Tea six months ago. I was formerly an officer in the cavalry. I trained at Sandhurst. I'd had enough of the military and decided to put the skills I'd acquired to another use and this job came up. I told you it was dull. Now your turn.'

'Nothing much to tell. I'm from London. Married just over three years. In India since.'

I could sense his proximity on the little sofa. He smelled

of something fresh, slightly citrusy, some sort of perfume or soap. I looked into my coffee cup to avoid making eye contact. Why did he make me feel so uncomfortable? It was as if I were afraid of him.

He laughed again. His laugh was deep and throaty and, as he did so, everyone turned around to look at us. Acknowledging the interest, he spoke to the room in general. 'I'm discovering that Mrs Tilman has a risqué sense of humour.'

I felt the blush rising, but this time it was in annoyance. The man was insufferable.

'Excuse me, Mr er...I need to get some fresh air.' I got up and went through the open door to the veranda. To my annoyance, he followed me outside and came to stand beside me, leaning against the wooden balustrade. He was not a tall man, not as tall as Tony, but that's not difficult. But he carried himself with a languid nonchalance as though he didn't care what anyone thought of him. Very different from the other Indians I'd met, but then they were mostly servants.

'Mistry,' he said.

'Excuse me?'

'My name. You'd forgotten it. It's Mistry. Jagadish Mistry.'

'I hadn't forgotten it.' I paused. 'I just wanted you to think I had.'

He laughed.

'You find me rude?' I asked.

'No, I find you interesting.'

'I can't imagine why.'

'You're not happy. And I'm wondering why.'

'That's ridiculous. You don't even know me.'

'No, I don't but I'd like to. And I can see it in your eyes.'

I looked away. 'You have an over-active imagination, Mr Mistry.'

'So my teachers used to tell me. But then my grandmother also told me I had the gift.'

'The gift?'

'The second sight.'

'You have second sight?'

He gave that funny little sideways Indian head movement, only it was so slight as to be almost indiscernible.

'According to my *daa-dee-maa*, I foresaw my father's death.'

'Your dar-dee-what?'

'My *daa-dee-maa*. It means grandmother.'

'What happened to your father?'

'He was in the Indian Army. Infantry. He was sent to fight in the war in Europe when I was nine. One night, I woke up crying in the early hours. I was inconsolable. My grandmother took me into her bed and tried to calm me, but I kept calling for my father. Months later, we were notified of his death. He'd been killed on the same day at the same time I'd woken up crying for him.'

'Gosh. Do you still remember it?'

'Not the waking up and crying. I remember my father though. He'd been so proud going off to fight. He thought he was doing it for the family honour and to fulfil his duty to the king. I remember him in his uniform when we went to wave him off on the train. The last time we saw him. Leaning out of the window, waving his handkerchief at us. What a waste of a life.'

I thought of my own father. 'What year did he die?'

'Nineteen-fifteen. He was killed at Neuve Chapelle. All my mother has are a few postcards and letters sent from the front. His name is inscribed on the Arch in New Delhi. What's that worth? Poor, deluded fool. Giving up his life for a cause he didn't understand, let alone believe in, for a king and country he didn't know, in a land that was strange to him. Just one of a million of my countrymen who went off to fight for your king and his empire. Fifty thousand of them died. Bloody awful waste. And now it's going to happen again. All that sacrifice—and your mother-in-law thinks we aren't even capable of governing ourselves? Capable of dying for Britain though.'

He turned away and looked into the darkness of the garden. I could hear the sound of crickets.

'She's not the most sensitive of people. A million men. I'm so sorry. I had no idea so many Indians were involved. I feel ashamed of my ignorance. I didn't even know any were involved at all.'

'You're not alone in that. They don't exactly broadcast that so many brave Tommies had brown faces.

We were silent for a few moments, then I said, 'It's terrible to lose one's father when one is so young. I know how that feels.'

'Your father died?'

'When I was a bit older than you. About to turn fourteen. He was in the war too. He was shelled and was never the same afterwards, according to my mother. Terribly nervy. It weakened his heart. That's how he died. A massive heart attack. He died in 1932, and I still miss him. Although I think about him a lot less as time goes by. It's harder to remember. That's awful of me isn't it?'

'Life moves on, and we must move with it.'

'I miss him though. When I think of him, I mean. We were close. I sometimes think I've lost my way a bit since he went.'

As I said the words, I wished I hadn't. I was revealing more of myself than I wanted or intended. But he didn't pry. He turned to lean sideways on the balustrade so that he was looking at me again. His expression was one of curiosity, but I wasn't about to divulge any more of myself.

The evening was cool and I shivered. He slipped his jacket off and put it around my shoulders. It was an act of surprising intimacy. I could feel the warmth of his body inside the linen jacket and I could smell him. I liked the feel of it and the way he acted so proprietarily towards me. Then, realising how inappropriate an act it was, I shivered again and the jacket slipped off my shoulders onto the ground.

'I'm sorry. I didn't mean...I'd better go inside. I'm neglecting the other guests,' I stammered.

He bent down to pick the jacket up and laid it over the balustrade. As I walked back into the drawing room, I knew his eyes were following me.

People were on their feet, getting ready to leave. Tony appeared irritated and distracted. I saw them to the door, trying to avoid Goddard kissing me goodnight. Slightly the worse for drink, he went to plant a kiss on my mouth but I managed to twist my head so his blubbery lips hit my left ear.

Mr Mistry was last to leave. He shook hands with Tony, then took my hand and bending low over it, touched it lightly with his lips. I jerked it away.

When the door closed, I turned to Tony and, to cover the confusion Mistry had created in me, said, 'Really, that Goddard chap is the end. I don't know who the heck he thinks he is. He kept trying to make a pass at me. The man has no manners.'

Tony had started to walk towards the bedroom, but he halted and, still looking ahead up the corridor, said quietly, 'Don't talk about him like that, Ginny. He's my colleague and a damn fine chap. He was certainly not making a pass.'

Then he turned and made his way towards the bedroom. I was about to follow when I sensed Marjorie behind me. She gripped my elbow, and said, 'You need to develop some manners yourself, Virginia. You're in no position to criticise Tony's colleagues when you allowed yourself to get so intoxicated you fell over and ruined the whole evening. The servants will be scraping sticky stuff off the floor for weeks. But what would you know about that? You have no idea what is involved in running a household. You can't even organise a dinner party without messing it up, or relying on other people. I know you called on Lilian to bail you out. And what do you think Tony's guests will be saying now? You'll be the talk of the Club tomorrow.'

'That's not fair. And it's not true. Everyone was understanding. Anyone could trip on a carpet edge.'

'Don't give me that, Ginny. You were sloshed. And it's not the first time either, I gather.'

Tears were pricking at my eyes and I fought to keep them back. *Don't let her see you crying. Don't let her know she can upset you.*

'I'm going to bed.'

She grabbed hold of my arm and her words came out in a hiss, 'And don't think I didn't see you talking on the veranda with that Indian fellow. He's an activist. Have you no shame?'

CHAPTER 16

NEXT MORNING my ankle looked as though it had been inflated with a bicycle pump and, when I tried to stand, the pain was so bad I cried out and Nirmala came rushing into my room. She summoned the doctor, who pronounced the ankle badly sprained and prescribed ice packs, a couple of days' bed rest and a ban on high heels until it strengthened.

'And the other matter, Mrs Tilman? How is that proceeding? You seem to have gained a little weight. That is encouraging. Have you begun to menstruate again?'

'Unfortunately, not, Doctor. I suppose it will take time?'

'When did you last menstruate?'

'I haven't since I saw you.'

He took out his stethoscope and came over to the bed. 'Please permit me to examine you.'

When he had finished, he pulled over a chair and sat down. 'I am happy to tell you that you are in the family way. I told you it would happen eventually. Once you stopped worrying about it.'

He took off his spectacles and polished the lenses.

I wanted to jump out of bed and hug him, despite my

reticence about Indians and his reserved and proper manner. But the disappointment of my phantom pregnancy was still fresh and I wanted to be sure.

'Your weight gain is due to the pregnancy. I'd say you are already about nine or ten weeks along. Once your ankle has mended, I'd like you to come to the surgery and I'll have a proper look at you, weigh you and work out a more accurate date.'

I clasped his hand. 'Thank you, Doctor Banerji. You've no idea how happy you've made me.'

'I'm delighted to be the bearer of such good news. Now, don't forget to rest that leg.'

Tony punched the air when I told him, then hurried out to the garden to inform Marjorie who was snoozing on the veranda. He had to go to Cochin a couple of days later and returned with a velvet box containing a necklace of tiny rubies twisted into a coil. I was touched he'd managed to choose it himself and, this time, had found something so delightful. He was solicitous in the extreme, treating me like a delicate piece of porcelain. Even Marjorie softened a little. She was basking in the prospect of her forthcoming grand-motherly status and, while she still wasn't exactly pleasant, she eased back on the constant carping.

And, then one morning a few weeks later, I had a stabbing pain and ran into the bathroom where I bent double with cramping. I was bleeding. I called out to Nirmala. I could tell by the look on her face she knew I was losing the baby. Tony was in the tea gardens and couldn't be traced immediately. I didn't want Marjorie anywhere near me, so I told Nirmala to telephone Lilian, who hurried round and drove me straight to hospital. All the way there I was panting, sweating and clenching my legs together, willing my body to hold on to my unborn baby. But it was no use. There was nothing could be done.

I was terrified of what Tony's reaction would be and couldn't stop weeping, but when he arrived, he sat beside my hospital bed and took my hand. His face was crumpled, the habitual hard set of his jaw softened and his eyes filled with tears as he shook his head.

'I'm so very, very, sorry, darling.'

I was grateful he didn't blame me. He just looked at me with sad eyes and patted my hand. Communication between us had never been strong and, in this case, neither of us was any better equipped than usual to talk about what had happened. I was beyond being comforted. It felt as if I'd failed in some way in my responsibility to care for my baby. My body had let my unborn child down. I tortured myself as to what I had done wrong. Hadn't I eaten enough? Had I drunk too much? Was it that stupid fall with the Queen of Puddings? Though she said nothing, I could read accusations on any or all of these things in my mother-in-law's face.

But grief and sadness were weaknesses in Tony's eyes. Once he'd observed a brief period of mourning, his lip stiffened and the capable general manager took control. All was business and activity. I envied him his ability to push what had happened to one side, and I hoped he knew he couldn't expect me to do the same.

Once more I discovered the kindness of Lilian Bulstrode-Hemmings. She told me she had experienced three miscarriages herself and lost her first child in infancy, before safely giving birth to her son and daughter.

'It was cerebral malaria. Three years old. Running about happily in the morning and dead the same night. Bloody India.' She looked thoughtful, then added, 'Not that I wanted to leave. No matter how tough it gets, India crawls all over you and digs its way under your skin. I was born here, so it's in my blood.'

'It must have been so hard, losing a child that way.'

'India is hard for women and children, especially on the plains. Burning heat in the dry season so one would pray for the monsoon and, then when it came, it was worse. Everything soaking all the time: shoes covered in mould. Horrible. Sickness always a threat. But I'm a tough old bird. Daughter of the Empire. Bred for it, Ginny. I'd have hated being stuck in a house in England—I'd have climbed up the walls or beaten my own brains out. And my miscarriages were nothing to do with India. And yours isn't, either. It's incredibly common. Even in the home counties. I could give you the names of half a dozen women you probably know. But it's taboo. No one speaks of it. One is expected to grin and bear it. The main thing, my dear, is it's not your fault. You've not been negligent in any way. You'll have a healthy child one day. Just as I did.'

I tried to believe her.

I dreaded telling Pud, so I kept putting it off. Her letters were all about the war and its impact on her own daily life. I felt guilty and disloyal in keeping the miscarriage from her, but I couldn't face the prospect of putting how I felt about it into words. And as I couldn't relate to what those in Britain were going through and yet had little in common with my fellow exiles here, I felt stateless, alien and alone. At the club, I read out-of-date English newspapers with their reports of sea battles, but it was remote and unreal. Tony was preoccupied with the plantation and, since the war broke out, he'd joined a detachment of the auxiliary forces, The Southern Provinces Mounted Cavalry. It was more of an excuse to play at soldiers than a serious contribution to the defence of India, but it meant I saw less of him than ever.

I found out I was pregnant again. This time I lost my baby after only eight weeks. I miscarried the day we heard about the evacuation of Dunkirk. We were at the club for lunch. Tony was in the bar discussing the situation in France, and I was with Lilian in the library. I felt a failure. People don't understand. They don't get that, even though you don't even see or get to hold your baby, she's still your child. It still feels like your heart has been ripped out.

I ached for the child I'd never know, for how life might have been. Anger. Grief gnawing a hole in my insides that would never be filled. And, through it all, a sense of utter uselessness. My fault. My fault. All my fault.

Tony tried to be kind, but he was absorbed by a virulent insect that was threatening the tea gardens and had to be eradicated before it spread and killed off the rootstock. His grief was absorbed into other activity. Mummy used to say men are better than women at putting things in separate boxes and getting on with one task at a time, while we women get overwhelmed with the enormity of that one big thing and allow it to colour everything. I don't know if that's true, but it did surprise me how easily he got on with his life, while I just wanted mine to end.

I lay in bed for days, lacking the strength to get up and get out. Life was pointless. If I couldn't even manage to do what most women did as easily as breathing, then what did that say about me? Everywhere there were women with swelling bellies clutching the hands of children. British and Indian alike. It was like a sting of a lash. Their happiness taunted me, and my envy consumed me.

Lilian tried to buck me up. I grew tired of her ever cheerful face and her jolly hockey-sticks manner. Damn it. If I wanted to grieve, I was damn well going to grieve. And, in my heart of hearts, I knew I was also grieving for my mother, even though I didn't admit it—even to myself.

I DON'T KNOW what caused me to get on with life again. Maybe the body has a trigger mechanism that jerks you back into living. All I know is, that from one day to the next, I woke up feeling differently. I was still grieving. I still blamed myself. I was still sad. But, somehow, I'd started to function again.

In the dining room, the sun streamed through the slats of the shutters, where Nirmala had left them apart after dusting. The house was quiet. I supposed she and Thankappan were in the *godown* or at the market. I opened the shutters and went onto the veranda and sat down on a wooden steamer chair. The pair of whistling schoolboy birds that lived in the African tulip tree were splashing about in a pool of rainwater in an abandoned plant saucer on the lawn. The two thrushes played like children, teasing each other with short, sharp whistles as they splashed. I realised I was smiling.

I wanted Hector to stride up the driveway. I felt terrible about the way I'd dumped him but, more than that, I missed his company. It was all well and good for Tony to issue diktats about who I could or couldn't see when he was at work and I was left here to rot alone. He wouldn't see it that way. He'd never understood my aversion to the other women at the club. He was easy with their husbands and was never happier than bantering at the bar, playing billiards or hunting game with them. He expected me to get on with his friends' wives. But I wasn't the kind of woman they'd call "clubbable".

I WENT to meet Tony for dinner. I left it until the last minute, so I wouldn't have to hang around in the lounge while he was in the bar. It irritated me that women were not permitted to enter its hallowed portal. Tony's justification for this policy was "a chap's got to have somewhere he can relax and say what he thinks, without worrying he might be giving offence to the ladies". Never mind that being excluded was offence in its own right.

Every year after the summer monsoon, we always got a few members of "the fishing fleet": single, English women out for a short stay in the hope of bagging a husband. I'd often wondered why Tony hadn't succumbed to one before we were married. He was after all the best-looking man in the place and, as the general manager of Tilman's, would have been seen as a good catch by the fishers. Tonight, as I walked into the lounge he was there rather than in the bar and it wasn't just the fishing fleet clustered around him like wasps around a jam jar: all the regulars were there as well, belting out "For he's a jolly good fellow".

I stood on the edge of the group, wondering what he'd done to merit this, but feeling pleased it was my husband who was the centre of attention. Theo Bulstrode-Hemmings clapped a hand on my arm.

'You must be proud of him, eh Ginny?'

I had to raise my voice to be heard above the din of the chorusing crowd. 'I'm always proud of him, but I've no idea what he's done.'

'He hasn't told you? Probably didn't want you to worry until it was all over.'

'Are you going to enlighten me?'

'Took down a big brute of a bull elephant. Gone rogue. Trampled through the tea gardens and crashed into one of the cottages in the Muduvan village.'

'He killed an elephant?'

'One clean shot. Great sportsman, Tony. Always been a bit of a poor one myself. Not so bad at the pig sticking in my day, but give me a gun and I'll end up blowing your head off.' He roared laughing. 'Good man, Tony. Any excuse for a spot of game.'

The bell rang to summon us to dinner, and Tony hove up

beside me and slipped an arm through mine. He was flushed in the face. Half the club had been standing him drinks. I took advantage of his still euphoric state and Marjorie's absence to steer him towards one of the few remaining tables for two and he sat down, grinning inanely at me.

'You seem pleased with yourself,' I said.

'Huh? Nothing much.'

'Doesn't sound like nothing to me. A marauding elephant on one side, and you with a great big blunderbuss on the other.'

He gave me that funny blank look of his, which usually meant he was trying to work out whether I was joking or not.

I carried on regardless, 'Gosh, you're brave. Nothing but a loaded gun to protect you. Did you tell it to put up its trunk and surrender before you shot it?'

'Anyone would think you were being sarky.'

'I thought you had to get the *maharajah's* permission to kill an elephant? Hector said the *maharajah* has elephants *rampant* on his coat of arms. Maybe he should change it to elephants *dormant*—blasted by rampant hunters.'

He sneered. 'Hector. But as it happens, he's right. Elephants are protected by the royal family.'

'Then why did you kill it?'

'Because it was rogue.'

'Couldn't you have rounded it up? Like those Muduvan fellows did with the one we saw on the road. Remember?'

'Rounded it up?'

I hated the way he repeated my words like that. 'I mean they could have led it back to the forest. I can't believe you shot the poor creature. I know everyone here seems to think you're bloody Sanders of the River, but I think it's frightful.'

'Have you finished?' He was practically hissing his words. 'Don't make a scene.'

We finished our meal in silence.

In the car I started to speak, but he cut me off. 'Not yet.'

When we'd driven a short way down the hill, he pulled up at the side of the road and I realised it was the same place where we'd stopped for the calf elephant when I'd first come to Mudoorayam.

He switched off the ignition. 'First of all, I have the sole licence to shoot elephants in the district. Granted by the *maharajah* himself. Secondly, I'm only allowed to shoot if it's a killer. It's about bloody time you lost your romantic ideas about this country. Elephants are dangerous. Not like the ones in your blasted schoolgirl storybooks. It was a fully-grown adult male. Smashed its way through half the tea gardens. Rumoured to have killed several people in one of the Muduvan villages.'

'Rumoured?'

'I wasn't about to go and conduct a full scale investigation, while it flattened my crops and threatened my workers.'

'Had it actually killed anyone?'

He replied through clenched teeth, 'As it happens, no. Made a calculated judgement. What I'm paid to do. Make decisions every day. It's my job.' He gestured back up the road towards the club. 'Those people there understand. Why the hell can't you?'

He was yelling now. I hated that. All I wanted was for him to stop.

'I'm sorry. I didn't realise.'

'No. You never do, do you? Plough straight in and make accusations before checking your facts. Bloody well sick of it.'

I'd expected him to ignore me that night. I thought his anger would mean he'd shun me in bed, something he was doing more often lately. Instead, it was as though the row in the car had dissipated his anger and maybe the adulation everyone else had shown him at the club had fuelled his testosterone. He was waiting for me in the dark when I came in from the bathroom. When I turned the light on, he told me to switch it off and, as I drew back the bedcovers, he pulled me to him and took me with an enthusiasm he hadn't shown for some time. For my part, I just felt sad. Sad that we'd come to this. So out of tune with each other and our relative moods, needs and motivations.

Next morning, over his soft-boiled egg, I asked him what would happen to the elephant.

'Told you, it's dead.'

'I mean its body? The carcass?'

'No idea. You and the Hindus can give it a bloody state funeral for all I care.'

He paused, thinking for a moment. 'There's the tusks of course. Have to offer them to the *maharajah*. He'll refuse politely, though. Suppose we'll get to keep them.'

He looked up as though picturing them on the wall over the fireplace. 'It was a big tusker with a fine pair.'

'I don't want them here. I've accepted you had to do it. I'm not going to raise that again, but I'm putting my foot down over you hanging tusks on the wall. I don't want them in the house.'

He shrugged.

'Right then. Piano keys and knife handles. Or I'll ask if they want them in the club.'

Best place for them.

OUR QUARREL over the elephant was forgotten when we found out Germany had begun bombing London. It was a day of vibrant sunshine in Muddy, following the end of the rains. He telephoned from the factory to tell me the news. That evening, the club was buzzing with it.

When we were getting ready for bed, I asked him what was going to happen. 'Do you think it'll go on for long? Thank God, we're far away from it all here.'

He looked away. 'Not far enough.'

'Don't say that.'

'The Japs know that, with what's going on in Europe, we're exposed here and don't have the means to defend India. And not just the Japs—the blasted Indians could rise up and start fighting us.'

'Gandhi's a pacifist. He's not going to incite anyone to start fighting us.'

'Not literally—far too cunning for that. He and those congress *wallahs* are always on the lookout for ways to mess things up for us. Bound to try and take advantage of trouble on the home front to make trouble here, too. Doesn't look good. Not good at all.'

CHAPTER 17

INDIAN WEDDINGS CAN LAST for days. Dr Banerji's was a less protracted affair, although still on a grand scale, with no expense spared. I loved the ritual and colour of it all.

Instead of exchanging rings, the bridegroom tied a *thali*, a sacred thread smeared in turmeric paste, around the neck of his bride, to signify the permanence of the union. Once the *thali* was secured, the couple walked hand in hand three times around a sacred fire. To symbolise the union of their minds as well as bodies, the groom bent forward and touched his forehead against his bride's and she flung puffed rice into the fire as an offering. The guests threw rice and flower petals over the couple.

After the ceremony, there was a formal presentation of the couple and a meal for hundreds of guests. It was, of course, an arranged marriage. But he looked happy. The bride gazed shyly at her new husband throughout the proceedings. I supposed a doctor of medicine would be seen as a desirable match.

They were a handsome couple; the groom as elegant as the bride. His white coat was encrusted with tiny seed pearls and sequins, and he wore a large, jewelled droplet in the centre of his forehead under a ceremonial turban. His wife's red sari was sumptuous, heavily embroidered; the gold thread, pearls and beads that covered the fabric shimmered under the lights of the hotel ballroom. Her arms were weighed down with colourful bangles, and she had a red *bindi* in the centre of her forehead. They sat garlanded with flowers on an arched throne, on a raised dais. As Tony and I joined the queue of people lining up to be presented, I thought of our own wedding and what a drab affair it had been in contrast to this, and of Dr Banerji's advice about my fertility. I hoped he and his new wife would be luckier than me.

Once we'd exchanged greetings with the bridal party, we followed the throng into the hotel dining room, where an enormous buffet spread awaited us. The meal was accompanied by the plaintive twanging of the sitar and the rhythmic beat of the tabla from a group of musicians. Marjorie had stayed at home. Evidently gracing an Indian family occasion with her imperial presence was a bridge too far in Anglo-Indian relations. I spotted Lilian and sat down with her, while Tony and Theo repaired to the bar.

As we were talking, there was a commotion behind us and we heard Theo's raised voice.

'Steady on old chap. You've had a few too many. It's time you went home.'

He was addressing Hector. My former pal was looking the worse for wear; his normally immaculate clothing was crumpled and his hair lank and dishevelled. He saw me and began lurching towards me.

'As for you...' his voice was slurred, 'fine friend you turned out to be. A bloody fair-weather one aren't you, Mrs Tilman?'

I blushed to my roots. He was right.

Theo Bulstrode-Hemmings grabbed his arm and steadied

him as he veered sideways into our table, spilling his drink over Lilian's sleeve. He brushed Theo off and turned to Lilian.

'Frightfully sorry, old girl. Always had a piss poor aim. Meant to get her.' He jerked his head in my direction.

Before he could say anything else, Theo and Tony each took an arm and propelled him out of the room.

'What on earth was that all about?' Lilian asked me.

'I'm so sorry. Did he soak you?'

'It's nothing. It's certainly not the first time I've had a gin and tonic all over me, and I dare say it won't be the last.'

'Hector's angry with me because I've dropped him.'

'Dropped him? I thought you two were thick as thieves?'

'Tony doesn't like him and thinks he's a bad influence.'

She looked at me over the top of her spectacles. 'And what do *you* think?'

'Well, I think that's rubbish of course. He's completely harmless.'

'I'm inclined to agree with you, my dear. Surely Tony doesn't think Hector's going to turn you into a homosexual?' She laughed heartily at her own joke, and slapped her knee.

'I suspect it's actually because Hector's so clever.'

'You could be right about that. He's a bit too clever for his own good. And he's not interested in the things the other chaps are. Theo's always saying Hector eats dictionaries for breakfast—in several languages.'

She hesitated, then gave me a quizzical look. 'But it does seem a bit extreme for you to drop him just because Tony doesn't like him. I'd got you down as a young woman who knows her own mind.' She patted my arm as she spoke.

I felt ashamed. 'I do, well I think I do, but I don't want to upset Tony. He found out I'd been going up to the Hindu temple to paint and blamed it on Hector. He thinks the Indians don't like me being there.'

She shrugged. 'I can't imagine they'd care.'

'And he found out Hector had taken me to an independence movement meeting, while he was in Coimbatore.'

'Oops.' She shook her head.

'It was only a demonstration on spinning cotton, with a dull chap banging on about self-sufficiency and Mr Gandhi's code for living. I thought it was all a bit daft, really. As if the government would give two hoots about a few people making their own cloth. And now there's a war on, it's likely to be the last thing on their minds.'

'You're right about that.'

'I'd thought at least it would involve someone ranting about violent insurrection. That would have been something. Bit of a let-down really to be in Tony's bad books just for attending a home economics lecture.'

Lilian roared with laughter, then placed a hand on my arm. 'We're joking, but we just don't know what will come of it all eventually. There are some real hotheads on all sides and, instead of concentrating on what's right for India and the people, they spend all their energy on infighting. Then, when you throw in the obduracy of some of our own countrymen, it's a recipe for disaster. I fear for the future.'

'At least we're not in Britain with bombs raining down on us.'

'There's that to be thankful for. It's such a worry. Thank God all mine are in the countryside. How about you, Ginny? Any family in London?'

'Not since Mummy died. I have an aunt in the Yorkshire Dales.'

She glanced in the direction the men had gone, dragging Hector between them. 'So Hector has the hump, because you've sent him to Coventry? No excuse for his behaviour. I can't imagine what got into him.'

'It does seem an overreaction. And he can normally hold his drink.'

I felt a hand on my shoulder, and turned to find Jagadish Mistry standing there. He crouched between Lilian and me, with a hand on the back of each of our chairs. She didn't seem bothered in the slightest at his over-familiarity.

'Ladies, are you enjoying yourselves?'

Lilian beamed at him. 'Who doesn't love a wedding, Mr Mistry? And Indian ones are so colourful.' She gestured at the heavily laden buffet table and the uniformed waiters. 'The spread is absolutely delicious and so generous.'

'They make a fine couple, don't you think, Mrs Tilman?'

I mumbled my agreement and then got to my feet and, making a hurried excuse, headed for the powder room. When I emerged, he was waiting for me, leaning against the wall opposite, one leg bent under him, foot on the wall, smoking a cigarette, one of those vile-smelling local ones.

I started to walk past him, but he reached for my arm. I pulled away.

'You really don't like me, do you? Have I offended in you in some way? Because that's the last thing I want to do,' he said.

'I have to get back to Lilian.'

'My offer still stands.'

'What offer?'

'To show you the High Ranges.'

I didn't know what to say. To refuse would be to make his offer seem inappropriate, to confer more meaning on it than was perhaps intended. But to accept was unthinkable. I looked around hoping Lilian would materialise, but she didn't.

'That's kind of you. Maybe I'll take you up on it one day.'

He was between me and the room where Lilian was waiting, so rather than squeeze past him, I nodded my goodbye and headed in the opposite direction. I glanced through an open doorway as I passed. My husband was inside talking intently to a woman I'd never seen before. They were sitting on a wide sofa, yet were so close to each other there was no space between them. They didn't see me. I hurried back to Lilian with a gnawing anxiety.

'Do you know someone called Daphne?'

She looked surprised. 'Daphne Bingham? She used to come up from Cochin for the summer months. Her husband was something important to do with water management but he died about six years ago—heart attack, I think.'

I decided to plunge right in, 'Did Tony want to marry her?'

She looked around as though hoping for an escape route, then gave me one of her motherly pats on the arm. 'I don't think it went that far. They were friendly—you know what it's like, Ginny, we all live in each other's pockets at the club. He was kind to her—we all tried to rally round when Cyril died. Has he mentioned her then?'

'No, but Marjorie has—she said something about her objecting to Tony marrying someone called Daphne. She implied she'd stood in their way.'

Lilian raised her eyes to the ceiling and sighed. 'Marjorie's such a trouble maker. Ignore her, Ginny. It was a long time ago. Long before you and Tony met. Daphne Bingham went back to Britain at the end of '35. I remember, because she took some packages for my grandchildren with her.'

'Who's the woman I saw Tony talking to just now?'

'What woman? Where?'

'In a little bar just off the corridor. They were deep in conversation. I've never seen her before.'

'It can't possibly be Daphne. That would be too ridiculous for words. She can't...'

Her voice trailed away, and I realised she was looking

past me. The woman, now alone, was standing in the doorway waving at Lilian. She came towards us her arms extended.

'Darling Lily. What do think of my surprise? Too exciting. I simply had to be here for the doc's big day.'

She was tall and carried herself with an easy elegance that made me feel as though I'd shrunk down to the skirting boards. Her dress of printed crepe de chine was cinched at the waist, and she wore a single rope of enormous pearls, perfectly offsetting brown hair brushed back and pinned at one side, so soft waves framed either side of her face. She was about fifteen years older than me and, while her individual features were perhaps not classically beautiful, all the eyes in the room were drawn to her.

She wrapped Lilian in an embrace, then turned to me with a quizzical look and Lilian introduced us.

'So *you* are Tony's wife. I've heard a lot about you.'

I felt myself flushing, and clenched my fists at my sides in anger. I say anger, but it was born of jealousy. It wasn't hard to imagine why Tony had wanted to marry her. And being an older woman and a widow, I could guess why Marjorie would have opposed it. And Daphne Bingham did not look the compliant, easily malleable type I think my mother-in-law had once believed me to be.

'Are you back in Muddy for good then?' Lilian asked.

'Not sure. I've been staying at the coast with some friends for a few months, and I'm trying to decide whether to come back here or take a place by the ocean. I'm at the Thomsons' house while they're on leave, so I'll be in Muddy for at least another month.'

My brain whirled. I saw Tony's frequent trips away in a different light. Within five minutes of meeting her, I was convinced she was my husband's mistress.

She wafted off to speak with someone else just as Tony

returned. I wanted to know if he'd mention that he'd been talking to her, so I asked him where he'd been.

'Theo and I had to send that fool Channing home. Pissed as a newt. Took us ages to find a *tonga* and put him in it.'

***

THE MORNING AFTER THE WEDDING, I was painting when Nirmala told me I was wanted urgently on the telephone. It was Hector's bearer, Uddi, in a state of near panic.

'Come quickly please, *Memsahib*. Mr Hector is very bad, very, very, bad.'

'Steady on, Uddi. Tell me what's going on?'

'I am thinking he is dying, *Memsahib*. Please, please come at once.'

'Have you called the doctor?'

'Dr Banerji is away visiting the family of his new bride.'

'Well, call the locum.'

'Mr Hector never sees any doctor than Dr Banerji.'

'Good grief, Uddi. If he's being that picky, he can't be dying.'

'Please come, *Memsahib*.' His voice was breaking.

'Very well, but as soon as I hang up I want you to call a doctor. I don't care what Mr Channing says. Do it, Uddi.'

'Very good, *Memsahib*. Immediately I am calling for doctor. I will later tell Mr Hector you made me do so.'

'Yes, yes, you do that. I'll be there as soon as I can.'

When I walked into Hector's room, he was on the bed wearing silk pyjamas. The first unusual thing I noticed was his eyes. The pupils were more dilated than I'd seen before in a human being or have ever seen since, turning his usually, clear, blue eyes into two dark saucers with a narrow blue border. He was staring into space with his mouth squeezed shut and his nostrils flared, like a runaway horse. Beads of sweat covered his forehead, despite the cool of the day. His skin was as pale as the pillow, and he resembled a crucified corpse with arms splayed out beside him. It was obvious he was seriously ill.

Uddi was wringing his hands in consternation and hopping between one foot and the other.

'How long has he been like this?'

'I am calling you as soon as I am finding him. This morning when I am awakening him, he is asking me to bring him some boiling water instead of tea. I am leaving it with him and coming back in half an hour to bring breakfast and am finding him like this.'

'The doctor?'

'Doctor is coming.'

I took Hector's hand. Cold and clammy. His body jerked into a spasm and he arched up in the bed, then his feet twitched and poked out from under the sheets and he collapsed back down again.

'Hector. Look at me. Can you hear me?'

His eyes rolled like a pair of marbles and thick, white foam coated his lips.

'Where the hell is the doctor, Uddi? Call him again. This is serious. Hurry up.'

Uddi ran from the room. I grabbed an embroidered linen cloth from the abandoned breakfast tray and tried to wipe Hector's mouth, but his face convulsed into a grimace like a gargoyle. Then he made a gut-wrenching cry. I was terrified. Uddi might be right about him dying. I looked around the room as though hoping a miraculous cure for his strange condition might manifest itself magically in front of me, but all I saw was an orderly bedroom; immaculately organised wardrobe, shelves stacked neatly with highly polished shoes, all with wooden trees inside, piles of books and a vase of white flowers on the table and hundreds more books in the book cases that lined all the walls. His pupils were still dilated and his eyes were full of tears.

'Hector, can you hear me? It's Ginny. Give me a sign you can hear me.'

I held his sweaty hand in mine, but he gave me no signal. The white foam frothed through his lips, even though his mouth was closed. He started wheezing, and I could see the now rapid rise and fall of his chest. I thought he was having a heart attack.

Then I saw the glass by the bed. It had half an inch of liquid in the bottom, over which was a soggy layer of what looked like crushed tissue paper. I picked up the glass and sniffed the contents. A sickly, sweet smell. Then, at once, I knew. I looked at the table and the vase filled with white, bell-like shapes of angel's trumpets. *Datura*: the flowers I'd admired when we visited the temple together, highly toxic blooms that covered the riverbanks and roadsides all around the town. He must have made an infusion with the petals.

Uddi returned with the doctor, a smartly dressed Scotsman of advanced years. I'd never met him, so he can't have bothered with the club. He was a retired medical officer from the Mudoorayam General Hospital.

He went straight to the bedside, gesturing to me to move out of his way.

'Doctor, I think Mr Channing has drunk tea made from the petals of these flowers.' I pointed at the vase.

He ignored me and poked and prodded at Hector, taking his rapidly racing pulse, listening with his stethoscope and examining his dilated pupils with a magnifying glass.

Finally, he acknowledged my presence. 'I'm admitting him to hospital to have his stomach pumped.'

'Oh, God. How terrible.'

As I spoke, Hector sat bolt upright in the bed and began to scream. His eyes were full of terror, and I could tell he was in severe pain and distress.

'*Datura* poisoning can have serious consequences. Even death. It's like deadly nightshade. We need to empty his stomach, then monitor him for a couple of days, assuming he pulls through. Right now he's in a hallucinogenic state. He'll have absolutely no idea what's going on. He probably won't even remember this afterwards.'

That didn't sound promising.

'He will pull though, won't he?'

'He seems fairly strong and healthy. That will help.'

Hector slumped back on the pillow and appeared to lose consciousness. The doctor was by the door making arrangements with Uddi for the transport of the patient to hospital.

'He's fallen unconscious.'

'That's normal with this type of poisoning. He may stay asleep for some time, or even go into a coma.'

'A coma?' A chill ran up my arms.

'Once we've pumped him out and got him on a rehydration drip, he should recover.'

He looked me in the eye for the first time since he'd arrived. 'Do you have any idea what caused him to do something so stupid? Didn't he know *datura* is poisonous?'

'Yes, he did. He told me about the plants once. That's what made me realise what he'd done.'

'But why did he do it? Mrs....?'

'Tilman. I don't know. I can't imagine what possessed him.'

'Is he the sort of person who take risks?'

I thought of him with his bearer and his cabinet minister —maybe he was? But I replied, 'Not as far as I know.'

'Does he experiment with narcotics?'

'Certainly not. Well, not to my knowledge. His preferred poison is gin.'

'There are only two possible reasons for someone to deliberately ingest *datura*: for a hallucinogenic experience or to take one's own life. There are manifest risks associated with the former, and as you will have observed, there are horrible side effects. If he pulls through, I suggest you tell Mr Channing that, if he wishes to kill himself, he'll find a gun or a rope brings about a more rapid and effective conclusion. If he wants a painful and slow death, then he should make sure he crushes the seeds with the leaves and avoids the petals altogether, and then take himself off to a place where no one will find him until his agonising death is concluded. That way, he'll help preserve the strained resources of the general hospital. Now, I think that's the ambulance I hear.'

Within a couple of minutes, the hospital bearers had Hector on a stretcher and carried him out to the waiting vehicle, accompanied by Uddi. I looked about me, searching for a clue as to what could have caused Hector to do such a thing? After his drunken behaviour at the wedding the previous day, I had a horrible feeling it might have something to do with me. I picked up the heavy vase of flowers and walked around to the back of the bungalow, where I tipped the contents into the gully behind the house.

CHAPTER 18

I JUMPED in a *tonga* and went straight to the hospital, but was told I couldn't see Hector until the following day. Walking along the disinfectant-smelling corridors the next afternoon reminded me of my mother lying dying in her hospital bed, so I was filled with dread at what I might find. But Hector was cut from a tougher cloth: he was sitting up reading a copy of *Decline and Fall of the Roman Empire*.

I grabbed his hands, relieved at his rapid recovery.

'Watch out. Don't make me lose my place.' He put the book to one side. 'I believe I have you to thank for saving my life, Mrs T?'

'Oh, Hector, what on earth possessed you? You knew those flowers were poisonous. What were you thinking of?'

'Just a little experiment, my dear. Not a well thought-out one, though.'

'I was totally terrified. I thought you were an absolute goner.'

'Like most things I do, I made a botched job of it.'

'You weren't really trying to kill yourself?'

'Of course not. I told you it was an experiment.'

'But why?'

'I was hoping to discover enlightenment.'

'That's absurd. Can you remember anything? The doctor said you may not.'

'Sadly, no. Not a bally thing. It was all a complete and utter waste of time.'

'Well, it's a jolly good thing you can't remember as I, for one, won't ever forget and it was vile. Absolutely hideous. You were in the most dreadful agony. It was positively terrifying for me and poor little Uddi, and can't have been a pleasant experience for you at that time, so it's not one ever to be repeated—promise me?'

'Don't worry, Mrs T. I won't be messing around with exotic plant life again. Now tell me what's new. I'm bored out of my mind here. Maybe you can convince that miserable excuse for a doctor to let me out. He says I have to stay at least another day for observation.'

I realised we'd both assumed, without saying, that this incident would mark the end of our hostilities. I decided not to probe why he did it, nor to question his behaviour at the Banerji wedding. I didn't want to push my luck. Without saying anything, we'd moved on and picked up our friendship as casually as if we were putting on a familiar shrugged-off, woollen cardigan.

'Gosh, I forgot. Have you heard the news? The war's taken off in a big way. They're fighting over Britain from the air. Can you imagine? Planes shooting each other down over the fields of Kent and Sussex? I was reading the papers just now and it's frightening. The Germans are sending hundreds of planes over every day, and our boys are up there too, and they're literally blasting each other out of the skies. Absolutely vile.'

'You disappoint me, Mrs T. I might have to rethink my

assumption that you're a selfish, empty-headed, little creature who cares not a fig for her fellow man.'

'Do you really think that?'

'But, of course. It's true.'

'I do care. I just don't always get politics. And the war didn't really seem like a proper war at first. But, now, it's different.'

'Rubbish. You understand far more than you let on. I'd be foolish to assume there's nothing going on in that pretty head of yours.'

'Do you really think that about me not caring a fig for other people?'

'Well, do you? Really?'

'Yes, of course, I do.' I hesitated. 'Well, apart from the bores at the Planters' Club...'

'They're not all bores, you know.'

'Lilian's a bit of a brick, really. And I suppose Rogers and his wife aren't so bad...'

'And...?'

I looked down and started to pick at the tufts of the candlewick bedspread.

'You find it hard to even remember their names, don't you? You really are entirely wrapped up in yourself. Maybe that's what I like about you. Unashamedly selfish.'

I could feel tears welling. I decided to tell him. 'While I wasn't seeing you, something happened. I was expecting a baby. It happened twice, and both times I lost the child. Do you think it's a punishment? For me being selfish?'

He reached for my hand and squeezed it. 'I'm so sorry, my dear. I had no idea. You poor darling.'

'I wasn't going to tell you. But I've missed you so much. And I've been rather down in the dumps.'

'Understandably.'

He squeezed my hand again.

I WAS glad I'd made it up with Hector, but resurrecting our friendship did little to lift my gloom. His run-in with the angel's trumpets was a source of anxiety, particularly as a part of me still doubted his claim his ingestion of the plants was purely experimental. Linked with his behaviour towards me at Dr Banerji's wedding, I wondered if he'd been depressed and my cold-shouldering of him might have been the cause. Had he tried to kill himself? It was incredibly self-centred of me to imagine my withdrawal of friendship would be enough to tip a man like Hector over the edge. But I had no other explanation.

Whatever the truth, Hector reverted to type and tried to lure me back to our gin-soaked afternoons. I was having none of it though. I'd come to the conclusion gin made me more miserable and encouraged me to dwell on my failure to have a child. Now Daphne Bingham had appeared from nowhere, I was determined she wasn't going to take Tony from me. I took Banerji's advice and stayed off the alcohol. Until I had established what was going on, I didn't want to antagonise Tony, so I only saw Hector when I was sure there was no risk of being spotted. I never found out who had told Tony about my trips to the temple, so decided to trust no one.

Then, one day, the story of Savita changed things for me —although I didn't know then her name was Savita. I was at the market with Hector and we were sitting at a beverage kiosk opposite the district court, while he smoked a cigar and I had a cup of tea. A group of people began to gather outside. Every now and then a man would emerge from the court building to relay a message to the growing throng, which became increasingly restless. Hector strolled over to speak with one of the men on the fringes, then returned, shaking his head.

'What's happening?'

As I asked the question, the court doors swung open and an angry crowd emerged. A man shouted and those waiting on the pavement began a chant in response. A police van emerged from behind the building and tried to get through the blocked street. This incensed the rabble and they hammered on the roof of the vehicle and the shouting grew louder.

I looked at Hector anxiously.

'This could get unpleasant,' he said.

As he spoke, John Simpson, the local police chief, emerged with a group of Indian policemen behind him, batons raised.

Simpson held a megaphone and spoke in Tamil in a slow, authoritative voice. A few men on the edge of the crowd— and they were all men—turned and walked away until eventually the whole gathering dispersed.

'Are you going to enlighten me?'

'The court has just passed sentence on a man for the murder of his daughter and on his son, her brother, who helped him do it.'

'They killed their own family member? How dreadful. Why on earth did they do it?'

'She was raped by a friend of the father's.'

I gagged. There was a bitter taste in my mouth. It made no sense. 'Then why did they kill her? Why didn't they kill him?'

Hector shrugged. 'They did that too. These things happen from time to time. Family feuds. Vengeance. It's hard to unpick all the reasons. Both father and son have been sentenced to death. The sentence is supposed to be a deterrent to this kind of crime, but the courts are fighting a losing battle.'

'And the woman who was raped and murdered?'

'I don't know any more than that. Come on, let's get

going. I want to get to the post office before it shuts.'

I didn't move. He walked off, then stopped when he realised I wasn't following.

My stomach churned and I thought I was going to vomit. Four people dead or about to be. How old was the girl? Raped by her father's friend. Murdered by her own family.

Hector sat down again. 'What gives, Mrs T?' He laid his hand over mine and squeezed it. I started to cry.

'Hey, hey! What's wrong? Tell Uncle Hector.' He passed me a handkerchief.

I blew my nose loudly and felt a bit better. I reached out and he wrapped his big hand around mine.

'It happened to me,' I said.

'What happened?'

'He was a friend of my father's.' I couldn't bear to look at Hector. 'He made me think I wanted it to happen. He worked on me over time, and I realise now he planned every move. But then I thought he was just being kind. I thought he loved me. I thought he was my friend.'

Hector was silent for a moment, then picked up my hand again. 'How old were you?'

Lying to Hector had always been impossible, but my voice was barely a whisper, 'Fourteen.'

'And how old was the man.'

'I don't know exactly. Fifty? Fifty-five?'

A look of disgust crossed his face, to be replaced with a more neutral expression. I said nothing, but began to scuff my shoes on the ground and wondered what to do. I felt like a little girl again. Scared but, at the same time, relieved. There was something about Hector made trusting him easy. 'I can't believe I'm telling you all this.'

'Perhaps you needed to get it off your chest? Did your mother know?'

'She had no idea it was happening at the time. She was furious when she found out. She said he'd done it to get back at her.'

'What did she mean?'

'He went out with her. Years before. They were engaged. It was before she met my father. Rupert—that's the man—was angry when she married Daddy rather than him.'

'You seriously think he went after you when you were still a child to punish her for marrying your father?'

'Yes. Well, that's what she thought.'

'And, yet, he kept it secret? How was that supposed to punish her?'

'I don't know. Maybe he knew she'd find out in the end. He'd started getting careless.'

'Did he force you?'

I sat rigid-backed in the chair and looked around, fearful we might be overheard. 'I didn't want to do what he wanted at first. I didn't like it. What he did felt wrong. Dirty. He made me to do things I hated. But, afterwards, he was kind to me. And he was always so interested in me. I thought he loved me. As the time went by, I thought I loved him too.'

I was screwing up the fabric of my poplin frock in my clenched fist. Hector was silent, leaning back in his chair, listening.

'But it was all a lie. He didn't care for me at all. He just used me. My mother said he'd had hundreds of affairs. An inveterate philanderer—that's what she called him. I felt so stupid, so used. I'm ashamed about what we did.'

Hector didn't offer any sympathy. If he'd tried to give me a comforting hug or words of kindness, I'd have felt worse and wouldn't have been able to suppress the tears. I actually felt better for having got it off my chest.

Eventually, he spoke, 'I was only nine when it happened to me. It was one of the masters at school. I know what it feels like, that feeling of being used. Of being ashamed. I used to ask myself why he picked on me. Was there something about me that was different from the other boys? Then I found out years later he was doing it to most of us. None of us told. We were all too scared. He was an authority figure. I thought no one would believe me. A snotty-nosed boy's word against a respected master's. Bastard.'

'Is that what made you...?'

He laughed. 'Made me what? A homo? No, my dear. That was ordained by the gods, from the womb. I've always known—and despite him. Exploiting children has nothing to do with being queer. And no matter what his orientation, a nine-year-old child is a vulnerable creature, who doesn't want to have his teacher taking him from his warm bed in the middle of the night and forcing him to do things he finds frightening and painful.'

I felt a sense of relief at having shared my secret at last. Now there was someone to whom I didn't need to lie. Someone who might understand me.

'Mine wasn't like your experience. Rupert was kind to me. I really thought I loved him.'

'Oldest trick in the book, darling. To cover you in kindness, reassure you, praise you, reward you, win you over so you'd never tell. He had you in his power.'

'I thought it was my choice.'

He spoke more gently, 'At fourteen?'

I looked away. I knew he was right.

EVERYTHING HAD GONE WRONG. I'd lost two babies and was petrified of another pregnancy. I was afraid I'd lost my husband. I was lonely. And the incident at the court brought Rupert Milligan back to me from the place where I'd shut him away. And it wasn't the Rupert I'd believed I loved, but the other Milligan—the one who had hypnotised a bereaved child, raped her and then convinced her it was a beautiful and loving thing.

Muddy was oppressive, especially now during the rains. The thought of a London pea-souper, of hailing a taxi instead of a *tonga*, wandering around a museum or art gallery and taking tea at Fortnum's, filled me with nostalgia and longing. I was cut off from what was happening back in England and wondered how the advent of War was affecting everyday life. Most of all, I missed Pud and worried constantly about her. But I knew returning to London was not going to solve my problems. I'd be running away from them. And running back into Milligan's world. That was unthinkable.

I could hear my mother saying over and over in my head, *"You've made your bed, Virginia, so you can jolly well lie in it."* I missed her too, despite all her faults and her terrible snobbery. I was so lonely.

CHAPTER 19

THE HIGHLIGHT of the Mudoorayam social calendar was the annual polo match between the planters and the summer government visitors. It took place on a maidan above the town and everyone who was anyone was there. It was also one of the few ostensibly British social occasions when Indians were well represented—probably because they invented the game.

Tony was captaining the planters' team. He claimed not to be a great horseman—more used to walking his horse sedately around the tea gardens—and wasn't awfully keen on polo as it didn't involve firing guns or sticking spears into pigs, but he loved a chance to compete, and the rivalry between the planters and the snootier government officials was rife.

I knew nothing about polo, but was soon caught up in the excitement of what was a fiercely contested match. Hector turned out to be something of a non-playing expert.

'I've had plenty of practice as a spectator, darling. It's a good way to sort the men from the boys.'

He ran through the rules with me and offered a running

commentary on the individual players' styles. Tony's second-in-command at the plantation, Jim Walters, was a bit of a miss-hitter and Hector diagnosed too strong a grip on the mallet, causing him to give away a series of fouls to the opposition. I couldn't work out the science, but I could certainly see the difference between Jim's swing and that of the undoubted best player on the field, Jagadish Mistry. The government team had a couple of good players but the planters, despite the handicap of Walters, were running away with the match. I was impressed with Tony's skill on a polo pony. While not in the same league as Mistry, he was making a respectable fist of it.

Mistry was fast and perfectly balanced on his pony, perched slightly above his saddle, the pendulum swings of his mallet cutting smooth arcs through the air and always making perfect contact with the ball, sending it on a straight trajectory. He was riding a grey thoroughbred, frisky and nimble, which he was able to turn on a threepenny bit.

'There's nothing I like more than a fine piece of horse-flesh—except, of course, an even finer rider.' Hector's voice had a salacious tone. 'What I wouldn't give for a few hours alone with that young man. "*As if an angel dropp'd down from the clouds, To turn and wind a fiery Pegasus, And witch the world with noble horsemanship.*" '

'Stop it, Hector. I hate it when you talk like that.'

'What? You don't like the Bard?'

'I don't mean the Shakespeare. I mean all that lovelorn, sighing, nonsense.'

'Alas, you have no romance in you, do you, Mrs T?'

'I'd just hate to see you making a fool of yourself.'

'Don't worry, darling. I know it's a hopeless cause. But allow me my dreams, won't you?

At half-time, we went onto the field with the other spectators to stamp down the divots. This was as much a part of the entertainment as the game itself, and the occasion for conversation and analysis of the highlights of the preceding chukkas. I was enjoying myself until I spotted Daphne Bingham on the other side of the field. She wasn't participating in the divot stamping, but was holding the reins of Tony's pony, while he changed the saddle. I stopped what I'd been saying to Hector midsentence.

'What's wrong?' he asked.

'Do you know that woman? Daphne Bingham. Over there. Talking to Tony.'

'The Black Widow? I'd heard she was back in town. I thought we'd seen the last of her years ago.'

'You don't like her then?' I tried to disguise the satisfaction in my voice.

'I wouldn't go that far. I just like to make sure I keep the fenders on when she's coming alongside.'

I couldn't stop myself. 'I think she's having an affair with Tony.'

He raised his eyebrows and then, in one uninterrupted movement, dropped them into an exaggerated frown.

'And what gives you that idea?'

'He wanted to marry Daphne, but Marjorie put a stop to it. And she's been back in India for months staying at the coast. I think he's been seeing her.'

'And do you have the slightest shred of evidence for that?'

'Woman's intuition.' I tried to sound worldly wise, but I'm not sure it worked.

'So Marjorie told you she'd put the cat among the matrimonial pigeons for Daphne, did she?'

I nodded.

'I think the lady takes too much credit. She may well have wanted to stop Tony marrying the merry widow but, as it happens, Mrs Bingham had ideas of her own and they didn't include your husband.'

I looked over to where she was standing stroking the neck of Tony's horse. 'So what were those ideas?'

'She has expensive tastes, does our Daphne. Cyril left her well-provided, but it wasn't enough for her. She may well have dallied a while with Tony but, as soon as she realised despite having his name over the factory door, he was just a hired hand, she wanted no more of him. Poor chap was dumped like a barrel of bad fish and was quite cut up about it. Till you came along, of course, and made him forget Daphne's dubious charms.'

I jerked my head towards the pair at the edge of the field. 'Doesn't look as though she wants no more of him now.'

'I wouldn't take any notice of that, darling; Daphne Bingham is a terrible flirt and loves nothing more than having her adoring acolytes around her. Your husband now represents a challenge. She won't be too pleased that he so speedily got over his broken heart and managed to pluck another apple from the orchard. And, of course, she'll hate the fact that, instead of an over-ripe windfall, he's bagged a bright and shiny new fruit from the top of the tree.'

I slapped him playfully. Hector always managed to cheer me up when I felt low. But as I looked across the polo field, I wished I could say his fruity metaphors convinced me. I turned back to the task in hand, pleased replacing the divots gave me a perfect excuse to stamp my feet.

When the next chukka began, I positioned myself so I could watch the unfolding drama on the field of play, but also keep Daphne Bingham in sight. She was a picture of casual elegance, in immaculately tailored wide-legged trousers and a simple, open-necked blouse. I was suddenly conscious of the creases in my linen skirt.

Hector went off at the end of the chukka to procure me a cup of tea. I was relieved to see Tony was alone as he changed his pony. Then, I felt a hand on my arm. It was Daphne Bingham.

'I thought I saw you over here,' she said. 'Tony is doing awfully well this afternoon. They're absolutely clobbering the government *wallahs*. Do you like polo?'

I muttered a greeting, then said, 'This is the first game I've seen. I'm enjoying it.'

'Didn't you come out a few years ago?'

Thinking she meant to India, I was about to answer, when she added, 'I remember. You weren't actually presented, were you? Some fuss about a painting wasn't it? I remember now—my late husband's niece is a chum of yours —Rita Carruthers. She said something about a cheeky painting. Well, jolly good for you, I say. And why not? You show them. A bunch of fuddy-duddies. It was that rather good society artist wasn't it? What's his name? Middleton—no Milligan—that's the one. Rita said it was a fine likeness. Do you have it? I bet it would look marvellous over the fireplace in the dining room. Tony used to say he was saving the space for a nice pair of tusks, but I'm sure a portrait of you would look much better. Terribly modern. What does Marjorie think?'

I was struck dumb. The woman was more or less threatening me. That was the only interpretation, despite the beaming smile. As I was wondering how to respond, Hector returned with the tea.

'Are you all right, Mrs T? You look a little pale. You're not causing trouble are you, Daffers?'

'As if. No, I was just asking Mrs Tilman about her coming out. It turns out she's a pal of my niece, Rita, who told me all about what a talented and interesting woman she is. Good stuff, eh? And how the heck are you, Hector, you horrible man? Still as catty as ever?'

'I couldn't pretend to be in the same league as you.'

She leaned forward and flicked the tip of his nose with her finger, then headed off.

The final chukka concluded with a series of goals in rapid and alternating succession from each side, turning the crowd of onlookers on the maidan into a fever of anticipation. But, despite this late rally by administrators, the victory was the planters'. Tony accepted the silver rose bowl from the Resident's wife on behalf of his team, then Mr Mistry stepped up to be awarded a carved ivory model of a polo player and his pony as Best Player of the Day.

As soon as the presentations were over, I said to Hector, 'I think Daphne was threatening me just now. She hinted she's going to let Tony and Marjorie know about the nude portrait. Marjorie knows already, but Tony hasn't a clue. What am I going to do, Hector? She wants to destroy my marriage.'

'For heaven's sake, darling, don't be so dramatic. She just wants you to know she has something on you. Daphne loves to have power over other people. It's how she gets her thrills. She won't do anything about it. It's just to frighten you and keep you guessing. And as for having an affair with Tony, I'd say it's highly unlikely. She's looking for a rich husband.'

I looked around and could see no sign of Daphne Bingham. I walked over to congratulate Tony on his triumph on the field of battle. He was handing his pony over to his *syce* to walk back to the stables. He grinned at me, and said, 'There you are, Ginny. Dinner at the club tonight? Bit of a victory party.'

I put his cheerful demeanour down to the result. I nodded agreement, and then noticed Jagadish Mistry rubbing down his pony nearby. On a whim, I walked over to him.

'That was an impressive performance, Mr Mistry. Where did you learn to play polo?'

He looked annoyed. 'Not bad for an Indian? Is that what you mean?'

'Of course I don't. Why would I think that?'

'Sorry. I just get a bit prickly sometimes.'

'Well, that's absurd. You just won the Best Player. I'm complimenting you. What's wrong with that?'

'Absolutely nothing.' He kept his eyes fixed on his horse.

'It's a perfectly innocent question. How *did* you learn to play like that?'

'In my regiment. I was in the cavalry. It was expected.'

He carried on grooming his pony. He was trying to be rude.

I persisted, 'I gather there's going to be a bit of a party at the club tonight.'

'Well, enjoy it.'

'Aren't you coming?'

'Not invited.'

'But that's potty! They couldn't have won without you. I'm going to speak to Tony.'

He reached out and grabbed my arm, holding me back as I started to move towards Tony. 'Don't. It's not his fault. It's down to the club secretary.'

'But why would the secretary object to you coming?'

'Normally he wouldn't, but someone else does.'

'Who?'

'Look, Mrs Tilman, forget about it. I already have. I'd have felt out of place anyway.'

He was stroking the nose of his pony as he spoke, and then I saw him glance across the field to where Marjorie was holding court to her witches' coven.

'It was my mother-in-law, wasn't it?'

His silence was enough.

'That woman is poisonous. Does Tony know?'

Mistry's face flushed with anger. 'Drop it, Mrs Tilman. I

don't want a fuss. I just want to get out of here. Good evening.'

And, with that, he led his horse away, leaving me looking after him.

When the party was in full flow and within earshot of Marjorie, I asked Tony where Mistry was.

'Had another engagement. Damn shame.'

'That's unfortunate. Didn't he know there's usually a party at the club afterwards?'

'Can't have done. Although, come to mention it—I'm sure Walters told him this morning.'

Marjorie responded in a stage whisper. 'It isn't appropriate to have him here. Official functions and visits of the *Dewan* or the royal family are one thing, but an Indian employee is another. I had a quiet word with the secretary and he took care of it without any fuss. So problem solved.'

I dug my fingernails into my palms and breathed slowly to control my anger. 'He was good enough to play for Tilmans, though. No quiet word with anyone about that. But I must say, Marjorie, you missed a chance there. Couldn't you have had a word with the Resident and got him to award the Best Player to someone else? Someone with white skin? Your behaviour is absolutely despicable.'

Tony stepped between us, and put his hands on my shoulders and shepherded me to the other side of the room. I was furious. 'I don't know how you can stand by and let her get away with it.'

'Look, Ginny, you're never going to change the mater. She's old school. It's just her way. Take no notice. Mistry won't care. Water off a duck's back.'

'I'm sick to the back teeth of her. You don't see the half of it. She's constantly carping and looking for ways to put me down. Trying to sap my confidence. It's unrelenting.'

'Don't be daft. She adores you. She's just a bit old-fashioned. Take no notice. You shouldn't be so sensitive.'

We were in a corner of the lounge, and I pulled him towards the door and into the corridor out of earshot of the crowd. 'I know about Daphne Bingham.'

He had his arm about me and suddenly dropped it. 'What about her?'

'That you wanted to marry her.'

He made a kind of hollow, fake laugh. 'Who told you that?'

'Your mother.'

'And what exactly did she say?'

'That you were going to marry her, but Marjorie stopped you and now she wishes she hadn't.'

He gave me one of his blank looks, so I blundered on, 'I saw you with her. At the Banerji wedding. And today at the polo. Are you in love with her? Are you having an affair?'

He took hold of my arms, and his grip was so tight I winced in pain. 'You silly little fool. I married you, didn't I? Daphne's just a friend. A very good friend.'

'But...'

Before I could say anything else, the dinner gong sounded.

Despite his denials, I was more convinced than ever Tony was in love with Daphne Bingham. That night when he went straight to sleep, ignoring the fact the date was ringed on the chart he kept on the back of the bedroom door, I gave myself no further room for doubt.

I would have to fight to win my husband back.

CHAPTER 20

THE SKY WAS PALE GREY, with a pattern of darker grey clouds laid across it like the rippled surface of a sandy beach when the tide has gone out. Even dull days here had a beauty smoggy London could never attain. I took the morning post out to the garden and set aside most of the letters for Tony to deal with, pouncing on one with a London postmark covered with the censor's stamps.

LEIGHTON SQUARE

MY DEAREST GINNY

I can't believe I've let nearly a month go by since your letter. It's certainly not for lack of thinking of you—I do that all the time and am missing you dreadfully, but life has been hectic.

I hope things are getting a little better for you as each day passes, and the pain in your heart, whilst it will never completely leave you, will at least become easier to bear. It seems cruel that you have had to suffer so much loss so early in your life. To lose both parents prematurely and go through successive hopes and disappointments in trying to start a family—my heart goes out to you, my darling. I can only say, from my own experience of loss, time does help us to bear it. I know it's a cliché—but, then, clichés are by definition clichés because they are so apposite.

I try to imagine you sitting out on your veranda in the sunshine. I do hope you are painting again? I know you'll say it's another cliché, but I think being creative also helps to heal a troubled soul. Do send me a picture of your garden so I will know exactly what you look at as you sip your tea every day. I loved the little watercolour sketch of the tea plantation you sent last year. Roger framed it and hung it in the bedroom so I see it every day and think of you.

Life goes on here. Well, war goes on. It's not easy—but then we never expected it would be, did we? We all make the best of things. As you will see from the postmark, I'm in London at the moment. I come down once a month to make sure all's well at Leighton Square. And I now have another reason, as I'm now secretary to a society dedicated to the resettlement of refugees. Most of it's dull administration and committee work (you know how I feel about that)—but it is a good cause and someone has to do it. It's the sort of thing your mother would have excelled at. She was always so much better at getting things done than me. A born organiser. So I try to do it with a willing heart in her memory.

Roger has joined the Home Guard and takes his duties seriously. He only joined recently as I think he still harboured the hope (not shared by me) he would be accepted into the army proper, but he has been told as a farmer he is ruled out completely—his is a 'reserved occupation' and needed for the war effort. Huge relief on my part. Still, he gets to wear a uniform and has attended training camps—it's all very pukka. Can't tell you any more, as it's all top secret.

The bombing has been going on for months now. It's every single night, but we're all getting used to it. The other big cities are

getting a hammering, too. Roger doesn't like me to be down here,
but the show must go on and all that. Mostly I stay only a couple of
days anyway, and it seems to be the poor old East End that's taking
the brunt of it. I'm getting to know the cellars here well. Haven't
been down there since your mother and I were children and used to
play hide and seek among Father's wine racks. Gosh, I still miss my
darling Fliss—as I know you do, too. Anyway I don't want you to
worry about me. It's all rather a lark. And if the Queen can brave it
out, then I jolly well can.

Give my good wishes to Tony. I do hope he's giving you lots of
love and attention. You are always in my prayers.

With fondest love,
Pud

DARLING PUD. I tried to imagine her doing administrative
work. It was far easier to imagine her caring for the refugees
than trying to organise placements for them. She was right;
organisation was more up Mummy's street. Compassion was
Pud's. As I read her letter a second time, I wished I could be
there with her, curled up in an armchair at Leighton Square
sipping a whisky, or hunkering down in the cellars listening
to the bombs falling.

I wondered whether to tell Pud about Tony and the
Bingham woman? She might offer some good advice. But she
had enough to worry about without me adding to her anxiety. She'd be upset that, far from giving me a lot of love and
attention, Tony had become distant and preoccupied. And
she'd have been horrified he was having an affair.

Instead, I imagined what advice Pud would have likely
given me had she been here. She'd have urged me not to give
up my marriage without a fight. Then and there, I decided to
go and see Tony. I asked the cook to make up a tiffin box
with his favourite treats, then saddled up Natana and set off

to the tea factory. It was a beautiful day, and I had in mind to surprise him with an impromptu picnic and save him the trip home.

When I walked into his office unannounced, he was at a large table adjacent to his even larger desk, poring over a map with Jagadish Mistry, Mr Bailey and a stout Indian man whom I didn't recognise. They all looked up as I walked in, and Tony was taken aback. For a moment I thought he was going to be angry with me, but then his face broke into a smile.

'Darling, what a delightful surprise! Is everything alright?'

'I thought I'd bring you some luncheon. I was hoping you could take a short break, but I can see you're busy.'

He looked at the other men and seemed to be about to agree with me, but then said, 'Give me a few minutes to finish off here and I'll join you. Just for half an hour, though. Mistry, take Mrs Tilman into the board room—she can wait for me in there.'

Mistry led me along a corridor through wooden, double doors and into a room panelled in wood and hung with animal trophies, guns, paintings of turbaned men on horse-back sticking pigs and a couple of portraits of white men, one heavily whiskered, the other sporting a trim moustache not dissimilar to Hitler's. Tony's grandfather and father. Mistry gestured for me to sit down, but I chose to walk about the room, examining the pictures and the stuffed animals with feigned curiosity.

I'd expected him to go back and join the others, but when I turned round he was still there, arms folded, watching me with an expression I couldn't read. Then he smiled. 'I was rude to you the other day after the polo. Please forgive me,' he said.

'On the contrary, Mr Mistry, it is I who must apologise

for my mother-in-law. I think she hasn't forgiven you for daring to disagree with her at the dinner table.'

'You have no need to apologise, and certainly not on behalf of your mother-in-law. I suspect it was not just my failure to agree with her, but the fact her dignity was offended by being seated next to me.'

'Well, then, for that you must accept my apologies as I'm the guilty party. I'm terribly sorry to have inflicted her on you.'

He laughed. 'You can make amends by affording me the privilege of sitting next to you next time.'

He bowed slightly and I decided he was mocking me. I turned away and moved to the window. It looked out over the tea gardens, which rose up the sharp incline of the hills to a tree-covered ridge at the top. I felt him come to stand beside me and, for a moment, I thought he was going to touch me, but he just stood there close to me, looking out over the green panorama.

'What are you two conspiring about?' Tony had entered without me hearing.

Mistry spoke, 'I was offering to show Mrs Tilman the High Ranges. I understand she's a painter. There is some beautiful scenery up on the ridge.'

I took a little step to the side in surprise. I didn't know what to say or whether to contradict him.

'Splendid—that's top hole, Mistry,' said Tony.

My heart sank. 'But it's not necessary. I know Mr Mistry is busy.' I was starting to feel annoyed with Mistry. His cheek was incredible.

'I thought I'd take her along when I do the boundary check next week,' he said.

'First-rate idea.' Tony turned to me. 'Darling, it's beautiful up in the hills. Plenty to paint up there. Better than washing lines and hovels.'

He addressed Mr Mistry, 'Been a tad neglectful about showing Ginny the sights. She's been reduced to painting the dark underbelly of Mudoorayam.' He started to laugh and clapped Mistry on the back.

'I'd be in the way,' I said. I knew I was sounding desperate.

Tony was not going to help. 'Not at all,' he said. 'Boundary checking is a straightforward job. All Mistry has to do is follow the Muduvan guide and make sure the boundaries are clearly marked and the fire boundaries are clear. You won't be in the way at all. Paint away to your heart's content while he gets on with it. Not a lot to do, eh Mistry? Most of it was done recently by Bailey. Just a few stretches he didn't get round to, up by the top station.'

'But Mr Mistry must have more important things to do.'

'Nonsense. Part of his job. Chance to see the full extent of the estate, eh Mistry? And Ginny, good to get out of the house for some fresh air. May even see a tusker up there. I know how much you like them.'

I ignored the barbed comment. 'But couldn't you and I go together some time?'

'Far too busy, darling. Already had to uproot a couple of thousand bushes because of the fungal attacks. Need to make sure we get the rest treated with sulphur or we'll lose the blinking lot. Mistry will look after you. Won't you, Mistry?'

'It will be my pleasure.'

'So that's settled.'

My heart sank.

***

I WAS DREADING IT. Terrified actually. Daphne Bingham was

throwing a party. The whole of Muddy was going, and I wished I wasn't.

Tony spent an inordinate amount of time on his ablutions and dressing—he wasn't usually the preening type, so this really got my hackles up, not to mention reinforcing my conviction he was in love with her. When he emerged, wrapped in gentlemen's cologne—a first for him, to my knowledge—shoes gleaming like polished steel, his evening suit without a crease and his white shirt as bright as a tooth-paste advertisement, he barely gave my own efforts a glance. I, too, had gone to some trouble, giving my apricot silk a rare outing and wearing my wedding diamonds. I might as well have worn jodhpurs for all the attention he paid me.

I'd hoped Marjorie would have plumped for a night at home—parties weren't usually her thing—she preferred smaller groups she could easily dominate—but she was waiting in the hall, an expansive vision in purple and about seven strings of pearls.

We parked at the end of a long line of motors that stretched half a mile down the hill. The Thomson house was a sweet little cottagey bungalow with roses round the door. Another re-creation of Britannia. There were far too many guests for the size of the place, and they spilled out through the open doors of the crowded drawing room onto the velvet-smooth lawn. Glasses chinked and the rumble of conversation mingled with the ubiquitous chirping of the crickets and the raucous rhythm of a dance tune playing on the gramophone.

To my surprise, there were several Indians there. Dr Banerji, a group of district office chaps, only one of them accompanied by his wife, and, in the corner talking to Hector, Jagadish Mistry. I saw Lilian and Theo out in the garden, and made my way to them. Marjorie had already made a beeline for the aging widows' club hogging the seats in the drawing room and Tony had vanished. I looked around for our hostess, but she was nowhere to be seen.

Lilian jumped on me joyfully, and began to recount a story about the ENSA concert she and Theo had seen in Madras the previous week. She happily listed the songs and sketches and gave me a critical appraisal of the qualities of the jazz band—excellent, the pianist—average, and the singer—poor. We were joined by a couple of women I knew by sight and whose names I couldn't remember, and so I had to spend the next ten minutes trying to avoid the need to address them. Theo took their arrival as a chance to slip away and get some drinks.

One of the women, a redhead who, I eventually remembered, was called Laura Winstanley, was speaking *sotto voce*, 'We were on library duty at the club this week.'

Lilian threw her head back and laughed. 'Gossip alert!'

'You know as well as I do, Lil, the library is the best source of scandals.'

The other woman spoke next. I was praying someone would address her by name before I had to. 'Yes. Hot off the press, ladies. That planter who lives on the road leading up to High Station? The one with the Scottish accent and a face full of freckles. Only about five foot nothing. Bandy legs. You know the one.'

'Angus MacBride,' said Lilian. 'Go on.'

'He's been barred from the club. Was just shy of his seven years, but they've blackballed him.'

'What did he do?' I felt the need to make some contribution to the conversational flow, no matter how minor.

'He's gone and married a local girl.'

There was a pregnant pause in which, presumably, Lilian and I were supposed to express shock and horror. Instead I asked, 'A local girl? What's wrong with that?'

The nameless blonde mouthed her words at me, 'An Indian, silly.'

'They've drummed him out of the club for that?'

'Of course. Club rules. NTDT.'

I looked puzzled, so Lilian helpfully translated, 'Not The Done Thing.'

Laura Winstanley said, 'I can't understand it. There must have been half a dozen *"Returned Empties"* when the fishing fleet last left. He could have had his pick of them.'

Lilian again interjected for my benefit, 'That's the grace-less, little soubriquet given to ladies who return to England sans partner.'

'So, because he's fallen in love and married an Indian woman, he's been shown the door? When the fellow's been a member for years. His friends did that to him?'

'Have to keep up standards, Mrs Tilman,' the nameless blonde said sulkily. 'It's happened before. There is precedent. You can't make exceptions.'

'Yes,' added Lilian. 'There have been a fair few chaps over the years who've fallen for the dusky charms of an Indian girl. Who can blame them? Some of them are jolly attractive.'

'What about women?' I asked.

Mrs Winstanley frowned. 'What do you mean?'

'Well, if a woman marries an Indian. Is it the same?'

The two friends burst into laughter. 'How absurd. As if! What Englishwoman in her right mind would ever fall for an Indian? Gosh, that's too funny for words.'

The other added, 'Besides, women aren't members of the club in their own right, so it couldn't happen anyway. But, really, Mrs Tilman, what an odd question.'

Theo returned with our drinks and the two gossips faded away into the growing crowd.

'Bloody chaos in there. Like Piccadilly Circus on a Saturday night,' he said. 'Had to stand in line to get the drinks. If Daffers had told us she was light on the servant front, we'd have lent her one or two of ours. Apparently, the Thomsons gave their bearer some time off. They thought Daffers would be able to manage with just two while they're away. Obviously forgotten how she loves to throw a party.'

I gulped down my drink. It was some kind of unfamiliar cocktail, and I started to feel unsteady on my feet. But it was my first drink so it couldn't have been that. I must have looked pale as Lilian said, 'My dear, are you all right? You're white as a sheet.'

The room began to spin and I felt a hand take my arm, then the next thing I knew I was being lifted and carried back to the house and set down on a sofa, which the widows' club vacated for me. I must have passed out for a moment but, when I opened my eyes, Mr Mistry was crouching in front of me, his eyes full of concern, while Hector behind him held out a glass of water.

'You all right, Mrs T?' asked Hector. 'Had a bit of a to-do there.'

I looked between them and past them to the circle of curious onlookers pressing behind them. 'I'm so sorry. I felt a bit faint. Nothing to worry about. Just a bit hot and dizzy.'

Dr Banerji pushed his way through the throng and took my temperature and pulse. 'Nothing serious, Mrs Tilman. You're probably tired. I think it would be a good idea for you to go home and lie down.'

'No, no. I'll be all right. I'll just have a few moments sitting here. I'll be right as rain.'

'I insist. You must go home. Where is Mr Tilman?'

He looked over his shoulder, but there was still no sign of Tony, and our hostess was also still conspicuous by her absence.

Hector spoke a few words in Banerji's ears and put a hand on his arm with what looked like practised familiarity. In that instant, with a jolt, I understood the reason for Hector's drunkenness at the wedding and subsequent flirtation with the toxic plant.

Hector spoke again, 'I'll run you home, Ginny.'

'No, I won't have it. I'm not spoiling the party for you.'

He winked at me. 'No lip from you, young lady. Uncle Hector is running you home and that's the end of it. I can be back here in no time, don't worry.'

'But what about Tony?'

'No point in breaking up the party for him. I'll tell him where you are when I get back and once you're safely tucked up in bed.'

At this point, Marjorie elbowed her way through the crowd. 'What's going on?'

'Mrs Tilman is unwell so I'm going to run her home.'

'Don't be ridiculous. Where's my son?'

Quick as a flash, Hector said, 'He's dashed up to the club to collect a few glasses as we seem to have reached the limit of the Thomsons's supplies.'

I didn't know whether this was true or if Hector was covering for Tony, but it shut Marjorie up. After tutting and shaking her head at me, she said, 'I'll come too, then. Too much of a crush here for my liking.'

On the trip home, Hector sustained what was practically an inquisition of Marjorie.

'I've heard some interesting news about you, Mrs Tilman Senior. '

'Don't call me that. It's impertinent.'

'Just anxious to avoid confusion with Junior here. But I do apologise. Let me start again. So, old girl, I've been...'

'You really are the most insufferable man. I don't know what possessed me to agree to travel with you.'

Hector slammed the brakes on. 'So sorry, we can't have you suffering.' He reached over his seat and unlocked her door. 'Only a couple of miles from here. All uphill though. No one could accuse you of being a slacker, Marjorie.'

'Really! Wait until I tell my son about this.'

'Changed your mind? Fair enough. The privilege of old age.'

I tried to suppress my laughter. I was enjoying this too much.

'As I was saying,' Hector began again, without waiting for the angry muttering to stop. 'A little bird has told me on good authority you are heading back to England's green and pleasant. Bet they're flying the bunting at the Women's Institute. Herr Hitler must be quaking in his jackboots and modifying his battle plans, and I expect Mr Churchill is readying a seat for you in the war cabinet, eh?'

'I have no idea what you're talking about, you rude man.' She turned her head and stared pointedly through the car window into the impenetrable blackness of the night.

I turned in my seat, unready to give in to the waves of relief sweeping over me. 'Marjorie, is this true? Are you really going back to England? Why didn't you say?'

'My plans are not finalised.'

'That's not what I heard.' Hector had her squirming on the hook and was not releasing her. 'My reliable source says you have a passage booked on a ship out of Bombay next week.'

When we arrived, Marjorie swept out of the car without a backward glance or a word of thanks to Hector. I stayed for a few moments, savouring the news that had already lifted my spirits.

'Are you sure about this, Hector? How did you find out?'

'My sources are secret, but let's just say they are impeccable.'

'Well, you've made my evening. Thank you.'

'I think most people will be glad to see the back of her. She's never been well liked in Muddy outside her little coterie of friends, and I expect they stick by her out of fear rather than friendship. If they're in her gang, they can join in the mudslinging rather than risk her chucking it at them.'

'You're right about that.'

'Are you feeling better now? Didn't want to ask, but I can't help wondering if you are...?'

'No, I'm not. I can say that with categorical certainty. In fact, that's probably what was wrong with me. Not wanting to go into the details, but I think you'll catch my meaning?'

'Yes, and thank you for your discretion. So, you didn't think much of the party?'

'Jolly crowded, but I can't say much more than that as I was there barely more than half an hour. What about you?'

'I had a most interesting talk with Mr Mistry. One of the few intelligent men to be found in Muddy. If only...'

'I don't think he's the only one. There's Walter Davenport.'

'Can't count him. Summer only.'

I hesitated, then said, 'And Dr Banerji. He seems an intelligent man. Of course, I don't know him well, not at all socially, but he has intelligent eyes. In fact, I'd go so far as to say he looks extremely clever and interesting. What do *you* think, Hector?'

'I think it is time I headed back to the party.'

He looked at his watch.

'I see Dr Banerji is there without his new wife.'

'Of course. She's in purdah. Very few Indian women come to social events.'

'Well, that's good, isn't it? It will give you plenty of opportunity to talk to Dr Banerji, won't it?'

'What are you trying to say, Ginny?'

I gulped, then went for it, 'That I think Dr Banerji may be a special friend of yours. That I think he may have had something to do with your drinking that poisonous tea. And that I think I realised that this evening when I saw you together.'

He took his hand away from the ignition key and put his head in his hands. 'Is it that obvious?'

'No. No one would guess in a million years. I was perhaps looking for it. Don't forget I'm the only one of them who knows what happened to you.'

'Don't breathe a word of this, Ginny. He'd be ruined. Shamed. Disgraced. Thrown in prison. So would I—not that I care for my own reputation. I think people have known for a long time that I'm that way inclined and choose to draw the veil over it. But, for him, it's everything. And he's an Indian, so they won't tolerate it at all.'

'Are you still...seeing him?'

'Not in that way. No. Well, not in any way really. He's taking his marriage seriously. And he cares for his wife. He very much wants a family. I don't figure in the plans. I just have to be content with a snatched conversation at occasions like tonight. And they're few and far between. Not everyone here is like Daffers, keeping open house including Indians.'

'I'm really sorry, Hector.' I gave his hand a squeeze.

'Oh, well. Hey ho. And talking of Daffers. She seems to have done a disappearing trick.'

'Along with my husband.'

'You don't seem too bothered about it.'

'Of course, I'm bothered. He's my husband.' But, as I spoke the words, I wondered if I really was upset.

'I'm sure you're wrong about them. You know I have no time for Tony. I think he's a dullard and not worthy of you. But I don't think he's an adulterer. And, I don't think for a moment, he's in love with Daphne.'

'Or she him?'

He shrugged. 'I doubt it. I told you she wants a wealthy husband. But she does like to have men in thrall to her. And Tony is a handsome chap. I will give him that. She wants to show her power. And, if it means upsetting you, then so much the better. It's all a game to her. Nothing personal.'

'I don't think it's a game. Tony barely glanced at me tonight. He was all spruced up in a way I haven't seen since our wedding day. He never bothers about that sort of thing. You'd have thought he was auditioning for a part in a film tonight. And he disappeared as soon as we got to the party. Just vanished. Theo had to get me a drink.'

'I'm sorry. He's behaving badly, but I'm sure there's a good reason.'

***

I WENT to bed as soon as Hector left. There was no sign of Marjorie. Maybe she was busy packing. I hoped so. It was after one when Tony got back. I could smell whisky on his breath when he bent over to kiss me and his tie was askew. I turned away and went straight back to sleep. Not for long. Next thing I knew he was undressed and climbing into my bed. Without preamble, he pulled up my nightgown and climbed on top of me.

'Let's make a baby, Ginny.' His voice was slurred.

I pushed him off, and he lost his balance and ended up on the floor. I used more force than I'd intended, and he was clearly very drunk.

I snapped at him. 'For God's sake, what the hell do you think you're doing? I have my period. I don't know what's got into you tonight. The moment we arrived at the party you disappeared. Where did you go? Off canoodling with your mistress? Did you know I fainted and Hector had to bring me home?'

He was still on the floor in the dark, but I was so angry I

couldn't stop yelling. 'And just when were you going to get around to telling me that finally your mother is going home?'

I leaned over the edge of the bed to look at him. He was sleeping, lying there on the bedroom floor.

Next morning, he went to work before I woke.

***

HECTOR TURNED up for a midmorning coffee to give me a blow-by-blow account of the rest of Daphne's party.

'You were wrong about Daffers setting her cap at Tony. Not that I'm one to say I told you so.'

'Really? He came home really late and very drunk.'

'Well, so did most of Muddy. That girl knows how to throw a party, I'll give her that.'

'Well?'

'She announced her engagement.'

My jaw dropped.

'She's going to marry a counter jumper from Calcutta.'

'A what?'

'A shop keeper.'

'She kept that very quiet.'

'Daffers likes to keep people guessing. She produced the gentleman in question and displayed him like a trophy. And I say gentleman, but some of the snobs around here will only ever see him as a wealthy *box wallah*. Terribly *infra dig*. He's the Managing Director of the Calcutta Provincial & General Stores. In fact, he's more than a shopkeeper, as the business, which has been going since Clive of India first arrived, is in his family, so he's worth a not inconsiderable fortune. More than enough to keep our girl in baubles and beads and fund the occasional trip to Europe. Well—once this bloody war's over. So, while the ladies of Muddy sneer in disapproval, the Black Widow will be cashing in.'

'Gosh.'

'Is that all you have to say, my dear, after impugning the reputation of your dearly beloved husband?'

'Well, I still don't know what they were always whispering about. And why he's still never mentioned her properly to me, or admitted they had a relationship before he met me.'

'Well, you'd better ask him, sweetie, hadn't you?'

CHAPTER 21

THE TRIP TO inspect the boundaries required an early start. I
was dreading the day ahead. When I rode out in the early
mornings on Naṭaṇa, I was alone and unobserved by anyone
other than children and tea workers—no one qualified to
cast a critical eye on my equestrian skills—or lack of them.
I'd learnt to ride as a child and had been an enthusiastic
enough member of the pony club, but had not ridden in
public since I got dumped off in humiliating circumstances
by a vicious little beast at a Boxing Day meet. I wasn't thrilled
at the prospect of riding beside someone with the horsemanship and arrogance of Mistry. I'd also be on an unfamiliar
mount as Natana was lame, so I was to ride one of the plantation horses.

Mistry was waiting at the side of the road where a cart
track through the tea gardens began. He held the bridle of
the grey thoroughbred he'd ridden at the polo match and a
bay horse that looked rather too frisky to me. I didn't want
him to see my nerves and prayed I wouldn't disgrace myself.

Squatting at the roadside was a tribesman who, I
presumed, was our Muduvan guide. He wore a turban, an ear

stud and a white *lunghi*. Close by, untethered and munching grass was a stocky mule, presumably his mount.

Mistry looked the picture of equine affinity. He was wearing jodhpurs and, the bagginess of the fabric around his thighs, drew my eyes to its tautness around his knees and to the cut of his shiny, black, leather knee boots. Apart from the colour of his skin, he'd have passed muster anywhere in the home counties. He held my bridle and gave me a leg up, then with practised ease, sprang onto his own horse. It took me a few moments to get the feel of the animal underneath me, then I relaxed into the saddle and pressed my calves into the horse's flanks, feeling her respond to the slightest pressure.

We circled around, getting the measure of each other as well as, in my case anyway, our horses. The Muduvan man ignored us. He appeared to be far away in another world, still down on his haunches, rolling a couple of pebbles back and forth through his hands, while mumbling as though in prayer.

'We'll ride for a couple of hours, then stop for a break. All uphill. Steady pace as the ground is stony. Sankaram will go at his own pace and may take short cuts, but he won't lose us. We'll take it nice and easy. It shouldn't prove too taxing for you, Mrs Tilman. Let me know if you need to rest or feel uncomfortable at any time.'

My tone was frosty as I replied, 'I won't need to rest. And I am quite comfortable. Shall we go?'

He nodded, and I saw the same slightly crushed expression cross his face I'd noticed before. But I told myself he needed crushing. He was too cocky by half. And I was annoyed he'd tricked me into this trip.

We left the tea gardens and rode single file behind the guide along a narrow pathway through a heavily forested section of the hillside until we got to a clearing, where we stopped and looked back through a gap in the trees to the valley below. The tea plantations were spread out below us, their swathes of green broken every now and then by the vertical rise of tall, silvery-green, feathered trees. At the tops of the surrounding hills, the trees grew more densely and were more varied, some with long thin trunks, others like low fat bushes, while clumps of pine trees marked the summits. Above the trees, a hazy, bluey-grey mist swirled, so it was as though the lower part of the sky was covered in a pall of drifting smoke. The tea pickers were already about their work, their brightly coloured *saris* dotted across the hillside. I could hear the faint sound of laughter, and possibly singing. The sight was almost mystical. Suddenly, I was glad I had come.

Mistry sidestepped his horse towards mine and gathered up his reins. 'It's a beautiful sight, isn't it?'

'It is. It is. Quite, quite, lovely.'

'And profitable. There aren't many crops that yield a return every couple of weeks for more than half a century after planting. No wonder the British planted tea gardens all over India.'

'So it isn't just because we love drinking the stuff?'

'Well, that, too.' He paused, then said, 'It looks as though tea plants were made for these hills—as if they've been growing here for a thousand years.'

'Haven't they?'

'Only about sixty. Tea is not indigenous to India.'

'Of course. I knew that.' But I didn't.

'Before the planters, this land was unexplored. Wild forests, teeming with wildlife. Not many people—just bison, elephants, tigers and leopards. When people like your husband's grandfather started to grow tea, workers came from the plains of Tamil Nadu for the chance to make a living.'

'Where did tea come from originally?'

'It's native to China. We're the beneficiaries of centuries of accumulated Chinese wisdom in its cultivation.'

I remembered how Tony had tried to tell me all this when we first came to Mudoorayam. What had seemed dull then was interesting now I was here at the top of the world, looking down on it. Or maybe Mr Mistry had a way of making it seem more interesting?

He turned his horse around and signalled to me to follow him. 'Tempting as it is to stay and gaze upon the beauty of the landscape, we have a job to do, Mrs Tilman. I can't have you telling the boss how easily I am distracted by beauty.'

I could have sworn there was a note of flirtation in his voice. I kicked my horse and cantered past him. 'Race you to the top of the hill.'

Tony was right; checking the boundaries was hardly an onerous task. Mr Mistry told me that more often than not it was done on motorcycles rather than horses.

'Bikes are faster and don't try to head for home when the day gets hot, and they get tired. But Tony didn't think you'd be comfortable riding pillion.'

I pictured myself astride a motorcycle, hanging onto the surveyor's back. I realised the prospect was actually an appealing one.

As though reading my mind, he said, 'I think you're made of sterner stuff than perhaps Tony credits.'

'I've never been on a motorcycle. It sounds like fun.'

'It is, as long as it's not during or just after the rains. You'd end up plastered with mud and looking like a coal miner. At this time of the year, it's safe enough.'

The guide emerged from a thicket of trees in front of us and I asked Mistry why the Muduvan were known as the back people?

'Some say, when they first came here centuries ago, they carried their children and household goods on their backs.

Others believe they carried a huge statue of the goddess Meenakshi on their backs over the mountains, and she blessed them and helped them to live in peace and harmony. Which they still do.'

We rode on in silence for a while, picking our way through a long stretch of rocky terrain. Mistry broke the silence, 'Not too tired?'

'Of course not.'

'Usually, when we do a boundary check, we're away for several days so we bring camping equipment and food. Today, we're just covering a small area we didn't get to last time. The survey team cut the last boundary check short, as everyone's needed back in the tea gardens to clear up the fungal infestation. As the new boy, I'm more easily spared.'

I suspected this expedition was more for my benefit than a serious task. I looked at Mistry and, felt again, he was reading my thoughts. Part of me resented his familiarity and, yet, I couldn't help being drawn towards him. He seemed to see me, to know me. It was uncanny. It made me feel uncomfortable.

Sankaram, the Muduvan guide, was often out of sight, taking different routes through the forest, but always managing to keep up with us. He signalled something to my companion and we rode into a clearing in the forest where we came upon a stack of white painted stones.

'This is the first boundary kern.' Mistry slipped off his horse and moved towards the guide. Sankaram took a can of paint and a brush out of his knapsack and started to apply a coat of white paint to the kern.

The rest of the morning involved more kern painting and, from time to time, the two men together tied up short sections of broken fencing, where the boundary backed onto cattle grazing land. I took advantage of the frequent stops to make quick charcoal and pencil sketches of the scenery.

Mistry made notes about any more major repairs needed using a leather-bound notebook he kept in his saddlebag. I watched him as he worked and, almost unintentionally, started sketching him and Sankaram instead of the scenery.

'Did you learn to ride, as well as play polo, when you were with your regiment?'

'I learned as a boy, that's why I chose the cavalry.'

'Where did you do your military training?'

'In England. I was trained and commissioned at Sandhurst. My father's brother paid for me to be educated at a military academy in Madras and, after my engineering degree, I was in the last batch of Indian nationals to be sent to Sandhurst. Now, all the officer training is done here.'

'What did you think of England?'

'I liked it well enough. What about you? I imagine you've been riding for a long time?'

'I rode as a child, but I haven't ridden seriously for years.'

'Well, you must take it up again. You look comfortable on a horse.'

'I hope that doesn't mean I have a big bottom and bow legs.'

As soon as the words were out, I wanted to take them back. What was it about the man? I kept saying things I didn't want to. It was as if I had no barriers with him. As if he didn't let me.

'If that were true, I would never have drawn attention to it. And it, most certainly, is not.'

I blushed, and said, 'Maybe we'd better get on? Those kerns won't paint themselves.'

We rode through the high ranges, enchanted by the beauty of the plains: open grasslands known as *shola*. We rode past streams and pools: natural watering holes where we watched bisons and wild goats drinking. My companion told me the wild goats with their backward turned curly horns were *tahrs* and the wild bison were *gaurs*. I told him about the lost elephant Tony and I saw on the road from the club, and how I'd been frightened by the experience. I didn't mention Tony shooting one. I realised he must have known anyway.

'It's unusual for elephants to wander so far towards town these days, so Tony was right to be cautious when you met one. They can be dangerous. Up here though, unless they're wounded, they'll do you no harm and it's a joy to come across one. I'm afraid the day will come when there are no elephants left in India, the way men hunt them for their ivory. Let me show you something.'

He called out to Sankaram and exchanged some words in a native tongue, then turned to me and said, 'Let's go.'

We rode into the forest until we reached a clearing. We pulled up next to an ugly, concrete building, painted in white and green. Inside, it was lit by a mass of tiny candles and the concrete floor was painted with strange shapes and patterns in coloured paint.

Incense was heavy in the air, but there was no one in attendance. I sensed Mistry beside me, and he took my hand and steered me inside the shrine. His skin was cool and dry against the heat of my own hand. The building was bare, save for the votive candles, a bowl filled with little sweets, a heap of red powder in a metal dish and a scary looking statue. The place was pervaded with the scent of sandalwood.

'This is Lord Ganesh, the elephant god.'

The brightly painted statue was grotesque, like a fairground attraction or an oversized puppet. Michelangelo it wasn't. And, yet, it had a strange charm, a sense of quiet mysticism that belied the gaudiness of its colours and the crudeness of the anthropomorphic features. It was a fat-bellied man with white painted skin and the head of an elephant, complete with huge, curling trunk, enormous, pink-edged ears and with one of his tusks broken off. One pair of human arms was extended in front of him, palms outward as though in supplication, while the other pair was raised above his head, one hand clutching a dagger and the other a short piece of rope. On his head was a golden crown, studded with brightly painted jewels.

'Why does he have an elephant's head?'

'He was said to be born with a human head, but the god Shiva beheaded him when he came between Shiva and his wife Parvati. Vishnu replaced the missing head with an elephant's.'

'What's he doing here? Stuck in the middle of the forest?'

He tilted his head to one side in a shrug. 'There are shrines and temples everywhere in India in all kinds of places. Ganesh is one of the most widely-worshipped deities. He's said to be the remover of obstacles and the god of new beginnings.'

'New beginnings?'

'When people embark on a new enterprise, such as a building a new home or beginning a new relationship, Ganesh can help make their new venture a success and remove any obstacles in the way.'

He looked at me and I sensed he was talking more than generally, and I turned away from him, afraid to hold his gaze.

'Why here—buried away in the forest?'

'Who knows? Perhaps the shrine was built to give thanks after a narrow escape from a herd of elephants. Maybe to ask Lord Ganesh to provide bountiful crops, or bring the rain after a long drought.'

He paused for a moment, then said, 'Or to help remove the barriers for a couple in love?'

He looked at me as though daring me to look away, so I tried to hold his gaze, but felt my cheeks reddening and had to lower my eyes. Then, he handed me one of the narrow tapering candles and motioned me to light it and place it with the others. He did the same himself.

'What obstacle would you like him to remove for you?' I asked him.

'If I tell you, Lord Ganesh may not answer my prayer.'

'I thought you didn't believe in religion anyway?'

'I don't. I'm an engineer and have too much respect for science, but I also have respect for the ancient traditions of my country. And one can always hedge one's bets.'

'This place is extraordinary. Hidden away in the middle of nowhere.'

Out of the corner of my eye, I saw Sankaram, kneeling behind us, his head lowered to the ground in prayer. There was something touching about the way he prayed, silently, devoutly, privately.

Mistry put his hand lightly on my arm and I stepped away, pretending I hadn't noticed his touch.

He turned back to the horses. 'Let's go.'

We left the little shrine and rode up to the crest of the hill, leaving the forest behind us. At the top, we looked down into a wide valley with a waterfall at one end and a large pool fed by a fast-running stream. Sankaram pulled a couple of tiffin boxes out of the bag he carried on his back and gave them to Mistry.

'We'll let the horses graze a while. Sankaram will look after them. We can eat our picnic down there by the water-fall. There's fresh water in the spring.'

'You seem to know a lot about this spot. I thought it was your first time here.'

'I could hardly risk bringing the boss's wife here without checking out the place first, could I?'

'So you've been here before?'

'Last weekend.'

He'd given up his free time just to prepare the ground for our trip. It didn't feel appropriate. I knew it was well beyond the call of duty. I knew I was heading for trouble but tried to suppress the thought.

As we scrambled down the hillside, he told me the names of some of the surrounding features and their meanings: the hill of winds, the river of flowers and Lord Shiva's mountain.

At the floor of the valley, the sound of the waterfall was loud—the cascade was at least a hundred feet high. He held his arm out to help me over the rocks to a flat grassy area, where we sat side-by-side and ate our tiffin. I was ravenously hungry for the first time I could remember since I'd been in India. Mistry filled a couple of tin bottles with spring water and handed one to me.

We leaned back against the warm rock and drank the cool water. All around us the hills rose, forming a circle around the valley, so it gave the impression of a secret, hidden place.

'These are part of the Nilgiri Hills. They stretch right up through Tamil Nadu. Hundreds of miles.'

'It's the most beautiful place I have ever seen.'

'*Nilgiri* means blue mountains in Tamil. I suppose it must be because of the *kurinji*.'

'What's the *kurinji*?'

'*Neelakurinji* flowers—they grow all over these hills. Blue flowers that completely carpet the hills. But they only bloom once every twelve years.'

I looked around me at the green vegetation covering the sides of the valley. 'Are these *kurinji* plants?'

'Yes, but they won't produce any flowers until 1946.'

'That's seven years away. I can't wait that long.'

I pulled a face at him, and he laughed.

'Well, you could be in luck. Sankaram mentioned a place not far from here. An isolated valley where they grow on a different cycle and their twelfth year falls this year. They should be flowering fairly soon. We could go together and see if he's right? I've never seen them either, and I'm as impatient as you.'

'I'd like that.'

'Of course it won't be as spectacular as it will be here and in the hills all around Mudoorayam—it's a much smaller area. Just a few plants that somehow mutated on to a different cycle.'

'I don't care. I'd love to go. I want to see them.'

Then he smiled at me, and I wondered why I'd disliked him so much when I first met him. He was the only Indian I'd had the chance to get to know at all. He was confounding my preconceptions.

We lapsed into a companionable silence, broken only by the sweetness of the birdsong.

Then I remembered the angry scene I'd witnessed outside the court house in Mudoorayam with Hector, and decided to ask him if he'd heard about it.

'Do you know what it was about? Hector said a father murdered his daughter aided by his son. It doesn't make any sense to me. I thought he must have got the wrong end of the stick, because he said the woman had been raped and that was why they killed her.'

'Yes. A sad story. For once, I am forced to agree with the hard line the British court has taken.'

'So what happened?'

'She was barely a woman. Just a girl of twelve. Her name was Savita. A man from the next village took a fancy to her. He was a widower and a friend of her father. He asked to marry her, but she refused because he was so much older than her. Her parents tried to persuade her, but the man grew impatient and withdrew his offer. Savita's family were angry with her, but finally respected her wishes and consulted the matchmaker to find another candidate to become her husband. One morning she was carrying wood from the forest back to the family home when the man came upon her and, still angry at her rejection of his marriage offer, beat her badly and raped her in the forest, leaving her barely conscious. She struggled home to her family, badly hurt and distraught and, when they realised what had happened, her father and brother took her to a pool in the forest and held her head under the water until she drowned.'

I clapped my hand to my mouth. 'That's horrible. She'd done nothing wrong. She was the injured party.'

'They stabbed the rapist to death in his bed. Tribal justice. Then the police caught up with them.'

'What about justice for the girl? What a hideous thing to happen. And I still don't understand why her own father and brother killed her.'

'They would see it as her bringing dishonour on the family.'

'But she was raped. How was that her fault?'

'Doesn't make any difference. In their eyes, she was at fault. She had been disobedient and disrespectful, and what was done to her meant now she was unclean and someone to be shunned. They probably believed they were doing her a favour. Her only future after what had happened was prostitution.'

I felt like crying. Savita's story was too close to home. I felt a stab of sorrow for the girl, a twelve-year-old child, trusting and innocent, suffering the horror of rape and then being killed at the hands of her own family, people she had loved and trusted.

'I don't understand. You mean, because she went with the man against her will, she had still broken a moral code?'

'That's how they would see it. But it's less about morality than about economics.'

'How?'

'No man would have accepted the girl in marriage after she'd been violated by another man, so she would have become a burden on her father, another mouth to feed, with no prospect of finding a husband. Killing her would mean saving the dowry money, as well as the family honour, and it meant one less mouth to feed. It's harsh. It's cruel. It's unfair, but that's the way it is. They'd probably have got away with killing her if they hadn't gone on and killed the old man.'

I wanted to hit him, the way he talked about Savita in such a calm matter-of-fact way as though it were the kind of thing to happen every day. It must have shown in my face as he laid a hand gently on my arm.

'I'm sorry, Mrs Tilman. I'm not proud this kind of thing happens. It makes me angry, too. Like you, I feel compassion for the girl and think she had every right to refuse to marry the old man and was an innocent victim. But, the fact remains, this is the way of the people. Right or wrong. Every life has its price and, when there's a struggle to put food on the table, some men make wrong decisions. I abhor and condemn what happened, but I can't say I don't understand why it did. And who's to say Savita wasn't spared a worse fate? Disowned, degraded, abused, forced into prostitution, starvation, cast out by friends and family, begging at the roadside. Given the choice, maybe she preferred death at the hands of her family.'

'Are there other women like Savita? When such a thing happens, are they always killed by their family?'

'Yes and no. Fortunately, it happens rarely. I'd hate you to get the wrong impression.'

'It's a bit late for that.'

'Mrs Tilman, the life of women in my country is very different from yours. It's not so many years since widows were forced to climb onto funeral pyres to burn to death beside their husbands' corpses. Again, it comes back to economics. This is a poor country, and we have many more mouths to feed than we can produce food for. A widow is a burden on her family and has no husband to support her. A girl who can't find a husband is a drain on her family. These things will change in time. But we have to change them ourselves. It's made worse by the fact we are a country occupied by a foreign power. When your countrymen eventually pack their bags and get out of here, we will start to put some of these things right for ourselves. It has to come from us. You can't force your British way of seeing and doing things on us. It will never work. It will never stick. Do you understand?'

I nodded. 'I think so.'

'Sadly, right now, the only people helping women in situations like Savita's are the nuns. They take abandoned women in. But at what price? Forcing them into Christianity.'

'You're angry.'

'Yes, I am. But mostly because I want to live in a country with our own government, where our resources are applied to the good of our own people, not siphoned off to boost the profits of a bloated empire.'

He picked up a pebble and hurled it into the stream, where it splashed and bounced to the other side.

I took this as a signal, and began to gather my things together. Then, he spoke again, 'I'm sorry. You didn't deserve that. Sometimes my anger gets the better of me.'

'It's my fault,' I said. 'I brought the subject up. I wish I hadn't now.'

We saddled the horses and rode in silence for a while. Then breaking the impasse, he leaned across and placed his hand for a moment on my arm and asked, 'I've made you sad? I've spoiled your day?'

As he spoke, the sun broke through from where it had

been hiding behind a cloud and, simultaneously, it began to rain heavily, the sunlight refracted in the downpour. We kicked our horses forward and headed for a clump of trees but, just as we got there, the shower stopped. India was like that. Or rather Muddy was. Rain on the sunniest of days without warning and, at other times, pregnant clouds that failed to deliver.

LATER WE STOPPED to drink tea that Sankaram produced from a flask in his saddle bag. I wanted to break the silence that was starting to feel oppressive.

'You know a lot about this place, Mr Mistry, considering you're not from Mudoorayam.'

'Maybe, but I'm not wholly a stranger. My grandmother came from a village a few miles away from Mudoorayam. It was one of the reasons I took the job here. Getting in touch with my roots, I suppose you could say. When I was a little boy, she used to tell me about the *neelakurinji* flowers. She taught me a few lines of a poem about them. I think I can still remember them.'

'Tell me.'

He spoke softly, his voice caressing the words.

'*What could my mother be to yours?*
What kin is my father to yours anyway?
And how did you and I meet ever?
But in love our hearts are as red earth and pouring rain:
mingled beyond parting.'

I felt he was addressing the lines to me. I thought they were beautiful. They moved me and made me want to cry. Then I remembered myself, and could hear the harshness in my own voice as I said, 'That's not about the *kurinji* flowers. It's just about love, surely.'

'*Just* about love? But isn't love everything?'

'But you said it was about those flowers.'

'According to my grandmother, the poem is about a love that came when the *kurinji* blossomed. It's from an ancient Tamil poem called *Kuruntokai*.'

Then, I couldn't help myself. 'Say it again.'

He repeated the poem.

'I like it. Especially the red earth and pouring rain. It could only be here.' As I said the words, I realised that for the first time I was thinking of India and Mudoorayam with affection.

'Why did your grandmother leave here?'

'She fell in love. She married my grandfather, who was on leave in the area from his barracks. He was posted to Lahore, and that's where my father and my uncles were born.'

'So it wasn't an arranged marriage?'

'No, it wasn't. I don't think my grandfather's family was happy. My *daa-dee-maa* was from a poor Tamil family. He was high caste. His parents thought she'd bewitched him.'

He laughed. 'And I suppose she had. Not really a suitable wife for a military man with good prospects. I think that's why she loved the poem.'

'Say it again.'

He repeated it, and I thought the words even more beautiful.

'I can see why she loved it. I love it, too.'

I looked up and saw he was watching me again, with that intent look he had when we talked at the dinner party. But now, it didn't annoy me at all. I wondered why it ever had. This time he looked away first.

'So you were the third generation of your family in the army? What made you give it up?'

'I don't like the idea of fighting. I don't like the discipline of army life. I hate taking orders. And I didn't like the uniform.' He laughed. 'Very scratchy.'

'You must have looked awfully dashing in uniform.' There it was again—words out before I realised they were inappropriate.

He looked at me quizzically, as though assessing me in some way. At that moment, we heard the voice of Sankaram calling, '*Chinna dorai!*'

'What's he saying?' I asked.

'*Chinna dorai*. He's calling to me. It means Little Boss. Your husband is the *periya dorai*.'

'The Big Boss, I suppose?'

He jumped to his feet and stretched an arm out to pull me up. 'It's time to go. We don't want the *periya dorai* wondering where we've got to and sending out a search party.'

When we caught up with Sankaram, the guide put something into Mr Mistry's hand. The little man grinned at me and repeated, '*Ten, ten, ten.*'

Mistry said, '*Ten* means wild honey. Sankaram would like you to try some.'

He held out his hand, and I could see it was covered in a sticky mass. 'Go on. Taste it. It's good.'

I leaned over Mistry's outstretched palm and scooped up some of the honey on my finger. As I did so, Sankaram hopped from one foot to another and moved his head from side to side.

The sticky goo was sweet and delicious and I licked my fingers, watching Mistry as he did the same. Something deep inside me made me wish I was licking it from his fingers, not my own. I could feel a blush coursing up my neck, and hoped he wouldn't notice or read what I was thinking.

'Do you like it?'

'It's delicious. Where did he find it?'

'There are wild bees all over the forest. The Muduvan collect the honey. It's a dangerous business. They have to climb high up in the trees where the hives are and smoke the bees out.'

He turned to the guide again, and they had a brief exchange.

'His brother-in-law hunts for honey. He's working on a hive just a short distance away. Would you like to go and see?'

I turned to Sankaram and said, '*Ten* very good. Thank you.' I tried to nod at him sideways. He roared with laughter, and Mistry laughed too. Then we got down from the horses and walked a short way into the forest, and there they were— the hives, hanging like sacks from the branches, high in the tree, about half a dozen in each of two neighbouring trees. Sankaram's brother was lying along one of the main branches high in one of the trees. He'd climbed about twenty feet, barefoot, a dangerous task. Mr Mistry took my arm, and pulled me back behind a thicket to watch without getting too close.

'I don't want the bees attacking and stinging you. Sankaram and his brother will be stung, but they're used to it. Years of practice.'

'Is it painful?'

He laughed. 'I got too close once and was stung and, believe me, it hurts like hell.'

We watched Sankaram clamber up the tree to join his brother, carrying a bundle of slightly damp leaves. When he reached the crown of the tree, he set fire to the leaves, held the bundle under the entrance to the hive and let the smoke drive the bees out. Meanwhile, the brother chopped a hole in the biggest hive and reached his hand in to grasp the honey. All the while, bees were attacking the pair of them in a demented frenzy. I wanted to cry out and beg them to stop, but Mistry whispered to me that by now they were immune to the poison, if not to the pain. After a while, the two men shimmied back down the tree and pulled on a rope to lower a basket in which they'd placed the honey.

Sankaram, smiling, despite his stings, took a honeycomb and wrapped it in a couple of leaves and handed it to Mistry, who said, 'He wants you to have it. A souvenir of the day.'

I turned to the tribesman and did my best effort at the little sideways head shake, mumbling my thanks, and saying, 'Good *ten.*'

Returning to Muddy, I wanted the ride to go on and on. I didn't want the day to end. I didn't want to go home. As we approached the tea gardens, we passed a crocodile of native women, all bent forward slightly with bundles of wood perfectly balanced on their heads. They gave the impression the heavy branches were as light as balsa and showed no strain from their labour. I drank in the sight of them, and knew I would paint them from memory. My head was bursting with images from the day.

It was the best day since I arrived in India. It wasn't just because of the breath-taking beauty of the scenery or the freedom I felt out all day on horseback. It wasn't just the perfection of the weather or the deliciousness of the wild honey. It wasn't just the sight of the tea gardens in the mist and the sound of the tea pickers' singing. It wasn't just the peace and mysticism of the secret shrine in the forest. It was all those things and more. But, most of all, it was Jagadish Mistry.

That night, as I tried to sleep, I went over the day again and again in my mind. The words of the poem he had recited repeated themselves like a mantra. The beauty of the image of the mingling of red earth and pouring rain haunted me, and I lay there listening to the remembered sound of his voice as he spoke the words. A voice I'd heard as an arrogant drawl when we'd first met, now wrapped around me like a soft, warm shawl. But then the story of Savita and her brutal murder pushed its way to the forefront, and I couldn't help thinking how closely her story paralleled mine, yet how different the outcomes. We had both brought shame and disgrace upon our families, but I had got off lightly, thanks to a caring mother, a privileged background and the fact people didn't murder their children with impunity in Britain. But, most of all, I knew I'd been lucky. I looked across the gap between our beds to the silhouetted outline of Tony's sleeping body and told myself to be grateful my violation by an older man had led to marriage and security, not to death and the destruction of a whole family.

CHAPTER 22

THE WAR in Europe felt unreal. The drama of the Battle of Britain, while it shocked us all when we watched the newsreels, seemed more like a film than something happening over the familiar hills and fields of southern England. But, when the Blitz began, there was talk of little else at the club. Everyone had someone they were worried about back home. We gathered around the wireless, listening to the updates on the progress of the war on *All India Radio,* and watching *India News Parade* during the weekly film night at the club, with its chirpy updates of smiling cockneys standing amidst the rubble and maintaining Hitler and his hardware would never defeat the East End spirit. But, otherwise, here in Muddy, nothing much changed. We were told to expect it would. The increasing threat from the Japanese was bound to affect us eventually and we feared might push us into the front line.

On the club lawn, I watched Hector drink his gin and tonic while I nursed a lime juice. It was a perfect afternoon, not too hot, with brilliant sunshine. We were doing what everyone did these days: dissecting the news.

'The war's given the viceroy the perfect excuse to fob off

the Congress Party. Most Indians are too damned decent to take advantage of it. And Linlithgow knows bloody well.'

'Yes, but at least he's promised dominion status once the war's over.'

'They want full independence, not some tin-pot dominion. Besides, the war could go on for years.'

'Surely not?'

'That's what they said about the last one.'

'Surely the viceroy will stick to his word?'

'You're talking about the man who declared war on Germany on India's behalf without so much as consulting them. And the way our politicians talk of fighting the enemies of democracy... conveniently forgetting, here in India, that's exactly what they are, too. It's hypocrisy of the highest order. We treat the population like children with underdeveloped brains, too immature to determine their own destiny. And we treat the politicians that way, too. Brilliant, highly educated men. I met Chandra Bose at Cambridge. He was at Fitzwillie. No one could accuse him of lacking intellect. Nehru too. It's insulting and makes me ashamed.'

'But Gandhi and Nehru have refused to support us in the war. And Bose has even suggested Indians should fight for the Germans.'

'Do you blame them? Apart from anything else, Gandhi's a pacifist, so what do you expect him to do? And why should they offer support for a war where they didn't even have any say on whether they were a part of it? Bose takes the view "my enemy's enemy is my friend". I can't agree with him on that, but I can't blame him for thinking it, either.'

'Don't let's talk about war and politics, Hector. It makes you so cross.'

'It's not the war that makes me cross. I hate Hitler and

fascism as much as the next man. It's the way it's allowed us to conveniently shelve the question of independence.'

'But everyone knows it has to happen. Tony says Linlithgow was on the point of granting it, when Hitler scuppered the plan by invading Poland.'

Hector rolled his eyes when I mentioned my husband's name. 'So it's back to "Tony says", is it?'

'Please, Hector.'

'Does he know we're friends again? Is he aware his wife is knocking about with a fairy?'

'Don't do this.'

'Very well, Mrs T.'

He took a sip of his gin. 'The government and the viceroy know self-determination must happen, but it's damned annoying they now have the perfect excuse to delay it. When the war's over, Britain will be bankrupt and won't be able to carry on running an empire.'

'Well, we're jolly lucky to be over here at the moment. I had a letter from Pud last week. They're rationing food and clothing. Everyone's been given little books they have to take to the butcher and grocer and get stamped when they buy anything. And it's tiny portions. At least, with Roger being a farmer, they have access to fresh produce. They took in a pair of children from Manchester at the beginning of the war. Poor little things. As if the war itself wasn't scary enough, I can't imagine how they must have felt having to live with grumpy Roger. Pud says the children cried every night for the first week, then just as soon as they settled down, their parents decided they should come back home. How terrible to be separated from their families like that. The little girl said to her, "I want to go home and die with me mam". It must be terrifying now they're bombing the cities. Having to sleep in underground stations. On the platforms. Can you imagine?'

'I can only think it will get worse.'

'Thank God we're in India.'

'You've had a Damascene conversion to life here? You were always so desperate to dash back to Blighty, and now you seem positively enamoured of our little paradise in the Western Ghats? How come? Do tell? I can't imagine it's fear of the war. You're the sort of girl who's always up for adventure. I can picture you driving a tank or, at least, a tractor. No, there must be some other attraction here in Muddy, and something tells me it's not our Tony.'

I could feel the blush spreading up my neck onto my face. Lord knows why. Ludicrous really, as there was no way Hector could have known of my new friendship with Mr Mistry—but, I suppose the fact I was now spending most of my waking hours thinking about the surveyor, meant I assumed it was obvious to everyone else.

Hector wasn't stupid. 'Something must have happened to change your views of dear, old Muddy. Or could it be you are once again in the pudding club?'

I wasn't. Since my two miscarriages, I'd now gone more than a year without any result. Tony still doggedly marked the dates on the calendar, and continued to approach our attempts to start a family as though it were a project. I approached the whole thing with a mixture of hope it would happen and, dread, that if it did, I would miscarry again. And, increasingly, I was asking myself if I really wanted to have a child at all.

'Hector?'

'At your service.'

'Remember the fuss in town about the sentencing of the men who killed that young woman?'

'I do.'

I told him the rest of the story. When I finished, he shook his head and looked at me soulfully.

'Alas, my dear, I can't say I'm surprised.'

'It's made me think.'

'God, that's a frightening prospect.'

'I'd like to do something useful. Help out in some way. I've heard the only help available to women like Savita is from the nuns, and they have to exchange their souls for that. There must be some other way.'

'What do you want to do? Solve centuries of female oppression singlehandedly without speaking a word of the local languages and as a representative of perfidious Albion?'

'Can't you take me seriously for once in your life? I haven't a clue what I could do, but there must be something? Surely?'

'Your best bet is to have a word with Lilian. You might be able to help out at the hospital. Or ask Tony if there's anything at the plantation clinic. But, to be honest, darling you'll be worse than useless unless you make an effort to learn some Tamil.'

So that was how I came to meet Neela, a schoolteacher from the primary school on the Tilman's estate, and began the process of learning Tamil. She was introduced to me by Lilian and agreed to teach me the basics two afternoons a week to ready me for helping Lilian out at the hospital. But, while I made steady progress in grasping some essentials in the language, Lilian's hopes of another recruit to swell the ranks of her volunteers were dashed the first time she took me round the wards. I nearly passed out when I saw a woman with leprosy. Her nose had been eaten away, and she had stumps where her arms were meant to be. I was ashamed of my squeamishness but, I knew if I were to help, I had to find something else to do. Lilian suggested the estate school. That meant asking Tony.

MARJORIE LEFT for England without fuss. I avoided saying goodbye by contriving an appointment with Dr Banerji— actually a game of chess with Hector at the club. I don't know how she managed to pull the strings to get a civilian berth on a ship, but she had lots of connections and I imagine plenty of them would have been only too glad to send her on her way. Tony took her as far as the train, and left her to nego- tiate her own way to and across Bombay and onto the ship. It was a minor thing, but I read it as significant. A little victory.

When he returned, he was unusually cheerful and I wondered if he, too, was glad to see the back of her. I grasped the opportunity to ask if I might help out at the school.

'I thought I could help hear their reading. Or read stories to them in English. What do you think? Neela says I'm making good progress with Tamil so that will help.'

I tried not to sound too keen as Tony was always so cautious, and over-enthusiasm on my part tended to produce a counterbalancing brake on his. But, to my surprise, he liked the idea.

'If the teacher's happy and thinks you'll be a help, I can't see why not. It'll be something to occupy you. Go ahead, darling. Good show.'

The school was the last in a row of three buildings, one of which was the tiny estate hospital—two beds, a dispensary and the doctor's surgery. Next came the crèche, an otherwise empty room where sheets were hung from the ceiling to make hammocks in which the babies were stored—and "storage" was the right word, as the bundles made the place look more like a grain silo than a dormitory. At the other end of the room, toddlers scrambled around the bare, clay floor with a couple of *ayahs* to watch over them. The school consisted of a single classroom, and the only teachers were Neela and an older woman, who was painfully shy and utterly unsuited to teaching. The children sat around low tables, cross-legged on the floor. Each table roughly approximated to an age group, but Neela had little opportunity to teach them separately so, most of the time, the older children chanted their times tables together or listened to the lesson, while the younger ones played with roughly carved, wooden toys and looked at picture books under the watch of the older woman.

My duties were enjoyable and I found them rewarding: I took groups in turn to one end of the room and listened to their reading, and then read them all stories. They clustered around me like iron filings to a magnet, reaching out their little hands to touch me and shyly asking me my name. At the end of my first day, I was exhausted but elated. As I rode home, I asked myself how I'd ever found Indian people frightening. These children, with their eagerness to learn, their curiosity, their happy smiles and infectious laughter, meant more to me than any of the shallow snobs at The Planters' Club.

When Tony came home that first evening I couldn't stop talking and put him through a barrage of questions and suggestions to improve the facilities at the school. His initial enthusiasm was soon tempered by doubt, and then annoyance.

'What do you expect me to do, Ginny? We're not damned missionaries. Already go well beyond the call of duty for the workers on the estate. Better off than most labourers in India. Defy you to go into any village that's not connected to a tea plantation and show me schools that are better supplied. It's what we planters do. Always thought it a bit OTT myself, but that's how it's always been done. Makes a happy, productive workforce.'

'But they need more teachers and more books. The class is huge and the way the estate is growing, the problem will only get worse.'

'Cross that bridge when we come to it.' He counted on his fingers as he made his points: 'They get housing, a nursery for their babies, subsidised rice and *ragi*, firewood, healthcare, two months' maternity leave on half their wages and a five *rupee* bonus for every baby that survives its first year. What more do you want? Besides, education wasted on most of them. The basics, that's all they need. If we go too far on the schooling front, they'll all bugger off and go to work in the cities and, then, where would we be? Be reasonable, old thing.'

I was so angry with him I feared what I might say, so I went out of the room and shut myself away in my studio. I couldn't help thinking Mr Important *Periyar Dorai* would have been a complete nobody back home in England. Probably a lowly bank clerk with limited prospects.

I DIDN'T SEE Jagadish Mistry for more than a month. I passed by Tony's office so frequently that he was beginning to wonder about my newfound interest in tea—or in him. But the surveyor was never there.

I tried to tell myself my feelings for him were a foolish whimsy. An invention. The beauty of the places we'd seen together, and the things he'd told me, had cast a more favourable light on everything to do with that day, him included. Was it a polar opposite reaction to my initial antipathy towards him? Like a pendulum, after swinging between these extremes would I eventually find the midpoint and see him as he was: no more than the first Indian person I'd got to know and like?

But, as I processed these thoughts, a vision of him swam into my mind's eye and, as I looked upon his face, the dark, silk arches of his eyebrows, the brown eyes, the long straight nose, the set of his mouth, I longed to be with him again.

How much my views had changed—when first in India, I'd feared and kept my distance from Indian people, slightly repelled by their differences from me. Now I wanted to know what it would be like to put my mouth against Jagadish's and kiss him slowly, taste him, feel his skin against mine, be held in his arms.

Then one morning, there he was. On the steps to my veranda. I was so startled when I looked up and saw him, I let out a little cry.

'I'm sorry, I didn't mean to frighten you.'

'Mr Mistry, you have a habit of coming upon me without warning.'

'Maybe I don't want to give you time to run away.'

'Why would I do that?' I looked down, as I felt myself beginning to blush.

He didn't answer me. Instead, he said, 'I've come to take you to see the *kurinji* flowers.'

'But...'

'I'm playing truant, Mrs Tilman. But with Tony's permission. I told him you wanted to see the flowers and, today, he suggested I might be spared.'

I must have looked surprised, as he added, 'He seems to think you need to be diverted. He told me you've been sad and preoccupied lately. He fears you are homesick for England.'

'I'm not at all homesick.'

'In need of diversion, then?'

'Not that, either. I've been learning Tamil and helping out at the school a bit. But I do so want to see the flowers and...'

He tilted his head on one side as he waited for me to finish.

'...And I suppose I'd better get changed. Are we riding?'

'It's quite far. I thought we'd go on my motorcycle. Is that okay? You don't mind?'

On the contrary, I felt myself shivering at the prospect. I ran inside and found a pair of trousers. A skirt wouldn't be a good idea. He called out to me, 'You need a warm jacket, it gets cold on the bike.'

I was nervous as we approached the vehicle; not about riding one for the first time, but at the prospect of being so close to him, body to body. Did Tony know we were going by bike? Probably not. As he didn't approve of me visiting Indian temples, he was unlikely to be keen on me riding pillion behind an Indian.

He handed me a pair of goggles and I clambered on behind him. He checked to see if I was comfortable, then fired the machine into life. We roared up the hill in the direction of the town but, about a mile short of there, he diverted from the road onto a dirt track, which led above the tea gardens. It was exhilarating. Fast and free. Hard ground bumping under us. Wind tangling my hair, cold biting my face. Hard to breathe. Eyes watering. His warm body against mine. So fast. Red soil track under the wheels. Colours blurring. Flying. Don't stop. Never stop.

I wanted to lay my head against his back and let my arms encircle him, but instead I held onto the edge of the saddle and looked over his shoulder at the road ahead.

The terrain became rougher and the going slower. Several times he looked back at me to see if I was all right. I grinned at him, unable to conceal my joy. I'd never been happier.

We pulled over and got off the machine. At the top, we could see more hills undulating in front of us. Out of a clump of trees, Sankaram, the Muduvan guide, appeared on his mule and my heart sank. I'd hoped we were going to be alone.

The two men had a hurried conversation. The Muduvan pointed to the distance and drew with a stick in the soil.

Then, with a sideways shake of the head, he went back down the hill towards the town.

'He's not coming?'

'He's not needed. There are no kerns to paint today. He's shown me the way, and now you and I will go together. I've told him to go to his home. He and his wife had a new baby last week. If I'm playing truant, why shouldn't he? He deserves to spend some time with them.'

I felt my heart banging inside the wall of my chest. Tony definitely didn't know about this.

We rode for about half an hour and, then, after rounding a craggy outcrop, we came upon the *neelakurinji* flowers. A big, blue sea across the hillside. I gasped. Without saying anything, we waded together into the thick of them. The flowers were like little bells, clustered on their stalks, a deep purpled-blue. One flower in isolation seemed insubstantial, nothing special, but, en masse, they formed a celestial carpet of colour. I told Mistry it was the opposite of the little pink and yellow *lantana* flowers that grew around the bungalow and only showed their true beauty close up.

He said, 'Like India, itself. Some things are best viewed from a distance, or close up you see the ugliness behind the flashy exterior, while others you need to linger over, to get up close and try to understand. Only then will they reveal their true beauty.'

I nodded. I knew exactly what he meant. I looked back at the field of flowers. 'And they really only flower every twelve years?'

'And only here. Nowhere else on earth.'

'Then they are indeed special.'

'They're said by the Muduvan to be sacred to Lord Murugan.'

'Who was he?'

'The god of war and victory. He's red with six heads and

rides on a blue peacock. He's sacred to the Tamils, and is worshipped out here in the woods and fields. He's much more important in the south than the north of India.'

'Six heads. He must have been very clever.'

'Well, clever enough to win the love of the woman he wanted. And that took some doing.'

'What does he have to do with the *kurinji* flowers?'

'He married a tribal hunter girl called Valli. He first tested her love by taking the mortal form of a handsome hunter but she refused him, so he took the shape of an old man and she refused him again. Finally, he called to Ganesh for help, and Ganesh sent a wild bull elephant after her. She was terrified and agreed to marry the old man if he saved her, which he did. He dragged her off into a thicket to make love to her, but turned back into his normal godly form and she was over-joyed. At their wedding, he wove a garland of *kurinji* flowers and placed it around her neck as a wedding *thali*.'

'Did they live happily ever after?'

He shrugged. 'Who knows? I'd like to think so.'

'And the poem you recited? Say it again.'

'*What could my mother be to yours?*
What kin is my father to yours anyway?
And how did you and I meet ever?
But in love our hearts are as red earth and pouring rain:
mingled beyond parting.'

'I've been thinking of it often. But I still don't see how it's about the *kurinji* flowers.'

'The flowers are the symbols of love, and their flowering is as the flowering of love.'

'So, it could be the words of Valli to Lord Murugan when he placed the *thali* around her neck?'

He looked at me with an intensity that made me look away. What was I letting happen here? I knew why I'd come, and I knew now that was his intent too.

Afraid everything was happening too fast and struggling to breathe, I moved out of the field of flowers. He followed me.

He lifted the tiffin boxes from his saddle bag and set them on the ground, then unrolled a rug and gestured to me to sit down.

As we ate, we spoke of the war and of India. It was a relief to me—and probably to him, too—to break the intensity of the previous moments. Things were moving beyond idle fantasies into something that felt real. Too real. I needed time to take stock. I couldn't let it lead anywhere. I was married. Anything other than a formal friendship with Mistry could exist only in my head; nothing more—not here, not now, not ever.

I forced the words out. I didn't really want to talk about war and politics. 'Hector Channing thinks the viceroy was wrong to declare war on India's behalf, and Nehru and the Congress Party are right to say India should have no part in it.'

He studied my face in silence for a moment, then answered, 'I hate the pettiness and venality of politics, but I love my country. I want to be a free man, governed, however badly, by a government of my own people I've played a part in electing. But I fear what will happen when the war ends and the British are, at last, gone. There's too much hatred and mistrust between Hindus and Muslims, stirred up further by the rivalry of our leaders and, without the steadying hand of the British, I dread to think what might happen. But I want to be free of the yoke of the British Empire. Anything is better than that.'

'Hector used to be a district officer, and said he had incredible power over so many people at a really young age. It made him feel guilty. But he admitted he loved it. That's the trouble, I think. Even well-intentioned people like him can end up enjoying the power, and then it makes it hard for them to let go of it.'

He frowned and looked angry, his eyes darkening. 'They think they have a God-given right to be here. Their arrogance is breath-taking.'

I reached out my hand and placed it on his sleeve. 'I'm sorry.'

'You have no need to apologise. I can't lay the crimes of British imperialism at your door, Ginny.'

I hadn't even noticed he had used my first name until he said, 'I am sorry, Mrs Tilman. I didn't mean to...'

'Please, please call me Ginny. We've got past all that I think.'

'Have we?'

His voice was quiet, 'Then say my name, too.' He smiled and gave a little nod of his head. 'If you can remember it, of course.' And then he was laughing at me.

'Jagadish.' It was the first time I'd spoken it out loud, and I pronounced each of the syllables, rolling them across my tongue as if they were sugar-coated sweets. 'Does it have a meaning? I know many Indian names do.'

He laughed his low rumbling laugh. 'It means "Lord of the Universe".'

'Of course. What else?' I started to laugh helplessly.

'Are you implying something, Ginny?'

I stopped laughing and looked at him. 'I'm afraid I did rather think you were arrogant when I first met you.'

'And now?'

'Now it's different. I think of you entirely differently.'

Our eyes locked and I thought he was going to kiss me, but he didn't. He got up and walked away from me to the edge of the field of flowers. He came back and sat down again beside me, facing out towards the flowers so I could not see his eyes.

'I'm thinking of rejoining the army.' The words were not what I'd expected.

'But you hated it. You told me you didn't like the life.' I could tell my voice sounded pleading.

'I don't. But I'm trained. I'm an officer. They need people like me.'

'But you despise the British. This war isn't your war.'

'This war is everyone's war.'

'I don't understand.'

I could feel tears of disappointment and confusion already pricking at my eyes. I didn't want what he was saying to be true. I wondered if he'd been toying with me.

He turned around to look me squarely in the eyes. 'Yes, I want the British to go. I long for the day when they leave forever. I may not like them, but I know they usually honour their word. Most of them anyway. And the British Empire has become too big to govern. Especially India. They can't keep control of a country as big as ours, with a population of more than three hundred million, and growing. They'll give us independence as soon as the war's over, and so I must help them bring about its end.'

'But they—we—have hung onto India so long. Do you really trust them?'

'They've given us enough reason not to in the past. But it's different now. We've become a burden, not a jewel to them. And it would be facile of me to see their colonisation of India in an over-simplistic way. I'm not so blind that I can't see there have been a few good things as a result of British occupation. They've helped catapult us into the twentieth century. We are like the child, and they the parent. A very bad parent. A very stupid parent. And now the child must grow up and find his own way. We need to pick up the reins of government and commerce and make our own way in the world.'

'Gandhi says supporting the war is wrong.'

'The Mahatma is a good man and his motives are good, but refusing to support Britain in its fight against Hitler won't further India's cause. I don't agree with Chandra Bose, either. He conveniently ignores that Hitler believes the white man is a superior race. How will India fit in his plan of a white master race? If we fail to help Britain in its hour of need and Hitler wins, then we'll open the doors to a new and, probably, more terrible oppression. We'll become slaves dancing to Hitler's tune, instead of being as we are now, within grasp of our own freedom. If we help do the job of stopping Hitler and the Nazi party, it will bring the day closer when we can hoist the flag of our own nation.'

'But to risk your life fighting?'

'My father gave his life fighting in Britain's last war. That was a war without reason, and he did it with honour. How then can I refuse this time, when it is to stop a man who will spread hatred and fear across the world and to bring forward the date when India is free?'

'But you'll be taking a terrible risk.'

'It's worth taking. There are untrained men joining up across the continent. At least I'm trained and skilled as an engineer and an officer. They've already promised to restore my commission.'

'So you'll be leaving here? You're not just thinking about it? You've made up your mind?'

'Yes. When they call for me, I will go.'

'Does Tony know?'

'Not yet.'

'Will he agree?'

'I believe so. Many of the planters will be volunteering.'

'I don't want you to go.'

He looked at me and smiled, but his eyes were filled with sadness. 'Enough of this. It may never happen. They may decide they have no need for me.'

But, as he said the words, we both knew they weren't true.

He jumped up and pulled me to my feet. 'Come on. Let's walk through the flowers. We'll have to wait until 1946 for another chance.'

We walked side-by-side, following a faint trail that wound its way through the *kurinji* flowers and up the other side of the hill. As we walked, we talked, this time avoiding the subject of war. We spoke of my painting, his childhood in Lahore, my former life in London. I told him how much I missed my mother. How I felt guilty I hadn't valued her enough when she was alive.

'I never really took the time to know her properly. I always presumed she wished I wasn't there, that she was sorry I was with her and not my father. My aunt told me she loved me dearly, but struggled to show it. I think I was probably transferring my own feelings onto her. I missed my father, and wished it were my mother who'd died and not he. Does that sound dreadful?'

'No. It sounds honest.'

'She was a terrible snob.'

'Then she wasn't alone in that. It's a common failing among the British.'

'It was probably just her way of taking control, of establishing order. She was always well organised. Liked everything in its place. And that included the social order.'

'The British empire runs on women like her.'

'Yes. She missed her vocation. She had nothing else to organise, so she organised me. I thought she was doing it to get rid of me, to get me married and off her hands, but now I wonder if she wanted to know I was settled as she had a presentiment of what would happen to her.'

'You think she, too, had the gift? The second sight?'

'Perhaps. I don't know, but I do think now she waited for

me to come to her before she died. I doubted myself at first—I thought she squeezed my hand, but she was unconscious so I told myself it was impossible. She died that night. I think she was hanging on for me to get there.'

I reached inside my collar and pulled out the little gold locket Pud had given me and showed it to him.

'She wore this always, and I never knew. It contains a lock of my hair from when I was a baby. Daddy gave it to her when I was born. I didn't even know.'

'How long have you and Tony been married?'

'Just over four years.'

'Do you love him?'

I looked up at him, surprised at the question, but suddenly sure about my answer, 'No. I don't. I never have.'

'Why did you marry him?'

'I thought it would make my mother happy. I thought it would be the right thing for me. He made me feel safe and cared for. He was good looking. He was kind. He came along at the right moment. I thought I'd eventually grow to love him...but I haven't. I can't, no matter how hard I've tried.'

'I thought not.'

'Is it that obvious?'

'He's a decent man. I'm fortunate to have him as a boss. There are many worse. He's fair. He's honest. He's respected. But he's dull. You're like a bright firefly spinning around him. He can't keep up with you.'

'He doesn't try. I can't love him, because he has no inner life. He lives on the surface. He does his duty. He does his job. He plays sports. But, whenever I've tried to get under the surface, there's nothing there.' I blushed. 'I feel bad talking about him in this way, but...'

'Don't feel bad. I understand.'

'Do you? Do you really?'

'I, too, am married.' Seeing my expression he said, 'No—

you wouldn't have known—I don't speak of my wife. It's easier to present myself as though I were a bachelor.'

'Who knows about this?'

'Just Tony. No one else here. I don't want questions from colleagues about why my wife isn't here. I married when I was eighteen. I had no choice. My mother has been little more than a shadow since my father was killed. My uncle was like a father to me and, as well as supporting our family and arranging my education, he also arranged my marriage to a woman of our caste, whose father was a superior officer in my uncle's regiment. A military marriage, I suppose. She was a sickly girl and sullen. She wanted the marriage as little as I did but, like me, she was an obedient child.'

'What happened?'

'We never got on. She spent much of her time in bed, too ill to do anything. She has no interests. She has no skills. I think she is actually a little slow and simple in the head. I knew at once she didn't like me. I think she was actually a little afraid of me.'

'Where is she now?'

He hesitated. 'She lives with my uncle and my mother, and the rest of my uncle's family. She would prefer to live with her own parents, but that would cause a scandal, so living with mine is a compromise as her family is close by. They tell people I'm away on military service. I make occasional appearances and it satisfies any curiosity. I think my uncle and his friend feel guilty about the lies they told me about her, so they don't make a fuss about us living apart. Like you, I tried really hard to make the marriage work. God knows I did. I felt duty-bound to my uncle after the sacrifices he'd made for my mother and me. She came with a sizable dowry, which helped repay some of the money he'd spent on us and helps with the support of my mother. But it's no use. I think marrying for love runs in my family—not only my *da-dee-mah*, but my mother and father, too.'

'You said your wife was sickly. What's wrong with her?'

He laughed a bitter laugh. 'You name it. All kinds of minor ailments.'

'I'm sorry.'

'So, Ginny, I know as well as you do what an empty marriage means.'

'And children?'

He looked away, then said, 'I hoped children would make a difference to her, that she might find some fulfilment in them, but she hated what it took to make them and it's hard for a man to have to force himself on his wife.'

I looked away, afraid of where we were heading, of what we were getting into.

'You have no children?' he asked.

'I had two miscarriages. Tony wanted a family, so I'm afraid I've rather let the side down.'

'You blame yourself?' His voice was shocked. 'Why?'

'I used to drink quite a lot. And I didn't eat enough. The doctor said I was seriously undernourished.'

He laughed a harsh laugh. 'If undernourishment was a way to avoid pregnancy, we wouldn't have an exploding population here. Do you want children? Not Tony, you?'

'I thought I did, but I think now it was mostly because I wanted to please him. And I don't think that's a good reason to start a family. What I mean is, it's not good to do it just to please someone else. And I'm not sure I'd make a good mother.'

'Very few people think they will until it happens. At least that's what my *da-dee-mah* used to say. But to have a child to save a marriage doesn't strike me as a good thing for the child—or the marriage.'

I nodded. 'You're right. Goodness, how did we get onto all this? It feels like I'm a Catholic in the confessional.'

He laughed, then more thoughtful, added, 'How has India been for you, Ginny? It must have been a huge change from the world you knew before.'

'I think I've been living my life on the surface, too. Going through the motions. Ever since I came to India. I couldn't get under the skin of the country. And, it's funny, because Lilian once said to me it's the other way around—India gets under your skin and never lets you go.'

'And has it now?'

'It took a long time. I hated it at first. Not the countryside I've always loved that. But the strangeness of it all. It was overwhelming. But yes it has now. Since...'

He looked at me, head tilted slightly to one side in that way of his.

'Since I got to know you, Jag. You have opened it to me. I feel as though I've been underwater and have burst through to the surface. I've come up for air. I feel alive. Today, and the day we rode the boundaries, I've seen more and felt happier than at any time since...well since Daddy died, actually. Does that sound awfully silly?'

He didn't reply, just shook his head. Then, as though he'd remembered something, he frowned and looked at his watch. 'We should be getting back soon. Why don't you sit down here, and I'll walk back and fetch the motorcycle?'

I started to protest, but he added, 'You must be tired— we've been walking for a long time. Wait here, enjoy the flowers and the view. It's your last chance for several years. I won't be long.'

I sat down on the grassy slope and must have fallen asleep, as the next thing I knew the sun had moved behind the high hills and there was a slight chill in the air. I jerked upright and felt something around my neck. I put my hand up to my collar bone and found the flowers. He must have twisted them into a plaited garland and tied them around my neck as I slept.

He said nothing. He was leaning back against a rock a few feet away from me, just looking at me, in that same way he'd looked me at me at the dinner party. Only this time, I was glad he was looking at me like that. I was looking at him, too, and wanted the moment to go on forever. He pushed himself off the rock face and moved towards me. My stomach lurched, and I sat still, my hand still touching the *kurinji* flowers at my throat. He reached his hand down to me and pulled me to my feet, and that was the last moment before. Before Jagadish. Before my life changed forever.

But we had to get back. Tony would be sending out a search party if we did not return at a reasonable hour.

I knew now I loved him. Madly, insanely, without rhyme or reason. I remembered what Hector had said on the subject of being in love, and I had no doubt at all in my head Jagadish Mistry was the one, the only one. I wondered why it had taken me so long to realise it.

The ride back to Mudoorayam passed in a moment. Just before we got to the main road, he pulled up. I had my arms around his waist and he placed his hands on top of mine and squeezed them gently. I wanted to ride away with him, behind him on his motorcycle, my face buried in the smooth leather of his jacket and my arms holding him so tightly he'd be unable to escape. He turned around in the saddle, and we leaned into each other and embraced under the branches and aerial roots of a *peepal* tree. He held my face in his hands, and pulled back from the kiss and locked his eyes onto mine. It felt as though he was looking into my soul.

Then, he turned round and fired up the machine. We were almost back at the plantation. I could see the factory in the distance and the long, low building that was the estate office.

I whispered into his ear. 'When will we see each other again?'

'I'll get word to you.'

'I love you.'

Instead of answering, he took one hand off the handle-bars and placed it over mine and squeezed them as I held onto him.

Tony was outside waiting for us as we rode down the hill. He waved as we approached.

'Damn good job I didn't know you were taking her off on that contraption, Mistry. I'd have been worried sick all afternoon. Thought you were going by car? You all right, Ginny?'

I nodded.

'Hope my little lady didn't cause you too much trouble? Get to see those flowers?'

Without waiting for an answer, he helped me off the motorbike and nodding at Jagadish, bundled me towards his waiting motorcar.

I twisted round to say goodbye, but Jag was already pulling his goggles on. I called out to him, 'Thank you, Mr Mistry. It was a wonderful day.'

When we got in the car, Tony turned to me before he started the car. 'Not sure I'm happy about you gadding about the countryside on a motorbike. Not very dignified,' he paused, then added, 'but it must have done you good. Colour in your cheeks again.'

He was unusually talkative in the car and wanted to know what I had thought of the *neelakurinji* flowering. I didn't really want to talk about it with him. It would have been an unwelcome intrusion on the beauty of the day. Instead, I talked vaguely about the beauty of the scenery, conscious of the garland of flowers around my neck and concealed under my jacket.

'Got along all right with old Mistry? Know you weren't that keen on him at first but he's a decent enough cove.'

The words "for an Indian" were implied, but unspoken. I forced myself to be the Ginny I'd been this morning, to step into her shoes and go back to the time I was already starting to think of as B.J. Before Jagadish. 'I still think he's a bit of a smart Alec.'

'A bit conceited, but a bright chap. Have high hopes for him. Thinking of stretching him a bit by giving him some of Goddard's responsibilities. A bit more dosh for him. Should keep him happy enough. Just as long as this darned war doesn't get in the way.'

'What do you mean?'

'He's ex-army. He'll be among the first to be called up if the Japs up the ante.'

'But that's not likely?'

He frowned. 'More likely than not. Could be in it for the long haul. Thought we'd never have that again after the last time, but the damned Germans never learn. As for those horrible little Nips...'

'But we're so far away from it all.'

'Shrinking world, Ginny. India's at war, too. Like it or not. At least, tea production is vital to the war effort so doubt I'll get the call-up myself. Many of the chaps are talking of signing up, maybe I need to think about doing the old duty for king and country and all that.'

'You're not serious? And, anyway, you're already in the Auxiliaries.'

'Let's not think about it now. Fancy a spot of grub at the club?'

When we got home from the club that night I was getting undressed when I felt him come up behind me. He placed his hands on my hips and began to kiss my neck. I jumped away in surprise. It was most unlike him these days. He pulled me back towards him, and encircled my waist with his arms and whispered in my ear.

'I was checking the calendar, and it's one of our nights.'

He kissed the back of my neck. My body stiffened, and I felt panic rising in me. Not today of all days. Not when every one of my nerve endings was still tingling with the sensation of touching Jagadish and longing to feel his body against mine, bare skin on bare skin. I couldn't stand the thought that instead, a pyjama-clad Tony would be going through the usual mechanical mid-cycle routine.

'I'm tired, Tony.'

But he was, unusually, not to be deterred. 'Come on, darling. Remember what the doctor said. How important it is to keep to the dates we've marked up and not to let what's happened in the past put us off. I promise to go easy on you, old girl.'

Any other time and I'd have found his complete lack of romance almost funny. But that night, it just made me feel sad and sorry for myself. Until I had a chance to speak again with Jagadish, I was afraid of Tony finding out about us. And, then I realised, I had no idea myself what was about to happen between us. All I knew was I wanted to be with Jag, and I didn't care how it came about. But he was still Tony's employee, and I was Tony's wife and there was a war on. I had a little money in London—as well as my share of the house in Leighton Square. I'd no idea how much cash was in the bank, as the probate on my mother's estate was held up by the war. I just wished it would hurry up and be over so Jagadish and I could go to London and start a new life. But, meanwhile, Tony was nuzzling at my ear.

CHAPTER 23

IT WAS MORE than a week before I saw Jagadish again. I was at the point of fabricating a reason to go over to the Tilman's office in the hope of running into him, when he rode up on his motorcycle while I was sitting in the garden. My heart almost burst through my chest as he walked towards me. Thankappan and Nirmala had just left for the market and were unlikely to return for a couple of hours. Tony was in Cochin.

He pulled me out of the chair and into his arms. We kissed, and then I hammered my fists into his chest.

'Where have you been? Why haven't you been in touch? I've been going crazy. I was so afraid. I thought you were regretting what happened.'

'Never. Things have been difficult and I couldn't get away. Tony's been stuck to me like glue. Today was my first chance. I've been waiting at the end of the driveway for your servants to leave.'

'How did you know they were going to the market today?'
'Never mind.'

He took my hand and led me into the house. As soon as

we got inside, we began to pull at each other's clothing. We were naked by the time we got to the end of the corridor and I steered him into the guest bedroom, empty since Marjorie's departure. He lifted me into his arms and carried me over to the bed.

My skin tingled under his hands and I shivered. His skin was smooth and firm and brown. If I lived forever, I'd never get enough of looking into his eyes.

Afterwards, lying in a tangle of brown and white limbs, I ran my fingers through his hair; it was thick and heavy, but soft as silk. I rolled onto my side and let my hands trace the bend of his knee and the swell of his chest, and the flat plane of his stomach; everywhere, trying to capture a tactile and visual memory of him that I could draw upon when he was gone. He looked into my eyes and laughed. 'What did I do deserve this, Ginny? You are the most beautiful creature. When I saw you at that dreadful dinner party, I wanted to take you by the hand and run away with you there and then. When you spilt that ridiculous pudding on your dress, I wanted to follow you to your room and take it off you to see what lay beneath. And now I can see.'

'I trust you're not disappointed?'

His eyes travelled over my outstretched body. 'Not bad.'

Before I could react, he pulled me into his arms and whispered, 'Beyond my wildest dreams. You are a goddess, Ginny, my own Valli.'

As we lay in each other's arms, he told me more about his life in the army, his closeness to his grandmother and his distant relationship with his mother after the death of his father.

'When my father was killed, my mother pulled away from all her children. I suppose she had some kind of mental depression, or was overwhelmed with grief. We couldn't understand—I especially, as the youngest. That's why my *daa-dee-maa* was so important to me. She brought me up.'

'I was closer to my father than my mother. I still find it hard to believe that she really loved me.'

I looked at him, then away again.

'Why do you find it hard to believe?' he said.

'I suppose I've always thought of myself as unlovable. I don't think I've always been the nicest of people. I'm still not.'

He didn't contradict me, but let me go on.

'I sometimes think maybe it wasn't my mother who struggled to show her feelings, but me. There was never any doubt how she and Daddy felt about each other. I felt a bit left out. Then when he died and it was just she and I, and she was so sad, I was at that awkward age. Too proud to show weakness. Afraid to display how I felt. So we kept each other pretty well at arm's length.'

'You're not, you know.'

'Not what?'

'Unlovable. I knew I loved you the moment I saw you. But you knew I loved you, didn't you? You must have been able to tell?'

'I knew you were interested in me, I suppose. I thought you were a bit full of yourself, actually. Rather a big head. Too jolly clever by half. What was it you said your name means? Master of all the Universe?'

He laughed. Laughter for Jagadish was something he threw his whole body into; an affirmation, a dance, an expression of joy.

'Don't spare me will you, Ginny, just tell it how it is.'

'How it is, is I love you. To distraction.'

I put my hands behind my neck and undid the clasp of my mother's locket. I handed it to him.

'Take this, Jag. I want you to have something of mine to keep with you always. There is a lock of my hair inside.'

'But this was your mother's locket. I can't take it from you.'

'Yes, you can. You must. I want you to. Whenever we're apart, you can touch it and think of me. You'll be carrying a piece of me with you everywhere. Keep it safe for me.'

He closed his hand around it. Then he jumped up from the bed and started to gather his scattered clothes together.

'I need to get a move on. Your servants will be back soon.'

'I don't care. People will find out sooner or later. But I do need to tell Tony first. I have a plan, Jag. I want to tell him as soon as possible—I can't go on living with him as man and wife. Not after this.'

I was talking excitedly, then realised he was frowning. But I blundered on, regardless, 'We could live in Bombay or somewhere until the war is over. It wouldn't be right to stay in Mudoorayam. Once it's over, we could go to London. I think you'd love it. I'll have my inheritance then. It's not a huge amount. I mean we won't be stinking rich or anything, but it should be more than enough for us for us to live on comfortably. And you can find work there.'

He moved towards me and gently pinned my arms against my sides. 'Steady on, Ginny. It's too soon to be making plans.'

My face must have fallen, as he hastily added, 'It all sounds wonderful, but you mustn't tell Tony yet.' His eyebrows were knitted in a frown and his face looked troubled.

'Why not? He has to know in the end. I can't live a lie.'

'I've told you, my darling, I may be going to war. We can't tell him and then have me go off to war and leave you here to face the music. We have to wait. I want to know you're safe here. Tony's devoted to you. I feel bad for him about what's happening. He'll be cut to the quick. He adores you and he's trusted me.'

'I can't stay with him. It's not possible. Not now. I can't stand the thought of him touching me. Of having to lie. You must see? I'd rather go back to England and wait for you till the war is over.'

'Of course, I don't want you to be with him. The thought of it makes me crazy. But we have to think it through carefully. Promise me you won't say anything yet?'

'But, Jag.'

'Promise? I need time to make plans. We have to be cautious. If we tell him, I'll lose my job. You'll lose your home. I have to send money each month to my wife and my *daa-dee-maa*. They depend on me.'

I slumped back down onto the edge of the bed, crushed with disappointment. 'I think Tony's been having an affair. He can hardly claim the moral high ground.'

Jag looked at me in astonishment. 'An affair? Tony? Not a chance.'

I didn't want to talk about Tony. I wanted Jag to see things the way I did. That we couldn't be apart for a moment longer. 'Jag, we love each other.'

'Yes, we do. And I'll work it out. We will have time to be together properly in the future. Meanwhile, it must be our secret. When I put those flowers around your neck, I was saying that you will be mine forever. And I will be yours.'

'But we're not together.'

'Patience, little Valli. It will happen.' And then he kissed me again.

A WEEK later he appeared in the driveway while I was pruning the roses. He was in riding gear and I saw the grey thoroughbred and the little bay mare tied up to the fencing outside the gate.

'Come on, there's only a few hours before dark.'

I dashed inside and changed and then hurried down the drive beside him, longing to touch him, but conscious of the risk of being seen by the servants.

'I have to check part of the top division. Elephants may have broken down the fencing, so I suggested you come along and Tony was keen on the idea.'

'I should feel bad about deceiving him, but I don't. And, anyway, he's having an affair.'

'I think you'd better tell me about this woman you think he's been seeing. I'm not convinced.'

'It's Daphne Bingham.'

He laughed. 'Daphne Bingham? She's just got engaged.'

I told him what Marjorie had said, how I'd seen them together at the Banerji wedding and Tony hadn't mentioned it, and how the two of them had disappeared together at her party. 'She's only marrying that chap from Calcutta for his money. It doesn't mean she's not having an affair with Tony. In fact, it gives her cover.'

'Tony disappearing at the party was no mystery. She pounced on him as soon as the two of you arrived, and asked him to run over to the club for more glasses and to pick up her fiancé. You were talking to Mrs Bulstrode-Hemmings so you didn't notice. I know because Hector and I were there when it happened. He returned not long after you left and had the man from Calcutta with him. He'd been staying at the club.'

'That proves nothing. Why did she ask Tony? There were plenty of other people she could have got to go with her.'

'They didn't go together. She was at the party all the time. Never left. It was crowded, but I'm surprised you didn't see her. Look, I don't know why I'm defending Tony. Believing him to be having an affair would make me feel a hell of a lot better about what's happened between us, but I can't have you impugning Daphne Bingham. She's one of the few women in Mudoorayam who doesn't act as if Indians are a lower form of life. She can be a bit full of herself, and she's a terrible flirt, but I'm sure she has no designs on Tony.'

I wasn't completely convinced, but I was beginning to accept there might be another side to the story, especially now I'd been told so by Lilian, Hector and now Jag. But, if he wasn't having a thing with Daphne, I had lost my self-justification for what I was doing with Jag. Daphne Bingham had been a convenient excuse for me.

But I didn't want to think about Daphne or Tony anymore. Today, there was only the man riding beside me. We rode through the afternoon, following the red earth tracks that bordered the tea gardens. The frequent piles of dung attested to the previous presence of elephants. As we rode he talked about them; how they slept standing up during the daytime, hidden in the depths of the forest; how they didn't eat tea because the leaves cut their tongues; that a useful escape route from a marauding bull was to head away from it into the tea bushes moving downhill as they couldn't follow downwards; how they could only see sideways so standing in front, invisible, would anger them.

We reached the boundary of the top division and followed it along to an area where the fencing was trampled flat. Jag noted down the map coordinates and then turned to me. 'Job done.'

He jumped down from his horse and helped me off mine, and we tied them up and sat together on a grassy mound overlooking the valley. Far below were the buildings of the tea factory and the estate office, the little estate cottage hospital and the long lines of blue-painted labourers' houses, clustered at the bottom of the valley. My own bungalow stood apart, on a rise above the rest, and a couple of miles further were the rooftops of Muddy. It was like a rumpled patchwork quilt: green tea bushes and trees, patches of red earth, the odd purple splash of a *jacaranda* tree with the dark threads of narrow roadways and tracks forming the stitching between.

We sat in silence, holding hands. I wanted to ask him if he'd thought any more about what we were going to do, but I didn't want to press him. I suddenly felt shy, unsure of myself. I even began to wonder if, perhaps, I had misinterpreted his intentions, if he were trifling with me. To me it was clear. We had to be together, war or no war, there had to be a way. We were meant to be together. But there was something still niggling at the back of my head. When he took me in his arms, I pulled away.

'I have to tell you something, Jag. I don't want any secrets between us. You may decide you want nothing more to do with me, so I'm very afraid. But I still have to tell you. I can't live with a lie.'

His eyes were full of concern and he stroked my hair. 'There's nothing you can say could make me love you less.'

'You remember what you told me about that girl, Savita?'

He nodded.

I avoided his eyes as I spoke, staring ahead of me down the valley without seeing. 'When I was just fourteen years old, a man who was a friend of my father seduced me. I had a relationship with him until my mother found out. It was just before I met Tony. Like Savita, I was disgraced. My mother had plans for me to marry well and was terrified of the scandal.'

I couldn't look at Jagadish, afraid how he would react to my story. I went on to tell him of the art exhibition and what Rupert Milligan had done to me over the years. I even told him about the stranger on the ship.

'So you see, I'm not the woman you thought I was. I will understand if you don't want me anymore. I won't be able to bear it, but I'll understand it.'

He was silent for a moment, and then he pulled me into his arms and covered my face with kisses. 'How could you think that, my darling, my love? I love you more than ever. I want to make that pain go away. I want to be with you. And I promise you we will be together all the time. Not yet, but soon. As soon as we can. Trust me.'

Then as he spoke, with a clap of thunder the heavens opened and torrential rain began, turning the red soil path around us into a rusty river. He clutched my hand and holding his jacket over us led me further up the track.

'What about the horses?'

'They'll be fine. They're used to the rain. They'll find cover over there at the edge of the forest. There's a hut up here, one of the estate's shelters. Come.'

We were soaked to our skins. It was a deluge, even by Muddy standards; so heavy it was hard to breathe. I tried not to stumble in the growing torrent beneath our feet and struggled to see what was ahead. My clothes clung to my body, chafing my skin as we walked. The rain had darkened the sky, blotting out the entire valley in a curtain of iron grey, turning the colours to monochrome.

In the hut we found blankets, a bit musty-smelling, but clean and dry. We peeled off our clothes like snakes shedding skin and fell shivering into each other's arms under the blankets. At once I felt renewed, naked, my limbs wrapped around his; as if I'd sloughed off my past, my guilt, my sadness, my pain, my shame. Jag didn't make me feel safe. He made me feel brave.

We made love, passionately, hungrily at first, then again, slowly, lingering, discovering. I felt like another person—I couldn't reconcile the way I felt now with the unhappy woman who had travelled out to India, with the woman who had found it so hard to adjust to life in Muddy, the woman who was fearful of putting a foot wrong. This Ginny was joyful, fulfilled, loving and loved, and terribly, terribly, happy.

We lay there as night fell, making plans and listening to the rain hammering a tattoo on the tin roof of the shelter. Not real concrete plans, but imagined ones, hypotheses. The uncertainty of the war and Jag's decision to fight in it, prevented anything other than what-ifs. I still couldn't understand why he wanted to fight with the British army, when everything he believed in was against that. But, at the same time, I respected his decision and loved him all the more for his sense of purpose and his refusal to compromise when faced with tough choices. But it couldn't stop every fibre of me crying out inside and protesting against him making such a sacrifice and risking everything.

We woke as the sun was rising. The air was fresh, new after the rain and the light was limpid and luminous. We found the horses and rode together as far as the bottom of the road to my bungalow. It was only then a chill came over me as I wondered what I was going to say to Tony about my absence all night.

But I didn't need to manufacture an excuse. I found him sitting in the drawing room, slumped in a chair, his head in his hands. He looked up at me and I saw his face was ashen. I stood rooted to the spot, shocked at seeing him like that, and my first thought was he knew about where I'd been and what I'd been doing. He stretched a hand towards me, his face gaunt.

'It's the mater. She's gone. Got word today. Ship sunk by a U-boat in the Mediterranean. She's gone, Ginny, she's gone.'

His voice was tremulous and he looked close to tears. I didn't know what to say, so I laid a hand awkwardly on his shoulder. He placed his hand over mine, and then pulled me towards him onto the sofa and laid his head in my lap so I could feel his warm tears through the legs of my jodhpurs.

'Should never have let her go. Knew it was too dangerous. But she insisted. Why did I agree? It's all my fault.'

Then he jerked his head up and looked at me, brushing his blonde hair out of his eyes. He looked just like a little boy, and I felt slightly repelled. But the moment passed, and the stiff-upper-lipped Tony I knew returned. He pulled out his handkerchief, dried his eyes and blew his nose loudly.

'You're all I have now, darling. Just you and me. Promise me you'll never leave me?' Then he pulled me into his arms and squeezed me so tightly, I thought he'd squeeze the breath out of me.

He left for the estate office a few minutes later, not even mentioning my overnight absence. When he returned that evening, he was all business-as-usual. Over the next few days, he organised a memorial service for his mother at the English church on the hill above the town. The grey, stone building was packed. Despite the dislike Hector maintained most people felt for Marjorie, they were prepared to give her a good send off—or maybe they needed the vicar's words to really believe she was gone. I listened to the eulogies with mounting disbelief, amazed people could find so many ways to praise a woman they disliked so much, all of them lies or, at best, elaborations of grains of truth. For my own part, I was relieved at her going. She was the cruellest, most unpleasant woman I'd ever encountered.

I HAD no word from Jag until several days later. I was sitting in front of the fire in the drawing room with Tony; he was reading a newspaper and I was browsing a book of poetry. Since falling in love with Jag, I didn't want to read anything else; in an endless quest to find something that summed up how I felt about him.

From behind the newspaper Tony said, 'War's definitely

335

hotting up. Going to have a struggle to keep production up at the plant. More than fifty of the workers volunteered for active service this morning. Half the town planning to join up. Jolly good show I suppose, especially with Gandhi rabbiting on all the time about pacifism and Congress trying to convince the natives we're the real enemy.'

I looked up and nodded, pretending to listen as he droned on.

'Bunch of damn commies. Especially that Bose fellow who set up that damn fool All India Forward party. All India Backward is more like it. Probably hoping while we've got our hands full, they can stir up civil disobedience. Stupid bloody plan. Fortunately, not a lot of the fellows have much time for him. That's why they're all joining up and showing support to the king. Know which side their bread's buttered on.'

His mother had used the same clichéd expression to Jag over dinner, and I smiled, remembering him telling her bread and butter was not something Indians were interested in. My eyes went back to my poetry book. Tony was in one of his rare talkative moments. The war and Indian politics had given my normally taciturn husband a taste for bluster.

'What's really put the cat among the pigeons is losing Mistry.'

'I beg your pardon?' I was listening now.

'A while ago, he arranged to rejoin his regiment if they needed him. Wasn't expecting the call so soon.'

I put down my book and walked over to the window so he wouldn't see my face. It was a struggle to conceal my emotions. But then he was never the most observant of people. Why hadn't Jag contacted me? 'When is he due to leave?'

'Gone already.'

'He can't have. Are you sure? When I saw him the other

day, he told me he wasn't likely to be called for months.' I struggled to keep the emotion out of my voice.

Tony looked at me quizzically over the top of his newspaper. 'I thought you weren't keen on him?'

I tried to sound normal and gripped the edge of the windowsill. I could see my knuckles were white as I dug my fingernails into the wood. 'He's pleasant enough, I suppose. But why on earth would he want to go back into the army?'

'Honourable chap. Wants to serve king and empire. Keep the old flag flying.'

'When did he leave?'

'Last night. Damned inconvenient. It's dropped me right in it.'

'Last night?' My words were little more than a whisper.

'Gone straight to join his regiment. Think they're planning on posting him abroad. Top-secret stuff, I gather. Wouldn't be surprised if it's North Africa. Top man, though. Can't blame the army for wanting to get their hands on him again. Pain in the neck for all of us at Tilman's, but needs must. Needs must. Hey, you all right, Ginny, old thing?'

'Just a little tired.'

He picked up the paper again, and spoke from behind it, 'Now he's gone, I can use his bungalow again for the Visiting Inspector. Save on hotel bills. The Valley Range put their prices up again last week. Damned profiteering if you ask me. Wife and children will have to go back to his family.'

'The Inspector's?'

'No Mistry's.'

My breathing almost stopped. 'But his wife is ill with tuberculosis and doesn't live here. She lives with his family. She's away in a clinic at the moment.'

He chuckled. 'Well, maybe, he has another wife? These Mohammedans often do. Although I had him down as a Hindi. Never entirely sure. Whoever they are, the family living in his bungalow has to be gone by the end of the month. Strange thing though, you thinking he has another wife. With TB, eh? Still the gossip machine always gets these things wrong. Heard it from Lilian did you? Often gets her facts wrong.'

While he waffled on, I fought back tears and was afraid if I said more I'd lose control. 'Look, Tony, I'm jolly tired. I'm think I'll skip supper and have an early night.'

'Of course. You turn in. See you in the morning. I'll be coming to bed late. I'll try not to disturb you, old thing. Got to catch up on some infernal paperwork.'

When I got to the bedroom, I shut the door behind me and flung myself on the bed. My nerve ends were jangling, and I realised I was in shock. I lay in the dark, unable to think; my head full of his face, the sound of his voice, the feel of his hands on me, the smell of his hair. I could make no sense of it. It was as though the earth had been ripped off its axis. I'd never been so alone.

Why had he gone without getting word to me? Then I thought of Savita and what Jag had said about how people viewed a woman who had been dishonoured. Maybe that's what he thought about me? I tortured myself that he'd seen me as a woman of easy virtue—just as the man on the boat had done. Perhaps I'd just been a diversion for him? And he'd lied to me. It was all lies.

I remember little of the days that followed, just a vague impression of Tony lurking anxiously at the bedroom door. Disembodied voices. I lay in bed for days, giving myself up to grief, wallowing in it, letting the tears blind me. Sheets soaked with them. Burrowing down into the bed, heart torn out, wanting the mattress to suck me in and make me disappear. Cruel, faithless, Jag. Stupid, gullible, Ginny. Grief, pain and betrayal gnawing me away like a rat devouring me from inside. Killing me slowly. *Can you cry yourself to death?*

Tony hadn't a clue why I was like this. I overheard him on the telephone to Lilian one evening, speculating that I was suffering delayed grief about Marjorie. As if! I didn't care a damn that she was dead. I wished I were, too.

One morning he caught me vomiting over the thunderbox in the bathroom and suggested I might be pregnant again, but he never suspected for a moment I was being eaten away from the inside by grief, loss, betrayal and a sense of utter loneliness of biblical proportions.

CHAPTER 24

MY DESPAIR TURNED to anger and, then, curiosity took over. I didn't want to believe Jagadish had lied to me about his family and left without leaving me word, and I hoped beyond reason it was all a mistake or a misunderstanding. I even thought Tony might be lying. Perhaps he'd found out about Jag and me, and had got rid of him and invented the story. I decided the only way to find out was to go to his house.

It was a square, timber-framed bungalow on the other side of the tea gardens, about two miles from the tea factory. I chose a day Tony was in Cochin at the tea auctions. I knocked at the door and waited a few minutes before it opened. She was short and, at first, I thought she was fat, until I realised she was heavily pregnant. Two children peered out from behind her; little hands gripping onto the folds of her *sari*. The older girl must have been about four, her ears pierced with tiny gilt hoops and a coil of brightly coloured beads around her neck; the sophistication of jewellery contrasting with the innocence and mischief in her eyes. The younger girl had a tiny topknot on her head and masses of coloured bangles around her chubby little wrists.

'My name is...'

'I know who you are.' She started to push the door shut, but I leaned towards her and held it open with my palm.

'Why has he gone?'

'You have no right to ask. You have no right to come here. Go away. Leave us in peace.' She said something in her language to the children, who ducked away into the gloom of the house. 'It is because of you my husband has gone away. Get out of my sight. I curse you. If he is killed in battle, it will be on your head. I curse you. I curse you.' She practically spat the words at me.

I backed a step away, relinquishing my hold on the door. Immediately, she stepped back and slammed the door shut behind her, leaving me standing on the threshold.

I WALKED home in the pouring rain; blind to the mud under my feet, oblivious to the way I was drenched to the skin. His treachery was absolute. He had lied. He had made love to me and made me believe he loved me and, all the time, he was concealing the truth from me. When I thought of the woman in the bungalow, I wanted to howl out loud; the mother of his children, with another child growing in her belly. It was cruel. It was too cruel. How could the man I loved from the depths of my being have done this to me? Why hadn't he told me the truth? Why had he led me to believe he loved me and one day we'd be together? Why had he told me a cock-and-bull story about a wife with tuberculosis who would give him no children?

When I got home, I asked Nirmala to draw me a bath, then I threw off my mud-spattered clothes and climbed in. I let the heat of the water warm my cold body, and then I leaned back and let my head slip under the water. *Let me drown. Let it all be over. Let me be Savita with someone to hold me under while I die. Breathe. Let the water in. Into the lungs. It's meant to be peaceful to die like this. Just breathe.*

But my body fought back, and I burst up to the air, coughing, spluttering, spitting the water out. Throat burning. Eyes stinging. I stayed there, tears mingling with the bath water until it was cold, and I climbed out, dried myself down and went back inside the house.

Nirmala stared at me as I walked along the corridor, trailing my muddy clothes behind me. I couldn't take any more of it. I flung the bundle of dirty clothes at her and screeched like a banshee, 'Why are you looking at me? Go away. Leave me alone.'

Then I went into my studio and fell asleep on the coach.

A hand was shaking me gently. Tony, sitting beside me on the edge of the daybed. 'What's wrong? Why are you in your dressing gown? What's up old thing? Not yourself these days. Nirmala's frightfully upset about something. Says you yelled at her?'

'Screw Nirmala.'

'Ginny, really.'

'I don't like her. She doesn't like me either. But she can go to hell. You can all go to hell.'

I saw sadness and disappointment in his eyes. He shook his head and left the room.

HECTOR WAS relentless in his efforts to cheer me. He was the only person I could face. If he guessed what had passed between me and Jag he never let on. As Mrs Mistry knew about us, I wondered if the whole town was aware. But Jag might have told her himself? Maybe she'd intuited something was going on and forced him to confess our affair.

Hector was a minor distraction from what was otherwise

my continual introspection and dissection of events as I struggled to understand Jagadish's motivations. I'd come to the conclusion he was yet another example of what I thought of as "the man on the ship syndrome"—that I must give unconscious signals that I'm ready and willing for an extra-marital adventure. My self-esteem was at rock bottom. At least the man from Birmingham had never done anything to disguise his motives. He wanted sex and that was that. Why had Jag told me he loved me? Why had he let me fall in love with him? I thought of the poetry and the garland of *kurinji* flowers and my stomach churned. How could I have been so gullible? Perhaps I wasn't the only white woman he'd used those lines on.

Hector never questioned me. He didn't tell me to buck up or pull myself together, the way Tony so frequently did. Instead he sought to divert me, offering books and magazines, which, when I refused to read them, he read aloud to me. He had a talent for acting and an ability to make things come alive. I only half-listened to him, but I was lulled by the rhythmic cadence of his voice—and anything was better than lying in a darkened room, a hostage to my thoughts and recriminations.

I couldn't keep food down. One afternoon, Hector offered me a glass of lime soda and, after a couple of sips, I ran for the bathroom. When I returned, he shook his head at me. 'You're in the pudding club, aren't you? Have you seen Banerji?'

I looked down at myself. I was thin as a rake. I couldn't possibly be pregnant.

'I don't think so.' I wanted to add, *I hope not*. Whereas, once I would have leapt for joy, the idea of another pregnancy—doubtless again ending in failure, was the last thing I needed. Since Jagadish, I didn't even care anymore about my marriage. I could barely look at Tony and did all I could to avoid him at home. The thought of his hopeful, but anxious reaction, to such news was hideous.

'I'll bet you a bottle of Gordon's you're gravid, Mrs T.'

Before I could answer, I was on my way to the bathroom again.

Dr Banerji confirmed Hector's diagnosis, but I didn't tell Tony. I had a fatalistic knowledge it wasn't going to end the way he'd want it. Three failed pregnancies and years of pointless hoping had convinced me I'd never carry a child to term. And, this time, I didn't even want to. I didn't want anything to keep me in India. My only wish was to escape, to run back to England, to Pud, to London, to be free of Tony and the memories of Jagadish, which would haunt me whenever I raised my eyes to the hills around Mudoorayam.

Then it occurred to me the child might be Jag's. I checked the dates against Tony's wall chart. Unlikely, but possible. I felt sick at the thought of it.

One morning over breakfast, I realised I was starting to show and couldn't really put off telling Tony. He looked up at me from the silver tray of mail Thankappan had brought in and said, 'Who do we know in Delhi, darling?'

'Why?'

'Letter here with a Delhi postmark. Typewritten, so no clue there.'

'Bunty Finchington? My mother's friend whom I met on the ship out. Husband's stationed in Delhi.'

I wasn't really interested. The only letters I ever bothered to read were Pud's, and it annoyed me he always insisted on playing childish guess-the-sender games before opening the damn mail.

He sliced the envelope open with his ivory-handled paper knife and frowned. 'Not from her. Royal British Legion. After money. Support the war effort and all that.'

He slipped the envelope into his jacket pocket and got up from the table.

The moment to tell him about the pregnancy had passed. About the baby that was showing no sign of giving up on me.

May God, if he exists, forgive me, but every day I prayed I would miscarry again. When Tony eventually found out about my condition, he was less exuberant this time around and treated me like a china doll, nervous and jumpy himself. He was probably no more optimistic than I was that I'd reach the end of my term. But the more I desired to be rid of the child, the more tenaciously it clung on. My morning sickness ended and my appetite returned. While I didn't want to eat, my body craved food. The child inside me was hanging onto life and not going to let go the way his unborn siblings had done.

I hated my pregnant body, the swelling of my belly and my breasts. I felt ugly and fat, and, yet, the mirror told me otherwise; my skin was clear and bright, my hair thick and glossy and my eyes shining. It was as though the child inside me was trying to make me better.

I'd kept the garland of *kurinji* flowers. As soon as Jag and I had returned from the ranges, I'd pressed the flowers inside the pages of the last book in a pile of heavy tomes in my studio. Many times I thought of burning the flowers, but something held me back. Maybe they were a symbol of my foolish vanity or a demonstration that, just for a few short days, I had truly believed myself to be in love and to be loved in return? It was all I had left and, maybe, one day, the sweetness of those days might survive the pain of what had followed them.

My tragedy was that in my foolish, youthful way, I still loved Jag. Despite everything he'd done to me. I knew if he walked through the door, I'd fling myself upon him and give thanks to the gods. I even thought of visiting the shrine to

Ganesh and laying a tribute there. Yet, I would never be able to find a way to forgive Jag his lies. He'd chosen his wife and his children over me. He'd abandoned me. He'd lacked the courage and strength of character to tell me the truth, face to face. But deep inside something in me cried out—*no it isn't true. He did love me. He does have a good character. This is not right.*

Worst of all, I missed him desperately. Pleading disturbed sleep due to the pregnancy, I took to sleeping in the guest bedroom and cried myself to sleep, night after night, trying in vain to recapture the happiness we had shared in that room. Trying in vain to smell him, to taste him, to find him.

WHAT PROVED to be a long and painful labour took place in the little general hospital in Mudoorayam. I still refused to reconcile myself that I was about to bring a child into the world, and I think I subconsciously fought against the baby to keep it from being born. Or maybe that was just my guilty conscience. Whatever it was, after hours of painful struggle, the baby stopped moving and its heartbeat became dangerously slow. My cervix stopped dilating so Dr Banerji, who was in attendance, along with the midwife, a nun from the local convent, decided to perform a caesarean section. They rushed about the room gathering equipment, putting on masks and I was frightened, not for myself but, suddenly, for the baby. Their faces were grim and determined. The whole thing had completely exhausted me and I was relieved to be put under, oblivious and uncaring that they were about to cut me open. I just wanted it to be over; for the pain to end. I didn't care if I died under the anaesthetic.

When the operation was done and I was brought around from my grateful sleep, a grim-faced Tony was sitting beside the bed. I looked about the room, seeking out the cradle and expecting to hear the cries of our baby.

'Where is it? Where's the baby?'

'You need to be brave, old thing.'

The door opened a crack and the nun poked her head around and nodded at Tony. He signalled her to come in.

'Why is she here? Where's the baby? I want my baby.' And I did. I really did. After all the months of wishing it wasn't there inside me, now I'd been delivered of my burden, I wanted to hold my child in my arms, more than anything else. I looked at the nun in her starched white apron and wimple.

'Please bring me my baby.'

Tony pulled his chair nearer the bed. 'There were problems, Ginny. The baby didn't make it. I'm sorry. He was stillborn.'

My voice rose as I spoke, 'That's not true. It's not true. He can't have died. That's why they did the caesarean. So he wouldn't die.'

Tony squeezed my hand and looked helplessly at the nun.

She approached the bedside. 'Mrs Tilman. The little thing never took a breath. He's with Our Blessed Lord now. All his pain is over. Thanks be to God in his mercy.'

'What do you mean, thanks be to God? What the hell are you saying?'

The nun frowned in irritation and spoke directly to Tony. 'Perhaps I should get Dr Banerji to give her a sedative.' She turned to me again and said, 'It must be a terrible shock, dear.' And then she left the room.

Tony hung his head and stroked my hand. I pulled it away from him.

Dr Banerji came in, his face grave. 'Mrs Tilman, I'm going to give you a little injection. It will calm you down. You're tired after all you've been through.' He had the needle in my arm before I could protest and I sank back into the pillows. 'I'm sorry. I know how much having a child means to you. I am still sure you can have a healthy child in the future. But this time, it was not to be.'

He looked towards the nun. She moved to the end of the bed and drew herself up to her full height. 'No point in beating about the bush, Mrs Tilman. It's all part of God's plan.'

'What are you talking about, you stupid woman? What the hell do you know about it?'

But, as I said the words, I felt a wave of tiredness sweep over me as the sedative took effect and I sank back into the pillows.

I remember nothing of that time. I suppose I was traumatised. In relatively quick succession I'd lost my mother, broken my heart and now I'd lost the baby I thought I didn't want.

Tony brought me home. We didn't speak on the short drive. We barely spoke at all in the days that followed. He didn't criticise me; he didn't try to coax me out of my misery; he no longer appeared to have any expectations of me. It was as if the birth and death of our child had driven the final wedge into the crumbling wood of our marriage.

CHAPTER 25

I HAD A NERVOUS BREAKDOWN. It was neither diagnosed nor treated. It was as if everything that had happened was too much for my mind and body to cope with. My system shut down, and I lost touch with the world and what was going on around me. I lay in bed in a catatonic state, unthinking, unseeing, shut off. Instead of thoughts, images, sounds, there was wet sand inside my skull.

Eventually, Tony arranged for me to go to Kashmir for a long break with the Bulstrode-Hemmings. They rented a little houseboat there and thought the change of scene would do me good. My time in Srinagar is a blank. It's as though my mind wiped it out. But something must have happened, even if only the passage of time, because when I returned home to Muddy I had started to function again.

I mourned the loss of the son I'd never held and never wanted, and I bitterly regretted I'd not seen his body before he was buried. Tony said he didn't look at him either. He confessed he was squeamish about such matters. There was a grave in the Anglican churchyard. I'd had no say in that. I wasn't even consulted—or if I was, I was in no state to express an opinion. There was a pair of graves on a path leading through the tea gardens, their inscriptions long ago eroded by wind and rain and covered with mosses and lichen. When I walked by them, as I often did on my way to paint up there, I'd wish my son had been buried next to those graves, under the shade of an African tulip tree, so the petals of its huge orange flowers would fall on his grave. I hated the idea of him being in the crowded burial ground of the Anglican Church. I'd never had much truck with religion. Yet, at least once a month, I passed by the church and left wild flowers on his grave.

Tony named him. It was during my breakdown. He called him Bertie, after his grandfather Bertram. I was glad he'd settled on the diminutive. Bertram would have been too cold and formal for a baby who would never grow up. All that was engraved on the undersized tombstone were the words *"Bertie Tilman, born and died June 25th 1941"*. I was thankful Tony hadn't had a sentimental tribute carved on the headstone. No words would have been adequate to describe the loss we felt over the son we'd never known. At least the loss I felt. I supposed it was the same for him. He worked long hours at Tilman's, and spent much of his time up at the club or shut away in his study listening to the wireless and reading about the progress of the war. I don't know whether he ever visited Bertie's grave. We didn't talk about such things. In fact, we talked of little at all, other than the usual pass-the-marmalade-please exchanges.

He tried to be kind. He sometimes brought me gifts, the way he'd done when we first married. He even found me art materials, which can't have been easy in wartime. It never occurred to me it must have been as hard for him losing Bertie as it was for me.

I WAS IN THE GARDEN, on the lawn, shaded by the purple *jacaranda* tree, where I settled down to read a letter from Pud.

I missed her so much. I thought about going back to London. I could move back into Leighton House and help with her refugee committee. Or go with her to Yorkshire? The idea of returning to war-torn London struck me as appealing, if slightly bonkers. What had Pud said? *It's all a bit of a lark.* I knew that wasn't true—just her putting on a brave face to save me from worrying, but facing Hitler and his airpower would at least be living. Anything was preferable to the living death of my existence here.

The following day I met Hector at the market, and over my lime juice and soda and his gin and tonic, I told him about my plan.

'You're quite mad, Mrs T. You do realise that, don't you?'

'I'm not mad at all. In fact, I feel saner than ever. And stronger than ever. It makes perfect sense.'

'The bombing of London is relentless. Theo Bullshit-Haemorrhoids told me on the QT last night morale in the cabinet is extremely low. They reckon the place will be flattened by Christmas if the Germans keep up this pace. Besides, you'd never get a passage and, if you did manage to get on a ship, you'd probably get blown up by a submarine just like poor Marjorie.'

I thought of the words of Pud's little evacuee, who preferred to die with her mother rather than be exiled among strangers. Maybe she was dead by now. Manchester had probably taken a pounding, too. But the little girl's sentiments felt right to me. Pud was my only family and the only person left in the world I truly cared for. I wanted to be near her.

'I don't think that will happen. I'm sure our airmen are

giving them a pounding back and they'll soon change their tune.'

'You're hopelessly optimistic and delightfully naïve.'

'And you can be so pompous. It's bloody easy for you to sit here with your gin in your hand, safely out of danger in India, while your countrymen are giving up their lives. And not only your countrymen.' I was thinking of Jag. 'Thousands of Indians are risking their lives so you can sit here enjoying a drink and, when the war's over, be free to stroll down the Strand without swastikas being draped all over the place.'

'My dear, you've found some passion again. I thought I'd lost my feisty little friend forever. And you're right. I'm an ungrateful coward and a heel. But you're mistaken if you think I'm neither aware nor grateful to the men and women who are dying in their droves in the name of liberty and democracy. But I do think you have to agree I'd look really lousy in khaki serge. And as for letting me loose with a gun in my hand?' He raised an eyebrow theatrically.

I laughed. He always managed to cheer me up. But I wasn't going to let him put me off. The only argument for me not returning to England was the one that went through my own head every day. It would mean leaving Bertie behind.

But my dreams of returning were shattered, in the form of a telegram from Roger. Pud was dead. The Luftwaffe dropped a stray bomb on Leighton House in a daytime raid. After leaving the house for her committee meeting, she'd nipped back to fetch some papers. The sirens sounded so she went down to the cellars, but they weren't protection enough for a direct hit. The awful irony was it was one of the last air raids of the war before the Germans switched their attention to Russia.

With Pud gone, I was now truly alone. Much as he may have loved my aunt, I couldn't count Roger as my own family and, after writing my condolences, our only contact was the annual exchange of Christmas cards.

The destruction of the house at Leighton Square and the loss of Pud severed any connection with my past life and the world I'd grown up in. My future, such as it was, was here in India, in Mudoorayam. I felt I'd exhausted my possibilities for happiness. It was as though I'd lived my life so far without leaving any tracks. I was just passing through, a bit player with a walk on part, watching helpless as more important characters disappeared from the stage one by one.

I went through the rest of the war years as though nothing mattered. And it didn't. If Hitler had sent his planes to bomb our house in Mudoorayam, I'd have run onto the lawn and offered myself up as a target. If he'd invaded Britain and marched his storm troopers into the Houses of Parliament, I'd have shrugged my shoulders. Yes, I was sorry for the loss of life, shocked as everyone was when I saw the photographs and newsreels of what had happened in the concentration camps and revolted by the senselessness of it all. But, somehow, I couldn't get myself to care, to really care. The war and the bereavements I'd suffered had killed my capacity for grief.

FOR A LONG TIME after Bertie's birth and death, Tony and I slept in separate rooms. Then one evening I was in the guest room in front of my dressing table, brushing out my hair before bed, and saw he was standing in the doorway watching me. He came up behind and me and took the brush out of my hand and carried on brushing my hair. Then he put the hairbrush down and began to massage my shoulders. He leaned down and planted a kiss on the top of my head.

'You look tired. It's been tough for you. I know I put too much pressure on you...about having a baby and all that. All I ever wanted was for you to be happy. I want to make you happy again. Will you let me try? Even if it's just you and me. No children. You're all I need. We'll get through if we pull together.'

He leaned across me and kissed me on the mouth and I let him pull me into his arms. To be perfectly honest, it was inertia on my part. That and cowardice. I just didn't have the fight in me anymore. And I told myself I might just find some comfort with him. Maybe he could help fill the terrible void of loneliness.

BUT WHAT OF JAGADISH, you ask? Did I ever see him again? Confront him? Accuse him? Every day I scoured the *Times of India* for any mention of him in dispatches. I pretended I wasn't really doing it. I excelled at the art of self-deception, convincing myself he was dead to me anyway. But I was unable to breathe until I got to the end of the list of fatalities.

Then, one day in 1944, as I reached for the paper I knew at once what I was going to find, as though I, too, had the second sight. And there it was in black and white. Killed in Burma with the Indian 19th Infantry in the 14th Army's successful campaign against the Japanese at the Irawaddy. What turned out to be a resounding victory for the Allies had cost him his life.

I didn't want to grieve. I'd done my grieving when he'd left me. I told myself I didn't care; it had been a brief affair and the lies he told me, his running away to join up without saying goodbye or writing, meant he'd lost all claim to a place in my heart. And, yet, I was filled with sorrow for his sacrifice; his belief he was doing this to help advance the freedom of his country. Then I wondered if this, too, was part of his deception. Perhaps he'd manufactured honourable motives for joining up, when all he'd wanted to do was extri-

cate himself from a tricky situation and escape the consequences of an affair with his boss's wife?

I wrote to Mrs Mistry, care of his regiment, to send some
money for herself and her children. It was unlikely she'd get
a very generous widow's stipend. She didn't receive my letter
or chose not to reply.

The night the war in Europe ended, the hills around
Mudoorayam blazed with bonfires with a huge beacon on
the summit of the highest peak, Aneimudi. Tony and I stood
on the terrace at the club and watched as the fires were lit.
He put an arm around my shoulder and squeezed me. 'We
came through it all then, old girl.'

I didn't answer. It didn't feel like something to celebrate. I
took no pleasure from the end of the hostilities, just relief
that, at last, it was over and sadness at the waste and loss
which the long years of war had brought to so many of us.
For India, it was the beginning of another terrible conflict, as
the journey to independence and the sectarian conflicts of
Partition lay ahead. So, I stood there beside him, passive,
silent, tired of it all. In the ten years I'd lived in India, I'd lost
my mother, Pud and Bertie. The war had been indiscriminate
in its victims, taking Pud whom I loved so dearly, Marjorie,
whom I loathed and, of course, Jagadish whom I'd loved to
the point of distraction and who had stolen my capacity for
hope, for joy, for trust, for love. The party started all around
me, but all I wanted to do was go back to the bungalow and
sleep forever. I cared not whether I lived or died.

The following year, 1946, I suffered a bout of influenza. I
moved back into the guest room and stayed in bed, listless,
fevered, wretched. When one morning I awoke late, but
feeling close to human again, I decided to take my tea on the
veranda. Tony had left for work and the house was silent. I
opened the door and blinked against the brightness of the
sun. My eyes took time to adjust after several days lying in a

darkened room. When I looked up to the hills and to the high peak of Aneimudi, I gave a little cry of shock. It was as if someone had taken a giant paintbrush and spread a purplish-blue wash over the hillsides, beyond the tea gardens. The *kurinji* had flowered. Nothing had prepared me for this. I'd had no idea I'd be able to see them from the bungalow. The little patch Jag and I had discovered was nothing compared to this, the main flowering. My legs buckled and I grabbed at the balustrade and then dropped into a chair, sucking in big gulps of air. *Oh, Jag, Jag, Jagadish, I've tried so hard to forget you and this is the cruellest way to force me to think of you.* I put my head in my hands to shut out the blue hills and my stomach knotted in pain.

THE BULSTRODE-HEMMINGS, like most of the expatriate British, returned to England when India gained independence in 1947. Hector decided to stay on. We listened to Nehru's historic words over the wireless at the club. *'At the stroke of the midnight hour when the world sleeps, India will awake to life and freedom.'* But already independence was tainted by the sectarian violence that accompanied it.

Hector was angry. Mountbatten had pulled forward the date for independence. 'We're just washing our hands of them. The war's knocked the stuffing out of us, so we can't even be bothered to sort it out properly. They waited two hundred years to get shot of us, and now we capitulate to Jinnah and the Muslim League and create a bloody mess for them to deal with that makes no sense at all.'

'It might work. It has to be better than being governed by us.'

'How can you possibly have a country divided in two as Pakistan will be, with a thousand miles of India in the middle? It will be ungovernable. It's a bloody shambles, and it's our fault. We may be world leaders at creating empires, but we're clueless, imbecilic meddlers when it comes to dismantling them. Masses of people trying to cross an invisible border, drawn up on a whim by a foreign power that's now buggering off and leaving them to sort it all out.'

I lay in bed that night, thinking of the future for this new blood-torn India and wondering whether Jagadish would have thought his sacrifice was worth it.

Tony still had the plantation and factory to run and, as there was nothing and no one any more for me in England, I stayed on with him. It wasn't because I wanted to be with him. We lived like fellow inmates in a guesthouse, nodding politely and otherwise ignoring each other. Since my influenza the previous year, we'd been sleeping apart and he never again tried to coax me back to sharing his bedroom.

Why didn't we divorce? It was part inertia, part the strong sense that prevailed in the 1940s that one just didn't do that kind of thing. And it was not as if either of us wanted to remarry. Divorce would have required us to manufacture grounds, have discussions with solicitors and reach consensus about how to go about it. It would have involved photographers in seedy seaside hotels, a dividing of the spoils, such as they were, and a lot of effort neither of us thought worth making. So, we just drifted on.

Maybe it would have been different if we'd had children. They might have pulled us together in our daily lives. Instead, we were two lonely planets in separate orbits.

THE YEAR AFTER PARTITION, Hector went back to England. Gandhi's assassination was the last straw. He admired the Mahatma, and the way he was cut down by his own guards filled him with revulsion and disillusionment. Besides, there were no longer any barriers to his returning. His cabinet minister had died without making it to PM. His father had died too, so the meagre trust fund had been supplemented by his inheritance. Enough for him to buy a place to live and to keep him in gin and tonic. I missed him like hell. Before he left, he playfully suggested I divorce Tony and marry him.

'You and Tony sleep apart, so why not sleep in separate rooms with someone you actually like and who likes you? It makes a lot of sense, my dear. You would provide me with a veneer of respectability, and I would keep you from getting bored. Just think, we could see every play in London, trot around the continent—well, the bits of it that are still standing - and keep each other amused. What do you think?'

I laughed. 'It's a tempting offer, Hector. But I can't leave Muddy. This is my world. However limited. I don't want to go back to England. I don't belong there any more.'

So I stayed on. Tony still went to the club most evenings, but I had no desire to join him. Without Hector and Lilian, there was no one there I cared to see. The new members were wealthy Indians who liked to emulate their former colonial masters and could match or even surpass them in snobbery.

So I became rather a recluse, pottering around the tea gardens and the garden at home. I flung myself into my painting. People probably referred to me as the funny woman with the paint-stained overall, as I was rarely out of my smock. My days of fine gowns and expensive jewellery were long over.

CHAPTER 26

1967

I'D ALWAYS EXPECTED that Tony and I would drift on in Muddy until he retired. Indeed I'd thought it unlikely we'd ever return to England. In the mid-fifties, the Christmas card from Roger didn't arrive and, not long after, a letter from a Harrogate solicitor informed me he'd died and left me the farm. I couldn't imagine ever wanting to live there. Not with Pud gone. So Tony arranged for it to be sold and the proceeds invested to supplement our eventual retirement. Year followed uneventful year, as we led our parallel lives, waited on in silence by the now elderly Nirmala and Thankappan, the rest of the servants having long departed.

Then, one morning, everything changed. Tony came home unexpectedly from the plantation as I was taking my mid-morning coffee on the veranda. He flung himself into a chair beside me, his face red with anger.

'It looks like it's the bally end.'

'The end of what?'

'Everything. The whole damn thing. We have to go home.'

I wondered what he meant. 'Home? This is home.'

'As if devaluing the *rupee* wasn't enough, bloody government is going to nationalise us.'

'What are you talking about?'

'They want to "Indianise" ownership. Bell's is selling Tilman's to Rajani Holdings. That's me finished.'

'I don't understand.'

'Of course, you don't understand. Never blooming try. One might think after thirty years you'd have cottoned on to what's going on in the damn country in general, and this town in particular.'

I was astonished at his outburst. 'That's not fair and not true.'

It was as though all the years of non-communication and polite trivia had piled up like fallen trees across a river and the waters had now broken through. He sighed and put his head in his hands. 'I'm sorry. Not your fault. Didn't mean to take it out on you. I suppose the writing's been on the wall for a while. We've hung on as long as we could. Thank God your money is invested in England and we didn't repatriate it. It'd be worth nothing in India now. I'm out of a job. Simple as that. On the bloody scrapheap. Two years from retirement with a rotten pension that won't keep us in postage stamps.'

I couldn't compute what he was saying. 'Why have you lost your job?'

'Because the Rajani people want to "Indianise" the management structure, too. I'm too expensive. Getting rid of me is a "cost saving". They're paying me off with a nominal sum that isn't even worth taking with us to Britain, even if the damned exchange controls allowed us to, which they don't. Thirty-six years I've given this company. Blood, sweat and tears. My father before me—and his. My grandfather will be spinning in his grave. Bad enough when the mater sold out, but this takes the bloody biscuit.'

I signalled to Thankappan, who was hovering by the drawing room door, to bring us a fresh pot of coffee, but Tony shouted across me, 'Never mind the coffee, man, bring me the Scotch.'

'Tony, it's not even eleven.'

'Who gives a damn? Doubt my pay-off will be enough to cover the trip home. Maybe our fares, but certainly not furniture and effects. We'll have to leave them here.'

I looked at him; the past few years had taken their toll on Tony; he'd thickened round the middle and his face had taken on that florid red bloom that blonde men with a penchant for whisky often acquire.

'I'm not leaving Muddy.'

He didn't seem to hear me, distracted by Thankappan's arrival with the decanter and a couple of glasses. I waved mine away. He poured himself a large one, and then said, 'What did you say?'

'I said I'm not leaving. I'm staying here.'

'Don't talk rubbish. You can't possibly stay here. Besides, they want the house back.'

'But it's our house. It was your grandfather's.'

'No it isn't ours. It's the general manager's house. Has been since the mater sold the firm. We live here solely by dint of my role as the PD.' He tilted back his head and drained his glass. 'A role I no longer occupy.'

'Surely you could stay on in another role? Even if you're not the *Periya Dorai*. You don't have to resign. Your pension's due in a couple of years and, in the meantime, if you accepted another role...I'm sure the new owners would value your knowledge and expertise.'

He gave me a look of utter disbelief, then poured himself

another slug of scotch and got out of his chair. 'I'm going to start packing. I suggest you do, too.'

I stayed on the veranda listening to the sound of the whistling schoolboys in the African tulip tree, watching them fly between there and a tall eucalyptus, sourcing twigs for a nest. Tony's words wouldn't sink in. Leaving was unthinkable. There was nothing for me now in England. I was forty-nine and had spent most of my life in India. I'd seen it as a prison when I first arrived, but now I couldn't bear the idea of leaving it.

But leave India we did. We went back to England and a bungalow on the downs outside Eastbourne where, after a while, I started to become fond of the sheep, the curving contours of the landscape and the grey-green, chalky sea. But I missed Muddy. I missed the warmth of the late afternoon sun, the intensity of the rains, the bustle of the market, the vast, undulating expanse of the tea plantations, the gentle cry of the Nilgiri pigeons, the sluggish, murky river, the blue of the skies and the even deeper blue of the morning glory, the soft, rainy mists on the horizon, the cry of the blue jay and the flash of its little crest, butterflies the size of small birds, the green patchwork of the tea gardens in more shades of green than I ever felt my palette could do justice, the sweet soprano trill of a thrush on the morning air—and the little plot in the English churchyard where my son was buried.

Once we'd paid our passage home, bought the bungalow and calculated what was left of our capital, I realised any idea I'd entertained of leaving Tony was not feasible financially. Times were hard in Britain and money didn't go anywhere near as far as it would have done in India. And what was the point of leaving him? We'd got into a way of muddling along together well enough, leading separate lives under the same roof; I with my painting, and he with a newfound passion for golf. The golf club became as important to him as the

Planters' Club. I was happy enough that he was rarely at home. He'd insisted on buying a dog. I'd resisted, knowing it would be likely to fall to me to exercise her, as proved to be the case. But it turned out, I enjoyed her companionship and spent long afternoons wandering over the downs or along the Cuckmere valley with her at my side.

I went up to London on my own just once. I wanted to make a pilgrimage to Leighton Square. They'd in-filled the gap where the house had stood with an incongruous and ugly concrete office building, sandwiched between the surviving Georgian houses. Ours had been the only one in the terrace to be hit.

I stood on the pavement for several minutes, trying to recreate the house in my mind's eye, remembering all the arguments I'd had there with my mother, the years with her and Daddy as I was growing up, the sad time spent with Pud, as we both grieved over Mummy. And I thought how strange it was both she and Pud should die there—or, in my mother's case, meet the cause of her death there. I was glad there was nothing left.

I walked away and slipped into a pub just around the corner. It was empty. I asked for a double scotch, and sat in the corner drinking to the memory of my aunt and my mother. All I had left of Pud was the well-thumbed copy of Wuthering Heights she had given me on the *Viceroy of India*. I wished I still had my mother's locket and hadn't given it to Jagadish Mistry, along with my foolish heart.

A young couple came into the bar, hand in hand, and stood leaning over the jukebox in the corner. It burst into sound, playing a pop song about needing nothing but love, over and over, drumming into my head. Yes, love was all I needed but it was everything I hadn't got. I got up to go and realised it was the same pub in which I'd agreed to marry Tony more than thirty years earlier. A lot of the original features had been covered up in a tacky attempt at modernisation. I hated the way London had changed. I'd left it as a girl and now felt tired and an outsider to its new "swinging" status. As I pushed at the door, the couple flung themselves down into a seat and began to kiss passionately. It was the same table where Tony and I had sat.

***

THE REWARD for me in returning to England was seeing Hector again. He lived in Hove, just a short drive along the coast. We'd meet for tea and cakes, which nearly always degenerated into gin and tonics and maudlin conversations. The spark had gone out of him since leaving India. But it was he who persuaded a friend of his with a gallery in Chelsea to exhibit my paintings of Mudoorayam and the tea plantations. I took some persuading, too. Not least because of my previous unhappy experience of the London gallery world.

'But that's exactly why you must do it, Mrs T. You have to lay those ghosts to rest. You can't let a stupid incident from more than thirty years ago deprive the world of the chance to see your work. What happened is ancient history. And it's your opportunity to be in control. A triumphant return.' He swept his hand dramatically through the air in front of him.

I was dubious, but Hector engaged in a long war of attrition until I waved the white flag. I didn't tell Tony. I didn't see why I should. He'd never been keen on my painting. I told him I was going up to town to meet a school chum, and instead motored over to Hove to pick up Hector and we tootled up to town together for the opening—or *vernissage* as he insisted on calling it in his annoyingly pretentious manner.

The gallery was near the King's Road, well away from Cork Street and Mayfair, to my relief. It was also a younger, more casual crowd, the women in mini-skirts and the men in kipper ties and flowery shirts—so different from the formal event that had marked my fall from grace. Within an hour of opening, the little red stickers were everywhere, like an outbreak of chickenpox, with only one or two paintings unsold.

Hector appeared at my shoulder.

'A triumph, Mrs T - a veritable triumph. In the words of the great Napoleon Bonaparte *"Victory belongs to the most persevering"* and, from what I first perceived was a somewhat modest talent, has emerged, thanks to your perseverance, a confident and vibrant touch and a record of dear old Muddy that brings tears of nostalgia to my eyes.'

I punched him playfully and grinned. I did feel a bit like the cat who'd got the cream. I remembered my abortive interview at the Byam Shaw School and wondered whether Mr F.E. Jackson would think I'd finally made the grade. Sadly, I'd never find out as he was dead—run over by a motorcycle in 1945, just before the war ended.

I felt a tap on my shoulder. I turned around smiling, to find I was looking into the face of Rupert Milligan.

Time had not been kind to him. His spine was bent over so he looked like a taller version of Quasimodo; his face was as heavily lined as a ploughed field and his eyes were rheumy and clouded. Cataracts, I guessed. I should have felt triumphant, to echo Hector's words, but I felt sad and old myself, despite the fact he had over thirty years on me. I paused, wondering whether to give him the cold shoulder, to repeat the door-slamming treatment I had meted out to him before but, as I looked at his wrinkled face, gnarled like an old olive tree, all I felt was pity for him.

'Surprised to see me alive, eh Ginny?'

'I didn't expect to see you at all. Least of all tonight.'

He sighed, and then spotted Hector beside me and nodded at him, unable to disguise the dislike in his eyes. 'Channing.'

Hector merely nodded.

Milligan grunted, then grasped my arm. His hand was a claw. Wrinkled skin, brown liver spots and bruising on the back of his hands. He was repulsive, like a newt. 'I don't get out much these days.'

He began to wheeze, and I could see his chest tightening and the pain in his eyes. He was seriously ill. The wheezing turned into a coughing fit and, involuntarily, I drew away from him. *How had I ever done all those things with this man? Spent so many hours in his company? Let him take my virginity? Screw up my life?*

He fumbled in a carrier bag, incongruously adorned in psychedelic flower patterns, and pulled out a brown paper parcel and handed it to me. It was roughly wrapped: the brown paper used before, crinkled and still bearing an old postmark. It was badly folded and held together with a sliver of adhesive tape on one fold. He pushed it into my hand, wrapping both of his around mine as he did so. His skin felt rough and scaly.

'Take it, take it. I should have given it to you years ago. I always meant to, but there just wasn't the chance. I brought it with me when I came to see you before you ran off and got married, but you locked me inside the house and buggered off. Not that I can blame you... never mind. I can't expect...'

I pulled my hands back from his and let the parcel fall to the ground, realising as I did so, from the feel and sound of it, that it was a book.

Hector moved beside me and crooked his arm in mine protectively. 'What do you want Milligan?'

Rupert nodded at him. 'Didn't know you were a friend of Ginny's, Channing.'

'Well, there's a lot you don't know. But you need to know this: you're not a friend of hers. Now leave her alone. This is a private viewing and you were not invited.'

I touched Hector's arm. 'It's all right. I can manage, Hector.'

I looked at Milligan. 'Why did you come?' I asked.

'To apologise. I was fond of you. I never wanted to hurt you. I never wanted to come between you and your mother. I was a thoughtless fool.'

I looked at the brown paper wrapped parcel lying on the floor between us. 'What's that? What did you want to give me?'

'It was your father's. His favourite book. He'd have wanted you to have it. I borrowed it from him and never got round to reading it before he died. Then, when Celia died last year, I found it on her bedside table. She was reading it before she died. Poems.'

He started coughing, then recovered. 'Ashamed about what I did to you. Your father was my friend. I shouldn't have done it. And Celia. It wasn't fair to her, either.'

He bent down and picked up the parcel and pressed it again into my hands. 'Funny what age and illness does to one. Even an unmitigated bastard like me.'

He tried to laugh, but it turned into another violent coughing fit. He gestured at the walls of the gallery. 'I'm impressed, Ginny. You have real talent. But then you always did have that spark. And India looks beautiful. Never got there myself. Did quite fancy the idea of it.'

He paused, then said, 'Maybe after all, things worked out for you?'

'If they had, it would be no thanks to you.'

He nodded solemnly, turned and went out of the gallery.

I slipped the book into my handbag and thought no more of it until later that night when, after dinner with Hector and his gallery-owning friend, I climbed into bed in my London hotel room and remembered the parcel. I tore off the flimsy wrapping and found a small, leather-bound volume entitled *Classical Indian Love Poetry*. It was inscribed *"To Hugh with all my love, Fliss"* in my mother's familiar spidery handwriting. The volume fell open on a well-thumbed page and I saw the words red earth and pouring rain. I thought my heart would burst through my chest.

CHAPTER 27

About three weeks after my London show, I decided to paint the *kurinji* flowers. My father's poetry book filled me with an overwhelming conviction my love for Jag and his for me was real. All the facts were against this but, I knew in my heart, I was right.

I had no photographs from that day to draw upon. Only my still vivid memories. I'd never painted the flowers or mentioned them to anyone. In 1946 I hadn't been able to avoid them as the grasslands above the tea gardens in front of the bungalow had turned blue, and I was forced to confront the sight every time I stepped outside or looked through the window. Twelve years later, when the flowers bloomed again and turned the hills blue, I couldn't help myself from crying. It was as though nature was mocking me, reminding me what a fool I'd been.

I painted entirely from memory. The curve of the hills, and the bare rock peaks were so different from the gentle, curvaceous slopes of the Sussex downlands. The purplish-blue floral carpet was engraved on my brain. When I'd finished, I stood back from the easel and looked at my work.

A wave of happiness swept over me. I looked out of the studio window and saw it was drizzling; a dull, dirty, mist of rain partly concealed the top of the downs as they rose up behind the house. Dreary. Gloomy. The afternoon already darkening to dusk. Yet I was joyful; wrapped in a blanket of happiness and wellbeing.

On impulse, I went into the room Tony used as a study and where most of our books were housed. I scoured the shelves and eventually found the volume: the *Collected Plays of Shakespeare*. It was the weightiest tome we owned, so perfect for pressing flowers and a book I'd believed there was no risk of low-brow Tony picking up for a casual read.

Inside was the remains of the floral garland; the *thali* Jag had tied around my neck, binding me to him forever. The petals were fragile and desiccated and their colour faded, but I could still see the tiny yellow hearts inside the little, blue, bell-shaped flowers and the dark core beyond. I wondered about making another painting and incorporating one of the pressed flowers into the composition. When I eased the flowers away from the page, I saw underneath them was an envelope. I hadn't put it there when I pressed them. Curious, I turned it over. A Delhi postmark. My hands trembling and my heart pounding, I slipped the paper out of the envelope and read the letter.

My dearest darling Ginny, my Valli, my love,

Please forgive my sudden departure. How can I explain to you, my love? How can I expect your forgiveness? I deserve nothing but your contempt for what I am doing.

I never intended to fall in love with you. I never expected to. When Tony invited me for dinner that evening I went with a sense of duty, hoping it wouldn't be too dull, but believing it would. Although, when I think about it now, I was also intrigued to find out more about you after our earlier meetings. Instead, the moment I set eyes on you again I was lost. Hopelessly, insanely, gloriously lost. When you fell over with that pudding, I knew then you were the only woman I could love and ever would love. I knew we were meant to be together. I don't think you knew it then, but I do think you were starting to feel something for me. Or maybe that's just my foolish vanity?

But reality has intruded and I know now it is not to be. You are married and, my love, this is hard to say, but I must tell you, I lied to you. You may already have heard by now my wife has come to Mudoorayam with our children. Believe me, I had no idea she was coming. She was at the house waiting for me when I returned from our night in the hut. She always refused to leave my uncle's home. I do not and have never loved Tanika. Before anything happened between us, I wanted to tell you the truth about the children but I was afraid I would lose you, so I came out with that stupid lie about having none. Once I had said it, there was no taking it back. I tried so many times but I could not find the courage. And what I said about her otherwise was true. I feel nothing for her—at least, not in any way resembling what I feel for you. Our marriage was arranged. We did not choose each other. Our relationship was cold. We do have two children and a third on the way, but what I said about her making me feel as though I forced myself upon her was true. I am a coward and I still don't understand why I didn't tell you, but I can only try to excuse myself by telling you I did it because I didn't want to hurt you. Tanika is not a bad woman, and I respect her as the mother of my children and I am ashamed that I have betrayed her trust. But I had no choice. You and I had no choice. I know as you read this you will be angry with me and will say that I have also betrayed you. This is true, but it was never my intention.

I did not know what to do. When you spoke of our moving to live in London after the war, my heart dared to dream of this as a possibility, but my head knew it could not be. Tanika and the children depend on me. She has done nothing wrong. She deserves better. And you, my love. You do, too.

I hated to live with a lie, so when I found her waiting for me after we had spent the night in the shelter I told her about us. I was so consumed with my love for you that I suppose I was hoping she would release me, that she would think of a way I could be free without bringing dishonour upon her—particularly as she has never shown any love or affection towards me. I dared to hope she might actually welcome our parting. But she took it badly, made threats to go to your husband, to tell my grandmother, my uncle, and her father, who is an important man with much influence. And my children. I couldn't hurt the children. I love my daughters dearly. They are innocent parties in this. It was not right I should punish them and bring disgrace on them. Ours is a very traditional society and family is more important than anything. I should never have dragged you into all this. I know I pursued you. I know you took persuasion. I wanted to win you. I needed you to love me. If I'd shown some self-control, I could have spared you this pain. But I had none. I could not stop myself. My love for you consumed me. It still consumes me.

And, why, you may ask have I gone away? I could do nothing else. I knew I could not stay in Mudoorayam, if not with you. I could not have borne to see you and not to be with you. The army needs men like me and the war will be a distraction from my constant pain at not being with you. As I told you before, I believe by fighting alongside the British, I will be doing my bit to help to bring it to a more rapid conclusion. I confess I was also afraid to tell you face-to-face about my personal circumstances, because I know what I have done is unforgivable. You will say I am a coward, and you have every right to, but I wanted to remember your face looking at me in love and not in anger.

In a way, our story mirrors that of Murugan and Valli. I didn't tell you he, too, had another wife, Devasena. Her name means "army of the gods", and she is said to symbolise the power of actions *while Valli is the power of dreams and aspirations. I choose to think she stands for mundaneness and duty, while Valli is hope, love and dreams. You will always be my dream. Every night, when I sleep, I pray to dream of you. Every morning when I wake, I cry out for you, but you're not there.*

All I can say, my darling, is please try to forgive me. Tell yourself this—I love you with my whole heart and soul and will do until I breathe my last breath. I carry you with me in my heart. Remember the words of the poem. "in love our hearts are as red earth and pouring rain: mingled beyond parting".

With all my love, forever,

Jagadish

I FELL to my knees in the middle of Tony's study and screamed. I poured out all the pent-up anger and frustration and love and grief I had blocked up inside me over the years. I cried for Jag, for doubting him, for blaming him, for loving him, for his death in a foreign country, for the fact he had never lived to see a free India. And I hammered my fists into the carpeted floor with anger at my husband.

I don't know how long I lay there. The next thing I knew Tony was standing there, looking down at me. He said nothing. Then he turned and walked out of the room. I pulled myself up and ran after him.

'Why? Why? You read my letter. Why did you keep it from me? Why didn't you confront me about it? How could you just hide it away like this? How could you be so bloody cruel? You total bastard. You absolute shit. You miserable coward.'

I had never spoken like this to anyone before. He went white. He sat down and put his head in his hands. When he looked up, I saw he was crying.

'I wanted us to be happy. What's wrong with that? I'm

your husband, damn it. I thought it would be all right in the end. Thought you'd get over him. Why couldn't you care for me? How you could love an Indian and not me? I thought you'd feel differently about him when you found out about his wife and children. Knew you'd be angry and hoped you'd then forget him. If you'd read that letter, there would have been no hope for us. You must understand that. It was for the best. He didn't deserve you.'

I couldn't find any words that made sense. I stared at him, unable to recognise the man I'd been married to for more than thirty years.

He went back into the study and returned with another envelope. A brown, official looking one. He handed it to me. There were two slips of paper inside and my mother's locket.

The first page was a brief letter.

JUNE 1946, Huddersfield, England
Dear Mrs Tilman

I was a friend and colleague of Captain Jagadish Mistry. We served together in the North Africa campaign, and then in Burma. He asked me to send you this if he didn't make it. If the news has not yet reached you, I am very sad to tell you he was killed by the Japanese in fighting there last year. He was one of the bravest and kindest men I ever had the pleasure to serve with. I have kept this with me until my demobilisation so I would be able to send it safely to you.

With respectful condolences,
Michael Johnson, RSM

FOLDED INSIDE WAS a handwritten note from Jag

My darling Ginny,

I hope you won't ever read this, as it means I won't have made it, but you know I have the gift and, last night, I awoke after dreaming of my own death. I've asked Mike Johnson to send your mother's precious locket back to you. I've kept it close to my heart every day since you gave it to me. Each night, the last thing I do before I sleep is to touch it and wish that instead I was touching you. Every morning, I wake with your name on my lips. Not a day has passed since I last saw you, my love, that you have not been in my thoughts and in my heart. I long for you. I love you. I hope that now in my passing you can at last find a way to forgive me.

Your Jag

I stood up. 'Did you read this too?'

He looked away.

'You cruel bastard. May you rot in hell.'

I ran out of the house and fumbled in my pockets for the car keys. He followed me onto the driveway, pleading with me to stay. I got into the car, ignoring him as he hammered on the windows.

I drove up on to the downs, parked and stared out to sea. I stayed there, oblivious to the increasing dark, punctuated by the regular beam of the lighthouse. When it got cold, I drove to Hector's. He opened the door raising his eyebrows when he saw my tear-stained face. He poured me a stiff drink and sat me down in front of the fire.

'Come on, then Mrs T, tell all.'

'Don't call me that. Not anymore.'

I showed him my father's book and the poem and, little by little, began to tell him the story of my short-lived romance with Jagadish. It was the first time I'd spoken Jag's name out loud in more than twenty years, and I had to fight back the tears. When I told him about the letters and the locket and how Tony had hidden them away, he was silent at first. Then he asked me a question, 'If Tony didn't want you to know about the first letter, why would he have hidden it with the flowers?'

'I don't know.'

'How did he even know the flowers were there?'

I shook my head.

'Maybe he chanced upon them, and put the letter with them on the assumption you would find it there.'

'But why not just give it to me?'

'Perhaps he thought, if you really loved Jagadish, you would find it. After all, you'd kept the flowers. If you'd gone to the trouble of pressing them, maybe he reckoned that meant you'd go back to them.'

I shrugged. I didn't care what my husband's motives had been.

Hector persisted, 'So what are you going to do about Tony?'

'I don't want to think about him. Oh, Hector, I can't tell you how much reading these letters means to me. I really loved Jag, and now I know he really loved me, too.'

'So you have a heart after all, Ginny? You always manage to keep it well disguised.'

'I don't have one anymore. It was ripped out of me in Muddy. Losing him was terrible. Worse than my parents dying and Pud. Even though I only knew him for such a short time. I remember once you told me I'd know if I ever fell in love. And I did. I really did. The pain of it nearly killed me, but if I had to go through that pain all over again I would. It would be worth it. I'd happily trade a life of sorrow to have had those few weeks of happiness.'

'I'm so sorry, Ginny. For everything. Especially for him dying. No one has any idea of the sacrifice men like him made. It's already been brushed away under the carpet of history. Two and a half million Indian volunteers.'

'He only did it to help bring about independence.'

'We'd never have won the war without people like him.'

We sat there sipping our drinks and watching the sun go down.

'What will you do now?'

'I can't stay with him. Not anymore. Not after what he's done. He held back the truth from me and watched me suffer. He let me live believing Jag thought nothing of me. That he'd walked away without bothering to let me know. And not just that. He kept my mother's locket from me. The only thing of hers I had. The only possession I cared for. Don't you understand, Hector? It's too much. I'm going to go back to the house and pack my bags. Could I stay with you for a while? Just until I can sort out solicitors and things and extricate my money from his. Then I can buy a little place to live.'

'You can live here, darling. Nothing would give me more pleasure. Don't waste your money on another property. We'll rub along nicely together. And my offer still stands. If you decide to divorce the man, then I'd be delighted if you'd do me the honour.'

I dropped a kiss onto the top of his head. 'Dearest, Hector. You never let me down. Despite the fact I gave you cause for it often enough.'

'You never did. Well, apart from the short spell when his lordship made you send me to Coventry. But you saved my life. That means I'm in your debt forever, Mrs T.'

'I've told you, Hector, don't call me that again. Never. Not even in jest. My name is Ginny. Ginny Dunbar.'

***

I WALKED BACK into the house and found a half-empty bottle of scotch on the kitchen table. The house was silent and, for a moment I thought Tony had gone out, then I heard whimpering from his study. I walked slowly towards the room and found the dog stretched out across the open doorway, like a barrier. I stepped over him as he continued to whine. The first thing I saw was the black leather bag, lying empty on the floor. I recognised it at once, even though I hadn't seen it in thirty years, since the night Tony took it out of the glove compartment when he went to move the elephant off the road.

I didn't want to look at the desk. I knew that's where he would be. But I made myself look. He was slumped back in the chair, blood pooling behind him on the parquet floor from a gaping hole in the back of his head. The gun was still in his mouth. Blood and bits of brain tissue were splattered over the stuffed animal heads on the wall behind him.

The police and ambulance came quickly. I sat at the kitchen table with Hector, finishing off the whisky. After they'd done what they had to do and a police officer had taken a statement from me, another person, his boss I think, handed me an envelope. It was after two in the morning.

'We had to open this, Madam. It's a suicide note, addressed to you. We've done all we need to do here, so we'll leave you in peace. They've taken his body away. Very sorry for what you must be going through. Is there anyone you can stay with tonight?'

'She's staying with me,' Hector said.

When they'd gone, I opened the envelope. There was a folded printed document and a note in Tony's spidery handwriting on his familiar pale green, printed Tilman's stationery—he'd taken a supply with him when we left India, rather than let the new owners have it.

DEAR GINNY,

I want you to know I am very, very, sorry for what happened. Try to understand everything I did was for you. I have always found it hard to express my feelings. I'm not sure how I can do them justice now. I love you and have always loved you. I have never felt worthy of you, or good enough for you, and our failure to have a child made this worse as I know the problem was mine, not yours, as will be clear when you open the enclosed. I realised this evening that this last secret cannot be kept from you any longer. Daphne Bingham urged me to tell you the truth, but I wouldn't listen to her. I know you thought that she and I were up to something—and probably the mater had a hand in that—but the time I spent with Daphne was always in seeking her advice about how to win you back, how to make you love me. You see, from early on in our marriage, I felt I'd rather buggered things up. I felt I was a disappointment to you. Getting drunk on our wedding night was the start of it—I think it gave you a bad impression. I never managed to redeem myself, and I know I never was much good at the sex business.

When you read the attached, you will probably want to know more. You can ask Dr Banerji. It's not his fault though. The fault is only mine.

I can't go on living. Not with you hating me. I know I let you down—in fact, I've let the whole side down, haven't I?

I love you,
Tony

I DROPPED the letter on the table as though it was contaminated. My heart was hammering and I was afraid to open the enclosed folded paper. Hands trembling. *Pick it up. Deep breath. Read. Words make no sense. Meaningless symbols. Brain can't take it in. Read, Ginny. Read. Read it.*

When my brain had at last processed the contents, I passed it to Hector and slumped forward onto the table, head on arms.

He read it quickly. 'My God, Ginny.' He read aloud, '*Born June 25th, 1941. Sex – male. Mother - Virginia Tilman née Dunbar. Father – Unknown. Sent to St Joseph's Orphanage, Mudoorayam.* Ginny, this is incredible. How is it possible?'

My world had been ripped off its axis. Nothing made sense any more. I was so overcome, I struggled to speak. Hector brought me a glass of water.

At last I spoke, the words tumbling out as I tried to make sense of what must have happened a quarter of a century ago.

'I don't understand. It's another huge lie. My son, Bertie, is buried in the churchyard in Muddy.'

'And why is there no name for the boy on the document?'

But I knew the answer. 'Bertie never existed. My baby was Jag's, and he was taken from me at birth. Tony did that.'

Hector reached for my hand.

'He stole my baby and sent him away to an orphanage.'

'But how the hell was it possible without you knowing?'

'I had a difficult labour and needed an emergency caesarean section, so I wasn't conscious when the baby was delivered. They must have seen at once it wasn't Tony's child.'

'But to take it away and have it adopted?'

'I don't know. I don't know anything anymore. My whole life is a lie.'

Hector jumped up from the table, looked at his watch and said, 'Just after three—that means it's about seven-thirty in Muddy.'

'What are you doing?'

'I'm going to call Rajiv.'

'Who's Rajiv?'

'Banerji.'

I'd forgotten about Hector's past relationship with the doctor.

He disappeared into the study and was gone for about fifteen minutes. When he came back, he took my hands and held them between both of his. 'Raj was horrified, but went along with it all at the behest of Sister Calista and Tony. Your baby had jet black hair and golden-brown skin, so they knew at once Tony wasn't the father. You were still unconscious from the anaesthesia, and Rajiv wanted to wait till you came round to ask you what to do about breaking the news to Tony. But Sister Calista was outraged. She took the baby and showed him to Tony. According to Raj, Tony was devastated. In a terrible state. He had to give him a sedative. Then, the nun suggested sending the baby to the orphanage.'

I couldn't take it in. None of it made sense to me.

Hector went on, 'The child buried as Bertie Tilman was the stillborn son of a half-starved beggar, taken in by the nuns. She died in childbirth. The nun suggested substituting the pauper's baby for yours so it would have a Christian burial. In the end, Tony wanted to save face. He didn't want the scandal of you having a child from a liaison with an Indian. Raj says Tony was determined to protect your reputation.'

'My reputation? Was that more important than my own child?'

'I know. Rajiv was appalled and tried to argue, but Sister Calista held sway and convinced Tony it would be the best thing for the child and for you. She was obviously also motivated by the fact Tony agreed to pay the orphanage a generous allowance each year, considerably more than the cost of the child's upkeep. He went on paying until the boy ran away, sometime in the early to mid-fifties. That's all he knows. He asked me to tell you how sorry he is. Please don't blame him, Ginny.'

'I don't blame him. I blame Tony. I blame that bloody nun and her bloody God. And now I'm going to find my son.'

CHAPTER 28

I DROVE up to town to India House to sort out a visa and book my flight. Hector offered to come to India with me, but I needed to go alone. I hugged him tightly when he saw me off at London airport. He was the nearest I had to a brother and my only friend. I clung to his jacket, rubbing my face in the tweedy warmth of it.

'Wish me luck, Hector. And pray next time I see you, I'll have my son with me.'

His eyes were sad. I told myself it was because he was sad to see me go, but I knew it was because he thought I was on a fool's errand.

The long flight was a torment. I replayed the events of the past couple of weeks over and over in my head; discovering Jag's letters, Tony's betrayal, the horror of his death and the thing I still couldn't get my head around—I was actually the mother of a son who must now be twenty-seven. A stranger.

I ricocheted between sorrow, anger, happiness and excitement, as well as fear. What would he make of me? Would he look like Jag? Like me? Would he accept me?

Would I recognise him? Would he think I had disowned him, given him away? Would he even be alive?—

But I refused to dwell on that. I was tortured that, for years, until he ran away, my son would have been living just a few miles away from me. I might have passed him in the street or the marketplace. What kind of a life had he had? I prayed he had been happy, but feared he had not.

I made plans—just like the ones Jag and I had made that night in the storm shelter—weaving a fantasy future; how happy we would be to find each other, what he would do for a living, who he would marry, would we live in England or India? Then I realised he may well be married already, may have his own plans and dreams I could play no part in.

Amidst these thoughts, the image of Tony's bloodied body kept pushing its way into my head. His funeral had been a quiet one. Hector helped me hush up the cause of death and the police were cooperative. I put a notice in the *Telegraph*— Tony's usual paper—and the *Times of India* to say he'd died "suddenly at home". Some of his school chums and a couple of old Muddy hands showed up in Eastbourne for the funeral, including Lilian and Theo. I didn't actually lie to them and they didn't ask a lot of questions, and I suspect Hector had put it about he'd had a heart attack.

I traced the miserable history of my marriage and tried to work out where it had all gone wrong. Should I have believed Tony's last words that everything he'd done was for love of me? He had always been a purposeful son of the empire, doing his duty to king and company. He'd been out of his depth with a flighty eighteen-year-old bride with more than a few of her own problems. And I suspected the loss of his father so early in his life and the expectations of an unreasonable and demanding mother couldn't have helped. In the end, he had paid the price. *Should I feel guilty?* Probably. But I'd spent most of my life feeling guilt for other people's actions. Ever since Rupert Milligan. Not anymore.

In Cochin, I hired a driver to take me the four hour drive to Mudoorayam and, as we crested the hill and began our descent into the little town in the valley, I felt I was coming home. There were blood-red rhododendrons at the roadside and butterflies in the air and the skies were clear. The shabby little town and its rich wrapping of tea-covered slopes looked beautiful. My head was repeating, over and over again, the mantra: *We have a son. We have a son, Jagadish, and I will find him.*

St Joseph's Orphanage was an ugly, concrete-block construction, painted in green paint and tacked onto an older red brick house, presumably the convent. The front door was open and I heard the distant sound of children playing outside coming from the rear of the building, but inside it was quiet and dark. I knocked on the door marked "Superintendent". A tall, bespectacled Indian lady in a nun's habit opened it and looked at me with suspicion.

'Can I help you?'

'I'm looking for Sister Calista.'

She frowned and crossed herself. 'Sister Calista is in heaven. She was taken to join Our Blessed Lord last year.'

I wanted to tell the poor fool that, if there is an afterlife, it will be hell she's in, not heaven.

Instead I asked, 'Are you the Superintendent?'

'Yes, I am Sister Mary Michael.'

'Then I need your help, Sister. I'm trying to trace a child. He was born in June 1941 and brought here as a baby.'

She looked at me with an inscrutable expression and said nothing.

'Can you check the records and tell me where he is now?'

'Our records are confidential.'

I fought the urge to shake her. 'The child is my son.'

'You are mistaken. There are no white children here. This is an orphanage not a boarding school.'

'My son was born by caesarean section in the General Hospital at Mudoorayam on June 25th, 1941. I was told he was born dead, but he was alive and your sainted Sister Calista brought him here, with the collusion of my husband and the doctor in charge, because it was evident he was of mixed parentage.' I handed her the adoption form.

She glanced at it, handed it back, then started to back away from me so I grabbed her sleeve.

'He was a child born of love. It was bigotry that took him from me. I've lived without knowing my child existed for the last twenty-seven years. Now go and check your records, and tell me what happened to him.'

Her contempt was now undisguised. 'How dare you come here and say these terrible things. You dishonour the memory of Sister Calista, a holy woman who served the convent, the hospital and the orphaned children for most of her lifetime. Take your horrible stories and go. Go and see a psychiatrist.'

And with that, she stepped backwards into her room and slammed the door in my face.

I went back to the Valley Ridge Hotel, wondering what to do next. I shouldn't have let myself get angry. I had closed off my options by alienating the nun. I sat on the bed with my head in my hands and wished I'd let Hector come after all. I slept for a few hours, then went to run a bath. Just as I was about to step in to the steaming tub, there was a quiet knock at the bedroom door. Cursing the intrusion, I bundled myself into a dressing gown and opened the door to find a woman standing there. She was exceptionally pretty, with delicate features, dark skin and extraordinarily beautiful green eyes. I guessed she was in her mid-twenties.

Her voice was mellifluous, 'I hoped I would find you,

Ma'am. They told me downstairs you are the only English lady staying here. I'm from the orphanage. May I come in for a moment? I can't stay long. My name is Padma.'

I nodded and she followed me into the room, perching on the edge of the only chair, while I sat on the bed.

'I heard what you said today to Sister Mary Michael. Is it true you are the mother of this child?

'Of course, it's true. Why would I lie about something like that?' Then I checked myself. *She's your only hope, Ginny. Don't antagonise her as well.*

'I'm sorry, Padma, I'm tired and didn't mean to sound cross. I've managed to upset the superintendent and I'm sorry about that, as now I don't have a clue what to do next.'

She held out a piece of paper. 'I work as Sister Mary Michael's secretarial assistant. I copied this from the admissions register. The dates match.'

I looked at the torn scrap of white paper and then at her. 'You think this is my son?'

'His was the only admission in that month and year. And he was born in the General Hospital. It says mother unknown, deceased.'

I squeezed my hands together into two tight fists and closed my eyes, then read the paper again.

'Hemanga Joseph. His name is Hemanga?'

'Yes. Not common in this area and, unusual, as most of the orphan children are given saints' names by the nuns. In his case, they gave him both.'

I rolled his Indian name around on my tongue and decided I liked the sound of it. 'Hemanga. Hemanga. So where is he?'

'Well, that I can't tell you Mrs...'

'Dunbar.'

'I am afraid Hemanga ran away from Saint Michael's when he was thirteen. We have no record of him after that date. I've been through all the books. I was able to do it as Sister Mary Michael always visits the hospital on a Thursday afternoon.'

'You have nothing else? There must be something? Why did he run away?'

She hesitated a moment, then said, 'It seems he was a naughty boy. He featured frequently in the punishment book. Always in trouble.'

'Why? What did he do?'

'The usual things. Talking in class, climbing trees, not saying his prayers. Reading books when he should have been at prayer. Most of the children misbehave, but he seems to have made a vocation of it. He was in the punishment book on almost every page for the most of the time he was in the home.'

'What were the punishments?'

I didn't know whether I wanted to hear her answer.

'Sometimes working in the kitchens or scrubbing the latrines. When he was younger, it was withdrawal of privileges.' She looked down. 'And often the *ferula*.'

'What's a *ferula*?'

'A whalebone stick covered with leather. The nuns hit the child across the hands or the back of the legs with it. It can be extremely painful. I think Hemanga must have got too much of it, and that's what probably drove him to run away.'

I shuddered and fought back my tears. 'So, what will have happened to him?'

'Who knows? Runaway children are all too common on the streets of India. He will probably have become a beggar.'

The bile rose in the back of my throat, and I went into the bathroom and dry-retched over the toilet.

'I am so sorry I have not been able to bring you happier news, Mrs Dunbar.'

'It's not your fault, Padma. I'm grateful to you for finding out what you have and I hope Sister Mary Michael won't find out you helped me.'

'She already has. She caught me searching the records. I need to find a new job.'

'Padma, I'm so sorry. This is all my fault.'

'Not at all. I have never been happy there, and now I have a good reason to find a new and better job. I could not have stayed anyway. Not after what I heard today. They still speak of Sister Calista there as if she were a saint. To do what she did to you and Hemanga is unforgivable. She must have been a very bad woman.'

'What will you do now, Padma?'

'I will seek another appointment. Something will turn up. Like Dickens's *Mr Micawber*, I am always a philosophical person. Things always happen for a reason.'

She smiled and I thought again how pretty she was.

As she got to the door, on impulse I spoke again, 'Wait a moment. Maybe things do happen for a reason. How about helping me for a while? To find my son? How much did they pay you at the orphanage?'

'One hundred *rupees* per month.'

'Then I will pay you one hundred and fifty. Plus any expenses. It will tide you over while you look for a permanent position, and you can be a great help to me as I never learned to speak Malayalam and my Tamil is limited and rather rusty. You can speak both, I suppose?'

'Of course. That would be very good, Mrs Dunbar. Very good indeed. I will be most happy to try to help you find your son. But I must say I am not very optimistic. The words "needle" and "haystack" are coming to my mind.'

I clasped her hands in mine. 'You and I will find him, Padma. We will. And please call me Ginny.'

Next morning, I went to look at the tin-roofed bungalow that had been my home for more than thirty years and saw it was shuttered up, the lawn overgrown and the roses unpruned. I went to the Rajani Holdings estate office and asked to speak to the *Periyar Doraii*. A smiling man called Mr Gupta ushered me into Tony's former office and offered me a seat. It looked much the same as it had in the old days, but the new occupant had removed the family portraits and stuffed animal heads. Instead there were sun-faded posters of Hindu deities and graphs of crop yields.

'I'll come straight to the point, Mr Gupta. I'd like to know if the general manager's house is available for rent as it seems to be unoccupied.'

'May I ask on whose behalf you are making this enquiry?'

'My own. I used to live there. I was married to your predecessor. I've decided to return to Mudoorayam for a while, and I'd like to live there.'

'I see no reason why not. Mrs Gupta prefers a more modern house. The company has been planning to sell it for some time. We just hadn't got around to it.' He shrugged. 'Maybe it was because it was ordained you would come?'

'Maybe it was.'

We shook hands on a deal for me to rent back my former home with an option to buy it longer term, and I moved in the next day. Most of our furniture, the heavy Victorian mahogany of Bertram Tilman and the more recent additions of mine, were still in the house.

Padma and I set up our headquarters on the dining room table. She arranged the connection of a telephone and hired a woman from the town as a cook-housekeeper. Meanwhile, I made a further deal with Mr Gupta for the rental of a car. The new housekeeper brought in some helpers to spring clean the house and eradicate the cobwebs that had made their home everywhere in the year since Tony and I had left. I made the former guest room my bedroom and set up the back bedroom once again as my studio. The room Tony and I had once shared could be the guest bedroom. I dared to imagine the possibility one day Hemanga might visit me and stay there. Meanwhile, I shut the door and forgot about it.

Once the housekeeping was in order, we set about the seemingly impossible task of trying to trace my son. All we had for him was his name, age and date of birth and the date that he'd run away from the convent orphanage.

'I have a clue.' Padma grinned at me across the table. 'I did some research in the library and found out Hemanga is a Bengali name and very unusual around here. It means "golden-skinned".'

I gasped. 'He would be, wouldn't he? Golden-skinned. Of course. That should really help us.'

'Maybe, but Anglo-Indians are not that rare. There are plenty of lighter skinned Indians around. Not everyone has dark skin like mine.' She gestured at her own arm.

I sighed. She was right. I felt overwhelmed by the hopelessness of the task we had embarked upon.

Padma saw my reaction. 'Cheer up, Ginny. It's not hopeless. The name itself could be a useful clue. People may remember it. Now let's write down everything we can think of. We'll make a list of places to go to and we can start to work our way through them.'

I nodded at her, perhaps less than enthusiastically.

She tapped my arm. 'We will put ourselves in Hemanga's shoes. We must imagine him leaving St Michael's. What would he do? Where might he go? He'd have no money and he'd probably want to get as far from the orphanage as possible.'

'You're right. He wouldn't have had money for a bus. How far could he get in walking distance?'

Padma reached into the leather satchel she carried with her everywhere and produced a map. We set to together, debating distances and times and drew a circle around

Muddy within which we would start our search. It looked daunting, but she pointed out that a lot of the surface area within was tea plantation or forest. The actual roadways and settlements along them were relatively limited, as there were basically only two roads in and out of the town, one going north and the other southeast.

We went to the police station, the churches—although I thought it unlikely he would have sought refuge in a church after the treatment meted out to him by the nuns—and the market places. Unsurprisingly, no one we spoke to had any recall of a light-skinned boy named Hemanga Joseph from nearly fifteen years earlier. We met a sea of blank faces and puzzled frowns. I began to believe it was hopeless and woke to a tear-drenched pillow every morning. It was too cruel to have had been given the knowledge of my child, only for it to be wrenched away from me because the knowledge had come too late.

One morning, just as I was about to give up the exercise, pay Padma off and buy myself a ticket back to London, she came running up the path, her face lit up.

'Ginny, I've had an idea. Remember how he kept getting punished?'

I shuddered. 'I don't like to think about that.'

'What was he punished for most often?'

'You said it was the usual things. Not paying attention in class. Talking. That sort of thing.'

'And reading. He was always reading. When he shouldn't have been. When he was supposed to be attending to his lessons or to the chores he was set. He loved books.'

I shrugged. 'And?'

'Well, where would a boy who loves books go if he didn't have any?'

'A library!'

'Of course.' She was jumping up and down on the spot.

'Is there one in Muddy?'

'Yes, but it's right next to the orphanage. And it's a private one.'

I groaned.

'But there's a public one in Poombachola, endowed by the widow of a coffee planter. It's about twenty miles from here.'

'How would he have known that? It seems unlikely don't you think?'

'Never say never, Ginny. I have a hunch. And my grandmother always told me I had the gift. The second sight.'

I gasped.

'What's the matter?'

'Nothing. Just that someone else told me exactly that once. Hemanga's father. He called it the gift, too, and said his grandmother told him he had it.'

'Well, then. Let's get in the car and find out if I'm right.'

The library at Poombachola was gloomy inside, dusty and quiet. It didn't look as though many people in Poombachola bothered with books. An elderly woman sat behind the desk, stamping her way through a pile of volumes and stacking them on a wobbly trolley, ready to restore to the shelves. She told us she had been the librarian there for forty years.

Padma explained our mission and asked whether she remembered a young boy passing through around 1954, likely hungry and possibly dirty. She shrugged her bony shoulders.

'We don't let children in the main library.'

She jerked her head towards the rear of the room, where there were some miniature chairs clustered around a low round table piled with picture books.

'The little ones go over there.'

'No. He would have read adult books. He was thirteen.'

I looked around the room, strangely certain he'd been here.

Padma placed her hand over the woman's bony one and whispered something to her in her own language. The woman closed her eyes and thought for a moment, then spoke in English, 'I think I do remember him. Hemanga Joseph, you said? That name means nothing to me. But there was a boy, very light-skinned. He was the adopted son of Mr B.J. Varghese. Yes, yes. Now I remember. One evening, I had just shut up the library and was almost home when I realised I had left my pen behind. My fountain pen. It was a gift to me from the library's benefactor, Mrs Gwendoline Roberts; a particularly fine pen; I still have it. A Conway Stewart. With a gold nib. So, of course, I had to come back. And it's a long way—nearly five miles. I think it's the only time I've ever had to do that. I'm most particular with my property. One cannot be too careful.'

I tried not to show my impatience.

'Yes, I do remember now,' she continued. 'When I opened the library door and switched on the light, he was lying on the floor over there under the table, about to go to sleep in the dark. I threw him out and locked up behind him. We can't have people sleeping here. Out of the question. Next morning when I arrived, he was waiting on the steps outside. I shooed him away but he kept coming back. Mr B.J. Varghese came to the library every day and he noticed the boy sitting on the steps, and took pity on him and took him home for a good meal. He and his wife were childless and they liked the boy and, eventually, decided to adopt him. Unofficially, of course.'

'Where do they live?'

She shook her head. 'The wife died a few years after they took him in and then, about ten years ago, the old man went too. He had made no provision for the boy. Never very organised, Mr B.J. Varghese. I don't know what happened to the boy. He must have been about eighteen then I suppose.'

Padma interjected, 'Where did they live?'

The woman gave us directions and we headed there in the car. It was a settlement of houses stretching along one side of a road that edged a tea plantation. There was a primary school, a cottage hospital, the tea estate office, a few estate properties and two rows of blue-painted labourers' houses. Mr B.J. Varghese's bungalow was set slightly apart from the others. He had been the estate doctor. The present doctor had no knowledge of his predecessor, but sent us to the cottage hospital to speak to the pharmacist. She remembered the golden-skinned boy and told us he'd won a scholarship and gone away to study at university, not long before his adoptive father died. She was unable to tell us which university and said he had never returned.

I was jubilant. Although we had no idea where Hemanga Joseph had gone, just knowing he had survived and gone at eighteen to university filled me with pride. My son hadn't become a beggar. He hadn't died, starving at the side of a road. My heart was filled with gratitude for the kind old man and his wife for taking him in, giving him a home and an education, giving him a chance. Now, I would find him if I had to spend the rest of my life searching every education establishment in the subcontinent.

We returned to Mudoorayam and set to working out the most likely candidates for the university. We settled on Kerala—as the University of Travancore had been renamed, Mysore, Bangalore and Madras as the most probable and Padma crafted a letter to the admissions officer of each. Then, all we could do was sit back and wait.

But Padma was not a patient girl. Following another of her hunches, next morning she urged more drastic action. 'Think how far we have come in such a short time, Ginny. We can't possibly slow down now and trust to others. Not now we are so close. I know what these administrators can be like. They are often lazy people, who will do only the tasks they see as most important and a request to find a student from many years ago will find its way to the bottom of the pile. I have thought about the possibilities, and I think we must go to the University of Kerala and do our research ourselves. Trivandrum is about 180 miles by road.'

I looked at her fondly. In such a short time, I'd become close to the young woman and couldn't imagine how I'd have got this far without her. And I didn't like to think of the day when she wouldn't walk down my front drive, swinging her satchel and smiling, ready to start another day's searching.

I jumped to my feet. 'You're right, Padma. I'll go insane if I have to sit around here waiting. Kerala it is.'

The journey south took us almost to the tip of India, along the coastal plain with the Ghats on our left and the ocean on our right. I drove and Padma read the map and kept me from drifting off by telling me about herself and her life. My search for my son meant a lot to her, as she too had never known her father. Like Jagadish, he'd died in Burma. My eyes welled up when she told me she was born the day after her father was killed. Her mother had never remarried and had died herself when Padma was twelve, so she was brought up by her aunt and uncle.

'Aunty was kind to me—but it's not the same as having my own mother and I dearly wish I'd had the chance to meet my father. I don't even have a photograph.'

She looked away, and I reached over and squeezed her arm.

OUR RESEARCHES WERE FUTILE. There had been no student with the name Hemanga Joseph registered at Kerala University at any time in the past fifteen years.

Padma put a brave face on it and said, 'One down, three to go—Mysore next.'

I wondered if I had the strength to face more disappointment.

We were walking aimlessly along a corridor inside the Natural Science Faculty of the University, unwilling to admit defeat and return to the car, when Padma gave a little cry and stopped in her tracks. I looked round to see what was the matter, and she was jumping up and down on the spot. 'Look, look!'

She pointed at a door. Inscribed on a wooden panel was the name of the occupant. Dr B.H. Varghese MSc, DPhil.

'It's him. It's him! It must be. Remember what the librarian said. The man who adopted your son was called Mr B.J. Varghese. He must have taken his first and last name. The H is for Hemanga. He probably dropped the Joseph after the convent. Who could blame him?' She was whispering, but barely able to contain her excitement. 'I knew we would find him. I told you I have the gift. Go on, go on. Knock on the door.'

I realised I hadn't actually got as far as working out what I was going to say to Hemanga, when or if I finally found him.

'What do I say?' I looked at her desperately, my stomach hosting a swarm of butterflies.

'Just say what you feel. Tell him the truth.'

At that moment, the door opened and there he was. It was the most terrifying and mystical moment of my lifetime; the moment I first laid eyes on my son. Mine and Jag's.

Jag's eyes. *Jag in the rich, dark, lustre of your hair. Jag in the rise of your cheekbones and the dark silk of your eyebrows. My nose. The same curve of the jawline I saw in the mirror. And your skin. Rich, golden-brown, sandalwood. No doubt. My child. My son. My Hemanga. Can't breathe. Can't speak. Feel only Padma reaching out to stop me falling.*

But he didn't even notice the two dumbstruck women standing outside his door and went to walk past us. I reached out my hand and placed it on his arm to pause him. 'Hemanga?'

He stopped dead. 'Who are you?'

I could barely get the words out, 'Hemanga, Hemanga.' How I had longed to say his name to his face.

'Why are you calling me that? My name is Bharat.'

I swallowed, and felt as though the earth was spinning faster, and I wasn't keeping up with it. 'I'm your mother, Hemanga.'

He looked from me to Padma and then turned to her and spoke, his voice sharp, 'I don't know who this woman is and what she's talking about. My parents are dead. I don't know this Englishwoman.'

The word Englishwoman was spoken with contempt. He was rejecting me. I grabbed at his sleeve in desperation, but he shook my hand away.

'Maybe you think this is some kind of a joke, but I don't find it funny. Now, if you'll let go of me, I have a class to teach.' And he was off down the long corridor and around the corner before I could take another breath.

Padma took my hand in hers and squeezed it. 'Come on, Ginny, let's go back to the hotel. We can talk things over there. We'll find a way. He just needs some time.'

We returned to our hotel in silence, and I turned down her suggestion that we have a cup of tea together and then an early dinner. I went to my room and flung myself on the bed and lay there, desperate and desolate. I couldn't even cry.

Then I told myself to stop the self-pity and think of him. He was the one who had been rejected. He didn't know why his mother had abandoned him to the orphanage. He didn't even know his mother was a white Englishwoman. There had been no warning for him when a complete stranger walked into his life and claimed his parentage.

And then I thought how proud I was of him, and how proud Jag would have been. To have walked out of the orphanage with nothing but the clothes on his back, and achieve what he had achieved. A doctorate. My heart swelled. My son.

I changed my clothes and went to find Padma. There was no reply when I knocked on her door, and I couldn't find her in any of the hotel's public rooms. I sat in the lounge and had a lonely gin and tonic, wishing Hector was there. I was about to head back upstairs for an early night when I looked up as Padma walked into the room. Then my heart stopped. Hemanga was behind her. I moved as though in a trance to meet them and this time he didn't push me away. He spoke softly and said, 'Padma has told me everything. I had no idea. I'm sorry. Forgive me.'

And then we were holding each other, until I had almost squeezed the life out of him.

His hair was like Jag's; thick and black and silky, and I buried my hands in it and pulled him closer to me, breathing in the smell of him and knowing without a doubt he was my son, my own, my love. After what felt like an eternity, I pulled back from him and said, 'I loved your father more than my life. And I love you and have missed you every second of every day since the moment you were born, even though I didn't know you existed until a few weeks ago. A part of me has always known. I'm so sorry for everything you went through in that terrible orphanage and, I swear to you if I'd known about you, I'd have moved heaven and earth to be with you. Can you ever forgive me, Hemanga?'

For a moment, I thought he was still angry with me. Then he leaned forward and took me in his arms again. As he did so, I noticed he slipped his left hand sideways and took

Padma's hand in his. He pulled her in and the three of us stood there in the middle of the hotel reception, hugging each other as though it was the end of the world. And I suppose it was. The end of me living numb, empty and alone. He was there, too. My Jag. His arms around me and around our son. Red earth and pouring rain.

EPILOGUE

I STILL HAVE the pressed *neelakurinji* flowers. And not a day goes by when I don't think of Jag. We were lovers for such a brief time, but he was and always will be the love of my life. It was exactly as the lines in the poem. We two were as that parched red earth and the monsoon rain, opening ourselves to each other.

I know nothing of how he died except what Sergeant Major Johnson wrote—that it was bravely. I can believe that. The only time his courage failed him was in telling me the truth about his family. I don't want to know the details of how he died. I like to think his passing was quick; picked out by a sniper so he wouldn't even have known it was happening. I recently saw a heart-breaking film clip from the war in Burma. It showed the Japanese using Indian prisoners of war for target practice; tying them up, kneeling them down and picking them off like coconuts in a fairground, then bayonetting the survivors. Somehow, I can't imagine that fate for Jag. He was too wily to be taken prisoner and as Johnson said—he died in combat.

Next year, 1970, the *kurinji* will flower again and I will

walk again through those fields of blue flowers. This time I will walk there alone. Although I know I won't be. He will be there with me in my heart and in my head.

So that is my story. There's no more to tell other than I still live here in the bungalow amidst the tea gardens I never tire of painting. I had another successful exhibition this year and flew to London for it at Hector's suggestion. He persists in asking me to marry him. I've told him I'll give him my answer soon. He's not getting any younger, and I'm all he has now. He's the person who has known me longest and knows me best. The brother I never had. And I have so much now, it would surely be mean-spirited of me to deny him a little care and companionship in his remaining years. With the proceeds of the picture sale, I've paid for a ticket for him to fly out next year to meet Hemanga and his wife and my new-born granddaughter, Sunetra. Her name means "girl with beautiful eyes". I often think I see something of Jagadish in her features, but there is no doubt she has Padma's eyes.

ACKNOWLEDGMENTS

Jo Ryan – as always my patient and number one reader of first drafts. Beric Davis, Michelle Van Vlijmen, Anne Tattersall, Clare O'Brien, Tom Flynn and Anne Caborn who all read early drafts and gave helpful feedback.

Darlene Elizabeth Williams, my patient and painstaking editor.

Sulochana Nalapat, whose book, *The Story of Munnar*, was full of useful references and helpful background to life in the area. And to Anna Carusi, who made me a gift of the book.

The staff at Tallyar Valley Bungalow, near Munnar, for looking after me so well when I stayed there to work on the book. I confess to stealing a couple of their names.

The staff of the Grand Hotel, Eastbourne were very helpful, giving mea tour of the building and a copy of Peter Pugh's book about it – another source of period detail.

To Jane Dixon-Smith for her beautiful cover.

And thanks to all who bought and read my first novel, A Greater World and encouraged me to keep writing.

ABOUT THE AUTHOR

Clare Flynn is the author of five historical novels and a collection of short stories. Kurinji Flowers is her second book. She lives on the south coast of England.

To connect with Clare
www.clareflynn.co.uk

ALSO BY CLARE FLYNN

A Greater World

Letters from a Patchwork Quilt

The Green Ribbons

The Chalky Sea

A Fine Pair of Shoes and Other Stories

Coming soon

The Alien Corn

Printed in Great Britain
by Amazon